THE HERITAGE OF MICHAEL MARTINIERE

AN AGRIPUNK THRILLER

THE PEOPLE OF THE MARTINIERE LEGACY

JOYCE REYNOLDS-WARD

EACH DAY WAS A GIFT.

Michael Martiniere was all too aware of that reality; had been since that fateful moment when he was five and his whole world changed. The depths to which he understood his mortality were almost as hard to explain as his intricate family relationships; how his son, grandson, and daughter were older than he was, and his great-granddaughter only six years younger.

But there it was. Like everything else Martiniere, the truth was convoluted and complex, made even more complicated by the fact that Mike was the clone of Philip Martiniere, the late megalomaniac head of both the Martiniere Family and the Family corporation, the Martiniere Group.

One day his world was stark and fearful, ruled by pain, terror, and the dread that he would follow in the paths of his Befores, a sacrifice to the grim-faced old man by whose orders he had been trussed onto a table and his blood taken, three times in all. He'd seen Larry's still body when he was just barely old enough to understand what death meant. Heard the worry in the voices of the six cyborged brothers meant to guard him.

"It'll be Michael's turn soon enough," Alexander whispered with Eric and Carl when they thought Michael was asleep, that last week when he was so sick, before things changed. "Philip's getting impatient. The limited amounts of plasma aren't working. He'll drain Michael next. This isn't right. Michael is *strong*. He's *smart*. He deserves better than dying for that foul old man."

"Can't we do something?" Carl murmured back. "Can't we reach Brandon? He was supposed to be one of us."

Just then the cough Michael was trying to suppress broke free. They fell silent.

Brandon. The one who was supposed to have joined the brothers—but somehow escaped. Brandon could save him.

That last blood draw left Michael sick and weak. The whispers of the brothers as they fussed over him let him know that things were getting desperate. That Philip would take more blood, and leave him…what?

Michael—or Thirteen, as Philip called him, because he was the thirteenth clone—didn't know. But the brothers did.

Dead, Carl and Eric and Alexander fretted. *And the latest clones aren't taking. They're failing in utero. That might be the only thing that saves Michael. He's the last successful clone that Philip made. He may not dare to drain Michael. But at some point he'll get desperate and do it anyway. We've got to find a means to reach Brandon. Maybe Brandon can help us.*

And then change happened. One moment they were careening down a mountain road, George's arm holding him steady while Carl drove as hard as he could. The next moment they skidded to a stop. A woman's voice barked out a command and George and Frederick froze, unable to move. The van door slid open, and a slender man who looked like Philip, except taller and with darker skin, stood in the doorway. Then he knelt, eye-to-eye with Michael. Michael's heart pounded with fear when he realized who this man was.

According to Philip, this man was dangerous. But he was the father of the Brandon that the brothers talked about.

I am Gabriel Martiniere, he had said to George and Frederick. *The true Martiniere. Your brothers have sworn loyalty to me and are freedmen.*

And then, to Michael. *Michael. I am Gabriel. This is Ruby. We're here to take you home with us. A real home.*

Gabe. Brandon's father. And…Philip's son, who adopted Michael as his own child.

From that moment on, Michael's life was different. That night in a strange bed, waking from a nightmare about Philip draining him. None of the brothers nearby to help as he sobbed, not sure what was real and what was illusion. Then Ruby crouched beside his bed.

I am your new mother, she said.

Philip says I don't have a mother, he said.

Philip's wrong.

That night was the first of many that Michael spent in Ruby's lap being soothed to sleep as she rocked the bad dreams away. If it wasn't Ruby, it was Gabe, one or the other rocking Michael and holding him tight until he went back to sleep.

He didn't need to chew on his hand to muffle his cries any more.

Until he was five, Michael hadn't known what it was like to be loved by anyone other than the brothers, definitely not what it meant to be part of a family. But after his existence became known to the Family? He was loved fiercely and passionately by the Martiniere clan as one of their own, even if his origin was—different, and his progenitor destructive and the creator of harm to many of the family members.

He returned that love with loyalty.

CHILDHOOD AND YOUTH

2059-2073

Age: 5-18

1 / FIRST DAYS AT THE DOUBLE R

OCTOBER, 2059

Age: 5

MICHAEL PRESSED HIS NOSE AGAINST THE AIRPLANE'S WINDOW, UNABLE TO look away from the snow-covered mountains below. He hadn't been allowed to gaze through an airplane window before.

Snow. Real snow.

He couldn't help bouncing with excitement.

"You like snow, Michael?" Ruby asked.

Sorry, bud, but we have to keep you from getting sick, was what Frederick or George would usually say when he looked wistfully out the window at snow wherever they were staying.

He looked away from the window. "Yes! It's pretty!"

"What do you like to do best in snow?"

"I don't know."

"You don't know?" Ruby repeated.

Michael shook his head.

"You've never played in the snow?" Sadness replaced puzzlement.

He shook his head again.

"You'll get plenty of chances to play in the snow this winter," Ruby promised.

"Yay!" And then Michael turned his attention back to the window, unable to stifle further wiggles.

Snow. Real snow. And I get to play in it.

Soon enough they started their descent, flying in front of tall mountains and pivoting over a lake with a town clustered at one end, then over brown fields. No snow there, he saw, slumping against the window.

But there were other things. Big black creatures in a field. Were those *horses*? He wanted to see a *horse*.

As they landed, he saw other things. Buildings. Two different kinds of animals in fields. Machines. So much to see. So many new things. Then his chest got tight and he started coughing, fear closing back in on him. Larry had been coughing before he—went still. Died. Did this mean he was going to die too? Before he could play in *snow*?

"Michael. Breathe," Ruby said from her seat next to him. She smiled at Michael. "Here. Use your inhaler." She fished it out of her purse.

Ruby had been scary as the Matriarch in the meeting yesterday, face stern and hard, especially after Philip—died. But that daunting woman was gone today. Smile lines crinkled around her eyes and lips, and the freckles that spread across her nose and cheekbones weren't covered with makeup. It made her seem more human, less the authoritarian Matriarch whose vocal tones could command compliance.

"Come on. We're home now. At the Double R." She tucked the inhaler back after he used it.

Michael unsnapped his seat belt and stood. Gabe smiled down at him.

"Ready?" he asked, holding out his hand.

Michael timidly took it. Gabe was still scary. Even though he knew Gabe wouldn't hurt him, Philip had said so many nasty things about Gabe. And yet Gabe joked. Ruffled his hair like Al and Daniel would. Like Ruby, he'd been intimidating in yesterday's meeting. But Gabe had held him after. Had rocked him last night when the nightmares woke him.

They descended the stairs from the airplane. Michael caught his breath again as two large creatures with big teeth charged toward him and Gabe, making loud sharp noises even as their stubby tails flicked back and forth.

"Rusty! Crimson!" the older man waiting by the machines snapped. The creatures whirled and ran back to him.

"Are they horses?" he asked Gabe, trying not to let his voice quaver. How could anyone ride something this small?

"Those are dogs," Gabe said, an odd expression on his face. "Charlie and Martin's dogs, Rusty and Crimson. Heelers. Rusty's a boy dog and Crimson's a girl." He snapped his fingers. "Rusty. Crimson. To me."

The *dogs* bounded back silently toward them, less scary now that they weren't making noise.

"Sit," Gabe commanded. He pointed to the darker red and gray dog. "This is Rusty. The other dog is Crimson." He knelt next to Michael. "Hold your hand out to them like this." He extended the back of his hand toward the dogs. Rusty licked it, his whole body wiggling.

Michael copied Gabe. The other dog reached for Michael's hand, and he laughed at the ticklish, warm touch of Crimson's tongue. Gabe rubbed Rusty's head so Michael did the same with her. Crimson scooted close to him, then started licking his face. Michael tensed in surprise, but that didn't last long because the tingles from her tongue made him laugh again.

"Easy, Crimson," Gabe said. "They'll know you now, Michael—Mikey. If you don't mind being called that."

Mikey. It seemed friendlier than *Michael.* "Sure."

The older man called the dogs back. "Hey, Ruby. Gabe."

Gabe rose. "Charlie. This is Mikey. He lives with us now. Mikey. This is Charlie. He manages the ranch for us. His husband Martin runs the labs here."

Labs.

Mikey tightened up. Had he escaped from one fate to another equally bad?

"Labs for the RubyBot and other agricultural biobots, as well as Gabe's microbials," Ruby said as she joined them, her hand resting casually on Mikey's shoulder, almost as if she read his mind and knew he was worried.

"Pleased to meet you, Mikey," Charlie said, pushing back the brim of his big hat before he extended his hand for Mikey to shake, like he would to a C-19 safe adult. Mikey took it. It was harder and firmer than Gabe's hands, almost like the flesh hand of the brothers. "We'll be seeing a lot of each other."

"He needs to learn a lot of ranch and outdoor safety behavior," Ruby said. "They've kept him locked up in a bubble."

Charlie smiled at Mikey. "We'll fix that. He'll be tearing around like Brandon used to do in no time."

"Brandon was here?" Mikey asked.

"He grew up on the Double R, Mikey," Ruby said. "Come on. Let's go up to the house. Need to get you situated with clothes and a bed and all. You've got plenty of time to learn about your new home."

"And it's all beautiful, including the lady whose ranch this is," Gabe said, a twinkle in his eye as he smiled at Ruby.

"Flatterer." Ruby grinned back at him, a quick flash of dimple in her cheek.

They walked to two squat machines smaller than the vans and cars Mikey was used to seeing, with tracks in place of wheels. Security loaded Gabe and Ruby's big suitcases and his small pack onto the other and took off.

"What's that machine?" he asked, pointing at the remaining one.

"Crawler," Charlie said. "What we mostly use to get around the ranch and do light farm work. Easier on the ground than full sized tractors. We save those for big jobs like haying."

"Haying?"

"Hay is the dried grass that we feed to horses and cattle in the winter," Ruby said. "We have to cut and bale it."

Mikey took that in. He poked at the crawler tracks. "How do these work?"

Gabe chuckled and squatted next to Mikey, explaining the process.

They climbed into the crawler. Ruby sat in front with Charlie while Gabe sat in back with Mikey. He pointed at things and asked questions as the crawler climbed up the slight rise to a big white house with several buildings around it.

He saw tractors, trucks, and cows. But no horses.

"Can we see horses?" Mikey asked finally.

"Ruby?" Gabe raised his brows at her as she turned toward them.

She grinned. "Sure, we can see horses. Charlie, let's take the crawler to the winter pasture. Mikey's been sick so walking isn't a good idea."

"Got it."

They drove past the house to a big metal gate.

"I'll wait here," Charlie said as Ruby and Gabe got out.

Gabe picked Mikey up as Ruby opened the gate and they went through it. "You'll see better," he said. "Plus it's safer for someone your size. At least until you learn how to be around horses. They won't mean to do it, but they're big and can hurt you bad by accident. They won't always see someone as small as you."

"Horses!" Ruby called.

Mikey strained to see as a group of large, long-necked animals at the far end of the field raised their heads, then moved toward them. Golden and brown and red and white. Then they began to run, and he caught his breath. So beautiful. So powerful.

So free.

This wasn't like watching the dogs charge toward him. A yearning he couldn't quite put words to throbbed through Mikey. He wanted to be on the back of one of the galloping horses.

Free.

The horses slowed before they reached Ruby, a big red and white horse tossing its head with ears flat back at the others. Ruby laughed and scratched that horse's head as the others crowded around her. Gabe and Mikey made their way toward her. Mikey reached out to the golden horse with white mane but it jerked away.

"I wanna pet one," he said.

Ruby grabbed the mane of the red and white horse that had led the others and guided it over to them.

"This is Crystal," she said. "She's the herd leader." She rested her hand on Crystal's nose while still holding her mane.

"Don't pet her face first," Gabe said. "Pet her neck. Horses don't see like humans or dogs. A hand coming right at their face can scare them. Touch gently, maybe even scratch a little. Horses like their necks scratched, and each horse has a different favorite place."

Mikey reached out. Crystal's coat felt softer and fluffier than the dogs' fur had been.

"Crystal's favorite scratch spot is right here, under her forelock," Gabe said.

Mikey scratched under the poufy long white hair that hung down between Crystal's eyes. Crystal shoved against Ruby's hand on her nose and her eyelids drooped slightly, making her look sleepy. He laughed.

"Can I ride?" he whispered.

"Just sit," Gabe said. He raised his brows at Ruby.

"Crystal's steady," she said.

Gabe eased Mikey onto Crystal's back, still holding onto him. Mikey rested his hands on her neck. He wanted to take off running with her. Wanted to be part of her strength and power. He leaned forward to hug her, joy flowing through him.

Horses. Freedom.

He wanted to be part of that wild power racing across the fields.

To break away from the pain and tiredness that seemed to drag at his every step.

Freedom.

"THIS IS YOUR ROOM," RUBY SAID A LITTLE BIT LATER, AFTER SHOWING Mikey around the downstairs and where the kitchen, living room, first floor bathroom, and her and Gabe's offices were. It had taken them a while to climb to the third floor because they had to pause several times to let him catch his breath. Ruby looked more worried with every stop.

Mikey gazed around the room. Big. So big, from the open space to the dresser and vanity, to the bed itself. Much bigger than any bed he'd ever slept in.

"Mine?" he asked, voice quiet and a little squeaky.

"Yes. It was Brandon's room when he was little." Ruby pointed to a second doorway. "That leads to a bathroom. You share it with me and Gabe. Our bedroom is on the other side of the bathroom."

"My room. By myself." Mikey's voice quavered as he turned in a circle. He was already dreading bedtime. Would either Ruby or Gabe hear him when he had a nightmare? And what happened when the pain struck? He shivered and wrapped his arms around himself. He'd never slept alone in a place this big.

Ruby squatted next to him. "Mikey. I know you're not used to this. We have a little bed for you in our room until you're ready to sleep here. We'll look at it next. But this is where you keep your toys and clothes and stuff. Your room. Your space. All right?"

He nodded. He'd never had his own space before.

She hugged him. "I know what it feels like to not want to sleep in a room alone at your age. Come on. Let's look at your bed."

She led him through the bathroom. To his surprise it wasn't all white and chrome like he was used to seeing. A big brown star in a twisted wire circle hung on one of the pale blue walls, and assorted metal and ceramic horse heads and figures on the others. A white tub with sliding glass doors took up most of one wall with a toilet next to it. A white sink sat inside a checkered blue and white counter. A big mirror over the sink. Assorted brushes and tooth care items on one side of the sink, while small boxes lined the other side. Ruby pointed to a small stool tucked into an open cabinet.

"If you need a stool to reach for washing your hands or brushing your teeth, there it is."

He nodded, not knowing what to say.

Then they went into Ruby and Gabe's room. This one was bigger than his, though like his room it had windows on two walls. A bed with the head elevated sat against one wall, like the one in Ruby and Gabe's room at Moondance, Gabe's ranch. A pair of dressers faced the foot of the bed, next to the door, a mirrored vanity between them. A recliner, a rocking chair, and a small table were placed by the west-facing set of windows. A tall, long screen blocked the view out of one north-facing window.

Ruby led Mikey there, and moved the screen slightly to reveal a small bed set underneath the window. A tiny nightstand holding a light sat next to the head of the bed, and several stuffed animals—one looking horse-like, another like a dog, and a third kind of like his

Stuffie Bear but not Stuffie Bear rested next to the pillow. Stuffie Bear was also there, though, on the pillow.

Mikey sighed with relief. Small. Just enough space for him and an adult to move carefully. And the moving piece of the screen enclosed the bed completely, so it was his own nest. He wondered if Ruby and Gabe would let him keep that light on.

"Why don't you kick off your shoes and check it out?" Ruby said gently. "You look tired."

He didn't need any more invitation to do that, crawling on top of the just-right firm bed to pull Stuffie Bear close. There had been *so much* today. Only now did he realize that he wanted to nap.

Ruby tapped a round device attached to the screen. It glowed.

"And this is a night light," she said. "If you want it."

He nodded again.

"You know how to find your way around in the house now, right?" she asked.

"Yes."

"If you want to lay down for a while, perhaps nap a little, then that's fine," she said softly. "Just come on down to our offices when you're done. Unless you'd like me to work in here?"

He shook his head. It would be all right to be alone during the day.

It was the nights that would be a problem.

After Ruby showed him how to move the screen—only one section actually moved, the other pieces were secured to the floor with cunning little feet that he admired as a logical design—and tucked him in, Mikey heaved another relieved sigh. He tentatively pulled the other stuffies to him, joining Stuffie Bear.

He had a nest here. A safe place. And maybe enough stuffies. Finally.

THE PAIN STRUCK ON THE THIRD NIGHT. MIKEY WOKE SCREAMING AS HIS arms and legs burned and his joints twinged with sharp needle-like prickles.

"Hurts," he moaned as Gabe and Ruby hovered over him. "*Hurts.*"

"This is the pain that Al was talking about," Ruby said softly. "I'll get the pain syrup."

Mikey burst into tears. "Makes me throw up. But hurts. *Hurts.*"

Gabe gently sat next to him. "Pain syrup makes you sick, even when you eat something first?"

"Eat something?" He'd always been given the pain syrup without food. Once he stopped throwing up, a second dose made the pain go away.

Gabe scowled. He took the bottle and dispensing spoon from Ruby, studying the label.

"This med needs to be given with food. Same one I was on for the G9. No wonder they went through so much if he's puking it up."

"Figures," Ruby snapped as Gabe gave the bottle and spoon back to her.

"Mikey. I'll take you down to the kitchen and fix you something to eat before you take the syrup. I know what you're going through. I had the same problem with this med. Feed you, then we'll try the first dose and see how things settle, okay?"

He nodded, just hoping to get through the misery.

Gabe gently wrapped Mikey in a blanket before lifting him. Ruby preceded them, opening doors until they were in the kitchen. She set bottle and spoon down on the table as Gabe eased Mikey into a chair. Then he went to Ruby.

"I've got it now, hon. You rest up for tomorrow's meeting."

"You sure?"

Gabe nodded. "I know how these painful nights are first hand. I'll get Mikey settled."

She hesitated, then kissed him. "All right." She went to Mikey and kissed his brow. "Hope you're feeling better soon, Mikey." She patted his head before leaving, hand resting there for just a moment, a soothing caress she did regularly that he was starting to like.

Gabe prepared a slice of toast. "Get that down," he said to Mikey, his tone matter-of-fact. He poured Mikey a glass of milk. "Drink half of this before I give you the dose, then finish it after. That always worked for me when I had to take this stuff. It's awful. But if you have something in your stomach, you're less likely to get sick with it. It's just plain misery to have to puke on top of the pain."

He understands.

Somehow Gabe's calm comments were just what Mikey needed to hear. That he wasn't the only one who had this kind of hurting. Neither Gabe nor Ruby were panicking about it. That helped the agony fade slightly. It could be managed. It wasn't scary. Just something to work through.

Mikey chewed the toast—mostly dry, with just enough butter to add a little flavor. He drank half the milk. Gabe poured the dose and handed the spoon to Mikey.

"Gulping it down all at once works better," he said.

Mikey made a face but cooperated.

Gabe handed him the milk. "Finish it."

He did.

Gabe gathered him up again. "We'll go into the living room. It's closest to the downstairs bathroom if you get sick, and there's still some heat from the wood stove which should help with the joint and bone pain until the med kicks in. Just tell me if you need to puke. Okay?"

Mikey nodded.

Once they were in the living room, Gabe sat Mikey on the couch while he moved the rocking chair close to the wood stove. Then he picked Mikey up and they sat in the rocking chair.

"It'll get better," Gabe said softly as he rocked. "Do you want me to tell you a story? To keep your mind on something other than hurting?"

"Uh-huh," Mikey said.

"Let's see. How about I tell a story from when I was a bronc-riding cowboy, and a pretty redheaded rodeo queen caught my eye?"

"You were a cowboy?"

"Uh-huh. It was an—interesting time in my life. But it's how I met Ruby. She was barrel racing, and her horse was bucking a lot instead of running."

Mikey frowned, trying to figure out what connection there might be between horses, racing barrels, and bucking. "How do the barrels run?"

"Barrels run?"

"They're racing, aren't they?"

"Oh." Gabe chuckled softly. "That is a good image, though. No, barrel racing doesn't have the barrels do anything other than sit there. People race horses in circles around them. We'll show you."

"And a rodeo?" His voice was very small now. There were so many strange things about his new world.

"Rodeo—it's a competition based on some of the stuff that cowboys used to do out on the range. Bucking horses, with and without saddles. Bucking is when the horse jumps and kicks. Some horses will do it with a rider. Rodeo horses like to buck. They're bred to be good at it."

"Oh."

Gabe kept talking in that quiet steady voice.

Mikey eventually fell asleep. He stirred a little when the rocking stopped.

"Putting you back to bed," Gabe said. He carried Mikey upstairs and eased him into the bed. Mikey grabbed Stuffie Bear and the other stuffies to his chest before going back to sleep.

2 / FIRST RIDE

NOVEMBER, 2059

Age: 5

IT TOOK A FEW WEEKS OF LIVING WITH RUBY AND GABE BEFORE MIKEY GOT to *ride.* They needed to get the right helmet for him and boots. And more. He got to sit and watch when Ruby rode. That wasn't enough. He wanted to get his hands on the horses. Wanted to brush them and feed them treats like Gabe and Ruby did. But Mikey could barely walk to the pasture without his joints hurting, much less stand long enough to brush any horse. And he was so tired.

"Can't have you riding until you can move better," Ruby decreed.

Mikey pouted. "Don't want to see a doctor." Doctors were scary. He hadn't felt like he could protest to Philip and the brothers beyond biting. But if he never saw another doctor again, it would be too soon. Bad enough that Ruby and Gabe were talking about taking him to a *counselor.* Whatever that was. Some sort of doctor, but not quite a doctor either.

Ruby crossed her arms. "Can't ride until you're cleared by Dr. Sheri."

"Why?"

"We need to manage your pain better before you start riding." She smiled ruefully. "I'm not being mean. But I don't want to keep giving you the meds from Philip's doctors. They aren't working. You move like you hurt all the time. That's not right for a kid your age. And it's not safe for riding. You need to be able to get around more easily. Otherwise, you could get hurt. Bad." She set her jaw, her blue eyes meeting his without flinching.

He looked away first. "Okay," he whimpered, cringing at the thought of seeing a doctor, all the same.

But Dr. Sheri wasn't like his old doctors. For one thing, she came to the ranch for their first meeting. Her white hair was soft and fluffy, and she didn't stink of chemicals. Her round, lined face had a friendly, open, expression, and she smiled. A lot.

"So, this is Mikey," she said, after spending a few minutes with Ruby in her office while Gabe and Mikey waited in the living room.

Mikey sat on a straight-backed chair. The only thing that was similar to his doctor visits from before was that he was stripped down to his underpants. But even that was different. He wore a bathrobe over his underpants instead of a gown open in the back. It still didn't banish the tightness in his gut. Not even when Dr. Sheri came in the room.

She bowed politely to Mikey. "I am Dr. Sheri. I hear you want to ride horses?"

He bowed back and nodded, fighting an urge to tell Dr. Sheri everything. Her face was smiley, *really* smiley, not fake.

She pulled out a stethoscope. "I know this is old fashioned," she said to him, "but sometimes the old ways work best. We'll do a scan next. I like to do both. If you could undo your robe and slide your arms out of it, please?"

No doctor had ever said *please* to him before. Mikey did what she asked without arguing. She gently turned him sideways on the straight-backed chair, pressing the metal device to his chest and then his back in various places, sometimes asking him to breathe deep. She frowned as she straightened up. That frown didn't look right on her face.

"Does your chest hurt sometimes?"

He nodded.

"Show me where."

He tapped his breastbone.

"When does it hurt worst?"

"After—after they take blood."

"I see." She bit her lip and exchanged glances with Ruby. "Is it hard to breathe sometimes?"

He nodded.

"When?"

"When my chest hurts."

"Any other time?"

"The week before the blood draw. When I'm on the stuff that makes me sick. And I get tired a lot. I have to stop and catch my breath just walking around the house." That was a good thing to add. He knew that worried both Ruby and Gabe.

"I see." She pulled out a scanner. "Let's have you stand up for a moment."

Mikey obeyed. She ran the scanner over his arms and legs, and then his chest.

"Go ahead and put the robe back on." She studied the results as he did it. "All right. Mikey, I know you have problems with blood tests. But I need a little drop of blood to see what is in it, okay? I'll show you what I'm going to do."

She pulled out a device as big as one of her index fingers. A light tap on one end, and a small needle popped out. "I'm going to use this on a fingertip, okay? See?" She poked her finger and squeezed it until a big drop of blood oozed out. She touched the needle to the drop. It sucked it up. Dr. Sheri ejected the needle into a small cup, then brushed the end of the device. A readout popped out over it. "This is what the tester does. It tells me what the levels are of certain chemicals in your blood. Right now, I'm a bad girl because my cholesterol is too high, along with my blood sugar. I'm a bad, bad girl." She grinned at him. "Shall we see if you're better behaved than I am? Check on how many cookies Ruby and Gabe are sneaking to you?"

"It shows that?" he asked timidly.

"Pretty much."

"And that's all you'll take?"

Her face went serious. "Mikey, I don't dare take any more than that one drop. You're still recovering from your last blood draw. I'm hoping the blood tester will tell me what I need to know so I can give the right medication to stop you hurting so much, without making you sick. That's why I want to check your blood."

He studied her. She *sounded* sincere. And Ruby and Gabe were here.

If he didn't do this, he wouldn't get to ride horses. And he *wanted* to ride horses, more than anything else in the world.

Mikey extended a trembling finger. The tester stung his fingertip and he flinched, but didn't jerk it away as the tester sucked up the blood drop.

"Good job," Dr. Sheri said. She studied the readout, chewing her lower lip. "Aha. Perfect. We can do something about the pain without making you fuzzy or sick."

"I'm worried about his joints and his bone density," Ruby said.

"He has arthritis, but I have a better pediatric med on hand than what you were given for him." Dr. Sheri sighed. "I don't usually see this blood profile in someone Mikey's age. It fits—his circumstances. There is a mix of pediatric and geriatric concerns to think about. I'd like to keep treatments as non-invasive as possible, considering the circumstances."

Mikey listened tensely as they talked further. At last, he couldn't restrain himself any longer.

"Can I ride?" he asked.

"You need to get stronger," Dr. Sheri said. "And I want you to drink some medicine every meal. I'm afraid it doesn't taste that good, but if you really want to ride—you're going to have to take it. Plus a shot."

"But I can ride?"

"Take your medicines for a week. Then we'll check your blood levels again. If they're better—then yes."

THE MEDICINES WERE BITTER AND ONE WAS A *SHOT*, WHICH MIKEY HATED. Another was a full cup of chalky liquid that he had to drink with meals. But Mikey tolerated the shot and choked down the yucky stuff faithfully, thinking about *horses*.

They went to Dr. Sheri's office for his next appointment, a homey, small, comfortable place with two waiting rooms. Dr. Sheri smiled as she ran the scanner over Mikey this time.

"He's responding," she said to Ruby and Gabe. "Mikey. How have you been feeling this week? Pain anywhere?"

He shook his head.

"Are you as tired?"

"No."

She grinned. "Okay. I think I know what the blood test will tell us."

He closed his eyes so he couldn't see the pinprick this time.

"Much better," Dr. Sheri pronounced. "All right. Mikey. You have to promise me you'll keep taking your meds."

He grimaced, but nodded. "They taste like yuck. And I hate the shot. It hurts."

"They *are* making you better. The only other alternative is an infusion—where I hook you up to a bag and needle and we pump it into your blood. I don't think you really want to do that."

He shook his head violently. "No!"

"I thought so. Keep it up with the yuck and—happy riding."

THIS TIME MIKEY WAS ABLE TO WALK TO THE PASTURE WITH RUBY AND Gabe without stopping to catch his breath. Gabe still picked him up as the horses galloped toward them.

Ruby haltered Crystal and led her out of the field, into the barn. Mikey stood on a stool with Gabe nearby to help brush the Paint mare —he had learned that was the right word to describe Crystal. Ruby put a saddle tinier than hers on the big mare and attached reins to her halter, while Gabe helped him pull on the helmet. They walked into the arena. Gabe put him on Crystal's back, then adjusted the stirrups so they fit.

"Ready?" Ruby asked, still holding the reins.

Mikey nodded. She tied the rein ends in a knot and put them over Crystal's neck. Then she led Crystal, Gabe walking alongside. Mikey didn't know where to put his hands. He had already figured out not to grab the horn—Ruby and Gabe never did. At last, he put them on his thighs, staring straight ahead, between Crystal's ears, one red, one white. His body rocked slightly from side to side as she walked along, but he could feel every step she took.

It was *so big*. So much bigger than any walking he could do.

"Kid's got a natural balanced seat," Gabe said finally, as Ruby halted the big mare.

She looked up at him. "Like it so far, Mikey?"

He nodded enthusiastically.

"Let's take the next step." She picked up the reins and handed them to him, gently placing his hands into the proper position.

"You're going to cluck to Crystal and squeeze with your calves like this." She gently pressed his heel and calf against Crystal's side. "Only with both legs. She will go in a circle around me because I have her on the lead rope. But you need to keep her at the end of the rope. If she comes toward me, pull on the outside rein. If she pulls away from me, pull on the inside rein. Okay?"

"Okay." His voice squeaked.

"All right. Send her on. You'll take her out to the end of the rope."

He clucked and squeezed his legs against Crystal's side. She moved away from Ruby. It took him a couple of moments to figure out how to work the reins, but soon enough they were walking around Ruby and Gabe in a circle.

"All right, Mikey," Ruby said finally. "Pull on the rein toward me and turn her around to go the other way. You'll need to keep pulling until she's completely turned, then correct her with the other rein."

Somehow, he managed to do it, though Ruby and Gabe had to back up a few steps.

"That's enough for now," Ruby said after a few more circuits.

They walked back to the gate together, but Ruby didn't take the reins away from Mikey until Gabe lifted him off of Crystal. Mikey happily brushed Crystal after the little saddle was removed, then gave her a big hug.

"You like riding?" Ruby asked.

"Uh-huh!"

He couldn't stop grinning for the rest of the day. Even the icky meds didn't seem so icky now.

He was *riding*.

And if it meant choking down the yucky stuff and tolerating the shot every other day…he'd keep on doing it. Forever and ever.

Anything was worth it if he could keep riding horses.

———

AFTER HIS FIRST RIDE ON CRYSTAL, MIKEY WHIPPED THROUGH HIS morning house chores as quickly as possible so that he could ride with either Ruby or Gabe after breakfast. He got the routine down of dressing, making his bed, hurrying downstairs to set the table for breakfast, then helping clean up afterward. If he got his chores done on time, then he could ride.

Mike didn't figure out until he was older that Gabe and Ruby dawdled about the kitchen to give him whatever time he needed to get chores done, especially on those mornings when he hurt. He remembered it as a pleasant family time, Ruby and Gabe often joking back and forth, lingering over coffee as they discussed their plans for the day, hugging each other and then him.

Soon enough, once their last cups of coffee were drunk and the dishes were washed and put away, either Ruby or Gabe would glance at him.

"Want to ride today, Mikey?"

His answer was always *yes*.

The next step was catching Crystal and another horse. Once Mikey could ride in the small indoor arena without being on a lead, Ruby and Gabe alternated days riding with him.

Ruby often brought in Legacy to school her, training her in reining movements at the lope while Mikey and Crystal plodded around on the rail at a walk. Then she would give him a brief lesson where he would get to trot or lope—that is, if he could persuade Crystal to move out of a lazy jog.

Gabe usually rode Casey or Red alongside Mikey and Crystal, and jogged or loped with him. Crystal was more willing to pick up a lope on those days, as long as Casey or Red kept moving.

He fell off a few times, usually when riding in a lesson.

"Gotta fall off a few times to become a rider," was what Ruby said as she brushed Mikey off and helped him back up on Crystal. "I've had my share of spills. Your own head can mess you up pretty bad if you let it. Best to get back on as soon as you can, so you don't think about it and get afraid. Just remember *not* to repeat what you were doing before you fell off."

"The trick to falling is to go loose and protect your head and neck," Gabe said. And since Gabe had once been a saddle bronc rider in rodeos, Mikey listened to him as well as Ruby.

But he got better at staying on. Soon enough, he wasn't falling off.

After two weeks of this routine, Ruby glanced out the window and nodded to herself, exchanging a grin with Gabe. Mikey was getting used to the way that she studied the outside every morning, assessing the weather. But something about this felt different. Maybe it was the way their smiles lingered.

"Looks like it's going to be the last day of good weather before we get some snow," she said as Gabe put the dishes away that Mikey had dried. "We've been working pretty hard. Time to take a break. Maybe we should ride up to the Homestead field?"

Mikey froze, clutching plate and towel tightly. An outside ride? Would he be able to go? He wanted to ask but was afraid they might say no. He hadn't been up that far even in one of the crawlers, and it hadn't been *that* long since Dr. Sheri had approved his riding.

"You think Mikey can handle it?" Gabe asked. "It's going to be a longer ride than he's done before."

Ruby shrugged. "Worst case scenario is that you or I end up sticking him in the saddle in front of us because he got tired. Leave a halter and lead on Crystal so we can pony her if need be. It's time." She grinned at Mikey. "He's been trying, and I'd sooner do that first outside ride before snow flies. You up for it, Mikey?"

"Oh yes," he said, his voice barely above a whisper. "Oh yes."

Gabe plucked plate and towel from his hands. "Better go brush your teeth and get your boots, then."

"And put some long johns on!" Ruby called as he bolted toward the kitchen doorway. "Gonna be cold! Wool socks and base layers top and bottom."

IT SEEMED TO TAKE FOREVER TO CATCH RED, PARD, AND CRYSTAL, THEN get them brushed and tacked. After that, Mikey followed Ruby and Pard out of the barn, proudly leading Crystal by himself. Ruby checked his helmet before she helped him into the saddle, then tied Crystal's halter rope to the saddle horn. She paused before turning back to Pard.

"Now Mikey. This is supposed to be fun. If you're having problems with Crystal, or get worried about something, say so. If you want one of us to take her halter rope and lead her for a while, just tell us. Nothing wrong with that. Crystal can be a little different outside than she is in the arena—any horse will be. You shouldn't have any problems keeping her moving like you do inside. Okay?"

He nodded, grinning at her, too excited to say anything.

"I *will* put you on the lead when we lope. Okay?"

He nodded again.

"All right." She gathered up Pard's reins and mounted him with a smooth, flowing motion. Gabe and Red came up on Mikey's right side.

"Let's ride next to Ruby," Gabe said.

They headed out, three abreast, on the crawler track. Crystal walked bigger than she did inside, and Mikey decided that he liked it better.

He wasn't sure what was more exciting, the fact that he was actually, finally, riding *outside* or that they were going beyond the complex of buildings that made up all he had seen of the Double R so far. Mikey really wanted to look around more, but he remembered what Ruby said about paying attention to his horse.

But oh, the glimpses he got of the world around him were beautiful. Fast-moving clouds overhead alternately blocked and opened up the sunlight. The light breeze was just cool enough on his cheeks that he was glad for the warm layers and gloves he wore. And the air smelled fresh, clean, and crisp.

They came to a big metal gate. Ruby opened it from Pard's back and held it wide so that Gabe and Mikey could ride through, then closed it.

"Always leave a gate the way you find it, Mikey," Gabe said. "Basic ranch rule. You don't always know what stock is in which field."

Mikey nodded. Did this mean he might get to go riding on his own someday? He sure hoped so.

They reached a fork in the track and turned to go uphill. As they approached a line of leafless trees Mikey saw wooden planks ahead of them. "What's that?"

"Bridge over an old irrigation ditch," Ruby said. "Here. Hold up, Mikey." She made Pard step sideways until she could reach over and untie the halter rope. "Crystal can be kinda funny about crossing that bridge. I want you to hang on because she might decide to jump."

Jump.

Now that sounded exciting. Mikey leaned forward and grabbed a hunk of mane—gripping the saddle horn didn't put him in the best position if he started sliding. Ruby took a tight hold of Crystal's lead rope, pulling her close until Crystal's nose was almost on her leg.

"One bad thing about this mare is that she doesn't like bridges, this bridge in particular," she muttered. "Mikey. Shorten your reins and hang on."

He shortened his grip on the reins until Ruby nodded.

"Here we go," she said. He felt Crystal go tight underneath him as they approached the bridge at a walk. Gabe dropped back to follow as Mikey and Ruby went across the bridge. Crystal and Pard's front hooves went *clop-clop* on the bridge and Crystal hopped, turning sideways, making a loud clatter.

"Quit, damn you!" Ruby growled, popping the lead rope.

Mikey clutched to mane and reins, clinging with his legs like he'd learned to do in the arena. Crystal shook her head against Ruby's grip, alternately hopping sideways and plunging into Pard. One hind leg dropped off the bridge and for a moment he thought they were going to fall. Crystal scrambled. Ruby's grip loosened. Crystal reared, yanking the lead rope free. Then she bolted.

Only his grip on the mane kept Mikey from falling off backward. He leaned forward as Crystal ran up the track, holding on with legs and hands as she galloped, fast enough that it whipped up tears in his eyes. Oddly enough, he didn't feel afraid. It was *fun*, even if it was bumpy. But the power under him as Crystal thundered along was exciting. Fast. So different from riding in a vehicle. He *felt* the effort it took as Crystal ran.

Soon enough she dropped to a fast trot, and then a jog. Mikey let go of the mane and sat up.

"Whoooa," he said, his voice shaking a little as he turned Crystal to ride back toward Ruby and Gabe, who were now long-trotting toward them.

"You all right, Mikey?" Ruby reached him first, worry in her voice.

He nodded. "It was *fun.*"

Gabe grinned big. "We've got ourselves a horseman here, Rubes. We've got ourselves a horseman. I'm gonna tell Donna-gran. She'll be tickled to death."

Ruby rolled her eyes as she gathered up the lead rope and retied it to Crystal's saddle horn. "Could have gone a lot worse. Next bridge, we switch saddles, Mikey goes up on Pard, and I school the heck out of Crystal. God damn it, I think I aged ten years in thirty seconds. Didn't expect her to blow up *this* bad."

"Eh, I think Mikey has it, Rubes," Gabe said, still grinning at Mikey. "But I think we'd better show him how to *properly* handle a gallop."

Ruby scowled at him. "On the lead line!"

"Of course. And maybe we should let Mikey take Crystal across the next bridge—one of us crosses first, then Mikey and Crystal, then the other. He has to learn how to do it someday, and schooling Crystal doesn't work for today. Let's not get her riled up."

"Yeah, you're right," Ruby said reluctantly. "He's not ready for Pard. Crystal's big issue is the bridge. Mikey needs more hours in the saddle before he can ride Pard and make him move." She frowned at Mikey. "Okay, you did a lot of things right. Grabbing mane was perfect. That kept you forward. The other thing? You kept your legs on her, so you stuck to her back."

"It was pretty bouncy," he admitted.

"It will be. There are a few tricks to make a gallop easier. We'll show you soon. Right now, I want to be sure you can stick on if Crystal jumps." Ruby shook her head. "That was a bigger reaction than she's done in years."

"You might have cranked her down too hard," Gabe said.

Ruby sighed. "Yeah, I did. Being overprotective. But if you give her too much lead it can be just as bad. Damn mare. I *am* gonna school her at some point, though, because this is bullshit. Gabe, can you show Mikey how to pick up two point while I describe it?"

"Sure," Gabe said.

Gabe shortened his reins, resting his hands on Red's neck. He rose a little in the saddle, leaning forward while arching his back slightly.

"See how Gabe has his lower leg against Red's belly?"

Mikey nodded.

"That keeps him on and steady. He lifts his seat off the saddle. Because we're riding Western, he's also arching his back so the saddle horn doesn't get him in the gut. And he's got his hands down solid on Red's neck." Ruby paused. "I don't know why I didn't think of this before," she said, sounding annoyed. "Let's whoa for a minute."

She dismounted and slipped her belt off, buckling it around Crystal's neck, yanking on it to make sure the buckle held.

"What's that for?" Mikey asked.

"A grabstrap. It's a little big—should be an English stirrup leather —but it's what I have. Grab hold of it when you come up to the ditch. Don't let go until Crystal's hind legs are off the bridge. Got it?"

By now Mikey knew that Ruby wanted him to repeat back her instructions.

"Grab hold of the strap when we come up to the ditch. Don't let go until Crystal's hind legs are off the bridge."

She nodded. "Okay. Let's do it."

When they reached the ditch, Ruby rode Pard across while Gabe waited with Mikey. She turned Pard sideways to block the path.

"Ready," she called back.

"Okay," Gabe said. He reached over to check the knot in the reins. "Get her started. I'll be right here. You ready?"

Mikey nodded. He rose a little in the saddle, legs tight, holding on to reins and grabstrap, and clucked to Crystal, kicking her a little with his heels. She tightened under him, her steps coming short and high, and he thought she might stop.

"Get on there, you old brat," Gabe muttered, bringing Red closer.

Crystal pinned her ears and tossed her head at them. Gabe backed Red off a step. "Keep tapping her sides with your heels, Mikey."

Crystal raised her head high and stopped at the bridge. Mikey kicked but she wouldn't move. Ruby clucked, annoyed.

"You want to play it that way, old girl?" Gabe muttered. "Mikey. Hold tight. I'm gonna slap her butt. She's likely to jump big when I do."

Mikey nodded and tightened his grip.

Gabe smacked Crystal. She launched herself high and Mikey gasped, hanging on for dear life. He slid sideways in the saddle as she landed hard and his feet slid out of the stirrups, but he managed to catch the saddle horn with his elbow and straighten himself up. Then Ruby took hold of Crystal's bridle and Gabe came up on their other side. Mikey fumbled for his stirrups, laughing with relief.

"That was FUN!" he finally exclaimed.

Gabe and Ruby exchanged glances, rolling their eyes at each other. Gabe chuckled and after a moment, Ruby joined in, both grinning.

"Don't develop too much of a liking for that stuff," Gabe said. "That leads to bronc riding and rodeo queens." He smirked at Ruby.

"Or a taste for bronc riders," she laughed back at him. "Ready to go on, Mikey?"

He nodded.

They picked up a slow jog up the track, until they reached the top.

"Want to gallop?" Gabe asked.

"Oh yeah!"

Gabe reached over and undid the halter rope. "Hey, Rubes, you've got the best galloping form. We'll go about halfway, then Mikey and I will get off the track and you can run by us so he can get a quick look at you."

"Lemme put the reins on the snaffle loop before you ride off," Ruby said. "Pard'll gallop better with both hands on the reins if I do that." She leaned forward and unsnapped her reins, one at a time, to move them up the shank to the higher loop.

Gabe and Mikey rode part way down the track, then Gabe pulled them off.

"All right. Get up in your stirrups. Take a firm hold of her reins as well as the neck strap. When Ruby comes by, we'll follow. You ready for this, kiddo?"

Mikey nodded, excited. This was the best thing ever! Just like he had dreamed of when he first saw horses.

Ruby spun Pard around. "Yaaahhh! Yaaahhh!" she yelled.

Pard took off as Ruby leaned forward. A big grin split her face as they galloped toward Gabe and Mikey. Red pranced as Pard and Ruby drew near, and Mikey felt Crystal get tight again. But he noticed how Ruby rode—in two point, like Gabe had shown him.

He didn't need to urge Crystal forward as Ruby and Pard thundered by them. He took a tight hold on both reins and grabstrap, rising in his stirrups as Crystal and Red took off after Pard.

This was different from before. Smoother, with Crystal's neck stretched out, running head-to-head with Red. He felt her muscles tighten and extend, tighten and extend, and the pounding of hoofbeats echoed his heartbeats.

All too soon, Ruby and Pard slowed in front of them.

"Sit up!" Gabe hollered, sitting up himself, slowing Red.

Mikey sat up and pulled back on the reins. They slowed to a canter, then a jog, and finally a walk.

Ruby leaned forward and switched her reins back.

"Like that, Mikey?" she asked as they joined her.

He nodded, once again speechless.

It was everything he had dreamed of. Freedom. Speed. He wanted more of it.

OCTOBER, 2060

Age: 6

Despite health problems all winter, Mikey managed to get riding time in. After the New Year, Crystal was retired from carrying Mikey because she was due to foal in April. He spent time on the other ranch horses—mostly Blaze and Cisco. They required Mikey to pay more attention than Crystal did, especially Blaze because he would buck a little if Mikey did something wrong. Sometimes he got to ride Casey as a treat, but only in the arena because she was reactive to the slightest touch and not a good beginner mount.

By summer, Mikey was able to ride along when Charlie or Terri rode out to check cows. It was frustrating in some ways because he wasn't big enough to saddle and bridle either Blaze or Cisco by himself, in spite of having a block to climb on. Sometimes he could slip onto a horse's back in the corral and ride without a saddle. Even then, they were big for him, and neither Blaze nor Cisco wanted to stand close to the corral fence so that Mikey could climb on.

Someday I'll be big enough. Someday, he told himself.

Other kids had ponies that they could saddle themselves and ride out on their own. Mikey longed for his own pony. Something he could take care of by himself, and didn't need help with saddling and getting on.

But adding a pony to the ranch herd might be a problem. Ruby and Gabe had bought a stallion and some mares in the spring. Star was the stallion's barn name, because he had a big spiky star on his forehead, bright white against the color that looked black to Mikey but that Ruby called dark bay.

Star was friendly enough to Mikey, but there were new rules to learn about being around a stallion. And there weren't any open stalls, not with the new dogs Smudge, Tip, and Cody living in one stall as a temporary nighttime dog kennel.

As fall came, Gabe had a kennel built closer to the house. It seemed to take forever for it to get finished. The dogs still spent the night in the barn, as Mikey's Gotcha Day approached. Ruby had announced that Gotcha Day would be Mikey's official birthday, and she and Gabe clearly had plans for it.

At last, Gotcha Day dawned. Mikey bounced out of bed, excited. Brandon, Kris, baby Lily, and the cyborg brothers had come to the ranch the night before, along with Gabe's sister Justine and his cousin Serg. The only person who wasn't there that he hoped to see was Donna-gran.

As he hurried downstairs, he heard Donna-gran's voice. Mikey raced into the kitchen. Gabe's grandmother sat at the table across from Justine, talking.

"Donna-gran!" he called. Once he'd been afraid of her. Now he wasn't, and ran to her open arms. "I was afraid you weren't gonna be here!"

"I wouldn't miss this day for the world," she said, holding him tight. He took a deep breath of that soft powdery scent that was hers.

"Can I let Smudge in?" he asked Ruby as she and Gabe hustled about making a big breakfast.

Ruby shook her head. "Too many people this morning." Mikey opened the lower dish cabinet to set the table like he always did, but she shooed him away. "It's your day. Go visit with Donna-gran."

Mikey obeyed, chattering away to Donna-gran about Smudge and riding and the first days of online class. He was supposed to meet up with his classmates in person next week—they did this every two weeks. The other kids were like him, schooling online because of health or security reasons, and came from around Northeastern Oregon. They were planning to do a trail ride on the Double R this time. That made him wish for his own pony more than ever, like the others.

At last Brandon stood next to them, grinning down at Mikey, Lily cradled in one arm. "Okay, little bro, it's time for breakfast."

Mikey sat at the head of the table in Gabe's usual seat when they had big family meals, Donna-gran on one side, Ruby and Gabe on the other.

Finally, breakfast was done.

"Well," Gabe said. "Maybe we should let the dogs out, eh, Mikey?"

"Sure." He turned to Donna-gran. "Smudge is getting big, Donna-gran. He's really pretty."

"Well, I guess I'll have to see him," she said, smiling.

It took longer to walk to the barn with Donna-gran leaning on her walker. Mikey noticed that Brandon, Kris, Justine, and Serg joined them. He wondered why, and then noted that Ruby wasn't there. Hopefully she wasn't doing the dishes all by herself!

Then, as they approached the barn, he saw Charlie and his husband Martin, Terri and Julie, Beck and Rick, Al and the other cyborged brothers. They all stood around the dog stall, grinning, under a banner that read *Happy Gotcha Day, Mikey.*

His heart hammered. No. It couldn't be, could it?

Gabe gestured toward the partially opened stall door. "Go ahead and open it."

Mikey slid it open the rest of the way, and froze. Ruby stood inside, holding the reins of a brown pony with cream mane and tail, with a big white star on its—*her*—face. His saddle was on her back, his helmet hanging from her saddle horn, a fresh Double R freeze brand shining white on her clipped left shoulder.

"Happy Gotcha Day, Mikey," she said, grinning.

"Mine?" he whispered. "Mine?"

Ruby handed the reins to him. "All yours, Mikey. Her name is Rose, and she's a silver dapple Shetland-Welsh cross."

"Mine." He stared at Rose. Then he extended his hand. Rose stretched out her neck and sniffed it. He scratched the big white star on her forehead. Her nose wiggled as she leaned into his fingers.

"Why don't you take her for a spin in the arena?" Ruby said.

Quick as could be, he pulled on the helmet and led Rose out. Gabe opened the arena gate and Mikey marched in with Rose on his right side. He stopped and checked how tight the cinch was—by himself! Then he put the reins over her head, carefully raised his left foot to fit in the stirrup, and swung onto her back.

Mine.

Much as Mikey wanted to thunder around in a gallop, he knew not to do that at first. Rose wore a snaffle bit, so he held the reins in both hands, gently tightening them until he felt her mouthing the bit. Mikey squeezed his legs and she walked off, not pulling hard on his hands like Cisco would. He guided her in circles using his legs first, shifting his weight. It took the lightest of weight shifts with a little leg to make her turn. So different from cranky old Blaze or Cisco!

Her jog was quick and fast, bumpy enough that he posted it. Then Mikey sat, and asked for lope. After two loops of the arena, he asked her to walk and changed direction, then asked for lope in that direction. Smooth, almost as smooth as Crystal. Smoother than Blaze.

How fast could she run? He leaned forward a little more, made a kissing sound to her like Ruby had taught him, and moved his hands forward. Rose accelerated smoothly, her strides shorter and faster than Crystal at a gallop and a little bit rougher. He let her run for half an arena circuit, then sat up and asked her to slow down, taking a firmer contact.

Rose shook her head and tried to pull for more rein. Mikey held firm. She kept shaking her head, then kicked up her hind end before launching into a series of hopping leaps. It wasn't a real buck, not a hard buck like he'd seen Flash do with Ruby when he started out under saddle. But it was exciting.

At last, she settled into that jouncy trot, then a walk. He eased his grip on the reins.

Mine.

He rode up to the adults at the gate, grinning. Ruby joined him.

"She's still green, Mikey, so we'll have to work with her. But she's pretty gentle, and big enough that I can school her if need be." She smiled up at him. "Like her?"

"Oh yes," he breathed. "She's wonderful."

"We'll move her back to the corrals so she can move around more than in the stall." Ruby made a face. "You'll need help catching her at first but that should get better as you two learn about each other." She scratched Rose's neck. "Typical pony."

Donna-gran came up to them with Gabe, smiling wistfully. "He rides like you did at that age, Gabriel. Almost exactly like you."

And those were just about the best words Mikey could ever have heard. One thing he had learned about his progenitor was that Philip didn't like horses.

But to hear that he rode like Gabe—that was just about perfect. Another way that he was different from his progenitor.

3 / CLONE ONE

Age: 10

MIKE HAD ALWAYS KNOWN THERE WAS SOMETHING DIFFERENT ABOUT HIM. His Befores. He quickly learned that having Befores who looked just like him was not normal. His studies in the Double R labs exposed him to basic cloning techniques. But when he asked about the possibility of human cloning, there had always been a hesitation. A pause.

Gabe, Ruby, Brandon, and Justine had always been careful to speak of his *progenitor* Philip. Not father. Progenitor. Mike knew he was related to them somehow, but they were cagey about the details.

That changed the summer of his tenth year, when he was learning more about the cloning techniques tied to the creation of the biological part of the RubyBot. A file he hadn't saved popped up in Mike's research directory. He opened it, curious, wondering if it was something new that Martin, Beck, or Julie from the labs had forwarded for him to read.

It described something that sounded like real experiments, not a simulation. But it was a *good* simulation because it sounded so realistic. He started getting nervous when he read the file about a clone called Larry. Larry had been one of his Befores. Mike had seen Larry's still body.

And then he reached the next section. Labeled *Clone Number Thirteen.*

The header was *Subject PJM-M-13-Michael.*

The picture was *him.*

Mike screamed. Memories from Before flooded over him. The brothers whispering that he was Philip's last viable clone. His Befores looking so much like him. Clone. Clone. *Clone.* He shrieked to try to block out that word pounding through his thoughts. He now knew what *clone* meant. How he was tied to Philip. Memories. Memories. Memories.

I am Philip. I am Philip. IamPhilipamPhilipamPhilipPhilipPhilip….

Nononononono….

Mike fell to the floor in a fetal curl. He screeched, hands over his ears, trying to block out *cloneclonecloneclone IamPhilip Philip Philip* echoing through his head. Smudge desperately licked Mike's hands and face in an attempt to calm him. It wasn't enough. Even when Beck knelt next to him, trying to ask what was wrong, Mike couldn't stop howling, sobbing as the bad old memories flowed over him. Everything he'd tried to forget came rushing back. The pain. The fear. The being alone. That was why those first five years had happened the way they did. *Clone. Clone. Clone.*

Nonononononononono….

He tried to fold himself up to be as small as possible. He couldn't stop screaming. His chest hurt. He couldn't catch his breath.

And then there was darkness.

HE MUST NOT HAVE BEEN UNCONSCIOUS FOR TOO LONG. MIKE WOKE IN Ruby's arms. She sat on the lab floor, holding Mike tight. Gabe knelt next to them, rubbing his back. Smudge pressed against his legs.

"You okay, Mike?" Ruby asked softly.

He gulped and remembered.

Clone. I am Philip. No.

He didn't realize he was moaning those words until Ruby shook him a little.

"Mike. *Stop.*" The Matriarch's command tone hit him hard, almost as if she had slapped him. But he couldn't keep from sniffling.

"Oh, Mikey, Mikey," she whispered, rocking him back and forth. He gulped but couldn't hold back a tiny whine that Smudge matched.

Dr. Sheri joined Gabe. Mike couldn't understand what they were saying because he heard the word *clone* again and it kicked off a renewed chorus in his head. He tried to keep from shrieking, but he couldn't because his throat was raw. Ruby and Gabe's combined strength kept him from coiling up once more.

"Mike. Michael." Dr. Sheri's voice was familiar, her friendly round face unusually tight with worry. "I'm going to give you something to let you sleep. Okay?"

He couldn't answer. The keening controlled him.

Clonecloneclonecloneclone.

Sharp bite of a shot in his arm. Then things slowly fuzzed up. He couldn't keep his eyes open. It was getting easier to breathe, though, easier to sag against Ruby's comforting warmth. Then darkness again.

MIKE BLINKED. HE WAS IN BED, SMUDGE CURLED UP AGAINST HIM IN defiance of Ruby's usual rules. It had been light earlier—now it was dark outside, the curtains and windows thrown wide open, a gentle breeze whispering through his room.

"Hey, Mikey." Ruby stroked his forehead. "You feeling better?"

Better? Had he been sick?

Memory washed over him.

Clone. I am Philip. Clone.

And yet the accusatory chorus seemed distant and not as painful as it had been before.

"Here. Have some water." She held a cup to his lips. He took it with shaky hands. Ruby helped steady it as he drank. It moistened his throat, enough that he could talk.

"What am I?" he asked her.

"You are Michael Marcus Martiniere," she said firmly. "My adopted son, who I love very much." Ruby turned her head. "Gabe," she called, pitching her voice to carry into the neighboring room. "Mike's awake."

Gabe came in and sat on the bed, opposite from Ruby.

"What am I?" Mike gulped as he asked again.

Ruby and Gabe each took one of his hands.

"There is a reason why we call Philip your progenitor," Gabe started slowly, carefully.

Mike interrupted him. "I—I'm his clone, aren't I. I'm *him*. I'm going to be just like him."

He gulped and started to cry again, because even at ten he knew how evil and awful Philip had been. Not just from how Philip had treated him but from things he had already learned about Philip's treatment of other people.

"No," Ruby said firmly, projecting the authority of the Matriarch. "You may be Philip's clone, but you know damn good and well by now that that only means genotype. *You are not Philip. You are Michael.*"

"Donna-gran said you were nothing like Philip," Gabe murmured.

"Was she—my grandmother?" That was what she had told him then.

Gabe shook his head. "She was Philip's mother, Mike. In a sense— your biological mother."

"Then—who are you to me?"

"I am your biological son," Gabe said. "Justine is your daughter. Brandon is your grandson. Lily is your great-granddaughter. But. Most importantly. You're *our* son. No matter what your biological relationship is to me."

He studied them carefully. No revulsion. No anger. Just worry and concern.

And—perhaps—a little bit of love?

He burst out crying, but this time it brought relief and not panic. Especially when both Ruby and Gabe slid in close, sandwiching him between them. Smudge crawled into his lap.

At last, his tears slowed.

"Are you hungry?" Ruby asked. "You've been sleeping for several hours. Dr. Sheri gave you a sedative because we couldn't stop you from screaming."

"Tired," he whispered. But the mention of food made him stir.

———

Brandon and Justine were in the kitchen the next morning when Mike came downstairs. Brandon strode over to Mike, pulling him close in a hug.

"Little brother," he said softly. "My little brother. That's who you are to me. Don't you ever, *ever* doubt that. Ever. Got it?"

Mike blinked hard and sniffled a little. "Okay."

Brandon let go, except for one of Mike's hands. They walked to the table and sat, Mike next to Justine.

Justine smiled at him. "Michael. You are so not my father, and I give daily thanks for that." She reached over and gave him a quick hug. "As far as I'm concerned, you're my nephew. Okay?"

He nodded hard, tears blurring his eyes again. Justine pulled a tissue out of her pocket and wiped his eyes.

"Mikey." Ruby bent over the back of the chair and hugged him with one arm as she set a plate with pancakes and bacon in front of him, his favorite strawberry jam on the pancakes. "Here's breakfast."

Neither Brandon nor Justine talked further as they served themselves from the platters lined up on the counter. Gabe came back in with Beck. He and Ruby exchanged glances and she nodded. Gabe's lips tightened.

"Hey Mike. Can you help Charlie with the field monitoring and scans after breakfast?"

"What about my chores?" It was a relief to talk about something other than being a clone.

"Don't worry about it," Gabe said. "Just for today."

No. It wasn't a reprieve. They were treating him like a baby.

Ruby must have seen or sensed his scowl because she turned around from doing dishes. "Mikey, giving you a break after yesterday. That's all. You need to get out on the land. You'll feel better." She picked up her coffee cup and crossed the room to rest her free hand on his shoulder.

The land. One of Ruby's favorite things. *Getting on the land gives you perspective, Mike,* was something she often said to him during their rides.

He exhaled shakily. It couldn't hurt to try it. And at least Charlie wouldn't be talking about *clones.*

JULY, 2064

"How the *hell* did Mike find out about being a clone? That file was supposed to be secured!" Gabe glowered at Ruby, Brandon, and Justine from behind his desk. Mike was safely out of the house doing ranch chores with Charlie, and they had retreated to Gabe's office.

The offending file had just been sitting out in the open in Mike's study files.

Subject PJM-M-13-Michael.

The whole damn thing, leaving no doubt in lay terms about Mike's origins as Philip Martiniere's final clone. Not that Mike could be considered uninformed when it came to lab work and programming. Even at age ten, Mike knew his way around biobots and their creation processes. Understood cloning basics. The kid was brilliant. But he was also sweet and somewhat naive.

Gabe had honestly thought, before yesterday, that Mike had some knowledge of his origins. He was aware of the existence of his Befores, the clones who had preceded him. Mike knew that he was connected to Philip, that Philip was his progenitor—they hadn't hidden that fact. But he had never asked anything about the details of his connection to Philip, nor had he said one word about cloning. Or being a clone. Or even mentioned Philip's name, much less why they called Philip Mike's *progenitor*.

Repressed memories? Not wanting to put the pieces together until that damned file rubbed it in his face? Damn it, Mike was only ten. He had been through hell during his first five years. Just about half his life. They needed to remember that.

At least having Smudge around seemed to keep Mike from his tendency toward self-mutilation when stressed.

Gabe rubbed his face wearily as Ruby pressed her lips together tightly and both Brandon and Justine looked grim. He had no doubts about Ruby. Shouldn't have any about Brandon and Justine. But the only ones who knew about *that damned file* were the four people—and now Mike—sitting in this room. Someone had to have made it accessible to Mike...didn't they?

"Ruby and I wrestled with the accesses to that file for half the night," Justine said, her voice low and tight. "Gabie, someone fucked with that file to make it prominently visible to Mike. It should have only been available to someone with access to our fucking father's restricted files. Whoever did this was capable of erasing every single trace they might have left behind when they shoved it into Mike's folders." She shook her head.

"It's not any of us," Ruby said grimly. "Traces don't match. Whatever did it didn't even try to spoof one of our codes."

Whatever, not whoever?

Gabe raised his brows at Ruby. Such subtle nuance from her in this context was meaningful. Her lips tightened even more and she nodded very slightly, not enough for anyone else to notice. They needed to talk afterward.

"Except for Mike's," Justine said. "The file is coded very specifically to Mike's accesses and restrictions. I couldn't pry it open. And yet it apparently just autoloaded when Mike found it."

"Could be that it's Philip's codes and that's why they match," Brandon said. "That would be my suspicion."

"Philip's?" Gabe studied his son. "But how—wait. Matching biometrics. Of course. Mike as Philip's clone will have access to any of Philip's restricted files, because they're all under biometric lock."

Brandon nodded slowly. "I checked file accesses against mine just in case my overrides as the Martiniere might be able to bring it up. I don't match. Justine—" he glanced at his aunt— "you might be able to. Difference between daughter and grandson."

She shook her head. "No. I tried. Ruby's Matriarch accesses don't work either."

Gabe spread his hands. "So did I." He exhaled slowly. "We're definite that this was one of Philip's files we've not been able to get into?"

"Yes," Ruby said. "Neither Justine nor I can get back into it, no matter what we do." She sighed. "I had hoped to learn more about the protocols used to create Mike, especially since he has all those health issues. But—" she shrugged. "It's zipped securely back into that archive of Philip's records. And I won't ask Mike to open it for me unless it becomes really necessary."

"So that will be that," Brandon said. "Closed except for Mike. And I don't think it's a good idea for him to go poking around in that archive just yet. Not the way he reacted to this file."

"Agreed," Ruby said. "Bran, please check the extra blocks I put on the archive."

Brandon briefly smirked at her. "Same type you put up for me at that age?"

"Why do you think I asked you to check it out? Mike's at least as good at hacking as you were when you were ten. Find the holes. Tighten up any protocols I left out, please."

"With pleasure." Brandon sighed, the smile fading. "Kris isn't feeling well, so I'm going to take a crawler out to find Mike and Charlie and say goodbye to Mike. I think he needs attention from his big brother. Then head back to Moondance to run that check."

"How is Kris doing after the miscarriage?" Ruby asked.

Brandon shook his head. "It's—I need to get back home. She needs me." He stood up.

"I'll walk out with you," Ruby said. She and Brandon left Gabe's office.

Justine eyed Gabe. "Gabie. Don't look so forbidding. You've got that Martiniere glare going."

"I just—" Gabe sighed. "This was so damn bizarre. Why did this particular file show up now, and why can't we get into it?"

"A timer, perhaps?" Justine said. "A dead man's switch that finally triggered? It's a good question, Gabie. But I think you have to look to Ruby or Brandon to figure out the programming." She frowned as she stood up. "It's not often that I run into digital stuff that doesn't make sense to me."

That was worrying, if his sister couldn't understand this programming.

"That surprises me," he said.

"Ruby and Brandon know those algorithms better than I do." Justine scowled. "My hands are full with managing Pat's fundraisers. I'd stay another night to support you two, but I need to get back to LA for a New Dems fundraiser meeting."

Justine had taken over the financial end of the re-election campaign of Pat Markey, the current President and the sister of Brandon's wife Kris. As a former indentured worker, Pat had campaigned hard to eliminate indenture.

They were so close to ending that mess…for good, Gabe hoped.

"We should be fine now. Pat's re-election campaign is doing okay?"

"Doing just fine." A fleeting grin twitched Justine's lips. "But I've gotta go crack the whip because there's some problems, and I can't delegate that job."

They walked down the hallway to the kitchen and the back porch of the old farmhouse. Ruby was washing the last of the breakfast dishes now that their meeting was done.

"Hey Tine. Have a good flight to LA and give Dorie et al my regards," Gabe said. "I'd say I'd give more to the campaign, but I'm maxed out on what I can legally donate."

"That's fine, Gabie. We may ask you to make some calls to pull in more funds."

"I'm always available to do that. Safe travels, Tine."

"Good luck." And then his sister was out the door, flitting away like she always did once she escaped their father, incapable of remaining in one place for long.

Gabe turned to Ruby, just finishing up the dishes. "You okay, hon?"

She placed the plates in the drainer, then faced Gabe, leaning against the sink, raising her hands to rest her head into her palms, shaking it. At last, she shuddered, dropped her hands and looked at him.

"Mike's freakout was pretty intense," she said in a low voice. "More than I would have expected from exposure to that file. Something else is going on."

"I didn't realize he hadn't made the connection between himself and Philip. He talks about his Befores sometimes."

"I think there was a trigger of some sort in that file."

"A mind control trigger?" Even as he said it Gabe's gut tightened. Of course. Mind control mechanisms *were* one of the secret Martiniere Group technologies, had been for years. And Philip had devised many of them. That would explain Mike's reaction.

Ruby nodded. "I thought I knew Mike pretty well by now. We've served as his parents for half of his life. This extreme a reaction to learning he was Philip's clone was not what I anticipated."

"Me too. I thought he knew more than he apparently did."

They eyed each other as Ruby detached her emerald wedding ring from the silver chain around her neck and put it back on her finger. It wasn't just any wedding ring, but part of the emerald set that usually belonged to the wife of *the* Martiniere or the Martiniere-in-waiting. Gabe had been one of the few Martinieres to step down from the title before his death, handing control of the family and the family-held conglomerate, the Martiniere Group, over to Brandon. He wanted to focus on Ruby and Mike as well as their personal businesses.

But Ruby was still the official Matriarch of the Martinieres, the female counterpart to the Martiniere within the family (but not the Group). She had received the title from Donna-gran, who was Justine and Gabe's grandmother, Philip's mother—and biologically Mike's mother. And as the Matriarch of the Martiniere family, *that ring* helped Ruby use preprogrammed verbal mind control techniques on other family members as well as indentured workers, augmented body-modified workers, or cyborgs connected with the Martiniere Group.

"Any reaction from the ring?" he asked, hoping that maybe it might have detected some form of manipulation.

Ruby shook her head. "No. It doesn't work that way." She frowned.

"But tracing the links to that file—Gabe, it has the marks of some sort of worm." She bit her lip. "And my knowledge of the possibility of it being a worm comes and goes. Justine completely forgets it. I—I have to look into the ring to remember. And even then...." Her voice trailed off.

He took her left hand, gazing into the ring, wishing that he could force it to reveal its secrets. His grandmother had been far too secretive about what it could do, citing a desire to see those technologies forgotten. But damn it, knowing them could be useful if they were fighting one of Philip's creations.

"Yeah," he said. "And that's a problem." He looked back up from the ring and into her troubled blue eyes. "But we'll figure it out," he said.

"You've locked your *whatthehell* folder down solid? If this was bad —that might trigger a worse reaction," she asked.

The *whatthehell* folder contained information for her and Brandon about Philip's abuse and control of Gabe, just in case he was killed before he could explain to them how he had been under the influence of mind control strictures, which had silenced him for twenty-one years.

It detailed how Philip had abused Gabe as a teen, complete with pictures of the beatings Gabe had undergone to protect Justine. The folder included the testimony Gabe had given in *US vs Martiniere Group* about the Group's role in the development of illegal mind control technology, using indentured workers without their consent as test subjects. Additions described how the technology had been used to silence him after his testimony, written after he had broken free from its control.

"Tight as can be," he said uneasily, because he was always uneasy about mind control technology. Gabe knew too damned well what it felt like.

"We thought that about this file archive too," she said.

Gabe nodded. "I'll ask Bran to check those safeguards as well. I'm —reluctant to destroy that file, Rubes. Something tells me we might still need that evidence at some point."

"I hate to think of that necessity, but...." She sighed. "We need to create safeguards for Mike. If this *is* a mind control worm that has the ability to trigger him." Their eyes met.

Gabe considered the possibilities. "Something unpredictable."

"Smudge shows potential as a therapy dog. Mike didn't self-mutilate this time." Ruby tapped her lips with her index fingers.

Gabe cocked his head thoughtfully. "Are you thinking about gene mods?"

"Epigenetic augmentation of that tendency in Smudge's descendants, including cyber detection and support."

"Whoa. You think that's possible?" He jerked his head back in surprise.

"Been talking horse and dog training with Martin and some other folks. There's a couple of interesting new studies about canine-cyber interactions. Equine, too."

"What will they come up with next?"

She smirked at him. "It's *fun* to play with the Martiniere labs, especially the European subsidiaries."

"Can you keep it isolated? Otherwise, it becomes predictable and useless."

"I have been." Ruby shrugged. "But cyber interactions are the coming thing with show training, and since Mike is so hot to get into reined cowhorse competition, I've been doing the research."

"That does provide a good cover," Gabe admitted. "So, horses and dogs?"

"It's easier in dogs," Ruby said. "But yes. Doable using nanos. Have to calculate the dosage in horses. But there's existing sensitivity in equines, and—" she paused thoughtfully, tapping her chin with her index fingers. "Legacy and her daughter Herrie are two who show sensitivity indicators. It seems to match with the cutting genes."

Gabe chuckled. "Damn, woman, I love the way you think."

Her smirk broadened. "I know that."

He bent to kiss her, rejoicing at their similar thoughts, while regretting the years they had spent apart.

You were a damned fool in so many ways to let Philip split you apart from Ruby all those years ago, Gabriel.

He hoped he'd learned some wisdom by now. Enough to pound the *don't hide things from the person you love* lesson into Mike.

5 / ANGELICA

DECEMBER, 2064

Age: 10

"Gabriel, I found something you might be interested in watching," Great-uncle Gerard (biologically Mike's brother) said over Christmas dinner.

"Oh?"

Mike barely heard the conversation over the chaos of the big meal, seated as he was next to Ruby who sat by Gabe. Christmas meant that all of the Family leaders came to Gerard's big house in Paris—the ancestral home of the now far-flung Martiniere family. It was his fifth year attending, and he still struggled with the crowd and the noise—and the ease with which his cousins could move from English to French to Russian to Spanish. His French and Spanish were much improved but Russian was still something he wrestled with, even when he practiced with Gabe, Serg, or Justine.

"It's cued up in the theater," Gerard said. "We can watch it after dinner."

When dessert had been served, Mike was more than ready to find a place to nap after this movie because he was absolutely *stuffed*. If only four-year-old Lily would just *leave him alone* for once, instead of pestering him to play with her.

Gerard rose.

"Before we part," he said, speaking in French. "I have a treat for Gabriel that the whole family might be interested in as well. As many of you know, Gabriel's mother Angelica was a ballerina before her marriage to Saul. I was recently made aware of the existence of a partial clip from her final performance of *Swan Lake*. It is ready to play in the theater."

Gabe rubbed his face. "That's—Gerard, I didn't think any recordings existed. I'm amazed. Thank you."

On Mike's other side, Lily perked up. "Ballerina?" she chirped, drowning out Gabe and Gerard's further conversation.

"Yes, your great-grandmother Angelica," Brandon said softly .

"Wanna see."

Mike rolled his eyes. Ever since Lily had watched the Nutcracker in Portland last winter, she had been fascinated by ballet. Brandon and Kris had found a good instructor in Pendleton and set up a small studio at Moondance for Lily to practice. She kept showing Mike pictures of dancers whenever they got together, and more often than not she was wearing a tutu and ballet slippers around the house.

But he was also curious about Gabe's mother, despite being sleepy, so he joined the others to watch the clip. Lily insisted on plopping into Mike's lap as they sat in the front row.

"There's a montage of several clips," Gerard said in introduction. "I didn't realize that Angelica's first company had created a tribute to her after her death. It ends with shots of Angelica with Philip and Saul, her wedding to Saul, and her with Gabriel shortly after his birth."

Mike settled back in the seat. Lily didn't stay in his lap for long. She tried to follow the dance steps—even when Angelica was performing the famous Black Swan pas de deux.

Then the clip moved to afterwards, and Angelica with both Philip and Saul, chronicling their courtship of Angelica. Mike winced at the sight of his progenitor. Even when it showed the wedding of Saul and Angelica, Philip was present as Saul's best man, glowering at the couple throughout the ceremony.

It was a relief when the film ended with a short set of pictures of Angelica, Saul, and infant Gabe. By then, Lily had returned to Mike's lap and fallen asleep.

Brandon smiled as he picked Lily up once the lights came on.

"My little dancer," he said softly, carefully nuzzling her hair so that he didn't mess up the three neat buns that Kris had created along the center of Lily's head. "Maybe someday you'll take after your great-grandmother, hmm?"

"She very well could be a dancer," Gerard said. "Lily reminds me of Angelica in how she moves. So graceful for a child her age. You've started her in lessons?"

"Lily's been mad about dancing ever since she saw the Nutcracker last year," Kris said. "And her instructor says she shows the discipline of a child twice her age." She exhaled as Brandon walked away. "I'm so glad we've found an outlet for her energy. It has been concerning."

"Yes," Gabe said, as they followed Brandon out of the theater. "A focus is good for Lily."

Something about Gabe's voice made Mike look at him sideways, concerned. But he couldn't figure out why Gabe's voice had that odd note about Lily.

6 / *BROKEN*

NOVEMBER, 2066

Age: 12

MIKE WAS TWELVE WHEN HE LEARNED THAT, JUST LIKE HIM, GABE AND Ruby had past experiences that left them broken.

The first indication was on a rainy fall day when he was poking through some boxes in the attic. Ruby and Gabe were working with Brandon at Moondance. Mike was in the last stages of a cold, so Ruby had decided it was all right if he stayed home. He wouldn't be alone. Charlie and Terri were working on the ranch, and then there was everyone in the labs.

"Can I play in the attic?" he asked. All sorts of treasures lurked there. Journals from Ruby's Ryder ancestors. Pictures of early days in Thunder County. Ruby's old show trophies and ribbons.

Ruby hesitated. "All right," she said. "But wear a mask to keep the dust from irritating your sinuses and lungs even more. And take a nap this afternoon. You're still recovering. Don't tire yourself out, and don't make a mess!"

"I won't," he promised.

He rummaged in the boxes, digging deep in one box that he hadn't been able to finish looking through the last time. It held assorted journals kept by Ruby's grandfather Ron. Mike had read through half of them, fascinated by Ron's accounts of ranching and life during that era. But there was one journal that was missing from the otherwise neat, chronologically-organized pile, a break in the history of Ruby living with her grandparents.

Mike dug through the box, about ready to give up, when he noticed a journal that had been shoved under a group of pictures. The dates written on the front cover identified it as the missing one.

A yellowing, tattered paper article fluttered out of the composition book as he opened it. He picked it up.

The headline read *INVESTIGATION INTO DEATHS OF LOCAL COUPLE COMPLETED*. Mike skimmed through the story. The conclusion was that Tony Barkley had beaten Beth Ryder-Barkley to death, and then been accidentally shot by their unnamed six-year-old daughter when he turned on her.

Mike put the clipping down carefully. Cautiously.

Ruby never talked about her parents except to say that they were methheads, and had died when she was young. Was this them?

With trembling hands, he opened the journal again. The entry for the date that matched the article was short.

Ruby cleared for killing that son-of-a-bitch. At least she saved herself. Damn Beth for not protecting her child.

He thumbed through the journal entries both before and after that. Nothing more—and that was the only mention of Beth.

Mike returned the journal to the box it had been in and went downstairs, a creepy-crawly sensation tickling his gut.

It was a long time before he ventured to investigate the boxes in the attic again.

MARCH, 2067

Age: 12

THE NEXT SPRING MIKE WAS AT MOONDANCE, STAYING WITH JUSTINE AND Lily while Ruby, Gabe, Brandon, and Kris made a grand tour of

Martiniere facilities in Europe. Mike had a programming project to complete for school and needed access to Moondance's production labs to make it work. Justine was staying at Moondance for work of her own and to watch Lily.

He was taking a break from programming, hiding out from pesky almost seven-year-old Lily, skimming through the Moondance archives, when he encountered a file named *WTH—GMR*.

GMR. Gabe adhered to the Spanish surname protocols to honor his mother, Angelica Ramirez, and often identified his files with those initials. Mike had never heard of a WTH file. He opened it. As soon as he did, he wished he hadn't...but couldn't stop scrolling. Even when tears blurred his eyes, he couldn't stop. Smudge's son Striker nuzzled his hand, but Mike kept sniffling as he read what had been done to Gabe by his progenitor, wiping his eyes often.

It wasn't until someone put a hand on his shoulder that he could look away.

"Fuck," Justine said. "How did you find this file?"

"It was in the archives," Mike gulped. He gestured at the picture on screen, a view of teenaged Gabe's back with open weals from being lashed. "Is this—"

Justine sighed. "I took the pictures after it happened, Mikey. I was forced to watch him do it to Gabie."

"Oh God." Mike buried his head in his hands. "How can he—my progenitor did this to him—how can he even stand to be around me? *I'm him.*"

"*No,*" Justine said, more sharply and harshly than he had ever heard her speak before. "Dear God, if anything, you are the exact opposite of Daddy-damn-dearest. My God, Mikey. You care about others." She gestured to the screen. "You understand that things like this are *wrong*. I don't think your progenitor ever grasped that, even when he was four times your current age. *You are not my father. You are not Philip Martiniere.*"

The intensity with which she said it rocked him back.

"But I'm his clone," Mike whimpered all the same.

"And *you are not him.* Trust me. If anyone would know, it would be both me and Gabie. You are not him, Mikey, and I give thanks for that on a regular basis."

"How do they stand it?" Mike swallowed hard. "Looking at me."

"For that you need to ask Ruby." Justine reached past him to close the file. "Don't ask Gabie. It's harder for him to talk about those days."

"And she has—a history too."

"Ask Ruby," Justine repeated. "She will tell you." She stood up. "But for now, it's time for you to take a walk with me and Lily. Family history can wait."

APRIL, 2067

Age: 12

BACK AT THE DOUBLE R AGAIN, SEVERAL WEEKS LATER. MIKE CURLED UP on the couch, binge-watching *Babylon Five* while recovering from yet another bout of pneumonia that had cropped up after his stay at Moondance. He *was* sulking a little because he hadn't been able to make the day trip to Swait Farms with Ruby and Gabe due to being sick. He'd become friends with Jeff and Kelsey Swait's youngest daughter JoAnn, and he had been looking forward to hanging out with her. Chat with JoAnn was okay, but he liked to see people face-to-face once in a while.

Ruby came into the living room, settling down next to him, pointedly ignoring that old, nearly blind Smudge and his son Striker had snuck up next to Mike on the couch, in violation of all the house rules about *dogs on furniture*.

"Pretty dark," she said finally, as the episode ended, putting her arm around him.

"Fits my mood," he said.

"I see." She paused. "Justine told me you found Gabe's *whatthehell* file a few weeks ago."

"Whatthehell?"

"A record he kept of his treatment after his parents died. And then more details supporting his testimony about misuse of Martiniere Group indentured contracts."

"How can you both stand to be around me?" Mike burst out. "I mean—I'm *his* clone. I'm *him*."

"Yes—and no," Ruby said. "You know that it's as much about environment as it is the genetics. We've studied the cloning process."

"I know, but all the same, I've gotta wonder. After my first five years, and all the problems I got from him. How can I not be the monster he was?"

"Mike. The fact that you can ask that question is a sign that you're not like Philip." Ruby sighed. "And as for your first five years—a lot can be overcome, with the right help."

"I—uh—saw your grandfather's journal. About your parents."

She sighed again, her hand moving to stroke his forehead and temple gently as he leaned against her.

"I still bear the scars from my first six years," she said softly. "Gramps and Granma got custody of me when I was four. But I was afraid of the monster that my father could be. And my mother. When meth had them, it was damn awful."

"But at least there was meth as an explanation," Mike said in a tiny voice.

"Explanation or excuse?" Her voice hardened. "I wasn't as important to them as their drugs. And when they kidnapped me, it wasn't because of parental love. Talk about learning things you don't want to know. I was about your age when I discovered the police report. My parents planned to sell me into indenture to buy more meth. It triggered that final fight. That information confirmed the self-defense verdict for me killing my father. It didn't keep me from having nightmares about it for years afterward. I was *only six* at the time, damn it."

"Like my nightmares about my progenitor?" Knowing this made a lot of things about his early days with Gabe and Ruby clearer. They *did* understand his experiences—more than he had realized.

"Uh-huh." She exhaled. "For me, it meant that I wasn't going to let myself get hit or hurt like my mother did. The first time Gabe got pissed and grabbed me, I decked him."

"What? You guys—*fought*? With fists? I don't believe it! Even when you disagree you don't get physical."

"Oh Mikey, Mikey, Mikey." Ruby shook her head. "We were very physical when we were younger, and we never solved the fighting during our first marriage. Both of us had things we hadn't worked out from our childhoods. In fact, we had a big fistfight just before our divorce that got us thrown into jail."

"Wow."

"We've worked through it, Mike. Learning that angry words don't need to lead to blows. Having you come into our lives gave us a big incentive to move away from that unfortunate habit. We had agreed to stop doing it before—but with you, with everything you'd gone through—it was an even better reason to manage our anger."

"You're angry?"

"A lot more than you think. Both of us. Gabe's letting go of more as he gets older, but me?" She sighed. "I am, at heart, a very angry person. And I have to stop and remember how and why I became an angry person, and choose different paths."

"Are you angry at me? Because I'm *his* clone?" His voice was very small this time, barely able to choke out the words.

"Oh no, Mike." She paused. "You're a kid. Most importantly, you're not *him*."

"How do I keep from turning into *him*?"

"Just what you are doing now," she said. "Thinking about actions and consequences." She kissed his temple. "Acknowledging that you are broken, and what that means for you." She squeezed his shoulders. "Donna-gran—your mother—was most firm in her opinion that you were not at all like Philip. If anyone would know, it would have been her. And Gerard."

Mike was silent for a bit, thinking about what Ruby had said. He had called Gerard *great-uncle*, though biologically he had been his brother. Gerard had been cautious around Mike because Philip had hurt him many times when they were growing up. It hadn't been until just before his death last year that he had been more than politely friendly to Mike.

"And what Gerard said?"

"The same as Donna-gran. I was afraid for a while. Donna-gran had said that Philip had been a very angry child. When I first saw you, I knew you had a right to be very angry indeed. But you didn't stay that way."

"I still have the nightmares sometimes."

"I know. And you will. I still have mine, just like Gabe does." She exhaled again. "We're all broken, the three of us. But somehow in our brokenness, we've found a way to help each other. And that, if anything, is the cure for being broken."

7 / INTERLUDE: FILE CONSULTATIONS TWO

APRIL, 2067

After talking to Mike, Ruby retreated to her office and buried her head in her hands.

I should have talked to Mike about this sooner, like right after Justine told me about his finding Gabe's whatthehell file.

But Mike had been so damned sick—again—when she and Gabe had returned from Europe that she had put it off. Then she forgot what Justine had told her, until seeing Mike looking so sad and depressed after they got back from the Swaits triggered that memory.

Her lips pressed together hard.

Was my forgetting another manifestation of that damned worm?

Her suspicions were growing that there was some sort of stealth mind control cyberattack happening. Even though she had no proof, just suspicions. Mike's discovery of yet another damned file was just too coincidental.

Ruby took a deep breath before going to Gabe's office. He looked up, his smile fading as he saw her expression.

"Mike all right?" he asked. "He seemed a little down. I thought maybe it was the latest bug."

She shook her head and dropped into a chair across from him.

I wish it was just as simple as an illness dragging Mike down.

"Our little friend has paid a visit again," she said.

"Which little—?" Gabe frowned, clearly perplexed.

"Another one of those nasty little files."

Gabe winced. "What is it this time?"

"Two things, actually," Ruby said slowly. "One isn't from the worm. Mike found a clipping and my grandfather's diary from when I shot my father. I had thought they were put away out of reach. Apparently, they weren't. My slip. I'd gone looking for them a while back to avoid just this sort of thing and couldn't locate them. I guess they were hidden pretty well, except from a teenaged boy."

"Oh crud. And the other—let me guess. My *whatthehell* file?"

She nodded.

"Today?"

"No. A few weeks ago, while Mike was at Moondance and we were in Europe. Justine told me about it right afterward. I was going to talk to him when we returned." Ruby studied her hands. "But he was so sick, and I forgot about it. Until now. He's been awfully depressed as part of his latest illness."

"He didn't have a meltdown this time."

"But he sure seemed to get sick fast after the exposure," Ruby said. "I wish circumstances had been different and I could trace the links sooner."

Gabe shrugged. "Maybe there wasn't a trigger in it."

"I don't know," she said slowly.

How could she convey the feeling of dread that had been clinging to her ever since she talked to Mike? Bad enough that Gabe's file had been involved. Ruby had no freaking idea that Mike had found *that volume* of Gramps's diary in the attic. Much less the damned clipping. The two disclosures so close to each other added a whole new dimension to her concerns.

Even though there was no possible means that the hard copy could have been manipulated by a digital worm. That part just had to be sad coincidence—or spoke to an awareness that Mike had come into that sort of information about her past.

Now that's just paranoid, Ruby, she chided herself. *How could a worm read Mike's thoughts and know that he was potentially vulnerable to this knowledge right now?*

And yet, before Gabe had told her the details of the mind control manipulation *he* had undergone and its effects on him, Ruby would have dismissed any serious discussion of the existence of that technology as nothing more than paranoia. But her husband was walking evidence that it was possible—and *those* physical and emotional scars showed no signs of fading.

So. Possible influence on Mike. And it worried her.

"It's been long enough that any trace of a worm has faded," she continued. "I poked at the record he showed me. Justine said he was crying when she found him looking at the pictures, but he didn't go into a full panic attack like he did when he learned he was a clone. He seemed to have resolved a lot of his feelings when I talked to him. I think Striker helped."

Striker. Smudge's son, with genetic modifications keyed to Mike to ensure loyalty and emotional support. Highly secret, highly experimental. Ruby had worked with Beck O'Toole to manipulate those genes in both Smudge and Crimson, Striker's dam. The modifications would need another generation, perhaps two, to come to fruition, but given Striker's current behavior, they were making progress.

"We need to be working on the equine version," Gabe said.

She nodded in agreement.

Mike had to be protected. She couldn't explain away that deep instinct as typical motherly protectiveness. Something made her more watchful about Mike than she had been while raising Brandon, and it wasn't just that Mike's health was frail thanks to being the clone of an elderly, vicious man who had only seen him as a blood transfusion source.

No. Her late father-in-law was capable of doing something absolutely evil to hurt Mike. She didn't trust that son-of-a-bitch to stay dead.

Ruby just wished she knew what it was that triggered her concern. Sometimes she thought she could identify what Philip had in mind, and she knew that damned mind control worm was part of it. But those brief moments flitted away, forgotten except in bits and pieces.

The best counter that she could conceive of, that she had vowed to do years ago when they took custody of Mike, would be to ensure that they raised him with as strong a sense of right and wrong as possible. She was certain that goal had been successful.

But had they defanged his ability to defend himself against unscrupulous family members as a result? That was her newest nightmare. Instead of Mike twisting to emulate Philip, that Mike was more vulnerable to whatever Philip's destructive scheme was.

"Rubes." Gabe's voice was gentle as he caught her attention. "Stop worrying about Mike being vulnerable."

"Am I that transparent?"

He got up, came around to the front of his desk, and took her hands. "When it comes to discussions about Mike and my father, yes."

"I just—Gabe, I worry."

"I know. It's your job as mother." He gently eased her up and took her into his arms. "And I will tell you this, from my talks with Mike and my role as his father. *My* deepest gut sense is that while Mike is gentle compared to his progenitor—that gentleness covers the kind of tough iron core that you have. That Bran has." Gabe looked deep into her eyes. "We need to have faith in him, Ruby. Keep molding him into becoming a good man, and not what my father was."

Ruby sighed and leaned her head into his chest.

She wanted to believe Gabe was right. She really did.

But all the same, she couldn't help being afraid for Mike. What would happen if something destroyed that gentleness and trust in him?

Age: 13

No. No.

Mike's hand crept up to his mouth and he began chewing on it as he stared at the screen. The pain didn't make what he read any better.

The Martinieres were slavers of the worst kind.

And it hadn't started with indenture and the stuff he *already* knew about from Gabe's files and past testimony. No. It went back to the very foundation of the Martiniere Group.

He had started this Haitian Revolution unit as part of his history class. At first, he'd thought it wasn't going to be a big deal. He *liked* history, especially the bits and pieces about the Martiniere Family that occasionally popped up in the early bits of American history. When a link to this article about the Group appeared, he'd followed it.

But it led to a research rathole that got worse and worse. Paul Martiniere, the Martiniere of his era, had made his fortune in the West Indies. Had owned a sugar cane plantation on Saint-Domingue. When the Revolution happened, he fled to Louisiana and continued working in the slave trade. Had been a synonym for abuse. So had his son Philippe and grandson Michael.

Looking at the portrait of Michael was familiar. He strongly resembled that ancestor; had known that since he was little.

No. He looked like that evil man.

It hadn't started with his progenitor.

His family had owned people like the Swaits. Like his friend JoAnn and her siblings. Like Kris and Lily.

No.

He was barely aware of rocking back and forth in rhythm with the gnawing on his hand, whimpering. Striker pawed at Mike's leg, gentle at first, then more demanding. Mike couldn't respond. Striker started barking. It seemed to come from far away.

Slavers for generations. And we did it again once indenture became legal at the turn of the 21st century.

The curse went deeper than Philip. It wasn't just Philip.

It was bred in the bone.

"Hey, Mike." Gabe's voice was worried. But Mike couldn't stop, no matter how much he wanted to, his breath coming short and fast as he screamed into his hand, his heart pounding in his ears.

Gabe rested one hand on Mike's shoulder. He inhaled sharply.

"End program," he said softly.

Mike shuddered as the articles faded away, but he couldn't stop shrieking.

Gabe's fingers carefully pressed against Mike's jawbone joints to release his hand. He guided Mike's hand free from his mouth as Mike gasped, the screeching and rocking now fading to moans and shaking.

"Let's get you cleaned up, hmm?" Gabe said in that same soft, reassuring voice. He got Mike up and guided him to the bathroom. "Can you stop moaning? We don't want Ruby to be getting worried now, okay? She'll be back from her ride soon."

Thinking of Ruby fussing over him helped Mike get control of the whimpers. She'd just gotten back on her feet after a bad fall with a half-trained colt this spring that left her with a broken leg. He and Gabe had been going out of their way to make things easier for her this summer, physically and mentally.

But he still felt numb and drained. He let Gabe cleanse, then wrap, his hand as he sat shaking on the toilet seat, tears not very far away. Gabe got a clean washrag and gently wiped his face. The coolness was its own shock.

"Come on, let's have you lie down," Gabe said. Mike didn't resist as Gabe steered him to his bed. Striker jumped up next to Mike, resting his head on Mike's leg and whining. Gabe sat on the bed next to Mike.

"S-s-sorry," he was finally able to mumble.

"I'm sorry," Gabe said. "I thought I had that section flagged for an alert so I could talk to you first." He sighed. "It hit Justine hard too. Me as well. Bran missed it because he didn't learn he was a Martiniere until he was older."

"It's-s-s real?" he stammered. "We're—we're f-f-fucking slavers?"

Gabe sighed again. "The original fucking Martiniere Family fortune was made through sugar cane and slavery. We do not come from nice people, and it goes back to our Medici and Borgia ancestors. Your progenitor admired Cesare Borgia and Lorenzo di Medici. He wanted to emulate them—amongst others."

Mike threw a forearm over his eyes, agony washing through him as he rocked his head back and forth.

"Hey," Gabe said, gently shaking him. "Just because our ancestors were slavers does not mean that we have to be like them. Or that we're cursed to be the same way. Learning this made me realize that I had a responsibility to fight slavery—and I was already upset about indenture."

"You were?" Mike dropped his arm.

Gabe nodded. "When I was your age my parents and sister had just died, and I was in Philip's custody—didn't know he was my real father. I was alone at military school. I knew kids whose whole families were locked into indenture. Slated to be indentured upon graduation themselves because the family was in so much debt. One of them was my roommate. Gabe Ramirez. Then I learned—this—" he gestured toward Mike's desk. "It's awfully fucking hard to read the truth about names that you know from whitewashed family lore and discover that a bunch of it is all pretty lies."

Mike gulped, nodding, remembering the Great Gallery at the ancestral home in Paris. Before Gerard had gotten too feeble, he had taken the younger family members on regular tours of the family portraits, explaining the history behind them. And then there were the monuments. The Martinieres in the Louvre galleries. The—

"D-did Gerard know?"

"Yes," Gabe said grimly. "And before you ask, yes, Philip knew. Nobody who holds power in the Martiniere Group is ignorant of our history. It's in the corporate records. The memoirs. Once Justine knew the lies that we were told about Family history, she and I argued about it with Philip and Joseph whenever I was on school breaks."

"So the Family was—tainted—from the beginning."

"Uh-huh. And none of the Family branches are free from it. The British members shipped slaves. Participated in the Highland Clearances with their profits." Gabe scowled. "Some members embrace that history. Some of us reject it. I started using the Spanish name protocols so that I was Gabriel Martiniere Ramirez once I learned about the Family history."

"M-maybe I should call myself Barkley instead of Martiniere?"

"Ruby would have *huge* problems with that because of her own history," Gabe said.

"Yeah," he said shakily. "So why did she keep the Barkley name?"

Gabe shrugged. "She didn't want to be Ruby Ryder of the Double R. I guess. It's not something she talks about or wants to discuss." He exhaled. "Bran needs to tell Lily before she comes across it herself. I think she'd take it better from him than me. Especially since it is entirely possible that we may have owned Kris's family in the bad old days."

Mike winced. He could just imagine Lily's reaction to *that* discovery. "I can't imagine wanting to be—like that—these days."

"Really?" Gabe raised his brows. "Knowing what you do about indenture, and knowing that we're still fighting with Family members wanting to hold on to it? Mike, it comes down to a choice. Are you going to embrace the Family's history, or are you going to try to overcome it?"

"Overcome it." The words came out firm without hesitation, from his deepest self.

Gabe's face softened and he smiled. "I had hoped to hear that from you, Mike. I didn't *think* you'd follow in Philip's footsteps."

"Just—the name similarities really got to me," he admitted

"The names get reused," Gabe acknowledged. "And we are direct-line descendants of Paul."

Mike shuddered. "I'm going to fight indenture too, Gabe."

Gabe patted his shoulder. "With any luck, it will be completely gone in a few years. At least that's what we're all working toward having happen. Feeling better?"

Mike nodded. He pushed himself up. "I'd better get back online. Teacher's going to wonder."

"Don't worry about it," Gabe said. "I'll write him a note saying you need a break for the rest of the day. You ought to go see if Ruby's back yet. I bet she'd appreciate it if you helped her untack. At the very least, getting outside should make you feel better."

"I'll do that."

His body hurt all over as a result of the meltdown spasms as Mike slowly descended the stairs, Striker following him. He grabbed a sweater from the hooks on the back porch and headed for the barn.

Despite the ache, it felt a lot better to be outside on the Double R. Outside, he could forget about his family's muddled history.

Or the picture of that one ancestor who looked so damn much like him.

9 / LITTLE DANCER

DECEMBER, 2069

Age: 14

Mike helped Brandon settle a heavily pregnant Kris into one of the seats in the Martiniere box in the remodeled Keller Auditorium in Portland. Then he took his place by Gabe and Ruby. Attending the Nutcracker's opening night had become a regular December feature for the family the last four years, ever since Lily's ballet teacher had referred her to Nutcracker tryouts in Portland instead of the local productions in Pendleton or Walla Walla. For two years that meant figuring out which angel Lily played. But now…Lily was in her second year dancing Marie's role.

He pulled up the program and skimmed through it. Lily's bio last year hadn't included a reference to Angelica, and she'd had a meltdown about it as a result on *that* opening night. *Artistic temperament,* Brandon had said nervously at the time. This year, the bio mentioned "Lily takes her great-grandmother Angelica Ramirez Martiniere as her inspiration, and dreams of dancing the role of Odile/Odette in *Swan Lake,* just as Angelica did."

Hopefully that would be good enough. She was nine years old to Mike's fourteen, but Lily in a rage still scared the heck out of him, especially since they were close in height despite the age difference. Something about those temper flares was just too close to what Mike remembered of his progenitor. If anyone should have that touchy, fiery rage, it should be *him*, as Philip's clone.

But he couldn't find the energy or the anger to blow up like Lily did on a regular basis. The last time he could remember being as angry as Lily was the day that Philip died. Mike finally found the nerve to yell back at Philip. And that was because he was finally free of his progenitor, so defiance was easy.

The lights dimmed and the familiar overture music started up. Mike let himself be drawn in to that magical world, absorbed by music and the dance. Even though he'd seen Lily practice in her studio at Moondance, she projected an aura of someone completely different now.

When the performance was over, he and Gabe went to meet Lily while Brandon and Ruby helped Kris to the van that would take them to Seafood Palace, a nice restaurant overlooking the Columbia that was now a family opening night tradition.

"I didn't get as many bouquets this year, Grandpa," Lily fretted as Gabe and Mike carried the armloads of bouquets to the van. She lugged several stuffed animals.

"It's been a bad year for flowers," Gabe said. "That's all."

"But I should have at least gotten more stuffies, then! Jeffy got more stuffies than I did." Lily pouted as they put the bouquets and stuffies into the back of the van. She had a rivalry going with the boy who played the Nutcracker Prince with her.

"You'll probably get more at other performances," Gabe said reassuringly.

"I bet they think he dances better than me," she grumbled.

"That's *enough*, Lily," Kris said, her voice tired. "As your grandfather said. It's been a bad year for flowers. And besides, how many more stuffies do you need? Really? Even if you give half of them to your baby brother when he's born, there's still going to be way too many for your room."

"That doesn't matter. Jeffy got more stuffies than I did." Lily's lower lip extended in a pout.

"Hey, hey, hey, my little dancer," Brandon said, reaching over to pat her hand. "It doesn't matter. You danced an exquisite Marie, and that's what counts. You are my number one dancer of all time."

"Even after my little brother comes?"

"Even after your little brother comes," Brandon said reassuringly.

Silence for a few moments.

"I'm going to be the best dancer ever," Lily said. "Better even than Angelica. When I am, will you date me, Mikey? Just like Philip did Angelica?"

Mike coughed. "I—um, that's not a good idea, Lily. After all, my progenitor was your great-grandfather."

"But maybe this time Philip can have Angelica." Lily gave him a sideways look and fluttered her lashes.

"That's quite enough," Gabe said quickly, before Mike could do anything more than make a disgusted noise. And then they were at Seafood Palace, and the conversation switched to other things.

LATER THAT NIGHT, MIKE WALKED PAST RUBY AND GABE'S ROOM ON HIS way to get a drink of water. He didn't intend to eavesdrop, but stopped when he heard his name.

"Mike needs to be firmer with Lily in discouraging that crush of hers," Ruby said. "Why did you stop him?"

A long sigh. "Kris is dealing with a difficult pregnancy and I didn't think we needed a battle between the kids in the transport. The mood Lily was in—that was too much like Philip at his worst. Kris didn't need that."

"I can understand that reason. But her crush worries me."

"It does me as well. Where is she getting those notions about Philip and Angelica?" Gabe sounded exasperated. "My mother was very explicit about not wanting to do anything more with Philip than she had. I can remember that."

"Is it coming from someone in the dance world?"

"I don't think so. Saul was a greater patron of the arts than Philip ever was—he cultivated that interest in me. And despite the way Lily talks, my mother was never that prominent a performer with San Francisco. Mama got injured and married Saul, just as she was starting to reach that point. No. I'm worried about Lily's obsession with her. But hopefully it's just a little girl thing and she'll get over it once she hits puberty."

"Hopefully."

Mike continued down the hallway to the kitchen. In some ways it was a relief to know that he wasn't the only one who found Lily's behavior disturbing.

But in other ways it made him more concerned that Ruby and Gabe saw it as well.

SEPTEMBER, 2070

Age: 15

"MIKE?" THE WORRIED NOTE IN RUBY'S VOICE CAUGHT HIS ATTENTION right away. "We need to go to Moondance. Immediately. Do you have anything that would keep you here?"

"Um—" He spun his chair back around and called up his calendar in the holoscreen. "Not anything that I can't do somewhere else. What's going on?"

Ruby swallowed hard. "Kris—she's collapsed with a heart attack. Brandon needs someone to watch over Lily and baby Ronnie. We're going but if you could help...."

"Absolutely." He typed a quick note to his teacher as he spoke, then strode to his closet to grab a duffle. He had some things at Moondance due to periodic stays when he couldn't travel with Ruby and Gabe, but it wouldn't hurt to pack more clothing in this circumstance.

"Thank you, Mike. Meet you in the kitchen in five."

Mike shut down his comp after his teacher confirmed his absence, and tossed it into the bag, along with underwear, socks, and lighter shirts than he wore at the Double R's higher elevation. Striker whined but Mike ignored him. He frowned for a moment, thinking about what clothing was already at Moondance, then added jeans and a sweat-shirt. He darted into the bathroom he shared with Gabe and Ruby to snatch his personal care items. A sweep of the meds on top of his dresser, and another pair of light shoes, and he was ready. There was food for Striker at Moondance, and he just needed to grab Striker's leash off the back porch.

He was the first one in the kitchen, Striker at his heels. When Mike looked out the window, he saw Gabe and Beck marching toward the house. Beck peeled off and Gabe continued inside.

His face softened as he saw Mike. "Ruby told you?"

"Yeah."

"Thanks for being so fast. Crew's unplugging the jet right now."

It was *bad* if they were flying to Moondance. Short flights like that weren't the most efficient for electric-powered jets, even Justine's newest fleet with solar skins to augment ground charging stations. Normally, they drove between the Double R and Moondance.

"Ruby told me that Kris had a heart attack."

Gabe nodded grimly. "She and Lily were arguing before Kris collapsed. Lily grabbed Ronnie when Kris went down. She called for help. But Lily's pitching a fit and Bran can't leave because he needs someone who can handle Lily. We've got to get there fast."

Oh God. Lily in one of her meltdowns. Mike drew a slow breath. "Ronnie's okay?"

"Lily kept him from hitting the floor."

Ruby joined them. "Let's go," she said.

THEY DROVE ONE OF THE WAITING CRAWLERS UP FROM THE AIRSTRIP AFTER a tense, silent, and blessedly short flight from the Double R to Moondance. Brandon met them at the door, holding baby Ronnie.

Ruby hugged him, then took Ronnie. "Go, Bran. We'll take care of things here. Where's Lily?"

Brandon swallowed hard. "In her studio. Dancing. I think. She stopped melting down and wanted to dance. I haven't dared—"

"We'll take care of it," Ruby repeated. "Go!"

Brandon quickly hugged Gabe and Mike. Then he took off running for one of the ranch trucks. It barely had time to unplug itself before Brandon was roaring down the driveway.

Gabe frowned after him. "Hope he's got the damn thing on auto-drive," he muttered. "Last thing we need is for him to crash."

"You could have gone with him," Ruby pointed out as she reached for her bag.

Gabe grabbed it first. "Not until we know what's happening. Bran didn't leave the kids with Al and Carl for a reason. You've got the baby. Mike, let's toss our bags in our rooms and see what's up with Lily."

Mike nodded. After he dropped his bag in the doorway of the room next to Gabe and Ruby's and told Striker to stay there, he joined Gabe. As they walked down the hallway, the strains of the Swan theme from *Swan Lake* grew louder from Lily's studio.

Dread tightened Mike's stomach and he was glad he was with Gabe.

Gabe opened the studio door . Lily was focused on a projection—Angelica, fluttering wildly, Lily trying to mimic her movements. Tear tracks stained Lily's cheeks and rosin dust from falling stained her black leotard and tights.

The music changed and Lily began a series of swift turns, whipping around faster and faster until she swayed slightly. And then her knees buckled. She crashed to the floor, burying her face in her arms. Sobs shook her body as Gabe and Mike hurried to her side.

"Lily. Honey," Gabe spoke quietly as he lifted her up.

"Grandpa?" she sniffled. Her face twisted and she wailed louder. "I killed Mama. I killed Mama. I didn't mean to!"

"Hush, honey," Gabe crooned. He looked up. "Mike. If you'd shut off the projection?"

As Mike got up Lily groaned. "I didn't want to eat lunch. I just wanted to keep dancing. Like the voices told me. I yelled at her. What the voices told me. And then she just—she just fell down!"

Mike froze in the middle of switching off the projection. His eyes met Gabe's. Gabe nodded at him to continue.

Lily screamed as the projection faded. "They're gone! The voices are gone! Where did they go?" She wrenched herself free from Gabe, who rocked back on his heels with a surprised expression. She ran to Mike and grabbed his shoulders. "Philip. Philip. You've got to turn the voices back on...."

What the—? Why does she think I'm Philip?

Shaken, Mike reached up to ease her hands off, but Lily sagged against him. Then she collapsed again, pulling him down with surprising strength. When he tried to pull away, she tugged at him, sobbing harder.

Gabe extracted Lily from Mike. "You'd better go switch with Ruby," he said softly.

Mike didn't need an excuse to flee the studio. Fear tightened his gut.

What's wrong with Lily?

He wanted to run away as hard and as fast as he could. Get away from Moondance, from Lily, from *you've got to turn the voices back on.* Something was wrong here, *bad* wrong, and it felt worse than Kris down with a heart attack and possibly dying.

He tore down the hallway, peeking first in the nursery to see if Ronnie and Ruby were there. No. Reluctant to yell in case that set Lily off, he charged into the vast great room. No Ruby and Ronnie—but he heard Ruby crooning in the kitchen. He skittered there, grabbing the doorway to keep from careening into the room. Ruby was feeding Ronnie a bowl of baby oatmeal.

"Ruby," he gasped. "It's Lily. It's bad. Gabe needs you."

Ruby looked up from spooning a bite of oatmeal into Ronnie's mouth. "What's going on?"

"We found her dancing. She thinks she killed Kris. And—" it was getting hard to catch his breath. His heart pounded so hard he thought it was going to throb out of his chest.

Ruby placed the spoon back in the bowl and got up, crossing the room to stand in front of him. "Mike. Slow down. Stop hyperventilating. Breathe with me."

He focused on Ruby's face, trying and failing to control his breathing.

"Go splash cold water on your face," she said.

He obeyed. Cool water helped ease the panic mode a little bit. Ronnie fussed and Ruby mumbled something to him before joining Mike.

"Look at me. Breathe with me," she said firmly.

Now he could slow his breathing, calm the panic within that he hadn't realized was building up.

"What's going on with Lily?" she asked, once his breathing was steady and his heart no longer pounded so hard.

"She was dancing along with a projection of Angelica. Then she collapsed." He repeated what Lily had told them. Then he swallowed hard. "She grabbed me after I turned off the projection because she stopped hearing voices. She called me by—my progenitor's name, and asked me to turn the voices back on."

"Oh *God*," Ruby sighed. "All right. Finish feeding Ronnie, then change him. I'll help Gabe." She pointed to the bowl. "Get the rest of that down him."

Mike nodded. He'd done his share of caring for both Lily and Ronnie. Babies weren't scary. Not as scary as—*this*.

Ruby took off running, confirming that sinking sensation in Mike's gut that *this was bad*.

The first few bites he fed Ronnie were mechanical, half-attentive and perhaps too fast as worry dominated Mike's thoughts. Then Ronnie blew a big oatmeal bubble, giggling at Mike as it splattered across the high chair's tray and onto Mike's hand and arm.

"Why, you—" But the big grin on Ronnie's face, so like Brandon's when he pulled a prank, was infectious enough to distract Mike from fretting. He blew bubbles back at Ronnie and was rewarded with more giggles.

Mike exhaled. He scooped up a smaller serving of oatmeal. "And here it comes, round and round and round—" He found himself mimicking Ronnie's open mouth as he inserted the spoon after circling it around Ronnie's face in anticipation.

No oatmeal bubbles this time. And by the time the oatmeal was more or less inside Ronnie, Mike felt calmer. He heard voices in the hallway—one that wasn't Ruby, Gabe, the brothers, or Brandon—as he washed himself and dampened the washrag. A doctor for Lily?

Ronnie's continued giggling and squirming was a welcome distraction. He'd taken a liking to Mike from birth, and Mike was beginning to enjoy it. The admiration from Ronnie felt different from Lily's.

After cleaning Ronnie, Mike let Striker out of his room. The presence of his dog helped him settle even more as he carried Ronnie to the nursery, closing the door firmly just in case Lily was wandering around. Striker was not fond of Lily and they didn't need any further issues. Striker settled in a corner of the room as Mike changed Ronnie's diaper, then settled to playing with his—nephew? Great-grandson? Either description would fit.

Nephew instead of *great-grandson* was much less complicated, just as *aunt* instead of *daughter* was for Justine. Mike smiled into Ronnie's dark brown eyes as he sat on a stool next to the playmat. Ronnie giggled as Mike held him while he bounced, pushing off with strong legs. His mass of dark curls against brown skin was just gorgeous and his laugh made Mike join him. Ronnie was a beautiful baby, just like Lily had been. But much more cheerful and happy a child, definitely less fussy.

Nephew, he decided. Not *great-grandson*. Not like with Lily, where *great-granddaughter* worked better.

Lily. Now he worried again. Striker raised his head and padded over to sit next to Mike. Ronnie squealed happily, lunging toward Striker, and Mike had to restrain him from being too aggressive in his pats. Striker tolerated Ronnie's attention as Mike held Ronnie around the waist.

"Doggie," he said to Ronnie.

Ronnie made a noise that sounded like "da-da-da."

"Doggie," Mike repeated. "Striker."

Someone knocked on the nursery door. Striker alerted, barking once and rising to his feet. Ronnie startled, beginning to wail.

"Striker! Quiet," Mike ordered. "Go ahead," he said to the person knocking. He juggled Ronnie on his knee. "It's all right, Ronnie, it's all right."

Gabe opened the door. "Everything okay here?" His face was grim and tight as he squatted next to Mike and Ronnie.

"Ga-Ga!" Ronnie squealed happily and reached for Gabe.

"Not now, Ronnie," Mike said to him, though Gabe's face softened slightly as he smiled at Ronnie. "Things are under control here. How about—" He let his voice trail off.

Gabe rubbed his face, the momentary relaxation gone. "Al and I are joining Brandon." He exhaled with a shudder. "Kris just passed away. At least Bran had some time with her before she died. Ruby's with Lily—got meds into her and she's calming down. Justine's on her way here to help get Lily into a hospital for a couple of days."

"I can take care of Ronnie," Mike said. "I can be Uncle Babysitter for however long you need me to be."

"Thank you." Gabe gave Mike a side hug. "You doing okay?"

"Lily scared me," Mike said. "Voices. Calling me—calling me who she did."

"I know." Gabe sighed. "She's been off her medication. I suspect that's what she was arguing about with Kris. We haven't been able to get much information from her just yet." He patted Mike's shoulder. "Don't let what she said get to you. I could tell that shook you up."

"The voices," Mike said.

"She's ill, Mike. Just what and how bad—is a diagnosis in process."

"Gabe?" Al came to the door. "We're ready now."

"All right." Gabe stood up. "Justine should be here in an hour." He started to leave, then paused at the door. "I'll close this, unless you want it open?"

"Not now."

Gabe nodded, and closed the door. Mike turned his attention back to Ronnie.

What was going to happen next?

THEY BURIED KRIS IN THE DOUBLE R FAMILY CEMETERY A FEW DAYS LATER. Brandon, Lily, Ronnie, and the new nanny hired to care for Ronnie and Lily spent the night. Lily was quiet and withdrawn, but clearly herself again after her hospitalization.

Mike had gone out to the pasture to spend some time with the horses to settle himself. On his way back to the house, he saw movement in the cemetery and changed course. A chill ran through him as he realized it was Lily, dancing. For a moment he almost turned away.

Don't be such a chickenshit, Mike, he scolded himself. *You have to deal with this. Yourself. Or you'll be ducking it forever.*

All the same, his steps slowed as he approached the wrought-iron fence around the cemetery. Lily had stopped dancing and now knelt at the foot of Kris's grave, sobbing. He slowly opened the gate and entered.

"Lily?" he asked tentatively.

"Mike?" she gulped, raising her head as tears streamed down her cheeks. Lily slowly rose and headed toward him. When she staggered, he forgot about caution and ran to steady her. Lily flung herself against him, shaking with tears.

"It's okay, Lily, it's okay," he murmured.

"No, it's not," she moaned. "I killed her, Mike. I know I did! I know Dad and Grandpa say otherwise…but if she hadn't been fighting with me…."

"Lily," Mike said firmly. "It's not your fault. Your mother had a bad heart. A legacy from her days as an indentured. All the implants and the body modification work done on her. That's all it was."

"Was it?" she gulped. "That's not what the voices told me. They told me to yell at her. That it would get rid of her."

"The voices aren't real, Lily."

"*That's what you think.*" She snuffled and wiped her eyes. "You and Dad and Grandpa and Grandma and Aunt Justine and those people at the hospital. But you're wrong. You're all wrong. The voices are real. They hate all of you." More crying shook her body. "And they hate you worst of all, Mikey. I'm afraid of them. I'm afraid of what they're gonna make me do. I can hear them whispering now. The meds I got in the hospital make it better, but they'll learn to beat the meds again." Her face contorted as she wiped her eyes again. "I don't know what to do! They're gonna make me—I don't know what to do."

This time Mike took Lily firmly into his arms, patting her back. "It will be all right, Lily," he said in an attempt to be soothing. "It will be all right."

But he had to wonder about that.

At last, she stopped crying. "Let's go back to the house," he said.

Mike took advantage of closing the gate to let go of Lily's hand. Fortunately, she walked on ahead of him. Brandon was in the back yard.

"Lily?" he called.

"I'm here, Papa," she said in a sad and resigned voice that made Mike ache.

Brandon embraced her. "I was worried when I couldn't find you in the house," he said, brushing a mass of tightly curled dark hair from her face. "I can't lose you too, my little dancer. You scared me." He looked up as Mike approached them. "Thanks, Mike."

"She was in the cemetery," Mike said.

Brandon nodded. "Thanks," he repeated, before turning and walking toward the house, his arm around Lily's shoulders.

Mike waited until Brandon had gone to bed before he talked to Gabe. Justine, Gabe, and Ruby had settled into the living room with screens and books.

"Gabe?"

Gabe looked up from where his head rested in Ruby's lap. "What's up?"

"Can we talk? Alone?" It wasn't that he didn't want Ruby and Justine to hear, necessarily…but both women would immediately ask him a dozen questions the moment he started talking and he didn't want to deal with that.

"Sure. Just a minute." Gabe sat up and put down his old tablet. He kissed Ruby, then rose. "My office or the kitchen?"

The office would be more private. "Office," Mike said. He followed Gabe down the hallway.

Instead of sitting in his chair, Gabe leaned against the front of his desk. "What's going on, Mike?"

Mike told him about finding Lily in the cemetery and what she had said. Gabe frowned thoughtfully, tugging at his beard.

"You're sure she said she could still hear the voices?"

Mike nodded. "Quieter. But she's afraid they'll get louder again. That they'll beat the meds."

Gabe's lips tightened. "She's only ten," he said softly. "Only ten." He shook his head. "God." He exhaled heavily. "Thanks, Mike. What did you think she was going to say they would make her do?"

"I—I think she meant the voices will make her hurt me," he said slowly.

"Yeah," Gabe said heavily. "That's what I think, too." He paused. "Lock your door tonight, Mike. And from now on, do it on any night that you're staying in the same place as Lily."

That more than anything else put a chill in his gut.

10 / SPREE

Age: 15

Mike was the first to see the red dun filly after her birth. He was on foaling watch that Saturday night, excited because he was now trusted to handle a simple foaling on his own and it was *this one*. He had pored over pedigrees and videos with Ruby last year to find the perfect match for Heritage, Legacy's daughter.

Herrie's udder was full, a waxy buildup on her teats, and the muscles around her tailhead were soft when Mike and Ruby did the pre-nightfall check in the small pasture that kept the mares due to foal separate from the rest of the herd.

"Likely to be tonight," Ruby said after checking Herrie's udder. She patted the chestnut mare's neck. "Going to give us a palomino like your mama, Herrie? Or a dun like proud papa Max?"

"I say it's going to be a dun," Mike said as he slipped the halter onto Herrie and led her to the foaling stall.

Ruby pursed her lips. "Could be. Genes are right. Well, do you feel comfortable handling the watch tonight, as long as it's routine? You might as well see this baby through to the birth."

Mike swallowed hard. "Yeah. I think so."

"You don't have to be awake the whole time, remember," Ruby said as she braided Herrie's tail, then wrapped it. Mike turned Herrie loose in the big stall bedded with fresh straw once Ruby had finished. "The monitor will wake you."

"Okay." He had things to do while on watch—homework, a programming project for the Northwest Tech Fair teen competition.

Ruby frowned sternly at him. "Don't stay up all night programming and chatting with JoAnn. And don't be afraid to buzz me if necessary."

"I'm not gonna take a chance."

"Good." She softened. "You've seen enough foalings by now that you know what is and isn't right. And Herrie is a pro at this—not her first foal. Don't worry, okay?"

"I'll try not to." But it was an important responsibility—and one he needed to know how to handle, if he was going to do what he wanted with horses. This was exciting—a foal whose creation he had helped plan. He wanted to see what the result would be.

"All right." She patted him on the shoulder, then left.

Mike watched Herrie explore the stall, through the bars that lined the top half of the alleyway wall. She sniffed around the straw, investigated her water bucket and hay rack, peed, then came over to nuzzle Mike. He scratched her forehead, then went to the small upstairs studio apartment over the tack room to let her continue to relax. Monitors for each foaling stall were mounted on one wall. A small table, a couple of chairs, a sink and counter with a tiny fridge set into it, bathroom, and twin bed took up the rest of the space.

Mike settled at the table and snapped up his homework screen from his comp. As he worked, he occasionally glanced over at the monitor. Not that he expected anything to happen until later. Herrie wasn't eating, but stood with one hind leg cocked, head low, drowsing.

Gabe swung by about ten o'clock. "You doing okay?"

"Just waiting," Mike said. His homework was long finished and he was now creating a prototype variation of the RubyBot for the Tech Fair. He'd been talking to JoAnn about it.

Gabe wandered over and eyed the 3-D projection that Mike was working with, resting his hands on the back of Mike's chair as he studied it. "Interesting idea."

"Hoping to enter it in Tech Fair this summer, and qualify for the Nationals," Mike said.

"Hmm. I see you've modified the base programming." Gabe leaned closer.

"Yeah, I have to do that if I want to enter it in NTF, then Nationals. I can only use so much of an existing program as the foundation. So...." Mike shrugged. "It's a wrestling match right now to get the bot working right. I keep looking back at yours and Ruby's notes from the RubyBot's development. I think I saw a different pathway."

"Huh. That's interesting. I see where you deviated from what we did. That could have some interesting results." Gabe straightened up. "There's a little bit of the Swaitbot in it as well."

"I've been chatting with JoAnn," Mike said. "I can get advice from other kids. Just nothing from adults."

Gabe patted his shoulder. "Well, I got told to remind you that you needed to get some sleep tonight." He grinned. "Ruby knows too much about how programmers think. Get some rest and don't get me in trouble with her, okay?"

"Sure." He closed down the program. He *was* feeling a bit tired, anyway—it hadn't been too long since he'd had another go-round with pneumonia, and it sure seemed to be taking longer to recover this time than usual.

Probably just growing up stuff.

He *did* feel tired just before a growth spurt.

"Good," Gabe said. "Here's to an uneventful foaling tonight."

"Thanks."

After Gabe left, Mike settled on the bed, switching off the light.

But he would text a little with JoAnn before going to sleep. She'd think it was weird if he didn't—and it made him feel good. He often daydreamed about holding her hand. Kissing her. Maybe the next time they got together.

—*Talked to Gabe about the new bot,* he texted JoAnn. *He finds it interesting.*

—*Hope you didn't ask for advice,* JoAnn texted back.

—*Nope. I remember the rules. I don't want to mess this up!*

—*Want to chat?*

—I can't. On foal watch and I need to rest. Herrie's going to have her baby tonight.

—She's the one you picked the stallion for, right?

—Right.

JoAnn sent a few heart emojis. He sent some back.

—Night now, he said. *Foaling probably something like two or three am.*

—I WANT PICTURES.

—I'll send them to you.

He sighed and signed out of his comm, staring at the monitor. Herrie wandered around the stall now, stopping to chew on some hay. Mike forced himself to turn away from the monitor and closed his eyes. He didn't think he was going to be able to sleep. But at least he should try.

A BUZZER WOKE HIM. MIKE STARTLED UP, HIS HEART POUNDING HARDER than usual. He glanced over at the monitor. Herrie was down on her side and as he watched, a pair of forefeet protruded from her vulva.

He pulled on his muck boots and crept down the stairs. The dim light in the stall allowed him to watch the uncomplicated birth. Once the foal was born, he slipped into the stall, waiting as Herrie passed the afterbirth, then got up, whickering deeply as she nosed the foal, licking it as it rolled onto its belly.

After the cord broke, Mike put the afterbirth in a bucket so Ruby could examine it in the morning to ensure that Herrie had passed it all, treated the foal's cord stump, checked to make sure the foal's nostrils were clear, then stood back and waited, not intruding. Ruby wasn't a fan of excessive foal handling at birth. All the foals became social with humans soon enough.

Filly. Not sure of her color yet because she was still damp. But was that a stripe down her back—yes. Dun, with a big white star on her forehead. But what shade of dun was she—buttermilk like her sire, or something else? He grinned to himself. He'd called the dun factor all right.

The filly struggled to control her long legs and stand up. She breathed a soft whicker that sounded like *"spree-hee-hee"* as she wobbled on legs spread wide. Then she fell.

"Spree," Mike said out loud. "That's your name. Spree."

He watched as Spree struggled to get up a couple of more times, finally managing to coordinate her legs and totter around. Herrie nickered softly as the filly bumped around her hind legs, searching for the teat. At last, she found the nipple and began to suck. No problems with her legs. Healthy-looking foal. Mike was about to leave when he remembered his promise to JoAnn and took a couple of pictures.

Then he went back upstairs, and sent a message to Ruby, marked non-urgent.

—*Herrie foaled at 2:30 am. Dun filly. Spree's her name.*

He sent the pictures to JoAnn.

Much as he wanted to watch dam and foal for longer, he was exhausted.

"Spree, huh?" Ruby said later on that morning, as they watched Spree and Herrie move around the stall. Spree was already bold, sniffing around the stall and trying out a few steps of canter. Her legs were sturdy and straight and she looked like she was going to be a big, stout horse.

Mike shrugged. "Her first nicker sounded like she said Spree."

Ruby rocked her head from side to side thoughtfully. "Okay. Sounds good enough. It'll make a good barn name."

"I thought so. Think she'll get lighter and go palomino with a dun stripe?"

"Nope. She's going to be a red dun," Ruby said confidently. "We'll leave them inside today because it's just too blustery for a baby. Tomorrow will be better weather for this little one to see the outside world. You done much handling of her?"

"Just a little."

Ruby opened the stall door. "Let's check her out further."

Spree skittered away from Ruby and careened into Mike. He took advantage of the moment and wrapped his arms around the filly's body, holding her still. Spree steadied, though she eyed Ruby cautiously. Mike set her free and Ruby went to catch Spree. It took her longer to settle in Ruby's arms.

"Huh," Ruby said. "Already showing a preference for you, Mike." A faint smile twitched her lips, the same smile she had when a programming tweak came together.

He grinned at that.

Once Spree and Herrie went out with the broodmare band, Mike found himself spending more time out there, watching Spree play with the other foals, and scratching her when she checked him out. Before long she'd amble over to meet him.

Weaning Spree that fall was easy. She settled down with the other weanlings, happy to see Mike when he worked with her between runs to Moondance to help Brandon after Kris's death. He taught her to lead and have her feet handled. Even if for some reason he was short of breath and had to lean a little on her after picking up each foot, she was quiet.

And in October, on his tenth Gotcha Day, his official sixteenth birthday, Ruby presented him with Spree's registration papers. Mike stared at the paperwork.

RR Heritage Spree. Owner and Breeder, Michael Martiniere.

He had to read it several times to believe it.

"Are you sure?" he asked Ruby, looking up at her and Gabe as he sat at the kitchen table.

"You chose Max for her sire," Ruby said. "You were there at her birth. She's yours, Mike."

He grinned and read the papers again. Even though the shadow of Kris's death and whatever was going on with Lily hung over this Gotcha Day, all the same—Spree was now his. He was on his way toward achieving his dreams of owning, breeding, and training good reined cowhorses.

Best of all, he got to sneak a couple of kisses with JoAnn when out with Spree because the Swaits were at the Double R for that Gotcha Day. Things were just about perfect. He could visualize JoAnn kissing him when he and Spree won the Reined Cowhorse Worlds.

Little did he know how soon those dreams would be shattered.

11 / CLONE TWO

Age: 16

MUCH AS MIKE LOVED THE DOUBLE R, THE PAIN THAT CAME ALONG WITH early winter and adapting to the cold was not something he enjoyed. It passed as he got used to it, but the process of adapting to the change hurt.

At least he wasn't the only one suffering from aches and pains in his joints. Mike, Gabe, and Ruby all moved stiff and sore in the mornings, drinking coffee and perhaps taking a med as they worked through breakfast preparation and cleanup.

But there were little things that started getting worse.

Many of Mike's jobs during morning stock chores with Gabe and Ruby involved hand strength and mobility, because his hands were more deft and agile, less affected by winter than theirs were.

But this December was different. He dropped and fumbled things like he hadn't done since Dr. Sheri had changed his medications ten years ago. His grip wasn't as bad as Gabe's, but was definitely weaker than Ruby. That was new.

It sometimes took all three of them to do certain chores, because hands gave out and all three of them got winded. And no matter how much Mike ate, it seemed like he got taller but didn't gain weight. He tired faster and it took longer to recover.

Just a growing spell, he told himself.

But it didn't ring quite true. Not the way that fatigue pulled at him.

Sometimes it became harder to breathe, coupled with chest pains like he hadn't had for years. Mike tried to hide that from Ruby and Gabe, though it scared him.

Just your imagination, he would scold himself.

After all, he occasionally had those phantom aches that mimicked real pain. His counselor had identified those as a manifestation of his PTSD. He tried to convince himself that this was just another version. Even when the meds that had helped banish them before didn't work now.

Gabe and Ruby had enough to worry about, helping Brandon with Lily and baby Ronnie after Kris's death. They didn't need to be worrying about him. Not since Lily was still blaming herself for what had happened to her mother. She had needed to go into the hospital again, for two weeks.

And Gabe was having heart issues too.

Mike was only a clone, young in years but not in body. Who besides close family would really mourn him if something happened? There were times when he retreated to his room with Striker, biting on a towel instead of his hands to muffle his whimpers. While pain helped drive away the shadows, even a distracted Ruby *would* notice if Mike self-injured. The towel was a partial solution, and gave him some relief.

That was how matters stood in early December, a week before the three of them would travel to Vienna for the Spanish Riding School's winter gala performance, then to Paris for the big Martiniere Christmas and New Year's celebrations.

Mike woke that morning to the wind rattling the windows on the north-facing side of his room, along with the clatter of ice pellets. Striker curled up at the foot of his bed, warming Mike's feet, and reluctantly hopped off when Mike got up. He patted the heeler's head, moving slowly and stiffly. Everything hurt.

He went to the window and pulled the curtains aside to gaze into a whiteout. His lips tightened as he tried to see what he could of the horse pasture, looking for Spree. Ruby had installed protective lean-tos, but would they work with this wind angle? He squinted and squinted, finally making out the forms of the horses sheltering in the lee of the line of cottonwoods that followed the ditch and nowhere near the lean-tos, of course. The weanlings and smaller horses used the bigger horses as a windbreak, huddled together in the center of the herd. All of the horses had their heads down, tails to the wind. He smiled as he spotted Spree in the shadow of her granddam Legacy.

First big storm of the season.

Mike shivered and dropped the curtains. He dug out his heaviest base layers and thickest wool socks, and put a set on before pulling on jeans and a sweater. Normally, they fed the pasture-kept cattle and horses a big square hay bale each afternoon, but Ruby might want to do it pretty early today, especially since some of the ranch workers were down sick. He grabbed his insulated coveralls out of the closet where he stored them last spring and tried them on, grimacing. Almost too short. He'd grown a bit over the summer. If he had gained any weight, they would have been too small.

Still, they were better than nothing. He slung the coveralls over his shoulder, planning to hang them on the back porch for the season.

Ruby was alone in the kitchen, cooking breakfast. She glanced at Mike as he came through, Striker at his heels. "How's the fit on those coveralls this year?"

"Barely long enough," Mike said. Last year they had been too long. "They'll do for now."

Ruby nodded. "All right. In a pinch, you're tall enough to wear Gabe's coveralls. I'll order you some new ones." She frowned. "Could you check on Gabe? He's in the living room next to the wood stove. I took him some coffee but he might want more. He's hurting bad this morning."

"Sure." Mike shivered in the chill as he hung the coveralls on the back porch. For some reason the cold bit worse than ever this year. On his way back through the kitchen, he grabbed the coffee carafe. Easier to take the coffee to Gabe.

Gabe sat next to the wood stove in his rocking chair, a blanket wrapped around him. He looked paler than usual as he studied the screen projected in front of him, his hands cradling the coffee cup.

"Need more coffee?" Mike asked.

"Sure." Gabe held out his cup. It trembled a little. Mike took the cup and filled it while Striker cozied up to Gabe for petting.

"You okay?" he asked, his voice quavering a little as he handed the cup back.

"I've just got a bug," Gabe said, a quick smile flickering across his lips before fading. "Don't worry, Mike. I know what it feels like. Not a heart thing."

"You're sure?"

Gabe nodded. "It's a cold. But it's not C-19, it's not G9, and it's not my heart."

"If you say so," Mike said reluctantly.

"I do," Gabe sighed. "Make sure Ruby doesn't overdo, will you? Charlie's down with the same bug, and you know how she is when we're running shorthanded. If I've got it, she'll get it too. You be careful! You don't need a cold."

"I'll be careful." Mike's sigh matched Gabe's.

All the same, he made sure to pat Gabe on the shoulder before returning to the kitchen. Hugging wasn't a good idea, but Mike didn't see where a pat would hurt. And maybe it would make Gabe feel better.

AFTER BREAKFAST, AS MIKE EXPECTED, HE AND RUBY WENT OUT TO TAKE care of feeding chores. Ruby fired up the larger tractor and speared one of the thousand-pound bales to haul out for the horses on pasture. Mike and Striker clambered into the cab with her, to open gates and help spread the bale once they got into the pasture.

Mike had just cut the bale strings so that Ruby could start scattering the bale in a feeding line, shooing back the impatient herd with Striker's help, when a hard, cold gust of wind body-slammed him, a clobber like he'd been hit by the full weight of the hay bale. Suddenly Mike couldn't catch his breath and his chest hurt. He stumbled away from the bale and fell to hands and knees, struggling to breathe as the pain radiated down his left arm, barely aware of Striker whining and licking his face.

This is not right. This is not right.

He gasped for breath, but couldn't get enough air.

His arms couldn't keep him up and oh God, he hurt, worse than he ever had before. Mike collapsed on his side in the snow, icy pellets pounding on his face, awareness fading even as he thought he heard Ruby yelling his name.

MIKE WOKE IN A WHITE ROOM, OXYGEN CANNULA IN HIS NOSE, TUBES AND PICC line hooked up to his arms, wireless monitors on his chest. For a moment he panicked. Had his memories of life on the Double R only been a dream? Was he actually still just five, having his blood sucked out to sustain his damned progenitor? He started to struggle but his wrists were restrained.

"Mike. Mikey. Stop." Brandon placed a hand on his shoulder.

Mike blinked up at him, confused. Why was Brandon here?

"What—" he groaned. It was hard to talk. To breathe.

Brandon patted his shoulder. "You collapsed in the field while feeding horses yesterday morning. I'm acting as your guardian because Mom and Dad are down sick."

"How—where?"

"You're at Lakeside Memorial. Mom dragged you into the tractor and called for help." Brandon sighed. "You should have told us you weren't feeling well."

"Didn't want—problems." He struggled to get enough air to talk. This felt worse than pneumonia. Were Gabe and Ruby also in the hospital and that's why Brandon was here? Surely, he wouldn't bother for just Mike. Not with Ronnie and Lily to take care of.

"Problems? Damn it, Mike. It was almost too late. We nearly lost you."

"Does it—matter?"

"Does it matter?" Brandon snapped. "Fuck. Mikey. You're my little brother. Of course it matters. We're all worried sick about you." He exhaled. "Sorry. It's just—Dr. Johns says you should have been showing symptoms for a while now. And Mom's beating herself up because she should have paid attention to your weight loss. So is Dad."

"Why? I—I'm just—a clone. I'm—*him*."

"Mike. No, you are *not*. You're my kid brother and that's the end of it. Look. Dr. Johns is coming in now that you're awake. You're old enough to sign off on treatment, and he wants your agreement first."

"For what?"

Brandon pressed his lips tightly together and shook his head, blinking hard. His hand tightened on Mike's shoulder. When he spoke, there was a catch in his voice.

"Mikey. I'm sorry. Mom's usually best at explaining this stuff. You've got cancer. Lung cancer. Identical to what Philip had, so it's a clone effect. But we might have caught it early enough that it hasn't metastasized. We hope." He gulped. "And it gets worse. There's been damage to your heart. Clone effect. You had a minor heart attack in the field. We have to be careful with your cancer treatment because of that. But Dr. Johns says the chemo now is less traumatic and more effective than it was ten years ago. If you haven't developed sensitivities because of what you went through before."

Chemo.

Try as he could, Mike couldn't choke back the whimper that escaped his lips.

Oh God, chemo.

He remembered the fiery burn of the infusions the week before the blood draws when he was in Philip's custody. And heart problems… he'd seen enough of those with Gabe already. And Kris dying of a heart attack.

"I'll be here for you, Mikey," Brandon said softly. "You're not alone."

"But—others?"

"Justine is with Mom and Dad, and Pat's taking care of Ronnie and Lily," Brandon said. "I'm here for you."

"No—need."

"Bullshit." Brandon glared at him. "Damn it, didn't you hear me?

You're my little brother. Taking care of you is exactly what I'm supposed to do as a big brother. I am not gonna let you go through this alone. Mom and Dad can't be with you."

To his surprise and shame, Mike burst into tears. Brandon slid onto the bed and gathered Mike into his arms. He murmured soothingly as Mike sobbed.

"It's gonna be okay, Mikey. It's gonna be okay."

God, he hoped Brandon was right.

THE PREPARATION FOR *REAL* CHEMOTHERAPY WAS DIFFERENT FROM WHAT he'd experienced as his progenitor's blood donor, especially given how touchy his heart apparently was. Among other things, besides being tested in just about every way that Mike could think up in preparation for the treatment, he ended up providing a semen sample. He hadn't wanted to do it at first, but Brandon insisted.

"In case you want kids after," Brandon said.

"Like—who's gonna—want kids—with—me?" Mike muttered. Thoughts of JoAnn fluttered through his memories but he banished them.

"Mike—" Brandon growled, then swallowed hard. "Look. Things change over the years. Lily was an accident, but Ronnie—God, I can't imagine not having them in my life. I wasn't planning to be a father at your age."

"Yeah. But. Look at—who I am."

"Who are you? You're Michael Marcus Martiniere," Brandon said. "And if Mom heard you talking like that, she'd jump down your throat for beating up on yourself."

Mike knew, all right. He didn't dare talk like this around either Gabe or Ruby.

"I'm a—fucking—ticking—time bomb," he said, gasping as he struggled to speak. "Who's to say—that I—won't—turn into—*him*—at some—point?"

Brandon gave him a glare with furrowed eyebrows that was purely Ruby. "You are *not* Philip fucking Martiniere and you never will be, thank God. Drop that bullshit. Or I'll tattle on you to Mom, and she'll get after you once she's cleared. Keep it up and I'll send Justine in to rip you a new one sooner. If anyone should know how different you are from Philip it would be her—and Dad."

"All right. All right. I'll do it," Mike muttered. He knew damn good and well that Ruby would yell at him for the mood he was in. And if Justine jumped into the fray? The possibility of both women nagging him was about the only thing that would make him cooperate.

———

But giving the sperm sample led to more drama. Brandon showed up the next day in Mike's hospital room, looking grim.

"What's wrong?" Mike asked. He knew that look. Brandon as the Martiniere, dispensing difficult news.

Brandon's expression softened as he took a deep breath.

"Bad news, Mikey. I suppose—depending on your perspective."

"What now?" Mike sighed and flopped back against the raised end of his bed.

"Your semen sample." Brandon's face tightened again. "As it turns out—Mike—you're sterile. No viable sperm. Not a one."

"Makes things—simpler—doesn't it?" Mike said bitterly. No, he hadn't really planned on having kids. He hadn't really thought about the prospect. All the same, hearing this news was yet another blow. "Not that—I need—to worry—about—long-term—relationships." JoAnn. No. She probably wanted kids. And someone who wasn't sick, who wasn't a clone.

"*Mike.*" Brandon's voice could be as expressive as Ruby's when he wanted it to be, though he didn't have the influence of her Martiniere command ring. "Look. I'm sorry. One hard thing after another. But don't write off having a future with someone you love because you can't have kids. Just don't."

"I just—" Mike's voice cracked. "God. Another. Fucking legacy. From him." He gulped, taking several shallow breaths. "Clone effect. Another—fucking—clone effect. Do we even—know if—chemo—will work—on me?"

"That we do know," Brandon said, exhaling slowly. "The one piece of good news. Dr. Johns told me while you were sleeping. He's going to administer a targeted chemo cocktail. It's proven for this particular variant and it shouldn't be too hard on your heart. That *was* one positive legacy from all the bullshit that you and your Befores went through. Releasing Philip's treatment files led to the development of this mix." A faint smile touched his lips. "We'll have you back on horseback sooner than you think, Mikey."

God, he hoped Brandon was right. The prospect of chemo still scared Mike to his core.

———

"WE'LL DO THE FIRST ROUND OF CHEMO BEFORE DISCHARGING YOU," DR. Johns said to Mike as the nurses set up the infusion. Brandon sat next to the bed, holding Mike's free hand. Mike cranked down hard on it to keep from losing control and bawling or whimpering as Johns talked, trying not to look at the bag or the tubes or the big needle in his arm. "There is a very faint possibility that you might have a sensitivity to one of the components because of past exposure, so I want to monitor you here for the initial treatment. Depending on your reaction, you could be discharged as soon as tonight."

Mike nodded tensely. He squeezed down even harder on Brandon's hand. Chemo. The stuff of his nightmares for years, returned in reality.

"I'm familiar—with the—side effects," he said. "Nausea. Fatigue." They had already discussed this.

"It shouldn't be as bad as what you went through before," Dr. Johns said.

Fortunately, Dr. Johns was right.

They didn't go to Vienna and Paris that Christmas. By spring, Mike was pronounced free from cancer.

But his heart wasn't behaving right, and he still had problems breathing. And scans over the summer revealed a galloping case of osteoporosis post-chemo, with the worst impact on his arms. At least his spine was all right—so far.

One problem down. Others arising.

He wasn't going to be able to deal with a young horse for a few years. And no matter what Ruby promised, Mike didn't think he'd be healthy enough in time to train Spree himself. And watching her move made him realize that while she wouldn't mind hanging out in a field waiting for him, Spree deserved the opportunity to let her ability shine. She was just that good.

It was painful, but he told Ruby to sell Spree to someone who could invest the time and training to live up to her promise. None of them were in the shape to do that, and who knew if he would survive what lay ahead of him?

All the same, Mike hid in the house when Spree's new owners came to pick her up, pleading that he didn't feel well—which was true enough. He ignored JoAnn's sympathetic texts because he just didn't have the energy to deal with anyone. Besides, why should he put JoAnn through his agony? She wouldn't have a future with him.

That was one of the times when Mike wondered if he would live to see his twentieth year, much less his next Gotcha Day.

If the sickness didn't get him, his depression might. It was so bleak that counseling didn't help, though he still tried to hide his despair from Ruby, Gabe, and Brandon most days.

No JoAnn. No Spree. Was surviving cancer really worth it?

DECEMBER, 2071

Age: 17

A SECOND CHRISTMAS AT THE DOUBLE R INSTEAD OF VIENNA AND PARIS. This time, Mike could barely move. He was on oxygen and wore so damn many slap-on monitors that it was ridiculous. His cancer made him ineligible for a heart transplant—and it became clear that he would need to have his lungs replaced as well.

"Cyborging's the only option we've got left," Dr. Renard had said when Mike, Ruby, Gabe, and Brandon went to the pediatric hospital in

Portland early in December to talk about his treatment options. "I can't get approval for donor regenerative cloning or synthetic cultivation with Mike in this shape. And Mike's own cells won't work, since they'd be a second-generation clone with all the same problems. We can't do gene edits because the problematic pieces are too enmeshed."

Mike shivered. "I'd just—as soon." He paused to breathe. "Not deal —with clone." God, talking was harder and harder these days. "Cyborg."

"There's still going to be a delay. Finding a facility that has the equipment and the right surgeon is going to be the challenge for you— for most people, the cyborging cost would be prohibitive."

"How common a problem is this situation?" Brandon asked. "Hell. Philip Martiniere was running bootleg cyborgs twenty years ago, and the Martiniere Group has been funding the use of cyborging techniques for limb replacement ever since I became the Martiniere. This is a situation that *should* be easily solved."

"The challenge is that limb replacements in isolation are different from what we're facing with Mike," Dr. Renard said. "At some point he *will* need limb replacement because of the nature of his osteoporosis, and that adds even more complications." He sighed. "What we're looking at with Mike goes beyond the traditional cyborging measures. It's not just heart and lungs. It's the overall impact on his body once we have to deal with his limbs. We have to be mindful about how much artificial materials his system will tolerate. Too far and it could be problematic—unless you want to make him a complete cyborg."

"But it can be done?" Ruby asked. "The heart and lungs?"

"Yes. Again, heart-lung cyborging is very specialized. Equipment, staff—it's very expensive to create something that won't cause more problems in the long run."

"How common a situation is this?" Brandon repeated.

"It's rare, but—we see at least twelve cases a year where having that capability would be useful. The waiting lists at existing central facilities—too many people die first. And none of them are in this region. The specialized heart-lung cyborging equipment can also be used for limb replacement and we are on a list to get funding for a combined facility. Until then, we don't have either set of equipment available in this region."

"How long are those waiting lists for other patients?" Brandon asked.

"At least a year."

Brandon glanced at Gabe and Ruby. They nodded. He tightened his lips. "All right. I need the specs as fast as you can get them to me. The Martiniere Group can fund the purchase of necessary equipment to have cyborging available to others who need it in this region—and finance its operations so that it's not just Mike who benefits from it."

Dr. Renard's eyebrows shot up. "That's generous, but—"

Gabe waved a hand dismissively. "The Martiniere Group has the ability—shoot, the Martiniere Family can afford it. Hell, as Mike's guardian, *I* personally can afford it."

"It—would be helpful to have access to the latest cyborging technology," Dr. Renard admitted. "We can share it with the university hospital and the veteran's hospital. Establishment of a regional center would guarantee plenty of use."

"Get us the specs," Brandon had said. "The Martiniere Foundation will make it happen from our end. You get us the surgeon. We'll fund that piece as well."

Now it was a waiting game.

Two months, Brandon had said. *Late January, early February, and everything will be ready. Just hang on until then, Mikey.*

Mike resisted the suggestion that he move downstairs, arguing that since he needed a float chair to go more than a few steps, it didn't really matter where he was in the house, since the floater handled stairs easily. He wanted to stay in *his* room if possible and have the comfort of the space that had been his, and his alone, since his rescue. Where Gabe and Ruby were next door.

Even with the addition of monitors, oxygen tanks, and a hospital bed, it was still his familiar place, where he could see the dresser that had once belonged to Ruby's grandfather Ron, then Brandon, and now him. The chair by the north window where he could watch the herd in the winter horse pasture on his good days, sadly without Spree. *His* horse pictures on the wall, including a rare still of Gabe on Skydancer during his bronc riding days, and shots of Ruby barrel racing and doing a Grand Entry run-in at the Pendleton Round-Up. Striker's accustomed place on the floor by the head of Mike's bed, when Mike wasn't letting him sneak up with him.

But everything hurt, not just physically but mentally. There were times when he wanted to make someone else hurt as much as he did. He'd lost so much of what mattered. So *damn* much. Spree. The likelihood of being able to do much with horses, even casually, any time soon, if ever. JoAnn. At least two Christmases in Vienna and Paris, which was something he had taken for granted and didn't realize he missed until now. Even being able to help around the ranch—except for programming bots in the labs, and he still couldn't *be* there to watch the implementation of his work. There was no guarantee that things would get better because after heart and lungs were fixed—he had to deal with the deteriorating bones in his arms and legs next. And who knew what else could go wrong with him?

He wasn't quite at the point where he cursed his creation.

There were times when he came close to it, though.

There were times.

THE SECOND NIGHT AFTER THEIR RETURN FROM PORTLAND TO SEE DR. Renard was one of those moments. Everything hurt so bad even with painkillers that Mike couldn't sleep. Despite oxygen, he had trouble breathing. He couldn't keep his focus on videos or books. All he could do was lie in bed with the light on, aching. It was so bad that Striker snuggling up close against him didn't provide much comfort. Mike stared off into space, fondling Striker's ears slowly.

Gabe appeared in the doorway.

"You doing all right, Mike?"

Mike sighed. For once he didn't want to hide his mood or the way he felt. "I feel—like shit. Like—fuck. Why am I—still fighting?" He knew he sounded whiny and self-pitying even as he struggled to speak and breathe, but at the moment he just didn't care. "What do I—matter to—the world? Why should—I keep on—fighting this?"

Gabe raised his brows and came into the room. He grabbed one of the straight chairs that had been moved in for visitors and staff to use, and pulled it up next to the bed, straddling it so that his arms rested on the chair's tall back. He let Mike rant until Mike finally couldn't say anything more.

"You matter to Striker," he said then, matter-of-factly. "You matter to Ruby. You matter to me, to Bran, to the rest of the Family. To Ronnie."

"What? As Philip's—goddamn clone?" He struggled for more breath. "Served up—for the Family—to exploit?"

Gabe's lips tightened and for a moment Mike thought he was going to snap a response. Then he sighed, his expression softening.

"You're a lot more than your origin, Mike." He reached out and took Mike's hand, squeezing it. "After Brandon—I wanted more kids but knew it wasn't a good idea. Not under the circumstances. And then—you came along, right after Ruby and I remarried. Long after we could have kids of our own." He paused.

Mike cleared his voice to speak but Gabe raised a finger to stop him.

"Save your breath and hear me out. You have been a gift to both of us, but most selfishly to me. I missed a big chunk of Bran's childhood because of my own damn stupidity. I regret that every damn day. But I cherish every moment I have had with you. Watching you grow. Watching you learn. Even the bad times have been a gift, because—" he fumbled for words, swallowing hard. "Damn it, Mikey, biologically you're my father's clone. But realistically, you are as much my son as Brandon is. I love you dearly, and it is just fucking *killing* me to see you suffer like this." He shook his head. "You do not fucking deserve this agony. God damn it. If I could take it on for you, I would."

Mike gulped, suddenly feeling *very* bad for projecting his anger on *Gabe*, of all people. "I'm sorry."

"For what?" Gabe closed his eyes for a moment, then opened them. "Damn it, Mike, I've not been as sick as you are now, but I've been an ass and pissed off at the world because I was clobbered with a life-changing illness. My heart and the G9. Asking myself the same questions. It's normal. Doesn't make it any better for you and those around you, but it's a perfectly normal reaction."

Mike pressed his lips together and shook his head, looking down. "Shouldn't have. It."

"Bullshit. It's not fair, Mike. It's not fucking fair. You are *so* much a better person than your progenitor was. He should have been the one suffering like this. Not you. *Not you.*" Gabe exhaled deeply. "So yes. You matter very much to me, Mike. You are part of my heart, my soul, just like Ruby and Brandon. And I am so fucking pissed that everybody, *everybody*, that I deeply love has been hurt by *him*. That includes you. His clone. That he saw as a disposable blood source. Because to me, you are not disposable. You are one hell of a lot more than Philip fucking Martiniere's clone. You are Michael Marcus Martiniere, my son, and you have a lot to offer the world."

Mike exhaled, blinking hard, fighting back tears. He hadn't realized how necessary it was to hear those words from Gabe. The bitterness that had been stalking him didn't completely go away—but it was much quieter.

And it never got quite so overwhelming again.

JANUARY, 2072

Age: 17

THINGS GOT SUFFICIENTLY BAD THAT MIKE WAS HOSPITALIZED IN PORTLAND to await the cyborging. He was barely conscious enough to realize that both Ruby and Gabe came with him, and that Brandon, the brothers, and even Lily, under Justine's supervision, dropped in every few days.

He missed Striker desperately.

But the comfort that came with opening his eyes to the familiar sight of Ruby and Gabe working with their screens in his hospital room was indescribable. Their presence kept the terror of death from descending on him with sharp claws; modulated the swings between wanting to keep alive and being too tired and depressed to struggle any further.

Some nights were only tolerable because Gabe held one of his hands and Ruby the other.

Nighttime was when *the fear* crawled back into his gut, when he found himself caught up in *those* memories from childhood.

He was barely aware of the world around him when surgery prep started.

THINGS ACHED, BUT FOR THE FIRST TIME IN AGES MIKE FELT LIKE HE COULD draw a decent breath. His chest hurt, but it wasn't the same scary thudding pain. This was sharper, like he'd been cut. He opened his eyes and looked around the hospital room. The world seemed clearer, without the fog that had been plaguing him for over a year. He startled as he realized that Gabe was also in a hospital bed next to his, apparently asleep, with monitors to match Mike's.

Ruby straightened up from her recliner between their two beds, snapping her screen shut. "Hey, Mikey." Her smile was tired but spread across her entire face. "How does it feel?" She stood and leaned over his bed, stroking his forehead.

He inhaled. Exhaled. "Things hurt but in a different way. I can breathe. I don't feel my heart pounding. And I can say more than two or three words without losing my breath."

"You're gonna hurt for a while, I'm afraid. Nature of this kind of surgery, or so I've been told." She leaned on the bed rail. "But your eyes look clear, not dull."

"Everything seems brighter." He gestured toward Gabe's bed. "What's up with Gabe?"

Ruby sighed. "He had to go into surgery the day before you. Bypass. Heart attack." She grimaced. "He'd had one before we remarried. At least we were right here when it happened. And as Martinieres, we have the bucks and the influence to pull strings to room you two together, so I'm not running between hospitals."

"So is he...." Mike let his voice trail off.

"We hope he's going to come through this all right," Ruby said. Sadness colored her voice. "But he's seventy years old, Mike. There's only so much they can do without full cyborging…and Gabe won't do that. Even if his system would hold up for it, which it won't."

"I'm sorry Ruby. Both of us down at once."

She shook her head, reaching down to squeeze his hand. "You're both gonna get better. That's what matters right now."

He nodded, suddenly feeling tired.

But it was a different sort of tired this time. A healing tired, not the sapping drag of a failing body.

MARCH, 2072 THROUGH AUGUST, 2073

Age: 17-18

STRIKER WAS ECSTATIC ON MIKE'S RETURN, YIPPING AND WHINING AS HE pressed close against Mike's legs. Mike knelt stiffly to pet him, still careful about his surgery site.

But that was the easy part. He had to rebuild his strength while being careful about his fragile bones. That proved to be a greater challenge than he expected. He got to know the physical therapy space that he and Gabe shared in the ranch labs very well.

Still, Mike tried to participate in ranch life as much as he could. While he couldn't lift things in the labs, he was able to work on programming. He didn't touch the bot he'd created for Tech Fair—too many memories of JoAnn there and he didn't want to get his hopes up again. Mike dated a couple of girls from Thunder County High. Not that anything went very far. It became obvious fairly quickly that his appeal was that he was a Martiniere, not *Mike*.

Soon enough it was clear that the bones in his arms would need replacing, before the muscles and tendons shattered them beyond simple repair.

Christmas in Vienna and Paris was bittersweet because there were so many things that he just couldn't do. This time Gabe arranged a private tour of the Spanish Riding School stables. The elegant white stallions were just different enough from Spree that they didn't evoke that aching sadness Mike had when he thought about her. At least not until one stallion gracefully extended his head over the stall guard to nuzzle Mike's shoulder as he sat in his wheelchair. Mike gulped and blinked back tears. The stallion blew softly in his face, and Mike gently blew back. He looked deep into the stud's dark eyes, and saw *knowing* as well as sympathy there.

Somehow that made things a little better.

In Paris, Mike found himself sitting with the fragile family elders instead of his cousins. At first he was silently grumpy about it—but then, as he listened, he learned more about the family. Against his will he was drawn into the Martiniere stories. The history. Not the white-washed versions he'd learned when younger. The real stories.

And yes, he discovered more about his progenitor.

The more Mike heard, the more he grew to accept that perhaps he was not growing up to be like Philip Martiniere.

All the same, there was a bitter, angry piece within himself that he recognized was clearly an element of Philip.

Someday he was going to have to face up to that.

THE ARM REPLACEMENT WAS NOT AS DIRE AS THE HEART AND LUNG surgery, though it incapacitated Mike for a lot longer, requiring more complex physical therapy. But the angry bitterness that had consumed him before his heart and lung surgery remained at bay. Especially once Ruby insisted that he make weekly counseling visits again.

But Lily took a turn for the worse.

Age: 18

MIKE, GABE, AND RUBY STAYED AT MOONDANCE THE NIGHT BEFORE HE had to report for his arm cyborging, as part of an early celebration of Lily's thirteenth birthday. He was nervous about the upcoming surgery, especially since his arms and hands hurt a lot. But Mike wasn't so distracted by the pain that he missed Lily's subdued response to presents after dinner. She'd gained weight and her hands and face were puffy.

The other thing he noticed was the dearth of dance-oriented gifts. That was new—or was it something that had happened while he was so sick and disconnected from everything? Had Lily given up her obsession with dance, and if so, when had it happened? Obviously sometime when his focus had been on surviving cancer and heart disease. He had heard about her going back into the hospital for longer periods. That must have ended her dancing.

Ronnie wanted Mike to put him to bed and read to him so Mike acquiesced, happy that his three-year-old nephew (*no! Great-grandson!* a part of him insisted) still preferred him. Even after the neglect during Mike's illnesses. Then again, even when Mike had been at his sickest, there'd always been a video message to *Unca Mike* from Ronnie when Brandon visited, something to look forward to.

Mike lingered with Ronnie until he fell asleep. Then he slipped out of the nursery, cautious in case Lily was lurking around the door waiting for him. But she hadn't shown any sign of her past obsession ever since he'd gotten out of the hospital that last round, so perhaps her crush was over?

Probably should ask Gabe about that.

And then he heard sobbing over distant strains of music coming from Lily's studio. Against his better judgment, Mike slipped toward the door, pausing.

"I don't want to give up dancing!" Lily moaned. "Even if I'm not white!"

Mike couldn't hear the speaker and it puzzled him. Brandon had been so proud of Lily's dancing. Surely that hadn't changed after Kris's death?

The music grew louder but Lily kept crying. Mike eased the door open. Lily danced as she sobbed, her arms around empty space that mimicked the presence of an actual dancer. She shook her head over and over.

A virtual partner?

Try as he could, Mike couldn't find any indication that Lily was wearing a virtual setup. Normal projections would be visible.

"No!" Lily yelled. She stumbled across the room and fell. It looked like she had been thrown by—what? Who? She cringed as if she were being struck. "I don't want to give up dancing!"

Mike slid back. He turned and hurried down the hallway to find Gabe, Brandon—anyone.

This wasn't right.

He found Brandon with Gabe and Ruby in the great room.

"There's something weird going on with Lily," he said.

Brandon sighed. "She's arguing with an invisible someone about quitting dance, and it looks like she's dancing with them?"

Mike nodded. "And she said something about not being white."

Brandon shook his head slowly. "It's the latest manifestation of her —problems. Al, Carl, Frederick and I have checked her studio. Nothing shows up on the house security scans." He sighed. "Part of it is the latest meds she's on. They interfere with her balance and strength. She can't dance any longer. This Christmas was her last performance. Dr. Soren thinks that this is her means of coming to terms with it. She's all right outside of the studio."

"It just looks like she's hooked into virtual."

"Trust me, she's not."

Mike sank into a chair. "Is she going to get any better?"

"I keep hoping she will," Brandon said quietly. "But we keep adding diagnoses to what's wrong."

"Meanwhile," Gabe said, fixing Mike with a stern look. "Remember what I told you a couple of years ago. Don't forget it."

"I won't," Mike said.

All the same, when he finally went to his room and locked the door, he ran his own scans of house security. Frowned at the results. There was something small that *wasn't quite right.*

But it could also be something weird in the Moondance security programming that he hadn't updated or had overlooked.

He meant to mention it to Gabe, but in the rush to leave in the morning, he forgot.

13 / GABE

Age: 18

FORTUNATELY, MIKE WAS AT HOME, STILL RECOVERING FROM HIS ARM cyborging, when *it* happened. A hot August day kept him inside his bedroom, air conditioning whirring as he peered at his screens, working on a summer class project as a makeup for the high school classes he'd missed while sick. Striker napped in his bed next to Mike's.

Mike heard faint murmurs from the shared bathroom with Ruby and Gabe as they prepared to go out for their thirteenth anniversary dinner.

Lucky thirteen, Gabe had chuckled at breakfast that morning, even as Ruby watched him with worried eyes. It bugged Mike that as he got better, Gabe seemed to be getting worse. Like he had found some way to trade his health for Mike's.

Still, the Old Man had made it to this year. He could still ride a horse, though he needed a walker to get around otherwise these days. That wasn't too bad for someone who had suffered from two severe episodes of the G9 virus, several heart attacks, and gone through the other stuff that Gabe had.

Then Ruby screamed, followed by the blare of Gabe's medic alert button.

Mike shot up from his desk and cut through the bathroom, Striker at his heels, already suspecting what had happened.

Ruby knelt by Gabe's inert form on the floor, keening as she performed CPR on him.

Mike didn't waste time offering to help with CPR. His arms were still too fragile. He yanked the AED off of the wall and ripped it open.

"Lemme get this on him," he said to Ruby, even as one of Gabe's nurses thundered into the room.

Mike had to grab Striker to keep him from attacking the man, then shut Striker into his room, paging Beck to get Striker and put him outside.

Ten minutes and multiple AED applications later, Gabe was pronounced dead.

Mike held Ruby as she wailed, inconsolable, while they took Gabe's body away.

Payback for all those years she soothed me.

Until the nurse finally administered a sedative, Ruby clung to Mike. And even when she finally surrendered to sleep, she still clasped one of his hands tightly.

He stayed with her. Much as he wanted to cry, he fought back his tears. He had to stay strong for Ruby now. But he just felt empty, like ice was forming around his deepest self, walling him off from all emotion. No. He couldn't give in. Ruby needed him. He couldn't believe that she had collapsed like this. Ruby had been rock-steady all these years. Mike had never thought he would see her fall apart. Not even for Gabe's death.

At last Brandon joined him, staring down at his mother as she moaned and tossed, whimpering despite the sedative.

"Doctor says it was immediate," he said.

"I was in my room when it happened," Mike said. "She was doing CPR and I got the AED on him right away, just before his nurse arrived. But I knew it was too late. He wasn't responsive at all. Not like I was even at my worst."

Brandon clasped his shoulder. "You okay?"

Mike blew hard. "Gotta be. Had to be for Ruby."

"You should probably get some rest."

"If she'll let go of my hand," Mike said.

"That's not going to mess you up, is it?" Brandon carefully worked his fingers between Mike's cyborged hand and Ruby's.

Mike flexed it carefully, once it was free. The fingers were cramped into a claw and wouldn't move on their own. "There's a reason why I gave her my left hand," he said. He used his right hand to pull each finger straight, then tried flexing them again. The hand locked back down into a claw grip.

Brandon winced. "That's going to be a problem."

"Just the joints," Mike said. "Fixable. I just need to reboot them. Easy enough to do. Not like—" his voice finally faltered, and he gulped. "Not like this." He blinked hard, fighting back tears.

Brandon held out his free arm. Mike leaned into him. "It's us now," he said. "You and me together, Mike. We have to take care of Mom."

Mike straightened up. "Yeah. Just—for it to be on their anniversary. Of all days."

Brandon nodded grimly. "You gonna be okay?"

"I'll survive. And you?"

"I've been through it with Kris," Brandon said softly. "I know how Mom feels, to have my other half torn away from me like this." He swallowed hard, blinking his eyes. "Knowing that there's no way I'll see her again. Oh God. This has to be worse than the divorce was for Mom. I am so damn glad you were here for her. Was he—did he say anything to you?"

Mike shook his head. "He was gone by the time I got in here. Unresponsive. No pulse, not breathing on his own."

Brandon exhaled. "I suppose we should be grateful that it was fast. But all I can think of is that he's gone."

"Yeah."

"Go get some food and rest. Justine's on her way here and she can spell us. At least until Mom's back on her feet."

"You think she'll be all right?" For the first time Mike let himself feel worry as he looked at Ruby's restless form in the bed.

"I think she'll be fine once she has to be," Brandon said. "It's not her first loss. It's just—I think it's the timing. On their anniversary. And she and Dad were so close this time around." He dropped his arm and patted Mike on the shoulder. "Better reboot your hand and get some food. Beck was grilling ribs when I got here."

"All right." Mike went back into his room. This was the first time he'd rebooted a hand by himself—either Ruby or Gabe had helped him before now.

Grow up, he grimly told himself, and placed his left hand in the form that sat on his dresser. *You aren't the little clone boy anymore. You are Michael Marcus Martiniere and you have a job to do. Responsibilities not just to the ranch but to the family.*

At least Gabe had passed the title of Martiniere to Brandon years ago, and Brandon's successor Seth was well-established as the Martiniere-in-waiting. They wouldn't have *that* to deal with.

Once rebooting was done and his hand operating smoothly, Mike went downstairs. In spite of sorrow clenching his gut tight, he was hungry. And he wanted Striker back at his side.

It seemed strange to see Beck in the kitchen instead of supervising the lab, blinking hard as tears ran down her cheeks while she sliced cooked ribs into sections. She dashed the wetness away with one wrist as he entered.

"Get some ribs, Mike. Potato salad in the fridge."

"Let me get Striker, and then I'll have some food." He went out and freed Striker from his kennel, kneeling carefully to bury his head in Striker's ruff for a moment, breathing hard. Striker whined and licked Mike's face. Mike took several deep, calming breaths. It worked. He felt better with Striker next to him. He stood up and went back to the house, Striker on his heels.

"How's Ruby doing?" Beck asked as Mike washed his hands.

"Brandon's sitting with her. She's not—not—" He gulped as tears threatened to overwhelm him. Striker pushed against his legs and he drew a shaky breath. "They sedated her. But she's still restless."

Beck nodded grimly. "Yeah. Would be. Especially Ruby. Once she and Gabe got back together, they were...." Her voice trailed off and she chopped hard at another rib section.

Mike suddenly remembered that Beck's partner Rick had died a year and a half after Mike had come to the Double R. Another person experienced with loss. He gulped and Beck looked up sharply.

"You doing okay, Mike?"

"I—" Mike blinked back his tears. "He's gone. Was gone so fast. I was in the next room and he was...." His voice trailed off. He really hadn't had time to think about it because he'd been so focused on Ruby.

"Eat," Beck said firmly. "You're burning a lot of emotional energy and you're still healing from the cyborging. Take care of yourself, all right? You've got to think about yourself as well as others."

"I'm just not very hungry."

"Even a little bit helps."

Mike took a few rib chunks and a scoop of potato salad, Striker following him until he sat down at the table. He felt heavy and stuffed afterward even though he'd not eaten that much. He was washing his dishes when he heard a crawler pull up, and looked out the window to see Justine hurrying toward the house. He met her on the back porch.

Justine was openly crying, mascara smeared, eyes red and swollen, face twisted in sorrow. She gulped when she saw Mike.

"Mikey. Oh God. Mike." Justine reached for him, even as he felt Striker against his legs.

"Careful of the arms," he said softly, holding her close as she sobbed into his shoulder.

"He's gone for real this time," she moaned. "Not just disappeared. Gone. Dead. Oh God."

Her tears staggered Mike because he had never seen Justine this reactive. He hadn't thought of her being someone capable of expressing this depth of emotion. Not because she didn't feel, but because she kept those feelings tightly controlled.

She sobbed for a bit longer, the tears gradually fading into sniffles. At last she straightened up, still clinging to Mike.

"Look at me," she half-laughed, half-cried. "Falling to pieces."

"He is—he *was* your brother," Mike said. "It's understandable."

Justine sighed, wiping her eyes. "You holding up all right?"

"Beck just made me eat and Brandon chased me away from Ruby," he said. "I'm supposed to take a break. I was right there after it happened."

"Oh God. Ruby. How is she doing?"

Mike shook his head. "Under sedation. Screaming and crying otherwise."

Justine closed her eyes for a moment, wincing. Then her arms slipped from around Mike. "I'd better eat too, then go see her. Tell me what happened." The commanding tone was back to normal Justine.

She ate less than Mike had. Beck joined them at the table and he described the events to both women, looking down at his clasped hands, especially the left one that he'd needed to reboot.

"So just like that." Justine snapped her fingers.

Mike nodded. "They worked on Gabe for ten minutes and he was unresponsive—" his voice caught and he choked for a moment. "Not even the AED did anything. Ruby said something about last words but he was gone in just the time it took for me to hear the alert and cut through the bathroom."

"I don't know whether to be grateful that it was quick, or wishing that he'd lasted long enough for me to say goodbye," Justine said, blinking hard again. "Oh God. Gabie's dead." She shuddered and buried her head in her hands for a moment. Then she looked back up. "Bran's with Ruby right now?"

Mike nodded. "I was with her until he arrived."

Justine sighed. "Thank you, Mike. For being here." She reached across the table and rested her hand on his. "A hell of a burden to land on you, though, even for a few hours."

"I owe it to them. Both of them. Ruby and Gabe have been there for me," he said.

And oh God, *that* suddenly hurt because he remembered how often Gabe and Ruby had brought him through hard times. Only now Gabe wouldn't be there, not just for the good times but the tough ones.

Gabe's dead.

That clobbered Mike hard and sudden, almost as hard as that heart attack he'd had in the field. He snuffled, then swallowed it back.

"Thank you again, Mikey. Thank you," Justine said softly. Then she straightened up and exhaled hard. "Thank you for being here for me, too." Another hard exhale. "And now I'd better get to work. Gabie left a funeral plan, and I'm his executor. I have to make the arrangements. Can I depend on you to help me and Brandon?"

"Whatever you need," Mike said.

Justine patted his hand. "Thanks, Mike. And yeah, I think you'd better go rest."

She got up and left. Beck fixed Mike with a stern look as he lingered at the table, so he went as well.

His screen was still in the middle of the project he'd left hanging when the alarm went off. Mike stared at it. His teacher's inquiry flashed in bright red letters across the middle.

—*You haven't been working on this for several hours. Is something wrong?*

Mike sighed. Then he sat down and typed an answer.

—*My father just died. Signing off for a few days.*

He gulped at that. It wasn't often that he called Gabe or Ruby by anything but their names. Something set in stone from their early days together.

Typing the word *father* brought home what had just happened even harder. He rubbed his face, fighting back tears, because he was afraid that if he let himself go, he'd be like Ruby.

A chime alerted him to a response.

—*I'm sorry. Take whatever time you need, Mike.*

—*Thank you.*

He shut off his screen. Then he walked to his bed, feeling as if the weight of the world had crashed upon him. After slipping off his shoes, Mike crawled under the light quilt, suddenly cold.

Striker jumped up uninvited and nosed his way under the quilt to snuggle up close to Mike. He wrapped his arms around Striker, breathing slow, breathing steady, like he had learned to do to calm himself. At last he fell asleep, Striker's nose under his chin.

MIKE WAS TOO BUSY OVER THE NEXT FEW DAYS TO THINK VERY MUCH. HE, Brandon, and Justine were the public face of the family as Ruby mourned. If he wasn't taking his turn sitting with her then he was talking to other family members and family friends—mostly relaying information to those his age.

Justine walked him through the legal protocols as well. "Brandon knows this stuff already, Mike," she said on the second afternoon after Gabe's death, the day before the ceremonies. "But with Gabe gone, I think you'd better learn how to handle procedures too. Just to be safe." She sighed. "This way you know what the process is, especially when it comes to transfers of financial authorizations within the Family."

It was one of the moments when he wondered about the degree to which cyborging affected his own longevity. And that night, Mike triple-locked his shields before he sat down to crack through the safeguards that protected the file about his creation. He'd peeked at it several times secretly before now. But not the area he wanted to check this time. Took a deep breath before opening it.

He skimmed through the records until he found the one he wanted.

PROJECTED CLONE LIFETIME:
Unable to clear PJM-M-13 variant from potential cancer, heart and lung disease, and osteoporosis without sacrificing other desirable characteristics. Unless remediated, death anticipated by age fifteen.

Mike snorted. He'd been able to beat that prediction by three years now, thanks to remediation.

Even with remediation, clone unlikely to survive past the age of 50 and will most likely not survive to the age of 45. Date to be affected by degree of limb cyborging and intensity.

He didn't read past that section. It had told him what he needed to know, in case he ran into JoAnn at the funeral.

No hope for *that* future. None at all.

AS BOTH BRANDON AND JUSTINE PREDICTED, RUBY EMERGED FROM HER mourning the morning of Gabe's funeral, still shaky but up and functioning. Brandon and Mike stood by Ruby during the short graveside service at the Double R's family cemetery, each taking an arm to support her as Gabe's coffin was lowered into the ground.

Gabe hadn't wanted anything big and showy, so there was a potluck afterward where first Brandon, then Mike, eulogized Gabe. Mike felt detached while speaking the words he'd written and memorized, somehow managing not to break down into tears until he was done. After a brief flurry of sobs, he was numb again, managing to stay unemotional while saying farewells to the majority of the attendees, until the only ones left were their core family members and the Martiniere Group leadership, which included Jeff Swait and his family because of their involvement in the Barkley-Martiniere-Swait company. Mike also suspected that because Jeff's wife Kelsey had died a month earlier, Ruby wanted to talk to someone who was experiencing a similar loss.

Lily and Ronnie went back to Moondance with their nanny, because Ronnie was too young and Lily too volatile to attend the post-ceremony business meetings. And JoAnn appeared to be involved in some sort of online game as she sat in a lawn chair near the adults in the back yard. That was a relief. Mike hadn't talked to JoAnn since he had gotten sick and he just didn't know what to say. It was his fault. He hadn't had the nerve to speak to her.

He took advantage of the distractions to slip off to Gabe's hammock hung between the Jeffreys pine trees in the front yard. Striker hopped up with Mike as he sat at one end of the big hammock, large enough for two people to share. Mike stared off at the mountains. What now?

He and Gabe had talked about college once he managed to wrap up high school, perhaps overseas at the University of Paris. Not something he thought was a good idea now, especially after talking to Justine the past few days. He felt like Ruby needed him, and besides— he still had a big chunk of high school studies left to complete.

Oregon State had a decent nanotech robotics program. Perhaps that was what he should be focusing on, something that would help Barkley-Martiniere Associates, Ruby and Gabe's—now just Ruby's— subsidiary. He could attend preliminary classes along with completing high school if he settled on OSU—Thunder County High had a cooperative program.

"Hey Mike," JoAnn said from behind him as Striker raised his head.

He stiffened. "JoAnn."

She walked to where he could see her and gestured toward the hammock. "Mind if I join you?"

He just nodded.

JoAnn slid gracefully into the opposite end of the hammock, moving with a lithe dancer's ease that added to his pain because it reminded him of what Lily had been. Instead of black mourning she wore forest-green culottes and matching sleeveless top with vest that enhanced the beauty of her dark skin. Longing stirred within Mike and he fought it back.

Can't afford a relationship. Too much to do. Besides, a beautiful girl like JoAnn won't want to be stuck with a cripple like me.

And then there was what he had read about his potential future last night. He liked JoAnn too much to subject her to his mess.

"I'm sorry about Gabe," she said.

"I'm sorry about your mom," he said mechanically. He'd ducked out of going to Kelsey Swait's funeral because he hadn't felt well—or was it because he didn't want to risk talking to JoAnn?

"Yeah." She sighed.

He swallowed hard, expecting her to ask why he hadn't answered her texts two years ago.

Strike first.

But he sure hadn't wanted this conversation.

"You doing okay?" he asked instead, hoping she wouldn't bring it up.

"It's difficult." Something haunted her eyes, made her look ages older. "And there's another big swarm of indentured issues to deal with. Keeps me busy. How are you doing?"

"Still making up high school after—everything," he said.

"That bad, huh?"

"I lost two years between cancer, heart and lung cyborging, and arm cyborging," he said bluntly. "I may never be able to ride a horse again. We still don't know what's going to happen with my legs."

JoAnn flinched. "I'm sorry."

"I'm sorry, too. I shouldn't be bringing you down like this."

She snorted. "We're at a *funeral*, Mike. Depressing subjects are allowed. Especially since it's Gabe. And with you—" she waved a hand at him.

"Crippled clone boys like me don't have much of a future," he said. "Why would you even want to waste your time with me?"

JoAnn scowled. "God, Mike, that's over-the-top depressing."

"It's true." He shook his head. "I don't have much of a future. That's a reality."

"You know, maybe I should leave you alone," she said. "Unless I can somehow talk you out of this mood?"

"I'm not fit company for anyone right now," he said. "Sorry."

She eased out of the hammock and started to walk away, then came back and rested her hand on his shoulder. "If you ever need to talk, Mike. I'd like to. But I can understand."

"Thanks," he said, not daring to look at her.

How could he explain how much her presence made his sense of loss more vivid? It wasn't just Gabe. It was the loss of a future where he had dreamed of Spree and JoAnn in his life, the two wound up together.

"Later." She walked away.

Mike exhaled. He should feel relieved that JoAnn hadn't chosen to confront him.

Instead, he just felt empty. Awful. He'd been rude to someone he cared about, and that wasn't right. He should have talked to her but— he just couldn't. He mechanically rubbed Striker's head.

He wasn't sure how long he had been sitting there when Striker raised his head to alert him of someone else approaching.

"Mike." This time it was Seth, the British Martiniere who Brandon had picked as his Martiniere-in-waiting. "Ruby wants to talk to us."

"Okay. Give me a moment. Down, Striker."

Fortunately, Seth held onto the hammock to make it easier for Mike to ease his way out. Seth patted him on the shoulder like he had earlier. But the two of them didn't talk as they walked back to where the family was gathered in the back yard.

Ruby stood alone under the big weeping willow tree as Mike and Seth found seats. The Martiniere emeralds glimmered bright on her, not just the necklace, earrings and brooch but a tiara that Gabe had given her years ago. It held the black veil covering her face in place. She drew a deep breath.

"I want to thank everyone here for your support and encouragement," she said slowly. "But especially for Mike, Brandon, Justine, Beck, Terri, and Julie. Without family and staff, I couldn't have made it through these last—horrible—" she choked and reached under the veil to wipe her eyes, looking down for a moment. Then Ruby raised her head again. "Justine. Come up here, please."

"Ruby, *no*," Justine said in a low voice. "Don't."

"*Justine*." Ruby's voice was firm, bearing the faintest trace of command.

Justine sighed and rose. Brandon sunk his head into his hands. Mike glanced at Seth, who was chewing his lower lip. What the hell had happened while he was off brooding?

Ruby exhaled a shuddering breath and took Justine's hands. "I—I know that the title of Matriarch of the Martinieres is not tied to marriage or to the current Martiniere. But I just can't find it within myself to continue in that role. Mike needs me. Brandon and his children need me. That has to be my priority now. I just—I don't have the strength or presence of mind to be the Matriarch anymore. I've talked this over with Brandon, Seth, and Justine. Brandon is widowed. Mike is too young to have a spouse. And Seth's wife Clarissa does not feel up to the responsibilities. That leaves you, Justine."

What?

Mike struggled to his feet. "Ruby. Not for my sake—" He hadn't a clue that she was thinking about this!

Ruby cut him off, shaking her head. "I've made up my mind, Mike, and you're not my only reason. Sit down."

He reluctantly obeyed.

"Bad enough that no one will take the emeralds because they think I have to keep them until I die," Ruby continued, her voice quavering.

"But, with Gabe's death, I am stepping down as the Matriarch, and appointing Justine as my successor."

Tears ran down Justine's cheeks as she repeated the Matriarch's oath of office, then accepted Ruby's vow of loyalty as she knelt to place her hands between Justine's for the swearing. Justine helped Ruby back to her feet, then kissed her cheek.

Next came Brandon, then Seth and Clarissa. Justine took a few moments with each of them, whispering something to Brandon and Seth in turn. Mike was unsure and uncertain of his place in line. Then the other Family heads stood aside, gesturing him forward.

I'm not part of the succession to become the Martiniere!

Nor was it something he wanted.

Perhaps it was his status as Philip's clone. Or as Gabe's adopted son. Mike wasn't sure which it was.

It's not my turn. It shouldn't be my turn.

All the same, Mike stepped forward and knelt in front of Justine. Had it only been two years ago that he'd sworn his oaths to Brandon and Ruby in a private ceremony, Gabe watching with that proud glint in his eyes? He choked out the words.

Justine helped him back up because his legs were wobbly. She leaned in and kissed his cheek, like she had done for Ruby.

"Take care of yourself, Mike," she whispered into his ear. "Take care of Ruby. Don't you *dare* shut down like you did after you got sick, and don't let her do it, either. Those are my orders to you as the Matriarch. Got it?"

"Yeah," he said.

Justine squeezed his hands. Mike stepped back, on the opposite side of Ruby from Brandon. He felt her trembling, and glanced sideways. Even though she stood there with chin raised, damp tear trails streaked her cheeks and she quivered slightly. He slid one arm around her waist. She didn't lean against him, but her quaking eased. Then she put her arm around Mike as the others completed their oaths to Justine.

THE DAMNED DAY WAS FINALLY OVER. RUBY STAYED UPRIGHT AS THE FAMILY left.

Brandon paused to whisper in Mike's ear. "You're okay with handling this by yourself?"

Mike nodded, his jaw set tight as Ruby clung to his waist.

"I'll come by tomorrow, then," Brandon said softly. He kissed Ruby's cheek and hugged her. "Tomorrow, Ma. The two of you be careful."

Ruby nodded curtly, an echo of Mike.

At last, only Justine remained.

"Do you want me to stay another night?" she asked.

Ruby wearily shook her head.

"I can, you know," Justine said.

"No," Ruby said, her voice still hoarse and scratchy. "I just want—I just want quiet. Mike's here. That's enough." She glanced over to where Beck, Terri, and some of the student interns were picking up after the potluck. "And there'll be Beck, Terri, and Julie here overnight, in their houses. We aren't completely alone."

"All right," Justine said, reluctance in her tone. "If you're certain."

Ruby's lips tightened. "I'll be *fine* now, Justine. I just had to get through—" her voice faltered again and her grip tightened on Mike.

"We'll be okay," Mike said. "I promise."

"You are *both* stubborn as hell," Justine grumbled. "Mike. Call me if you need anything."

"I will."

They watched as Justine loaded her suitcase into the waiting crawler to go down to the airstrip. Once it rolled away, Ruby sighed and leaned against Mike.

"What do you want to do?" he asked.

"Part of me wants to climb on a horse and ride hard," she said. "But after the past few days—" she paused and drew a shaky breath. "Not a good idea. Who's been checking the fields? Has anyone been up to see the broodmares and the cattle?"

"Terri's been taking interns out daily," Mike said. "I took a crawler to look in on the horses yesterday afternoon." A much-needed break, and he could still drive a crawler even if he couldn't ride. "And the cattle."

"Thank you." She guided him around so that they were facing the house. "I'm sorry. I'm just—" A faint, sad laugh. "I didn't think this would be so devastating, even when Gabe had problems. I really didn't. Much as I'd like to jump back into things, I probably shouldn't. I feel weak as a kitten. And my thoughts are all over the place. God. I just can't focus. That didn't happen with Granma and Gramps when they died. More like the divorce, but I haven't been sick."

"It'll be okay," Mike said gently. "You'll be fine and back to normal in a few days. Want to sit down outside or go inside?"

"Outside," she said. "Front porch swing."

They walked silently to the porch and sat down together. Ruby shuddered and leaned her head against Mike's shoulder. They rocked silently for a while.

"Your school," Ruby said suddenly, raising her head. "What's happening there?"

"Already told them. Teacher said to take whatever time I need."

"I'm sorry. It's going to set you back a few months."

"It's not going to matter. I've decided to do nanotech robotics at Oregon State. There's cooperative classes, so I can do a lot of remote work before having to go to campus."

"Gabe wanted you to go to University of Paris," Ruby said sadly. "Like him, and—" She left the rest of it unsaid but Mike could add it in his own thoughts. *And like Philip.*

"I don't need to walk that path," he said. "Besides. I'm also considering a master's program at Caltech once I graduate from OSU. If—" and now it was his voice that quavered. "If my health holds."

"Oh Mikey. Why wouldn't it?"

He hesitated.

Oh, what the hell.

Ruby deserved to know.

"I accessed my file. The one about my creation. Even with remediation, I'm likely to be dead by the time I'm forty-five. I've already outlived the projected lifespan without remediation."

"You accessed your file?" She straightened up a little bit more.

"Michael." A bit of chiding in her voice, but even more welcome was the switch from passive and sad to *Ruby with her ire up.*

"I wanted to know."

She poked at him—another good sign of revitalization. "I want a copy of it."

"Are you so sure that having a copy of my specs is a good thing to have floating around in our files?"

He didn't want *his* file out there in any other form than what already existed. And now that he was eighteen, maybe he could ask Brandon for custody of those locked files so they could be destroyed.

"Probably not." Her voice was firm. "Then print out what you can. I want to look at that conclusion myself. I don't accept that assumption. There's a lot that can be done with RNAi and gene mods, and besides, that damn thing is at least nineteen years old. Things have changed." Her voice went sad again. "Even without Gabe—Beck knows her way around a gene mod chart."

"Okay, okay."

Ruby settled back down against him. "I—I can still think. Everything's crashing down around me, but I can still think. It's—better. Thanks for giving me that to consider." She sighed. "Mike. Back to school stuff. I'm—could I ask you to work with the Barkley-Martiniere and the Barkley-Martiniere-Swait businesses with me for a few days before you get back to your academics? Just to run a few checks on what I do because right now I don't trust myself. And—Bran is so bogged down with Martiniere Group work that he really can't spend the time away from it. I'll need help sorting out what Gabe was working on. It's just—overwhelming to think about."

"That's kind of what I was thinking," Mike said. "I'd be here longer before going away to school if I went to OSU. They have co-op classes so I don't need to leave right away. Be able to help with things. Settling everything with Gabe gone is going to take a while."

"You're sure that you're okay with giving up the University of Paris?"

"And what happens when my legs fail? Better to be here than there. Closer to Dr. Pramula." He paused. "Besides. At some point, someone else is going to need to take over Barkley-Martiniere, whether that's me, Lily, or even Ronnie. This way I know what's going on with that company, at least."

Ruby was silent for a few minutes. "Mike, I would be thrilled for you to learn the management of Barkley-Martiniere," she said finally. "I don't know if Lily will ever be capable and Ronnie's so young. I just thought that you might want to go off on your own. Do something different."

"Why should I?" he said. "This is home. And right now, it's where I want to be."

"Thank you." She heaved a heavy sigh.

They stayed on the swing until sunset. Just before the last brilliant glow of the sun faded, Mike startled awake, realizing that Ruby was also sleeping. He nudged her awake. They went into the house and into the kitchen.

The house felt huge and empty with Gabe gone.

PREPARATION

2079-2083

Age: 25-28

14 / REUNION

Age: 25

It was one of those days when pain and lack of mobility reminded Mike that the reckoning for his legs was coming soon. But he wanted to put off that cyborg operation as long as possible. Most of the time, the support from his programmable leg braces was enough. Today, though, he needed crutches as well to walk from scooter parking to the lab building, while Striker's son Smudgie trotted proudly next to Mike, wearing his *Therapy Dog* vest.

Last night had been rough between unrelenting aches and the memories of Lily's meltdown when he wouldn't let her come with him to Pasadena. Her threats.

Just you wait, Mike. I'll make you pay for ignoring me.

He hadn't been able to sleep until he broke down and took a painkiller, later at night than he wanted. It would give him fuzzy brain for today's lab, but it couldn't be helped. Not if he was going to prove himself to some of the top nanotech scientists in the country here at Caltech. He needed the sleep, and he was more than capable of functioning well after taking meds—plenty of experience. Not so much with sleep deprivation.

Just because you have Gabriel Martiniere and Ruby Barkley as adoptive parents doesn't mean we're giving you a break, kid.

Oh, no one had *explicitly* said that to Mike. And his status as Philip Martiniere's clone also went unmentioned. But Mike was very aware that he was being measured. Assessed. Even though he'd graduated with honors from Oregon State's award-winning program in agricultural nanotech (the program funded in part by Ruby and Brandon), this was an entirely different environment.

If only the legs will hold out.

He would lose weeks of precious class time if they failed this fall and he needed to go in for the next round of cyborging. With any luck, his fragile legs would remain functional until after spring term.

"Mike? Is that Striker?" a familiar voice called from behind him.

Mike paused, negotiating the turn carefully. Any fast jerk or twist could bring about catastrophe.

"What—oh! JoAnn!"

JoAnn hurried toward him, grinning. "Boy is it nice to see a familiar face!"

"Same for you," he answered, as a matching smile spread across his face at the sight of her. "It's been—what—five, six years?"

"Not since Gabe's funeral," she said. "So, six years. I remember your eulogy for him. That was wonderful."

And then I was an ass to you later.

He regretted that.

They eyed each other. JoAnn had matured into a tall, elegant woman. Her dark, tightly curled hair clung close to her scalp. Mike and JoAnn had hung out together during Barkley-Martiniere-Swait business gatherings while her siblings Wesley, Deontae, and Rae rolled their eyes at "the little kids" more interested in building robots than music or video games.

And then there had been his crush on her.

But that was before everything happened. Sickness. Cyborging. Deaths. Memories of JoAnn and their first fumbling kisses were wrapped up with remembrances of Spree and the cancer and heart problems.

Then again, after several failed relationships with women who had been more interested in his money than *him*, maybe it was time for him to stop letting his screwed-up body hold him back. As near as he could remember, JoAnn had never cared about the fact that he was a Martiniere—probably because her family was in business with his.

"So." He gestured to Smudgie, sitting properly on his right side. "This is Smudgie. One of Striker's last sons." He swallowed hard. "He's my therapy dog. Keeps me safe in crowds."

And keeps me independent.

Mike wasn't about to mention that. Yet.

JoAnn frowned and nodded at his legs. "Because of your legs? They don't look good."

"Pretty much because of that."

He wasn't ready to talk about the bad nights, when Smudgie kept back the nightmares. Or the occasional panic attacks. Or the pain spells combined with the panic attacks like last night. He hadn't gotten *that* far in banishing the stigma of *crippled clone boy* in his own mind, despite ages of counseling.

"My leg bones look like Swiss cheese on any scan you want to choose," he continued. "I'm hoping to hold back cyborging until I'm past the core program this fall. Ideally after graduation in the spring."

"I'm sorry to hear that."

He shrugged and turned around. Much as he wanted to linger, he had places to be. "I have to get to the labs and it takes me forever on days like this. Let's walk and talk if you have the time. I'd like that."

"All right." JoAnn moved to the opposite side of him from Smudgie. "So your legs have to be cyborged?"

"Yep. It was more or less inevitable, I'm afraid."

It was only a question of *when*, not *if*, the bones in his legs failed. A stroke of luck that his spine wasn't involved. And whether the dire prediction he'd encountered in the file chronicling his creation would come true and he wouldn't live past age forty-five, in spite of Ruby and Beck's efforts to modify his DNA to offset further clone effects.

"I'm so sorry." She sighed. "I'm sorry that you had to sell Spree. Are you able to ride horses still?"

That was a tough one. "Not until after the leg cyborging happens. And we're not sure even then. It depends on how high up they have to extend the cyborg replacements for my legs and what technique they choose to use—the docs don't want to replace my hips unless it's completely necessary. I might look into taking up driving once I've graduated."

But driving horses wouldn't give him the same thrill as galloping across Thunder County's prairies and flats. He couldn't drive into the canyons or the mountains, not really. And as for working cows—well, forget that if he couldn't ride.

On the other hand, it *would* impress the French side of the family if he took up driving horses. The British as well, especially if he decided to do combined driving, the driving version of eventing. Maybe he would buy a team of Lipizzans.

"I'm really sorry about that. I remember, you used to be a pretty good rider."

"I'm sorry as well." Mike swallowed hard, wanting to change the subject. Thinking about not being able to ride hurt too much, even though it had been a reality for several years now. "What program are you in?"

"Robotics. And you?"

"Nanotech. I've got some ideas to take the RubyBot to the next level."

JoAnn chuckled. "Of course. Just like I do the Swaitbot."

"How's your dad? I haven't seen much of him since your mother passed away."

"He's hanging in there. How's Ruby doing?"

He sighed. "I delayed undergrad for a couple of years. Not just because of my arms and needing to make up high school, but to help Ruby through Gabe's death. It hit her really hard. She's doing better now."

And she'll be even better when I'm back at the ranch.

Another reason for him to push on through as best as he could.

"I'm glad to hear that. I miss seeing her." JoAnn's expression turned momentarily sober before she smiled again. "But I got into a great internship and study program at the University of Paris, thanks to Brandon. Busted my rear getting through it before coming back here for grad school." Her smile spread wider. "Can't argue with success, because here I am."

"Sounds good." They paused outside the building. "Hey. Jo. Want to get lunch or dinner sometime and catch up on old times?"

Worth a try to see if she actually still might be interested in a crippled clone boy.

"I'd love to do that."

"Let's swap numbers. Don't know how fast I'll be able to call, but if I don't call you right away, you call me. Otherwise, I'll get buried and forget."

JoAnn laughed as she snapped up her contacts. "And what else is new? Honestly, Mike, the same is true for me."

He had to chuckle along with JoAnn as he sent her his contacts.

And then they parted. He went inside and up the stairs slowly, Smudgie doing his job to keep Mike from being jostled too badly amongst the flow of students.

One bad fall and that leg cyborging would happen sooner rather than later. Just about any fall would be bad these days.

———

SUNDAY MORNING AT MIKE'S NEW FAVORITE COFFEE SHOP TURNED OUT TO be the first time they could get together. Mike arrived first, ordering his usual black coffee and the pain au chocolat that he saved for a Sunday treat. The barista slipped Smudgie his own cookie, which confirmed Mike's first hurried impressions from earlier in the week that this was going to be his new hangout. Mike settled at a table outside, clicking up a screen to scan the daily news.

But he couldn't concentrate. Was JoAnn going to ghost him, just like he had done to her when they were kids? He'd learned a lot more about socializing during his years at Oregon State, including the degree to which his Martiniere name attracted the less-scrupulous. He'd been ghosted enough by now to realize that he had been drastically in the wrong in avoiding answering her texts after he'd gotten cancer. Yeah, he'd been sick and unhappy and depressed then. Some of that was due to his physical conditions screwing up his thinking.

Excuses.

He should have known better. Should have at least tried to tell her what was happening. That weighed heavily upon him. And even though he hoped that JoAnn wouldn't be that petty, all the same, as the minutes ticked by and she didn't appear, didn't call or text, his heart sank.

Smudgie whined and nudged Mike's hand, picking up on his mood. Mike bent over to rub his head. He straightened up at the sound of hurrying footsteps—was it? *Yes.*

"Mike! You're still here! I was afraid you'd have left already." JoAnn rushed up to the table. "I am so sorry, but Dad called this morning and I needed to work through some programming with Rae."

Relief flooded through Mike. "I was planning to hang out here for a couple of hours, just scan the news and read, not study. Otherwise, I get sucked into classwork and programming with no time away. When I don't have ranch chores to do, I don't always give myself down time."

JoAnn grinned. "I probably should have texted but it was hard to escape Rae without telling her I had a date—which would have started the interrogation about *who, where,* and everything else that I didn't think she needed to know. I just ended the call when I turned the corner." She gestured at the pastry that Mike hadn't touched yet. "What are you having? Do you recommend it?"

"Pain au chocolat. It's not quite as good as you'll get in Paris but it's not bad."

Her smile spread wider. "Paris. Mmm. I miss Paris. Okay. I'll be right back."

Mike dismissed his screen and sipped his coffee. Unlike at the Double R, it was possible to get real coffee here, if one wanted to pay the price for it.

JoAnn glided out with coffee and pastry in hand. She settled at the table and exhaled.

"So. A break. It's pretty crazy for me. You?"

"Oh yeah," he said. "I thought trying to finish high school while also taking college classes and learning how to run Barkley-Martiniere was pretty intense. I had no idea that this would be more so."

"Juggling the University of Paris and the Martiniere internship was a challenge," JoAnn said. "But I agree. Nothing like this." She paused.

"I was really surprised that you didn't go there. I kept looking for you."

"If Gabe had lived longer, I might have." No need to talk about his legs. He'd said enough about that already.

"You gave it up for Ruby?"

He nodded. "It wasn't that hard. Not like I'm locked down on the Double R. We still go to Vienna and Paris for most of December, and now that I'm doing some management stuff for Barkley-Martiniere Associates, I travel on Ruby's behalf." He fiddled with his coffee cup. "Besides. She and Gabe rescued me from an awful situation. They were there for me when I needed them. It was time for me to start repaying that debt."

"You're stepping into BMA?"

He nodded. "Took out a loan against my interest. I'll need to work it off after graduation. Ruby and Brandon transferred Gabe's share to me, with my income in reserve until I've worked off what I owe the company for college. Beats worrying about indenture—not that it's much of an issue any more."

"It may be more of an issue than you think," she said in a low voice.

Mike snapped into alertness.

Fuck.

"What do you mean?"

She exhaled softly. "Until I went to Paris, I was actively involved in smuggling unlawfully indentured workers to safety. Part of my family's underground work."

"I—didn't know." A chill washed through him. "When did this happen?"

She gave him a sad smile. "Right when I turned fifteen. January, 2071."

About the time I ghosted her.

He exhaled through his teeth. "I'm sorry if I had anything to do with that choice. Really sorry, JoAnn. I should have answered your texts but it just hurt so damn much. Losing Spree. Losing the chance of maybe—" He couldn't say more.

"Mike." She reached over and rested her hand on his. "Gabe talked to me shortly after you went into the hospital that first time. He told me what was going on. That you were depressed as hell and hiding from everyone. That it wasn't your fault or mine either, but that you'd had something hard and heavy dropped on you and that it would take time for you to work through it. If you survived." She squeezed his hand. "I really did want to smack you at Gabe's funeral when you wouldn't talk to me, especially since I'd just lost Mama. But I remember how bitter you were that day, and how obviously hurting you were, above and beyond losing Gabe. It made me hurt, too."

"Yeah." He shook his head. How much did he dare share right now? Definitely not about his restricted lifetime. "Um. Depression does run in the family. I had to get counseling for a while."

No more than that, that cautious part of him warned, even though her sympathetic look encouraged him to say more. *Protect yourself. Too early in the relationship*. If there was going to be a relationship.

"I'm sorry to hear that, Mike."

"I'm past most of that these days," he said, forcing a smile. "And I am sure as hell glad to see you now."

"So am I," she said.

He missed her touch when she pulled her hand away. Their conversation veered into safer areas.

And when they parted, they made plans to meet again next Sunday.

NOVEMBER, 2079

Age: 26

AFTER A COUPLE OF WEEKS, MIKE AND JOANN DIDN'T EVEN BOTHER TO negotiate the time and date. One or the other would check the time, sigh, grin, and say "See you next Sunday" before leaving. They had different study loads and schedules, but Sunday morning was sacred.

By the first Sunday in November their meetings had become

routine—and Mike was, for once, enjoying a warmer climate which allowed him to sit outside this time of year.

Enough that he wanted to leave the Double R? Not really. But it did make him wonder about the possibilities for more frequent travel. It wouldn't be an issue for a while. Ruby had become more entrenched at the ranch, rarely departing Thunder County except for the annual Christmases in Vienna and Paris. He wouldn't leave her alone for very long once he was done with school. She was clearly getting frailer. Brandon couldn't stay with her, not with his obligations, especially Lily. Ruby had to be Mike's responsibility.

"Five more weeks," Jo said that morning, after they finished their pastries. Her hand rested on Mike's. Holding or touching hands for most of their visit was a new move that had started two weeks earlier. "You holding up okay?"

Mike grinned and wrapped his hand around hers. "These Sunday mornings sure help."

A smile touched Jo's lips, and she looked down as he gently rubbed her palm with his thumb. Cyborging had eliminated the arthritis in his hands. He enjoyed being able to move his fingers easily and do—this. Especially since Dr. Pramula had managed to keep his muscles and tendons intact and capable of working with cyborg bone structures so that it was still *his* flesh, *his* sense of touch, not a simulation like the cyborged brothers had.

"It's keeping me sane," she said, looking up. "After our talk last week, I went home and figured out what I was doing wrong in my last lab analysis. You'd think with all my work at home that this would be a cinch. But Dad's bots are sure different from what I'm working with in class." She grinned. "Remember the Tech Fair? Your comments really helped me figure things out. Just like last week."

Did he ever remember the National Tech Fair.

"Never forgotten it," he said softly. "It was wonderful—just before everything blew up."

Her hand tightened on his. "Sorry, Mike."

He shook his head. "No need to apologize. I've wondered if we might want to take another look at that project at some point."

"I'm sure it's out of date—" Her voice trailed off and she frowned, even as Smudgie rose to sit on his haunches and stare behind Mike. "Mike. Don't turn around, but there's someone standing about thirty feet behind you who is absolutely *glaring* at me."

Mike glanced down at Smudgie. His ears lay flat against his head and while Smudgie wasn't growling—yet—the heeler had raised his lips just enough to reveal his teeth. A sign that he sensed danger.

"Describe that person," Mike said, thinking through it.

He was armed, of course—knife and derringer tucked inside his boots, a stunner in one pocket, another derringer in a wrist sheath, heavy-duty pepper spray in another. No adult Martiniere walked unarmed in public, even though Brandon had calmed down the intra-family struggles these days. And rehearsing and training fight strategies to compensate for his physical frailties had been mandatory before Mike had left the Double R for Oregon State, even though Al had gone with him as bodyguard. Learning to take care of himself with ordinary Martiniere security staff—and where the hell were they?—had been the price for coming to Caltech without the cyborged brothers to guard him. He had, of course, informed his security of the regular Sunday mornings with JoAnn.

"Dark. Skin's pale in irregular patches like she's been using bleachers. Straight black hair. Looks a little like you."

"*Fuck.*" He inhaled sharply. "How the hell did Lily manage to get away from Moondance?"

"*That's* Lily?" JoAnn shook her head. "She's sure changed since I last saw her. A lot paler and skinnier."

Mike had told JoAnn about the meltdown Lily had staged before he left for Caltech. Just in case something like this happened. He had suggested she also advise her security about their meetings. Just in case.

"You're armed?" he asked tensely.

She nodded. "You think D would let me come here without protection?"

He let a faint smile twitch his lips at the mention of her older brother Deontae, the Swait security wizard. "Maybe we can get through this with a minimum of hassle. Let me send the code. Supposedly I've got security following me. But they should have been on alert and intercepted her—" Then his voice was the one to cut out as he spotted Brandon walking toward them. "And the troops have just arrived. Brandon's here."

Lily must be traveling with Brandon. Either that or Mike was being used as bait to capture an escaped Lily.

Would have been nice to have been told about this.

"Brandon's here?" JoAnn raised her brows but didn't ease her grip on Mike's hand.

"Hey, Bran," Mike said in answer as Brandon grabbed a chair and drug it over to join them.

"Mike. JoAnn." Brandon's voice was terse. "Sorry for the interruption. I was going to call to see if you wanted to meet for dinner, Mike. And then Lily slipped out last night."

A commotion started up behind them as Lily screamed.

"God damn you, Mike, and that bitch too!"

Mike half-turned to see uniformed Martiniere security surrounding Lily, forcing her toward a white van. He sighed and turned back around.

"What's happening?"

Brandon shook his head. "She's getting worse. I brought her down for an evaluation by Dr. Soren to see if it's time for permanent hospitalization. I promised her that we'd have dinner with you if she cooperated. She was good until last night. Obsessing about you when she's not focusing on Philip. But things—*had*—been calm. Something set her off." He rubbed his face.

"Mike's told me what's happening with Lily," JoAnn said softly. "I'm sorry. That's gotta be tough."

Brandon acknowledged her with a curt nod. "I appreciate it, JoAnn. You have security?"

Her face relaxed slightly even as she held Mike's hand tight. "Do you honestly think that D would let me go unprotected? Especially since Mike and I are having regular meetings? That's a BMS safety issue."

"True." Brandon's features eased slightly. "I'm sorry for interrupting. That was not my intention at all. We've been hunting her down since midnight." He sighed.

"It would have been nice to have a warning," Mike said.

"I was hoping it wouldn't come to this," Brandon said. "We almost had her at six this morning. Your meeting was our last resort for tracking her down." He paused, looking off toward where Lily had been. "And I guess that's it. Sorry for the interruption," he said a third time as he rose, patting Mike's shoulder. "We're heading back to Moondance *now*, since it's clear I can't trust her. You'll be all right. I'll tell you more later."

Mike exhaled as Brandon left.

"Sorry," he said. "I guess that counts as a Martiniere moment."

"That's the most distracted I've ever seen Brandon," JoAnn said. "You sure everything's all right?"

Mike flexed his fingers in her hand but didn't let go. "It sounds like Lily is getting worse since I left," he said. "And what makes it even more problematic is that she's not a half-bad programmer herself in spite of her mental issues. Who knows what she might be capable of hacking?"

JoAnn shuddered. "Do you know what's wrong?"

"It's a combination of in-utero exposures before Kris was able to get her indentured hormonal tags removed as well as family traits toward depression and bipolar syndrome." He heaved a heavy sigh. "As I well know." His depression hadn't completely been related to his physical problems. At least he'd been able to keep from going down the same path as Lily, but it had taken counseling to dig himself out of that pit. "Apparently that can also swing toward other problems. You'd think they could find a diagnosis, but it seems like every time someone comes up with a label, Lily finds yet another thing to add to the syndromes."

"That's tough."

"Especially since she seems to have an obsession with me." He paused. "She did manage to scare off one of my girlfriends at Oregon State."

JoAnn snorted. "Gonna take a lot more than Philip Martiniere's crazy great-granddaughter to get rid of me."

Words couldn't express the relief Mike felt when she said that.

DECEMBER, 2079

Age: 26

"Are you staying in town over Christmas?" JoAnn asked on the last Sunday of fall term. "Or going back to the Double R? Just wondered with all the reports of snow and such."

"Not the Double R," Mike said. "Christmas and New Year's are the big Martiniere family holidays. I'll be in Paris with Ruby and the rest of the family."

And the end of the year meeting.

Ron was too young to represent the US Martinieres, and Brandon as the Martiniere couldn't speak for their branch. It was Mike's job.

"Paris. Wow." She smiled wistfully. "I miss the city."

"It's business as well," he said. "Big family head meetings. Then Christmas and New Year's." Mike eyed her. He'd been thinking about suggesting they meet in Paris for the New Year, but had been—nervous—about bringing it up. He wasn't sure how fast she wanted to proceed. Well, she had spoken first. Had to be a safe subject. "So what are you doing for the New Year?"

JoAnn shrugged. "I haven't figured it out yet. I could stay home, but..." she shrugged. "Not been the same since Mom died. Christmas is one thing. New Year's...I'd rather be somewhere else."

"Want to spend it in Paris? There'll be room. Lots of room."

"You sure about that?"

"I don't know why not. Come over a couple of days before. We'll cruise the town. Eat great French food. Absorb culture. Show each other our favorite spots. Have a nice break before coming back to work our rears off winter term."

She hesitated. "You sure it's not going to be a problem?"

"David has a lot of space in that big old house of his. And not everyone stays over until New Year's. There's always a couple of extra rooms in the Martiniere's penthouse. Both Brandon and David told me several years ago to invite a friend if I wanted someone to spend New

Year's with me. Not Christmas—that's just for family. But New Year's? Yep. So I'm inviting you."

"It's tempting," she mused. "Just getting there from Arkansas can be a challenge, though."

"I'll have Justine send a jet to your airstrip."

JoAnn burst out laughing. "You Martinieres! It's always *I'll have Justine send a jet.*"

But she was smiling when she said it. And before they parted, the arrangement was in place.

Age: 26

MIKE IMPATIENTLY COUNTED DOWN THE DAYS BEFORE JoAnn's ARRIVAL. This was a busier business Christmas than usual. One of Brandon's concerns was the new regenerative cloning operation that Jeremy, one of the Canadian cousins, wanted to set up in Montreal. Brandon and Mike spent hours skimming the reports along with Seth.

Might as well be the Martiniere-in-waiting myself, Mike thought as he and Brandon did one last check of Jeremy's files, the day JoAnn was due to arrive. But he knew more about cloning than Seth, so perhaps he was just being jumpy about hidden motives on Brandon's part. He had been firm about turning down the position of Martiniere-in-waiting when Bran and Justine approached him about replacing Seth, once he reached legal age. There was a part of him that was too much like his progenitor for Mike's liking. He feared that getting too close to *becoming* the Martiniere might awaken that carefully restrained part of himself.

"It looks legit," Brandon said. "Not reproductive cloning at all."

"We'll need to keep an eye on it," Mike said.

"Dad?" Lily slipped into the room. Smudgie barked once, then hid under Mike's chair. "I want to take Carl and go shopping." She gave Mike a big smile. "Unless you want to go with me, Mike."

"Uh, no. My legs are hurting," Mike said hesitantly. There'd been far too many of these encounters with Lily to make him uneasy this holiday. When she didn't think he was looking, she'd stare adoringly at him. And her blouse necklines had been plunging lower and lower.

"Go ahead," Brandon said.

Lily lingered. "Sure you don't want to go with me, Mike?" The big smile turned pouty.

"I'm positive." He and Al were heading for the airport to meet JoAnn in two hours.

"You'll be missing some fun."

"Lily, I said *no*." His voice went sharper than he intended. Smudgie whined.

Brandon looked up. "Lily. You're not listening. Mike said no. He's got company coming."

"I bet he just wants to screw that Black slut of his!" She whirled around and stormed out.

"Lily!" Brandon snapped after her, then sighed. "Mike. I'm sorry. I don't know where she's getting this racist crap. She's been saying hurtful stuff to Ron, even though she's just as mixed race as he is."

"I'm sorry." Mike didn't know what else to say.

"It's not your fault," Brandon said. "I don't know how much of that focus on you is because you're Philip's clone." He rubbed his face, just like Gabe used to do when worried, like Mike sometimes found himself doing. "I didn't discover how much she's venerating Philip until we left Moondance to come here. I—found her stash of Philip stuff. Some of it is pretty explicit. Mom and I are going to do something with her when we get back. I just don't know what. Probably permanent institutionalization. Thank God Kris didn't live to see what Lily has become."

"I'm sorry," Mike repeated, and meant it

Sometimes a kindred spirit called to his very darkest impulses—legacy of whatever genetic element that had shaped Philip Martiniere's personality, and the reason why he didn't want to be the Martiniere-in-waiting, much less the Martiniere. He knew that Gabe had wrestled with it. Brandon and Justine as well.

But why could they fight it off when Lily couldn't? Why did their impulses lead to self-destruction, while Lily's reactions replicated Philip's in wanting to harm others?

He couldn't identify the factor that made the difference between her and them. And that nagged at him.

Especially when he remembered that trusting look in baby Lily's eyes. When had it changed?

The scary thing was that except for Lily as a baby, he couldn't remember a time when he *hadn't* been cautious around her.

MIKE AND THE CYBORG BROTHER AL MET JOANN AT THE PRIVATE Martiniere airstrip on the edge of the Paris suburbs. Once she descended from the plane, Mike swept JoAnn up in a big hug. Smudgie danced happily around them, the heeler pressing close and begging for attention as well.

"You do not know how good it is to see you," he said to JoAnn.

She bent to pet Smudgie, then rested her hand on Mike's as he wheeled the walker to the waiting car. "Legs getting to be that bad? I see you're using the walker as well as braces."

"Only a nighttime thing, to conserve energy. A lot going on. And even though there's been lots of pain au chocolat, there's not been the company to go with it." He'd been monitoring his blood sugar carefully. So far, so good.

JoAnn chuckled. "Yeah, you're not the only one missing Sunday mornings. Who all knows I'm coming?"

"Brandon and Ruby, of course. Ron—he's going to be happy to see you. Typical nine-year-old. Justine. Lily. I've tried not to talk about it around her." He scowled. "I thought things would get better after that last hospitalization. But Lily's showing signs of a worse than ever crush. She had a temper fit this morning."

"I'm sorry."

"It's harder on Brandon than me." He held the door open for her and Smudgie, then folded his walker and stashed it before he slid into the back with her. Al loaded JoAnn's luggage into the electric SUV's cargo space. "But you're in the secondary suite with me,

Justine, and Ruby. Lily's in the primary suite with Brandon and Ron."

"What is all that?"

"Oh, the way the penthouse suite for the Martiniere and his extended family is set up. Primary suite and several self-contained secondary suites, though we're only using one right now. Ours has its own living room. Bigger common penthouse living and dining room and a shared kitchen area. There's room for several visiting families in the penthouse, and because the Martinieres are the Martinieres, there's setups so that if anyone wants to evade someone else, they can do so. Secured locks on the external doors that face the main living area—and I reset the locks on ours and gave Ruby the override before I left. In case Lily decides to be a total brat and harass one of us. I don't trust her."

"Wow. You Martinieres are really paranoid."

"All things considered, and the way my progenitor treated Gabe— yeah, there's reason, that goes back even before that era."

Al climbed into the front seat and switched on the autodrive. "Good to see you again, JoAnn."

"And you too, Al. I'm surprised that one or the other of you or your brothers didn't join Mike at Caltech." JoAnn grinned at Mike.

"We wanted to," Al said. "But...Ruby prevailed. Said it was time that Mike had his own life. And then with Lily, well...she's been keeping us busy."

Al's message chime sounded. He turned back around, throwing up a privacy screen.

"It's been good except for Lily?" JoAnn asked.

"I have actually managed to be too busy to see much of her." He winced. "Except for her continually lowering necklines. But I've been careful not to be alone with her."

"Damn it." Al turned back to them, face set and hard. "Lily got away from Carl. And she's disabled her tracker."

"Shit!" Mike sighed and flopped back against the seat. Smudgie poked Mike's hand with his nose and he rubbed the dog's head.

"Carl's with Brandon. I'm with you two. The others are after Lily. I don't think she can get too far away," Al said.

"Wow. I'm sorry," JoAnn said. "Should I plan to head back early?"

"Absolutely not," Mike said, taking her hand. "This has nothing to do with you. And we are going to have *fun*, damn it. We earned it this term."

———

A HALF HOUR LATER, MIKE, JOANN, AND SMUDGIE ENTERED THE penthouse's main common room. Ruby and Justine sat on one of the couches, sipping red wine. Mike folded up his walker and stuck it in one of the closets along with their coats. His braces allowed him to hobble around the penthouse without it.

"JoAnn, it's lovely to see you," Ruby said, setting down her glass and getting up to hug JoAnn. "I'm so glad that you and Mike ran into each other at Caltech."

Was Ruby weaving a little? Mike glanced at the nearly empty bottle on the coffee table, then at the empty wineglasses. Oh. She and Justine had already hit it pretty hard. Not usual for Ruby these days, unless something bad had happened.

Oh God. What's going on with Lily?

"Seeing Mike been really helpful for survival," JoAnn said.

Justine rose and hugged JoAnn. "Very happy to see you here for the New Year."

"Thank you." JoAnn glanced at Mike. "We need to compare our favorite places in Paris."

"That sounds like fun," Ruby said, as she and Justine settled back on the couch. "Mike. The situation with Lily has been handled." She sighed. "We signed her into a Paris hospital, with transfer to happen as soon as we find a long-term, secure, *permanent* facility. No more of this in-and-out."

"How's Bran taking it?" No wonder Ruby was drinking hard. He wondered if he should check in on Brandon, too.

Ruby grimaced. "She didn't make it easy, and where they found her was—it just wasn't pretty. Electric Born cultists, drugs, and sex. But he's keeping it together for Ron. He said to tell JoAnn hi, but he's not up to seeing anyone but Ron tonight."

JoAnn shook her head. "I am so sorry. Especially if my coming triggered any of this."

"Oh JoAnn, it has nothing to do with you and more to do with increased opportunities for Lily to sneak out, since Christmas is over and there's less structure to what we're doing." Ruby tightened her lips. She eyed Mike. "Did you want to keep the lockdown going on our private area?"

"I'd prefer to do that for the time being," Mike said. "Just in case."

"All right."

"And now I've gotta show Jo the layout."

"Have fun, kiddos," Justine said, with that little edge in her voice that suggested she had been part of *dealing with Lily*, not just keeping Ruby company while she drank.

"As much fun as we can have, as jet-lagged as Jo is," he said, forcing a smile.

"Yeah, I'm *tired*," JoAnn said.

Mike took her over to the door and keyed in her handprint, followed by the code. "You're in the room next to me," he said as they walked down the hallway, Smudgie behind them. "Ruby's on the other side of you. Justine on my other side. Our rooms have connecting doors."

JoAnn chuckled as he opened the door to her room. "How convenient."

"Ruby and Justine set it up like this," he said.

"Oh my God, the aunties are at work." JoAnn rolled her eyes and looked around the room. "As if they needed to do it."

"Yeah," he said, swallowing hard. So a deeper relationship *was* on the table right now. He wasn't the only one thinking that way.

"Amazing view," she said, looking out of the big windows on one side of the room.

"One of the perks of being part of an old French family with a nasty but profitable history," Mike said. "Ruby's got the best room in this suite. Justine could claim it as the current Matriarch, but she doesn't."

JoAnn raised her brows. "Dad always said the Martinieres had money. I guess I didn't realize just how much until now. Sure is different from the Double R."

"Yeah, and I prefer to be at the Double R most of the time," Mike said. "I can handle small doses of the in-your-face nature of the family wealth here in France. After a while, it becomes too much. But if you think this is impressive, well, the Martiniere's personal suite is a whole different level. You can see the Eiffel Tower from there." He paused, suddenly nervous. "I'll let you get settled in. Smudgie and I will be out in the common room. Do you need anything?"

"Right now I think a shower."

"No food? Wine?"

"Maybe after a little bit."

"All right. I'll bring you some."

"Mike." She turned to him, and took his hands. "Thank you. This is really nice."

"I'm glad you're here."

They moved closer to each other, and Mike hugged JoAnn. For a moment, they almost kissed, but then he pulled back. They weren't kids experimenting in the barn any more, and kissing….

Before things got to this point, they needed to talk.

Mike settled for cupping her cheek in his hand. She smiled at him and pressed her chin into his palm before pulling away. "See you in a bit," she said.

"Why don't you open another bottle for us, Mikey?" Ruby said when he returned to the main living room. Smudgie trotted across the room and flopped on his bed.

"Sure you two haven't had enough?" He glanced at the now-empty bottle. Part' of caretaking Ruby when things like—*this*—happened. Unless Justine…no, the two of them together were notorious. She wouldn't be restraining Ruby.

"Well, maybe food first," Ruby conceded. "I haven't had lunch or dinner. I probably should eat, but…." Her voice trailed off. "I haven't wanted to."

"Let me give you a hand," Justine said. "There's already a tray made up in the fridge. Veggies, meat, cheese, crackers. We were going to start eating it when—Lily happened. If you'll get the wine, I'll grab the tray."

"Sounds good." Mike went to the wine rack and surveyed the options while Justine took the tray over to the coffee table. He picked a nice pinot with a pushbutton cork and grabbed a glass—on second thought, he grabbed two glasses, in case JoAnn joined them. "So it was bad with Lily," he said flatly as he tapped the cork open.

Both Ruby and Justine winced.

"Bran and the brothers walked in on an orgy," Ruby said finally. "Apparently part of a sex trafficking ring. With body-modded participants."

"Men modded to look like Daddy-poo," Justine growled.

"Psychotropic sex enhancing drugs," Ruby continued. "She was playing with mind control. Stuff I remember Gabe condemning."

Mike added more wine to his glass before pouring a much smaller amount into Ruby and Justine's glasses.

God. No wonder they're both drinking heavily.

"Was she being trafficked?"

Justine shook her head as Ruby picked up her glass, gazing deep into it before she downed half of it.

"She was the one doing the trafficking, Mike. She authorized the body mods," Justine said grimly.

"Oh, *fuck*." He forced himself to only take a sip from his glass. "How the hell did she manage doing *that*?"

Involved in that scene at age eighteen. Unbelievable. No wonder Brandon didn't want to talk to anyone tonight. Though he should try to talk to Bran privately in the morning, give him a chance to vent.

"One of her so-called *friends*," Ruby said. "Who happens to be tied to that Electric Born cult that worships Philip."

Mike slumped and smacked his head against the back of the couch. "What happens now?" He stared up at the ceiling. Fuck. This was bad.

"Serg is cleaning up the situation with the victims," Justine said. "Multiple violations of the laws restraining indentured service. Lily is locked in a criminal ward at the hospital. We can negotiate her out of charges *if* she goes into a high security long-term facility."

"Are her finances locked down? If she manages to get out it

wouldn't be that hard for her to get to the States, especially if she has friends that help her get into—that stuff. I don't know that location makes much of a difference." Mike sat back up.

"I've done my best to activate the defenses Donald created," Justine said. "I'd be more confident if he could have written more targeted protection himself, but...."

Mike nodded. Justine's ex-husband Donald Atwood had supervised the family financial defenses until his death. Seth had spent several years training with Donald, to step into his place. But he was not the hacker that Donald had been.

"It's a mess," Ruby said. "And for now, it's been dealt with." She sipped her wine, put it down, and methodically placed cheese and then meat on a cracker. "Right now, I prefer to think about something nicer. What are you and JoAnn planning to do, Mike?"

"Take a break from studies and work," he said. "Compare our favorite spots in Paris. Have fun. Get ready to work on our master's theses. We both have projects to develop and defend."

He helped himself to cauliflower chunks. Maybe it was time to make up a plate and go see Jo so he could talk about something besides Lily. It was obvious from the way that Ruby and Justine slowly nibbled on their food that they were thinking about the situation. Sooner or later, they'd be brainstorming solutions to present to Bran.

At least they were eating now.

On the one hand, I should be responsible and participate in creating those solutions. On the other, I have a guest.

And not just any guest, but a woman who he wanted to have in his life, long-term. He and JoAnn had their own serious talks ahead of them. He should butt out of this discussion about Lily.

Mike drained his glass and rose, hobbling over to get a platter.

"I'm taking supplies to Jo," he said. Both Justine and Ruby smirked. *Good. It distracts them, too.*

"Make sure you get this cheese." Justine pointed to one group of slices. "It's the best of the batch."

"Oh, and these smoked meats," Ruby said.

By the time the two of them were done, almost half the tray was loaded on the plate.

"I'm gonna need help," he said. "At least with the door. C'mon, Smudgie."

Justine snickered and got up, taking the plate. Mike poured a little more wine into Ruby and Justine's glasses, then took the bottle and glasses for him and Jo.

Smudgie sighed as only an exasperated dog asked to move after settling in for a nap could do, and followed, his lowered head and reluctant steps clearly communicating *make up your mind about where you're going to be, human.*

As Mike and Justine walked down the hallway to the small living area, he thought he heard the shower running in JoAnn's room. Justine winked at him as she set the plate on the coffee table and left. Smudgie settled on the dog bed in the corner with another deep sigh. Mike set wine and glasses next to the plate and went to JoAnn's door. No more sound of shower running. He tapped on the door.

"Jo? Hey Jo. I have food and wine out here," he said through it.

"I'll be right out."

He returned to the table and couch, moving both closer to the window.

"Hey Mike, I can help with that." JoAnn took the other end of the couch and helped him align it with the coffee table.

"Not the greatest view, but there are two old ladies working on getting seriously drunk in the room with the better cityscape. At least I got some food down them."

JoAnn raised her brows. "Oh?"

"Uh-huh." He sighed. "And I don't want to talk about it any further tonight. You are my guest, and I want to be alone with you." He took a second look at her and did a double take, grinning. "Damn, you look gorgeous." Slinky dark teal nightgown with matching robe that emphasized her beautiful brown skin. He swallowed as she straightened up a little and smiled at him. "Damn," he repeated. "We're not kids kissing in the hayloft anymore."

She laughed at his stunned reaction. They sat on the couch. Mike filled the wineglasses while JoAnn sampled the cheese.

"Mmm," she said, closing her eyes as a blissful expression crossed her face. "Lovely stuff."

"I'll have you know that Justine specifically chose that cheese to give to you," Mike said.

"She has good taste."

A few bites and he realized he was hungry as well. They methodically ate their way through the plate before picking up the wineglasses.

JoAnn finally slumped against the back of the couch, wineglass in the hand away from him. "Mmm. That was good. French food. Even if it's the same thing I'm eating back in the States, it still tastes better here."

"Agreed," he said, taking her free hand. They sat there for a few moments, studying the city lights.

"So," she said finally. "Here we are."

"Yes. Here we are."

"What happens next?"

"I—kind of thought we'd take the next few days to catch our breath and figure it out," he said. "If—that's what you want to do."

It's time for this talk.

"I'd like to do that, yes."

Good.

"And, there's things you need to know before we get much more involved," he said slowly, raising their clasped hands and studying them. "Just what you're getting into."

Don't hide anything in relationships.

That had been a lesson that Gabe had drilled into Mike over and over while growing up.

Trust me, I've been there and paid the price. Don't hide any of it from someone you choose to love, Mike.

Yeah, he'd been burned by that policy more than a few times. He'd been delaying having this discussion with JoAnn since their first Sunday together. But now it was time.

"I already know quite a bit about the Martinieres." She arched her brows. "Not the prettiest history, up to the present day."

"It's more than that. It's—me. Specifically."

"Oh Mikey." She gently raised their hands to her lips and kissed the back of his hand. "Don't you think I might have some idea of what's going on with you by now, just from our Sundays together and when we were kids?"

He winced. "I'm sorry. I was a shit when I got sick. I should have gotten back in touch after the surgeries, but…."

"Look. You told me what was going on that first Sunday and *I understand*. I had enough stuff of my own. You went through a lot." She took a deep breath. "So what do I know? Your legs are in bad shape. You've already had your arms, heart, and lungs cyborged and the legs are next. You're a clone of a nasty evil man and you are nothing like your progenitor. You have responsibilities to the Martiniere Group and the subsidiaries that Ruby and Gabe formed. You had a lot of dreams blow up in your face all at once as a teenager. And your great-granddaughter wants to drag you into bed even though you keep telling her no." She smiled at him. "That just about sum it up?"

He sighed. "Jo, there's more. I put on a good front. But there's more than one reason why I have Smudgie around, and it isn't just to keep me from being jostled in crowds. I have severe PTSD and anxiety as a result of everything that happened before Ruby and Gabe got me. Especially where medical procedures are involved."

He slid his hand free, took a drink, then set the wineglass down and rested his arms on his legs. *Ow.* They wouldn't take any weight tonight. He should take his braces off soon because he could feel them rubbing.

He leaned back on the couch instead, hands flat on the seat, not looking at her, taking a deep breath before his standard recitation at the slightest hint that a serious relationship was possible.

"Because my progenitor had a number of health issues when I was cloned, I am a somewhat unique blend of geriatric and—well—my biological age, health-wise," he continued. "I've survived cancer, but who knows if that will last. I'm sterile, always have been, so no babies from me if that's what you want."

JoAnn shifted sideways on the couch. "I'm the youngest of four kids. I have no need to reproduce because there are plenty of nieces and nephews, and that's good enough for me. I was a kid during the Indentured Wars, and a lot of those fights took place on our farm. I damned near got killed twice when I was helping smuggle indentured workers to freedom, so I have my own PTSD problems. And when you add in being assaulted and...." Her voice trailed off and she swallowed hard.

"It's a damned good thing those motherfuckers are behind bars," he said harshly. He'd learned about the assault that had happened shortly after Gabe's funeral.

"Oh, Mikey." She sighed. "I *know* what your progenitor was. I saw the results of Philip's policies as a young child, when Mom and Dad were helping indentureds escape illegal contracts."

He winced.

JoAnn continued. "I studied the Haitian Revolution, so I know about that part of the Martiniere history."

"It's pretty fucked," he said in a low voice.

"Still. You don't think I've got my own issues? I grew up Black in Arkansas. It wasn't what my parents and grandparents went through, but...it sure as hell wasn't perfect. Yeah, association with the Martiniere name protected us from the worst of the political upheavals, and the products from Barkley-Martiniere-Swait Associates more than made our lives comfortable. But I ain't anywhere near whole myself."

"There's more," he said slowly. "One reason why I was such an ass at the funeral? The night before, I'd gotten my hands on the files that detailed my creation. Seen a projection for my survival. Without treatment—I was expected to die before I was fifteen."

"But you did get treatment."

"The file also said I would be lucky to make it to age forty-five."

"Oh Mikey. Can't something be done?"

"Beck and Ruby have been working on it. They think that might be wrong. But. Jo. I don't want to break your heart. I saw what Gabe's death did to Ruby and I don't want to put someone else through it. I *am* a fucking crippled clone boy, and you might not have many years with me."

"Mike." JoAnn rested a hand on his cheek. "That is my fucking choice to make, *not yours*."

He blinked, then sighed. "Can you blame me for wanting to spare you?" He reached up and took her hand in his, kissing it. "It could end up being ugly, Jo. I've seen Brandon widowed. Ruby widowed."

"I *understand*, Mike. I've been through it with Dad. It's not easy, but give me the dignity of my own damn choice, okay?"

"I just—" He sighed again, leaning his forehead against their linked hands. "I want you to know what you're getting into with me."

"I get it. We're not going to get this all figured out tonight. Or even over the next few days. *It's all right.*"

She bent over and kissed him. He relaxed, savoring the contour of her lips, that faint spicy scent that was *JoAnn*.

She pulled back slightly, tapping his nose with a forefinger. "But you know what? I am quite interested in taking our time and exploring our options. I don't give a flying fuck that you consider yourself to be a crippled clone boy. That's not what I see in you. I see a brilliant man who struggles against a lot of odds that have been forced upon him. I see a man I want to know better."

He closed his eyes for a moment. Reprieved. For now. "You're sure?"

"Oh hell yes. I'm not in a hurry. We've both got a lot going on. But we are in Paris for the next three days, so—in spite of family complications, let's have fun. All right?"

"All right." He smiled at her, finally relaxing. Then he leaned forward and picked up their wineglasses. JoAnn took hers from him. "A toast," he said. "To us, whatever that may look like."

"To us," she said. They tapped their glasses and drank.

He leaned back and put his arm around JoAnn's shoulders. She snuggled in next to him. They sipped their wine and watched the city lights, without talking. At some point he put the empty glasses on the table as she wordlessly protested his moving. Then they settled against each other. JoAnn slipped her arm across his chest, and they drowsed.

It wasn't until Ruby and Justine came in, whispering loud in an attempt to be quiet, that Mike and JoAnn woke.

"Mm." JoAnn straightened up. "Tired."

"Me too. Been a long day."

They walked down the hallway with arms around each other's

waists, Smudgie trailing behind them. They stopped at the door to her room. After a few kisses, she eased back.

"I'd invite you in, but I want to save our first time for when I'm not so lagged," she said softly.

"I'm good with that," he said. "I've been on the run ever since I got here. Until now." But he stole one last kiss before she slipped through the door.

———

THE PROBLEM OF LILY TOOK UP THE NEXT MORNING. MIKE JOINED Brandon, Ruby, Justine, and Serg in the main living area as they worked through options. The best facility that had an opening was in Los Angeles, available immediately. For a fee that Mike suspected was tripled due to the Martiniere name.

"We're heading back now," Brandon said finally. "Ron and I will return to Moondance once I get Lily admitted. No need for the rest of you to speed home. Serg and the brothers will be enough support for me."

"You sure about that?" Mike asked.

"Yeah." Brandon sighed. "You have company, and in any case—I don't think you should be on that plane with Lily." He smiled wanly. "Enjoy your break with JoAnn."

"I'm staying through the New Year because there's a storm hitting the Double R and I don't feel like flying into it," Ruby said firmly. "Unless you need me for backup, Bran."

"Same for me," Justine said.

"Then it's set. You two have done plenty, and I appreciate it." Brandon got up. "I'll go tell Ron. Mike, a moment?"

"Sure." He followed Brandon out of the office. "What's up? Want me and Ruby to take charge of Ron? We could, you know."

Brandon shook his head. "Nah. I asked him already, just in case we had to go somewhere with Lily. He said he wanted to be with me. That's why I'm taking all the brothers, to protect him on the flight over. Cousin David's security should be sufficient for the four of you. No." He stopped outside the entrance to the Martiniere's suite. "I know our snoopy mother and our sneaky aunt too damn well, and I'm not going to be around to distract them from focusing on you two. If you and JoAnn want to have some time away from them—I added you to the code list for the Martiniere's personal suite. Just in case."

"Thanks," Mike said. He looked down, then back up. "We're not quite at that point yet, but—I have hopes. Taking it easy because—we both kind of want something that's going to last."

And this is so close to my teenage dreams that I don't want to take a chance on it blowing up in my face, like everything else I wanted for my life back then.

Brandon rested a hand on Mike's shoulder. "Then take advantage of the Martiniere's suite, whether it's for private talk or more. Good luck."

"You're going to need luck more than I will," Mike said. "I'm sorry about all this, Bran."

Brandon exhaled. "I'm glad that Kris didn't live to see this. Or Dad. So fucking damn glad. Bad enough that Mom has to be involved with this whole mess."

Mike patted Brandon's arm. Brandon pulled him close for a quick hug.

"You take care, Bran. And we will take advantage of the offer. Even if it's just a place to hang out privately."

"You have fun. The two of you just seemed like a pair when you were younger—one of the sad things about your getting sick was seeing that fade away."

"I did have dreams," Mike admitted. "A lot of dreams that died."

"Yeah. But you survived. Hey. I'll probably be seeing more of you with Lily in LA." Brandon said. "I hope that you and JoAnn work out. You need someone and so does she. I know that Jeff's been worried about her."

"So do you."

Brandon shook his head. "Kris—" He winced and swallowed hard, closing his eyes for a moment. "I don't want anyone but her. Just—stay safe, be healthy, and good luck." He turned away.

When Mike returned to the main living area, both Ruby and Justine were studying screens. Ruby had a silence shield around her as she talked to someone. He left them alone—clearly both were working—and went into their suite's living area, looking for JoAnn.

She was stretched out on the couch, reading something on a screen. He hobbled over and sat next to her with a sigh.

"I'm sorry I left you to your own devices this morning," he said. "I hope things haven't been too boring."

Jo laughed and snapped the screen shut. "You know what? I've been enjoying having some quiet time. No need to study. No nieces or nephews wanting Auntie Jo's attention. Heck, Dad's not been bugging me for advice about his latest robotics project." She slid over, making room for him to lie down next to her. "I'm sorry it's not been that way for you. Come here."

She held her arms open and Mike gratefully slid into them. He'd been looking forward to this.

"I'm tired," he said with a heavy sigh. "Even at Christmas it's been one thing after another. While Bran's officially made Seth from the British families the Martiniere-in-waiting, he still includes me in a lot of the decision making because Seth's specialty is finance and not tech. And there are issues. We didn't *need* Lily to crack right now—though I suspect as traumatic as it's been, the fact that it's finally happened is a huge relief. No more tiptoeing around the problem."

Smudgie whined from the floor behind him, begging to join them, but Mike ignored him for the moment.

"Things are going to be all right?"

He nodded, but before he could say more, Smudgie took matters into his own paws and leapt up on the couch, squirming between them until he found a space, looking lovingly up at both Mike and JoAnn.

"Smudgie," Mike chided. "Didn't invite you up!"

"It's all right," JoAnn said, grinning. "He's cute. And devoted. There's room for all of us."

"I guess this is a case of love me, love my therapy dog."

"Yep." JoAnn kissed him. "I'm all right with you dealing with responsibilities while I'm here, Mike. It would be the same thing for me if we were at Swait Farms. Only with added nieces and nephews, not just Smudgie, who is not only very cute but is very quiet in comparison. It is not a big deal, okay?"

"Okay." He exhaled. "Brandon and Ron are leaving today, along with the cyborg brothers. That does cut down on how much we can go into the city, because we have fewer bodyguards. They've found a placement for Lily in LA. I'm not thrilled about the proximity to Caltech, but it's the first open slot in a facility that fits all of our criteria, and it *is* secure."

"You all right with that?"

"I guess I am. I'm sorry we're going to be limited in getting around in Paris. We can do some meals out. I know a good nearby place for lunch. But extensive wandering around the city? Not going to happen."

"Hey. It's how things worked out. You're a Martiniere. I know stuff happens. And if you're tired, well, we do have a nice view while we rest."

"Yeah." He paused. "Brandon offered me the use of the Martiniere's suite. If we want privacy. I figure that if we go out for lunch, it might be ready for us to move into once we get back. If you want. It has better views than this suite. Nicer bathroom—big jetted soaking tub. With a view. That is private."

"You had me at nicer bathroom and better views." JoAnn grinned. "But more privacy would be nice. Gives me time to be around just you, and that's what I really want. Now did you say something about lunch?"

"BRANDON SAID THE SUITE'S CLEAR FOR YOU TO USE," JUSTINE SAID WHEN Mike and JoAnn returned from lunch. "Staff's cleaned and changed linens."

"Want to check it out first?" Mike asked JoAnn. "Or just get our things and move over? It'll take me a while because I'm completely unpacked—been here longer."

"Oh, let's take a look and you can code me in," JoAnn said.

Ruby chuckled. "Abandoning the old ladies, hmm?"

"Might as well spread out a little," Mike said.

He ignored Ruby's smirk and guided JoAnn to the door that led to the Martiniere's suite. He performed a quick code reset keyed to both of them, and then took JoAnn on a tour of the suite, ending up in the huge primary bedroom.

"Oh," JoAnn breathed, gazing at the view from the bedroom. "This *is* wonderful."

Mike spotted the ice bucket with a bottle of sparkling wine and a box of chocolates next to it sitting on the small round dining table in the bedroom. He eyed it.

Safe? Not safe? Probably safe. All the same, it was one time that he wished that he had activated certain parts of his arms' cyborg capabilities. Being able to scan everything like the brothers could do would be nice.

It was probably safe. The timing was such that Lily couldn't have messed with it.

You are being paranoid, he scolded himself, and snorted as he picked up the note card. *Enjoy,* Brandon had written. Definitely Brandon's handwriting. He stifled a snort. Clearly Brandon had been confident that they'd take advantage of this opportunity as soon as possible.

JoAnn joined him. He handed her the note.

"I think Bran is trying to do a little matchmaking," he said.

She snickered. "Does he need to?"

Mike kissed her. "Does that answer your question?"

She smiled enigmatically and went into the bathroom. "Oh my God, Mike, this is amazing! I am gonna get my stuff now and take a soak."

He leaned on the doorframe, grinning as she inspected the tub. "Did you check the soaking supplies?"

"No. I—oh my God, this is wonderful." JoAnn hugged him. "I'm moving in right now."

"Good. I'll be a few moments. But I'll leave you alone to soak."

"What, no champagne service?"

He snickered. "You aren't worried about me bothering you?"

She kissed him, long and lingering. "No." She tapped his nose with her index finger again. "We're adults. Consenting adults. We both know we're gonna hop into bed together sometime over the next few days. Timing and fatigue have just gotten in the way. I don't have a problem with you seeing me naked in the bath…hell, I hope you join me."

"Alas, I'm kind of limited on that front," he said. "My legs. Safety issue."

"Oh damn. I'm sorry, Mike."

"But don't let that stop you from enjoying it."

"I won't." She chuckled. "I'm selfish that way."

"I have no problems with that. You deserve it."

After JoAnn left to get her things, Mike messaged Brandon.

—*You left us chocolates and champagne? Thank you.* Didn't hurt to follow up.

Brandon's response was quick.

—*Yes. Al and Carl ran a check of the suite before we left. Justine was going to supervise the staff doing cleanup, and she placed the chocolates and champagne herself.*

Mike nodded to himself. All the same, he ran scans not only through Brandon's room, but the others. He was especially careful in Lily's room. Then he went into the penthouse's main living area. Justine was alone. She looked up from her screens as he sat down on the couch across from her.

"Bran told me you'd asked about the chocolates and champagne," she said. "And hinted you were concerned about security. It's clear. I watched the staff clean the suite for their own safety, because I was afraid Lily might have left a few traps before she took off."

He exhaled, shoulders easing from a tension he hadn't realized he was carrying. "Thank you. I'm running paranoid right now."

"As you should," Justine said. She shook her head. "Of all of us direct descendants, she's the one who reminds me the most of Daddy-fucking-dearest. She's him unleashed, without inhibitions. You just don't sneak into that kind of scene they found her in, especially as the one in charge. She's had help from somewhere and I suspect she's been into that sort of thing for longer than we realized. I've been trying to trace it."

"Yeah." He dropped onto the couch. "That's what worries me the most about her being in LA. Too damn close to me and JoAnn."

As if saying her name summoned her, JoAnn emerged from their secondary suite, pulling her roller bag. She left it and joined Mike, hugging him.

"I'm going to unpack and then take a nice long soak in that marvelous tub," she said, bending forward to kiss him.

He couldn't help smiling back. "I'll be there in a little bit."

"You owe me champagne and chocolate service." She smirked at him.

"Your wish is my desire." He kissed her back.

"And now I'm off to enjoy myself some luxury, courtesy of the Martinieres. Don't be too long."

"I won't." He watched JoAnn gather her suitcase and go.

Justine chuckled. "And so it begins, eh, Mike?"

"We'll see how things unfold." He eyed her. "Now don't go playing your Matriarch matchmaking games. I'm not even the Martiniere-in-waiting. That's Seth's job. I'm just training to manage Barkley-Martiniere and then the Barkley-Martiniere side of Barkley-Martiniere-Swait."

"Honey, you are still close to the throne, so to speak," Justine said. "And as the Matriarch, I am pulling for this relationship to succeed. You two were awfully cute together as kids."

"The line ends with me," Mike said. "I can't have children."

"No it doesn't. Ron is your biological great-grandson and the future for the American Martinieres. But he's young. And while Seth's brilliant, he's also a risk taker in his personal life, more than I'm comfortable seeing in the future Martiniere. I want to see you productive, healthy, and happy as a backup to Seth, and I'd just as soon steer clear of the French side of the family taking over. Too many problems there." Justine looked down at her nails, then back up. "More important to me, you are as much Gabriel's legacy as Brandon is—perhaps even more so, since Gabie had a greater influence in your upbringing than he did Brandon's." Her face tightened. "And until my last moments as the Matriarch, I am going to do what I can to preserve Gabriel's goals and vision."

"Sounds like you don't have much faith in Seth."

Justine shrugged. "You and Ron have important future roles, no matter whether it's Brandon or Seth serving as the Martiniere." A smile softened her stern expression. "Mikey, you look happy. Really happy. I hope this relationship works." She stood and stretched. "I'd better see what Ruby's doing. Alice asked her for help with a systems glitch, and Ruby got that obsessed programmer glint in her eyes. Now that she doesn't have you and Gabe to supervise, she goes off on programming tears regularly. Who knows what they're up to now?"

"Yeah, you'd better check on them." Mike rolled his eyes. He'd seen Ruby on a programming blitz often enough when inspiration struck her—had been part of them at times.

He went to his room and started gathering up his things. It was easier to transfer closet-to-closet, dresser-to-dresser. Sounds of water running in the bathroom told him where JoAnn was.

Before he retrieved his bathroom supplies, he paused. Got champagne flutes out, once again wishing for cyborg scanning abilities. Then he shrugged and washed the glasses. Paranoia was paranoia, and if he couldn't trust things here…still, it didn't hurt to freshly wash the glasses.

After opening the bottle and pouring a glass for Jo, he got a small plate, washed it, and put a couple of the chocolates on it. Then he carried glass and chocolates into the bathroom.

"Milady, your champagne and chocolate," he said.

JoAnn beamed at him, buried deep in bubbles, as he set the glass and plate within reach. "Only one glass?"

He shrugged. "I still have a few more things to move over. Enjoying your soak?"

"Oh yes." She nibbled on her chocolate. "Hurry up so you can relax."

Mike saluted her. "I hear and obey, milady." He paused to admire what he could see of her.

She flicked some bubbles at him. "Stop it. Get moved over here."

He snatched a quick kiss before he left.

ONCE HE'D BROUGHT THE REST OF HIS THINGS OVER AND REFILLED JOANN'S champagne, Mike poured himself a glass and settled into one of the recliners by the big windows, studying the cityscape below, since it appeared JoAnn was going to be in the tub a bit longer. Smudgie hopped up with him, and Mike rested a hand on his back while sipping from his glass. At some point after finishing his drink, he closed his eyes.

He woke to JoAnn in gown and robe, poking at him.

"Huh? What?" It was dark outside. How long had he been sleeping? It had been mid-afternoon when he sat down.

"Want some dinner?"

"I guess. How long have I been asleep? Should probably take Smudgie out."

"I did that. He was fussing. Ruby told me the dog walk was on the balcony."

"I guess I was tired. I should have felt him get up."

"Mike, you looked exhausted," JoAnn said firmly. "And he squirmed right out without bothering you—maybe with a little help from me." She grinned and sat on the arm of the recliner. "Seriously. I didn't want to disturb you. I figured you needed the sleep."

He yawned and stretched. "It has been a busy week," he conceded. "Even with Christmas."

"So come on over to the kitchen in the main area. Ruby fixed a stir-fry."

That got him up quickly. Ruby's stir-fries were good.

After they had eaten and taken care of the dishes, they returned to the private suite and cuddled on a love seat situated for the best view of the city. Mike ended up falling asleep again. JoAnn roused him enough to remove his braces, prepare for bed, and take his meds.

He woke with Jo snuggled close, her back to him, Smudgie at their feet. Had they—no. He would have remembered that. She stirred, and turned to face him.

"Now that we're finally both awake...." she said softly.

"Yes," he said. "If you're ready?"

"Yes."

AFTER THEY HAD MADE LOVE, THEY LAY FACE-TO-FACE, SAVORING THE afterglow. Jo stroked Mike's cheeks and forehead. He closed his eyes, savoring her touch, unable to keep from grinning. This felt so damn right, like she was a part of him that had been missing for a long time.

"I don't get it, Mikey," she said finally. "I'd have thought you would have been snapped up by someone else by now. Or did you use the *crippled clone boy* line on other women to chase them off?"

In her mouth his bitter self-description didn't sound quite so bad. "No, most of them were more interested in the Martiniere cash than in Michael." He opened his eyes. "I could say the same for you about not getting snapped up," he said awkwardly, unsure of this subject, wanting to divert it but realizing he shouldn't. "I really appreciate your patience with me all these years. And last night. So sorry I pooped out on you. But I'm afraid it comes with the territory. I can go great guns, work my butt off—until I can't. And then I go down just like that."

She shrugged. "Hey. Mike. No need to apologize for being tired. And as for relationships—I'm picky. I've been working my butt off to get where I am in robotics. I don't have a lot of time for relationships that are unlikely to work out." She shivered. "And I've had some bad relationship experiences too."

"I'm sorry," Mike said.

"It's—nothing you can do. I'm Black, female, and in tech. I remember Mama talking about how hard it was to find Daddy." She kissed him. "Plus you were always on my mind. I kept hoping we'd find each other again when you finally made your way past the depression and all."

"I'm flattered. Martiniere stuff plus the nanotech for me when it comes to the working my ass off stuff. And—add in the health issues as a relationship killer. First time most of my past girlfriends saw me get socked with a health thing—or the anxiety attacks—or the PTSD— that seemed to scare them off. The Martiniere money wasn't worth that, apparently."

"They're fools," Jo said. "But—my family intimidates a lot of people because of its size and closeness." She laughed, that deep chuckle that was so *JoAnn*. "At least I don't have to worry about that with you. And oh God, it was so damn wonderful seeing you that first day. Knowing there was a friend nearby."

"Do I ever know that feeling. A familiar friendly face. A friend. And now...." He kissed her. "As for family, well, I've gotten used to being swarmed by family. And possessive Family members. As you well know." Smudgie whined. "Just a minute, boy." He kissed Jo. "I'll take care of him. You stay right there!"

"Only if you bring me back coffee and pastries so I don't have to get out of bed!"

He grinned at her as he pulled on his braces, then his Caltech sweats. "Pain au chocolat?"

"What else?"

"Don't get dressed," he said.

She smirked back at him.

―――

THEY SPENT THE WHOLE DAY LOUNGING, READING, AND OCCASIONALLY talking, taking Smudgie to the balcony's dog run, and gazing out on the city together. Mike ended up removing his braces. Everything about the day felt really good.

"Did you want to go out for New Year's?" Mike asked after dark had fallen. They had made love again and lay on the bed.

Jo shook her head. "Happy enough to be hanging out here." She sighed. "But it's gonna be back to work soon."

"Yeah." He leaned on an elbow and rested his head on his hand, smiling down at her. "So what's next for us?"

She traced her fingertips across Mike's eyelids and he closed them, savoring her touch.

"We do have weekends," she said. "Friday and Saturday nights. Saturday and Sunday. I'd be open to saving those for just you and me."

Mike caught her hand and kissed it. "Sounds like a plan."

He was *really* looking forward to the year ahead.

16 / INTERLUDE: RUBY AND JUSTINE

DECEMBER 31, 2079

"Well?" Justine demanded as she dropped on the couch across from Ruby, while dusk fell over the Paris cityscape.

Ruby smirked enigmatically as she studied the bubbles streaming toward the top of her half-full glass of champagne. The good stuff, as always, when she came to Europe. Gabe had always insisted on *the best* here. At home, well, they had both lived pretty tight and close. Yeah, they could have shipped in luxuries. However, the frugal habits of a lifetime dominated at the Double R. Ranch life. But in Europe? That was one place where they lived like Martinieres. Mostly.

The thought brought back sad memories. Six years since Gabe died. And there were still some mornings when Ruby had those drowsy waking moments thinking he had gotten up before her and was in the other room. Then she fully roused and remembered that no, Gabe was out in the family cemetery. Those were hard days where she often ended up by Gabe's headstone, talking to him and crying. It was better when Mike was home, but she wasn't about to beg him to walk away from his plans. Not when he'd given up the University of Paris to take care of her, after Gabe's death.

Ruby shook her head.

Not now.

Not appropriate to think about Gabe, otherwise she'd be weepy.

Champagne could make her really teary. Not a mood she wanted for *this* New Year. Not when there was a budding romance that she wanted to see happen. There had already been too damn many problems thanks to Lily. And Mike would be back home soon enough, once he graduated from Caltech.

"Well what?" she said. Though she already knew what Justine meant.

"Mike. JoAnn. They've been locked up in that suite—haven't seen them since dinner last night except to take Smudgie out, and Mike grabbed food, coffee makings, and booze for them to keep in the suite this morning. Do you think something's happening between those two?"

Ruby arched a brow at her sister-in-law. "You'd know as much as I do. You talked to Mike."

"And you talked to JoAnn," Justine countered. "So. Do you think they're a thing for sure?"

"JoAnn did say that Mike fell asleep last night," Ruby admitted. "She took care of Smudgie. Sounds like Mike just plain collapsed."

God, Mikey, I hope this relationship works for you.

Her adopted son had gone through hell. But the expression on his face when he looked at JoAnn, or talked about her—she hoped that they could make a relationship work. Mike deserved to have someone like JoAnn in his life, something *good* for just him. Ruby hadn't approved of any of the other girls he'd been involved with so far. They had been more interested in Michael Martiniere and the money that came with him, not Mike as a person. Plus, honestly, Mike and JoAnn as a couple would solve a number of business issues, like what would happen with Barkley-Martiniere-Swait once she and Jeff had passed on.

Now if Brandon would only find someone to take Kris's place.

"Is Mike all right?" Justine frowned. "He's not having more health problems besides his legs, is he?"

"I think it was just his first chance to relax and let down his guard with someone safe since we arrived here," Ruby said.

Which might be an answer to the question she and Justine were pondering. If Mike trusted JoAnn enough to fall into that deep a sleep around her, if JoAnn could extract Smudgie from the chair he was sharing with Mike without waking Mike…oh God, she really hoped that was the case.

Mike and JoAnn as a couple. It fit. *They* fit together. And that was even more important than the future of BMS.

"That's—telling," Justine said. "They were awfully cute that first night. Sound asleep on the couch together. That's another good sign."

"They've been working pretty hard at school, from what Mike says, plus Bran has had Mike running ever since he got to Paris."

"It seems to me like Mike is head-over-heels about JoAnn. Just like Gabie was about you."

God. More talk about Gabe. Ruby swallowed hard. "I think Mike loved JoAnn even as a teenager."

Justine paused. "They already resonate with each other."

"Resonate?"

"Watch them. Lots of nonverbal language. Raised brows. Significant looks. Just like you and Gabie used to do. It sure looks to me like they're involved."

"As long as they're both happy," Ruby said. "But—they've gotta get through Caltech first."

"Brandon seems to think it's happening," Justine said. "He left them champagne and chocolates. The good stuff. He *specified* that I make sure they get the best available."

Ruby chuckled. "Bran's in on the conspiracy to get those two together, too?"

"It was his idea to have them take over the Martiniere's suite to have some privacy." Justine smirked. "And he told me to keep my nosey self out of their business and to tell you to do the same. Then Mike pretty much said the same thing to me while they were moving into the suite."

Ruby's chuckle exploded into a full-bore laugh. "Oh, Brandon. Oh, Mike. Damn it, my boys know us too well."

Justine laughed along with Ruby. Then she grabbed the champagne bottle in the ice bucket sitting on the coffee table, and poured herself a generous serving. She waved the bottle at Ruby.

"Want more?"

Ruby contemplated her glass. The odds were good that neither of them would remain awake until midnight to bring in the New Year, anyway. And if Mike and JoAnn were keeping to themselves…then no need to worry about staying up for their sakes.

"We should probably eat something," she said, even as she held out her glass.

Justine rolled her eyes. "Mike's busy and Brandon isn't here. No one to lecture us."

But she replaced the champagne bottle in the bucket after filling both their glasses, and rose to grab a tray of meat, cheese, and vegetables from the fridge. She paused to pick up a box of crackers, and placed the tray and box on the table next to the ice bucket.

"Good thing neither of us are into being formal."

Ruby shrugged and leaned forward to get some food. "Didn't really feel like cooking tonight."

"No complaints," Justine said. "You already do too much cooking when you're here." As Ruby shook her head, Justine continued. "I know, I know. You like doing it."

"Since Mike's been off at school, I've not had much call to cook," Ruby said. "Maybe when I invite the girls and security into the house for a weekly dinner." She sighed. "So many of my local friends are gone now. I've spent the past year going to funerals. People I went to school with. I'm *tired* of cooking for funeral potlucks. It's a pleasure to cook for family."

"We *are* getting older." Justine helped herself to a cracker. "Back to Mike. As the Matriarch, I have more than a minor interest in seeing Mike do well. He and Brandon are Gabie's legacy." She crunched down on the cracker, then sipped her champagne. "And I want to see Gabie's vision completed. I just—" she frowned down at her glass. "Lily. I fear that she's going to turn on Brandon. Even institutionalized. It's possible to escape those places."

Lily. A shared dread. "There is Seth," Ruby said cautiously. She picked up a thin slice of roast beef.

Justine's lips tightened. "Seth is a concession to the British branch of the family. He is far too reckless with his personal safety and those damn cars plus the mountain climbing. I worry that something is going to happen to him someday. But not just that. Mike and Ronnie are going to be Gabriel's legacy in the long run. What just happened with Lily worries the hell out of me. What she's already capable of doing. She's Brandon's weak spot. More so than her mother was."

Ruby tightened her lips. Lily. It hurt to see how flawed her beautiful granddaughter had become. So different from the cute dark-eyed baby and toddler with hair that Kris had carefully put up into three buns along the middle of her head. Who loved to dance.

What had gone wrong? By the time Gabe died, he had become suspicious of Lily. What had him worried?

"I hate to say it, but that's my concern about her as well." Ruby sighed. "I'm afraid we're going to have more problems with her in the future."

"Agreed," Justine said. "And as the Matriarch, I need to think about the survival of the family. Which means I want to see Mike settled and happy, and Ron kept safe. A hedge against things going wrong with Brandon."

"Amen," Ruby said, raising her glass.

"To Mike and JoAnn," Justine said. "May they have a long future together."

"To Mike and JoAnn," Ruby echoed. She got up. While Brandon had called quickly to tell them that Lily had been admitted, she hadn't heard from him since. And it *was* New Year's Eve. She had one boy settled. Time to check in with the other one. "Bran hasn't called yet today. I'm going to see how he's holding up."

"Want me to give you some space?"

Ruby shook her head. "I'm already on my feet. I'll go into the suite."

She went into their suite and sat down on the living room couch.

Brandon looked tired when he answered. "Hey, Ma." To her relief she saw he was in the informal office he had set up in his Moondance bedroom after Kris's death, sunlight spilling through the windows. He was home, in his casual office, and the sun was shining there. *Good.*

"I thought I'd call," she said softly. "See how you are doing."

He leaned back in his chair and ran a hand through his hair—a gesture so reminiscent of Gabe that it made her ache. "Lily's settled," he said. "Ron's got Jerry and Ken over. Lots of nine-year-old boy energy going on. It's keeping him—distracted. Al and Carl are riding herd on them at the moment. Pat and Dara are coming in a couple of hours to spend New Year's Eve with us."

"And how are *you* doing?" she repeated.

He sighed. "I feel like shit, Ma. I failed my daughter."

"I don't think there was much more you could have done," she said. "Lily was losing her grip on reality before Kris died. The two of you bent over backwards to help her."

"I still feel like a failure."

"Bran. She has a double genetic whammy from our side, above and beyond what was happening with Kris as a result of indenture. Not just the Martinieres but the Barkleys. Bipolar. Depression. Schizophrenia. And, to be honest, the Ryders as well." Ruby sighed. "You've done what you could. You gave her a chance. What she's gotten herself into is more than anyone can handle on their own. She needs professional help, and you're getting it for her."

"Dr. Soren says she needs to be institutionalized for the rest of her life," Brandon said grimly. "It's just that fucking bad, Ma. And now I'm worried about Ron."

"Ron hasn't shown any signs of the same sort of problem," she said. "Lily was already detaching by this age. He's probably going to be fine."

"I hope so," Brandon sighed. He leaned forward and picked up a glass—whisky, it looked like to her. He sipped it, then set it back down. His expression eased slightly. "How are Mike and JoAnn doing?"

Ruby let herself relax a little bit. "They disappeared into the suite yesterday afternoon and we've only seen them emerge for food, coffee makings, more booze, and to take Smudgie out. Mike crashed hard in the afternoon and JoAnn had to wake him for dinner. They're staying in for New Year's."

A faint smile twitched Brandon's lips. "He's getting some down time. Good. Kid's gotta learn to take breaks."

Ruby snorted. "He is too damn much like you and your father. All three of you run full bore until you can't keep it up."

Brandon shrugged. "He's a Martiniere. Still. With his legs he should be more careful. Hopefully JoAnn can get him to do that."

"He fell asleep in the recliner with Smudgie next to him. JoAnn was able to get Smudgie to move without waking Mike."

Brandon raised his brows. "That's huge. And good news. Even *I* can't get Smudgie away from Mike without waking him up."

Ruby contemplated her champagne. That was a good point. "Well, I'll be hoping to hear about—something—from them at some point." She looked up and fixed her son with a stern look. "Now. What about you? Don't you think you should be looking for someone for yourself?"

"Ma." Brandon tightened his lips. "What about you?"

"Point taken," she conceded. "But you're younger than me. And since Lily's institutionalized, you don't need to worry about her reaction."

"And you didn't get together with anyone when you and Dad were divorced. Ma. Look. Kris was the love, the light of my life. Yeah, Lily's sucked up a lot of my attention and concern. But that's not why I haven't found anyone. I haven't gone looking. In that respect, I'm like you. One person. Ever." He sighed. "And since that one person is gone —I haven't the heart to let anyone else in."

"Oh, Bran." He was *too* much like her. Gabe had found someone during their years apart, and cared deeply for her until her death. For Bran's sake, Ruby wished he had taken more after his father than her in this respect.

"Dad! Come on! We're gonna play football in the driveway! Come join us!" Ron yelled. "Hi Grandma!"

"Hi, Ron," she said. "Happy New Year."

"Happy New Year! Come *on*, Dad!"

"I've gotta go, Ma. You have a happy New Year."

"And you do as well."

He shrugged. "I have my son, and his aunt and her wife are going to be with us. I'll be *fine*, Ma. I'm not going to be alone and brooding. You take care, okay?"

"I will."

Brandon signed off. Ruby sighed and stared out the window. Things looked good for Mike right now.

She just wished that things were better for Bran too. She wanted both of her boys to be happy.

LATE JANUARY, 2080

Age: 26

MIKE WAS PLEASANTLY SURPRISED TO GET A MIDWEEK TEXT FROM JO. HE was working late in the labs, taking advantage of the relative emptiness to grow his latest nanobot design without having to deal with other students. It wasn't that he was unsociable. He just didn't want to talk about being a Martiniere or a clone, and it seemed like too damn many conversations went that way.

—*Need to talk F2F ASAP.*

Now that didn't sound promising. But they'd had a good weekend, lingering together on Sunday past their usual parting time.

Probably not a relationship thing.

Possibly a family problem. Her father Jeff wasn't in the best of health and Jo had been concerned because her sister-in-law had been fretting about her brother Wesley. They had regular cancer screenings after the death of their mother Kelsey. Wes was losing weight—and Wes was a big man, just like Jeff.

He pulled up the clock for the process he was working on. Another ten minutes. And then he'd need to set up for the next step so that all he had to do when he returned was push a button.

—*Half an hour at the bench?* he sent back. Sometimes they could snatch a quick lab break together. They didn't usually meet this late at night, though. —*I'll be there in twenty minutes, at the earliest.*

—*That works. Thanks.*

Mike shoved aside worries and went back to work. Fifteen minutes and he was ready to go.

"Wanna go to the bench, Smudgie?" he asked as he left the lab, unfolding his walker. Smudgie looked up from the bed that Dr. Olmos had allowed Mike to install in the hallway. He rose and fell in at Mike's right heel. Mike didn't bother with a leash after dark. No need for Smudgie to protect him from crowds this late at night. What protection he might need from Smudgie was best done off-leash.

George met them at the end of the hallway. "Taking a walk?"

"Jo needs to talk," Mike said.

George nodded and followed Mike and Smudgie.

Another worry popped up as they rode the elevator down to the first floor. Had Jo gotten another threat? Lily was confined and her communications restricted. But that didn't mean that Jo hadn't been harassed by Lily's associates. That pissed Mike off, but he'd been told by the cyborged brothers and Brandon that he couldn't do anything about the threats other than provide the brothers for Jo's protection. All the same, if he ever got his hands on a solid identity for Jo's harassers…Mike's legs might be messed up but his brain wasn't. And he was just enough of an Eastern Oregon cowboy underneath the Martiniere veneer to do something about it.

Mike settled on the bench, situated under a streetlight. Smudgie prowled around the bench while George moved into the shadows, a presence clearly there but out of sight unless he was needed.

Smudgie alerted, then barked a welcome as Jo hurried down the sidewalk toward them. Carl followed her, gliding into the shadows to join George. She took Mike's hands and kissed him before he could get up.

"Mikey." She sat next to him.

"Hey Jo. What's going on?" He rested an arm around her shoulders and pulled her close.

She sighed, snuggling in. "Dad's in town on Friday. He wants to have dinner. With us. Apparently, he and Ruby have been talking."

"I don't have a problem having dinner with your dad. Hell, my family knows about us. It's time that he got a chance to weigh in." That was a relief. He could handle dinner with Jeff.

"You sure about that?" Her voice quavered a little. "Daddy can be —a little over-the-top sometimes."

Mike laughed. "And Justine and Ruby aren't? It'll be all right, Jo."

"If you say so." She sighed. "I'm just nervous about this. He's been so grumpy since Mom died."

"That's understandable." Mike kissed her temple. "I can come to your place Friday night if you prefer." While it was her turn to come to his apartment for the weekend, it didn't matter to him. "Or wait until Saturday."

"I'd like you to stay at my place, if you wouldn't mind."

"I don't mind at all. Want to eat in? I'll bring some grass-fed lean-bred Double R steaks—I know your dad likes those. And a couple of bottles of wine. Perhaps more for the whole weekend."

"That would be great." Jo shook her head. "It's silly. I don't know why I'm so nervous."

"You should have seen me before you arrived in Paris. And before I came back with the wine and food that first night. I think it's to be expected."

She laughed, then winced as a chime sounded. "I've got to get back to the labs."

"So do I. See you about four on Friday, okay?"

"Okay." She kissed him and skittered off. Carl detached himself from the shadows and followed her.

Mike was eating a late breakfast and reviewing data at home to send to Dr. Olmos when his comm chimed the next morning.

"Ruby Barkley."

"Accept," he said, glancing around the room to ensure that things didn't look *too* messy. Not that he was inclined to be that way, but the life of a grad student did lead to clutter. Ruby didn't do clutter. It bugged her.

"Hey, Mike." Ruby grinned at him. "How are things going?"

"Research is chugging along. Otherwise, things are pretty quiet."

"Sounds like things are going to get stirred up for you and JoAnn."

"Oh, you mean dinner with Jeff on Friday night? Yeah, Jo told me. I'm going to bring steaks and wine. Been saving those good steaks you shipped me for an occasion, and this is as good a one as any."

"This call isn't out of the blue, then. Good." Ruby sighed. "I just got off the comm with Jeff and thought I'd better give you a heads up. You've got a protective papa incoming."

"I—kind of figured as much," Mike said. "Especially after what Jo told me about her last boyfriend. Don't worry. It's not my first rodeo with protective papas." He grimaced, remembering Gina and her father just a couple of years ago. "At least this time I don't have to deal with someone trying to sue me for child support."

"No, that wouldn't be Jeff's way. But he is worried about JoAnn. And he alluded to other family issues going on at the moment."

"Like what?"

Ruby shrugged. "Someone's health. He wouldn't elaborate."

Oh fuck. Either Wes or Jeff himself. One of them is sick.

"I know there's been concerns about Jeff," Mike said cautiously.

"He looked fine to me. The return of the Protector bots he had Deontae set up in her apartment, coupled with increased threats toward JoAnn, are what triggered the call."

"That's because I had them replaced with my protocols." Damn it, he should have at least talked to Deontae about it first. But between pain meds and being absorbed by research, he hadn't done that. "Lily can hack the Protectors, so we should assume that her followers know their way around them. Cost me a pretty penny to have our own equipment installed to Martiniere standards, but it's worth the peace of mind."

"I wondered what those big draws on your account were about, but figured it was your own damn business." Ruby pursed her lips. "I told Jeff that you aren't prone to casual liaisons, and that as far as the Martinieres were concerned, we're all supportive of you and JoAnn. He wants to see it for himself, so I figured I'd let you know what was going on."

"I appreciate it."

They chatted a little bit more about the ranch and his studies before disconnecting. Mike sighed when it was done, thinking about what it would be like to be back in the mountains. He did miss the Double R—now more than ever.

On the other hand, if he hadn't come to Caltech, he wouldn't have had the opportunity to reestablish a relationship with Jo. And that would have been a loss.

———

Setting up security to the degree that Mike wanted for Jo's protection had been a big challenge. His place had been designed years ago for residents with their own security. For Jo's apartment, he needed to have building systems retrofitted, buy permits, and otherwise negotiate setup with her building manager when they returned from Paris.

On the other hand, he suspected that being able to advertise Martiniere-quality security building-wide made the apartments more appealing to potential residents. Especially since the manager and building owner didn't protest very hard, and had given Jo a significant discount on the rest of her lease.

Mike noted approvingly that Carl was visible as part of the nighttime rotation as he entered Jo's apartment building. When they went to the tighter security, Mike had wanted the cyborged brothers on watch at night. Daytime…well, regular Martiniere security worked. He paid them well and there were bonuses for every reported problem prevented. Nighttime—he wanted the cyborged brothers on guard. They would guard his love as tightly as they would him.

George left after dropping off the steaks and wine that Mike had brought. Mike and Jo worked together in the kitchen, Jo preparing the main course while Mike made salads and served as her gofer.

Jo startled when the doorbell rang and Smudgie started barking. "I'll get it, Mike."

"Smudgie! Down. It's all right," Mike said, snapping his fingers. He grabbed his cane and hobbled after Jo. Smudgie reluctantly retreated to his bed, but stood watchfully as Jo opened the door.

"Daddy!" Jo said.

"Sweetie." Jeff Swait pushed his walker aside and hugged Jo. Mike studied him. Jeff looked older, true, but he didn't look sick. That was good.

But does that mean Wes—

Smudgie sat, still watching. His tail wagged, though.

"Smudgie. Stand down," Mike said. Smudgie lay down, still watchful.

Mike hobbled over as Jeff released Jo. They eyed each other, then Jeff extended his hand. "Michael. You've grown up since the last time we saw each other."

"A lot of life going on." Mike took Jeff's hand, squeezing back as firmly as Jeff did. "I go by Mike these days. Unless it's business or legal."

Jeff chuckled. "All right." He half-frowned. "I thought Ruby said your arms had been cyborged? Damn, your hands feel like they're the real thing."

"They *have* been cyborged. But the process Dr. Pramula used just replaced my bones. It's not full activation. That has complications with flesh."

"I see." Jeff nodded at Mike's cane. "What's with that?"

"Daddy!" Jo rolled her eyes.

"It's all right, Jo," Mike said, half-smiling. "He's just vetting me. Jeff, the bones in my legs are failing. I'm hoping to put off cyborging them until after graduation."

"Damn, kid, that's tough." Jeff shook his head. "The way you're falling apart, you sound like an old man."

"Technically, I'm a young man in an old man's body," Mike said wryly. "The joys of being an old man's clone."

"Yeah. About that," Jeff said slowly.

"It's a reality."

"You two behave," Jo said, fixing both of them with a stern glare. "I've got to put the last touches on dinner."

"You need more help?" Mike asked.

"Get Daddy settled and pour us all some wine. I think we're gonna need it tonight., Daddy, you be good!"

"All right." Mike gestured to the table. "Pick your spot, Jeff. We kinda tried to time the dinner to eat right away. Both Jo and I skimp on lunches, so we're starving by evening."

"You two are acting like old farmers," Jeff grumbled, but there was a twinkle in his eye that Mike recognized as teasing. "Skip the midday meal and eat early."

Mike shrugged and got the bottle of red wine. At least tonight he was moving better than Jeff. "Considering what we're going to be doing after graduation, we might as well start practicing."

Jeff's laugh this time was full-bodied. Smudgie sat up as Jeff laughed, squirming and half-whining, his tail beating hard against the bed as he begged for attention.

"Nice dog," Jeff said.

"That's Smudgie. Go meet Jeff, Smudgie."

The heeler trotted over to Jeff and sat at his feet, looking up, ears forward, his whole hind end wiggling. Jeff rubbed his head and Smudgie leaned into it.

"You like attention, eh, buddy?"

"He is a complete and total attention slut," Mike said, pouring a glass of wine for Jeff. "When he's off duty, that is."

"Duty?" Jeff raised his brows.

"Therapy dog, descendant of the original pup that Gabe got me as a kid. Protects me from being jostled too bad when I'm around a lot of people. When my legs hurt, he's trained to fetch what I need. And—" he decided to broach that subject right now. "A bit of extra protection."

"Good." Jeff patted Smudgie's head, then straightened up. "I notice there's a lot tighter security here than there was the last time I visited Jo."

"Martiniere quality. I'm not about to leave Jo vulnerable. Not when I'm responsible for drawing negative attention to her because of our relationship."

"I appreciate that."

Mike took a sip of his wine. "I'd be a real shit if I didn't make sure that my lady is safe. I don't operate that way."

"Gabe and Ruby raised you right."

"I'd hope so."

Jeff paused. "All right. Let's lay it on the line. Just what are your intentions toward my daughter? You gonna treat her right?"

"DADDY!" Jo bellowed from the kitchen. She came to the doorway, scowling, her hands on her hips. "You be nice! Or do I need to channel Mama's ghost and yell at you?"

"It's okay, Jo," Mike said. "He's your dad. He's entitled." He picked up his wine glass, took a bigger swallow. "We're still figuring out the details, Jeff, because it's complex given who both of us are. As far as I'm concerned, this isn't a casual fling. But there are bigger considerations that we have to think about above and beyond us." Another big gulp of wine. "Where I stand. I love Jo. She's smart and tough. She kicks my ass and keeps my head straight. We can hang out and read together—do you know how rare that is? I love her mind. We laugh together. I—" he shook his head. "I still can't believe that she puts up with me and my baggage."

Jo snorted as she brought in the salads. "Mikey is one of the few men I know who is not only a gentleman but respects my mind. I don't have any doubt about how he feels." She kissed Mike.

"Baby girl, I'm just trying to look out for you."

"I'm an adult now. I can make my own choices!" Jo put her hands on her hips again. "I do not need you scaring off another man! Especially Mike!"

"Jo. I'm okay." Mike reached over and squeezed her hand closest to him. "Believe me, this is refreshing after the other experiences I've had with the fathers of girlfriends. Your dad isn't trying to hit me with a paternity suit, for one. Or trying to run a scam on me because I'm a Martiniere."

Jo scowled. "All the same, Daddy, I've gotten past what's happened before. Mikey isn't just another white boy."

"But he *is* a Martiniere."

"Brandon and Kris," Jo said firmly. "Not like this is the first mixed race relationship in that family!"

Jeff sighed. "Okay, baby girl. I get it."

Jo patted Mike's shoulder. "I've got to get the rest of dinner. You two behave!" she repeated.

"It's more than the racial issue," Jeff said softly. "You're privileged and sometimes blindness to realities comes along with it. And yeah. I saw the two of you grow up together, knew this was possible. I just—" He paused, clearly gathering his thoughts. "Jo's been hurt in the past. Including when you cut off communications after you got sick. You hurt her bad, Mike. Jo is my baby girl. My youngest. And—my favorite."

"I was an absolute ass when I was sick, and I admit it. As for what happened to Jo in the past—" Mike gave Jeff a thin-lipped smile, baring his teeth. "Let's just say it's a damned good thing that neither of those men have given me cause to—do something more about them than the law has already done."

Jeff snorted. "Now you're looking and sounding like Gabe did when he was pissed off."

"I *am* a Martiniere. But it doesn't come just from Gabe. Ruby is pretty damn dangerous herself, and I grew up with both of them. There's more than a little bit of the redneck Eastern Oregon cowboy in me when someone injures one of mine. If I thought that it would do any good to make those men hurt for what they did to Jo, you're damn right I would do something about them." Mike tapped his legs. "Don't be fooled by this and assume that I'm weak. Too many people do just that."

"There's also the business piece," Jeff said. "Frankly, that's a big concern for me."

Mike nodded. That was a very real issue. "Agreed. And I'll get to that, but there's something else I want to bring up first." Mike took a deep breath. "My health is the biggest concern, followed by the business aspects of our relationship. Jeff, I'm not joking about being a young man in an old man's body. It's not just the cloning, but the things I went through before Gabe and Ruby rescued me. It's unlikely I'll be long-lived. Not unless I go full cyborg, and I'm not enthused about that prospect. And I'm sterile. There will be no children from me. No matter what."

Jeff frowned, but Jo scowled at him as she brought in the plate of roasted veggies.

"Mike, I keep telling you that I will take however long I have with you, and kids are *definitely* not an issue," Jo said firmly, before Jeff could speak. "Daddy. Mike and I talked about this at the beginning. He's not hiding anything." She went back into the kitchen and came back with the steaks, sitting down next to Mike after placing the platter on the table. "He's the one who is more concerned about his health and the impact it will have on me."

"Baby girl, it's not just his health. I'm worried about what else comes with Mike." Jeff speared a steak, then dished up a healthy serving of vegetables. "Are *you* ready to deal with what comes with being involved with the Martinieres, Jo? Not just on a business basis but on a personal level? Living that life and degree of visibility?"

JoAnn snorted again. "Daddy, I'm already affected by it. That ship left the dock ages ago. At least after New Year's."

Jeff pointed his fork at Mike. "You're in line to become the Martiniere. Jo, hon, what about that? Are you ready to become *the Martiniere*'s partner?"

"Actually, I'm not in the succession," Mike said. "I've been vocal about not wanting to be anything more than the manager of Barkley-Martiniere and the Barkley-Martiniere side of Barkley-Martiniere-Swait. Seth is the Martiniere-in-waiting, with the goal of moving leadership from our branch to the British side of the family. And even if that doesn't come through—there's Ron as a potential Martiniere. A lot has to happen before becoming the Martiniere falls into my lap, and trust me, I have no ambitions in that direction. I like life at the Double R too much for that." He winked at Jo. "The question is, will the Double R be enough for Jo?"

She laughed. "A chance to work in the Double R labs? Be still my beating heart."

He couldn't help but grin at her. "The two of us in those labs. Expanding them like we've talked about."

She beamed back at him, and for a moment they both forgot about her father as they gazed at each other. God, he could lose himself in her smile and that twinkle in her eye. He leaned in to kiss her because he just couldn't resist it.

Jeff cleared his throat. "All right, you two. I'm convinced. You mean it. Ruby told me that the two of you were head-over-heels about each other, but I had to see it for myself. Mike, no offense, but Jo *is* my baby girl, and she's had some bad experiences. And even though I've worked with Gabe and Ruby for years and know they're good people, that's no guarantee for your behavior."

"No offense taken." Mike grimaced. "And we have a prime example of a Martiniere gone wrong with Lily. Besides, you're right to be cautious, given who and what my progenitor was. I worry about that tendency in myself."

"Mikey, you are nothing like that girl. I keep telling you that," Jo scolded.

"What *is* going on with Lily?" Jeff cut into his steak.

Mike sighed. "We don't know. Labels don't fit."

"It's a sad, sad thing." Jeff shook his head. "I've talked to Brandon. It's a shame. She was such a cutie when she was little."

"Yes." He took a big swallow of wine this time. "And we are concerned about her connections. Therefore, the increased security for both me and Jo, as well as other family leaders. I'm not her only target."

"Brandon had mentioned that." Jeff took a bite of steak and smiled. "Ah. Nothing as good as your Double R grass-fed beef. So. Post-graduation plans?"

"I'm still holding to my commitment to Swait Farms for three years," Jo said. "Just because Mike and I are a couple doesn't mean I want special treatment on that loan I took from Barkley-Martiniere-Swait."

Mike nodded. "Agreed with that. I have the same loan condition from Barkley-Martiniere. It's only fair."

Yeah, he could use his trust to pay off the loan—and Jo's too, for that matter. But then he wouldn't have the funds for other things—like paying for Jo's security. Ruby and Brandon both had wanted him to take the loan.

A learning process, Ruby had said.

Get a feel for obligations, Brandon had added. *Learn what others who aren't Martinieres have to go through. Juggle budgets. For God's sake don't start a gambling habit. Don't copy me and Dad.*

They continued eating, chatting about their respective studies. Once they were done and Mike and Jo had cleared the table, Jeff sighed.

"Much as I'm happy to spend time with you two and see for myself what's happening, I did have another purpose for this visit. Baby girl, I have some bad news. Your big brother Wes has been diagnosed with leukemia. Late stage."

"Oh no!" JoAnn gulped. "Oh, Daddy. Just like Mama?"

"Uh-huh. 'Fraid so, honey."

Jo burst into tears. Mike instinctively put his arm around her. She leaned into him and buried her head in his chest, shaking with sobs. He wrapped both arms around Jo and held her tight. He couldn't say anything—he just didn't have the words.

At last she sat up, blinking hard. "How long? What kind of treatment?"

"He's refused treatment, honey. They're figuring eight months to a year."

She groaned and leaned her forehead against Mike.

"Is there anything he needs?" Mike asked. "Anything the Martinieres can do?"

Jeff shook his head. "Already had the talk with Brandon and Ruby when I told them this morning. We're good, but thank you, Mike. I just want you to take care of my baby girl for me."

"I can sure do that," Mike said.

He held Jo tight when they were in bed that night, as she cried some more. Smudgie snuggled up against her back instead of his usual position at their feet.

"The same thing as Mama," she whispered at one point, still crying. "The same damn thing. Almost enough to make me wonder about exposures."

Icy dread clawed at Mike's gut. What if he was to lose her? Selfish, but....

"Could be exposures, could be genetic. Or it could even be something that they share that you don't," he said softly. "You are getting checked by a doctor regularly, aren't you?"

She sniffled. "We all do, Mikey. Except Wes. Damn it. Damn him. Maybe if they'd caught it sooner...."

Smudgie whimpered. He oozed higher and nuzzled Jo's neck.

She gulped and half-laughed, rolling onto her back. "Oh Smudgie. Oh Mikey. I'm so glad both of you are here tonight. So damn glad. Oh God. Wes."

Mike stroked her forehead gently as Smudgie settled in between her arm and her torso, the heeler enthusiastically licking her shoulder.

"I'm glad we're here too," he said. "Do you want to go home on the weekends? I can get a plane."

Jo half-laughed, half-cried. "Oh Mikey." She gulped. "I want to see Wes, but...I want to be with you too."

"Nothing says I can't come along," he said. "I'm sure there's a corner where I can hide out and work."

"Not every weekend," she said. "But next weekend for sure? And then once a month?"

"We can do that." He kissed her forehead. "A Martiniere boyfriend is good for many things. Summoning a plane to visit your sick brother whenever you want is just one of them."

That made her laugh louder through her tears.

18 / DISASTER

APRIL-MAY, 2080

Age: 26

MIKE LET HIMSELF ENJOY THE BLISS. FOR ONCE HE WAS WITH A WOMAN who didn't care about his cyborging, didn't care that he was a clone, didn't even really care that he was a Martiniere. And while his studies were demanding, he enjoyed the research challenges.

He could almost forget the doom hanging over him. And Lily's followers were somehow getting information from her about him and Jo, at least from Al's reports. But nothing to worry about—so far.

But at the end of March, reality crashed down hard. He and Jo had spent part of spring break at the Double R with Ruby and part at Swait Farms, visiting Wes. They got back late on the Sunday before spring term started.

Mike fixed dinner for himself and Smudgie at his place. He set Smudgie's bowl down. Then he picked up his bowl of mac and fake cheeze, resting his hand for support on the half-wall that divided kitchen from dining area. Suddenly the world swayed around him and it was hard to catch his breath. Not a heart attack. Cardiac problems didn't have these bright, pulsating colors and distortion of vision, and the cyborging should have taken care of that anyway.

Shit. Some sort of psychotropic—damn it, what happened? How?

Mike turned sharply, trying to catch his balance as everything wobbled around him and he couldn't tell which way was up.

His braces gave way. Sharp pain knifed through his right thigh. It buckled under him. Mike tried to keep from falling, grabbing at the divider, but a second, blazing pain lashed through his left thigh and up his body into his chest before blackness descended on him.

He woke on the floor, lying on his back, sweaty, braces twisting his legs at wrong angles, food scattered around him, Smudgie licking his face and whining. Pain seared his legs from mid-thigh down. He bit back a scream at its intensity.

Mike tried to straighten his legs. The agony burned. He gasped. Tried again. Spots flashed in front of his eyes and he realized that he would pass out once more if he kept pushing.

"Smudgie. Comm," he gasped.

When Smudgie dropped it into his outstretched hand, he tapped the first link that came to mind—not caring who it was. Brandon. Carl. George. Ruby. Justine. Someone.

"Mike?" Jo sounded perplexed.

He groaned. He had *not* meant to call Jo first, of all people. She already had enough on her mind with Wes.

"Jo," he gasped. He didn't have it in him to call someone else.

"Is everything all right?"

Smudgie whimpered, and Mike struggled to find words as agony flared through him. "*Jo*," he moaned.

"I'll be right there," she said.

Oh God. He didn't want her to find him like this. Mike tried again to straighten his legs, but the pain was so intense that he blacked out a second time.

CONSCIOUSNESS RETURNED. HE STARED UP AT JO'S STRICKEN EXPRESSION.

"Mikey. Oh God. Mikey."

He blinked at her. Tried to form words but the pain knifed through him.

"Don't move. Don't say anything. Help is on its way. And Brandon knows."

"Thanks," he was finally able to gasp. "Don't touch divider. Something there. Sor—" He couldn't finish the word as more pain pounded through him.

"I'm here," she said softly. "I'm here." She started to take his hand but he pulled it away.

"Best—not—" he gasped. "Cyborging—controls. Exposure on hand. Wrist. Better." His hands tightened into fists in reaction to the waves of agony crashing over him.

"Should I kennel Smudgie before the paramedics get here? He's frantic."

He nodded.

It seemed an eternity before she was back beside him, one hand on his forehead, the other on his wrist. Her touch didn't banish the hurt, but at least it gave him something else to focus on.

JoAnn. Jo. Oh God, how can someone as gorgeous as you stand to be with someone like me?

"Because I love you, you silly fool," she said softly, and he realized he'd said it out loud. She slipped her hand down on his cheek and he turned his head slightly to kiss her palm.

In spite of the pain that movement sent burning down his body.

The agony was worth it.

AWARENESS CAME IN FLASHES AFTER THAT.

Brandon's voice. "JoAnn's taking care of Smudgie."

Jo's voice. "Bran took Smudgie for a walk."

Other statements he couldn't remember, as agony seared him every time he woke, followed by the warm fuzziness as more painkillers pumped into his body. But more often than not, it was Jo by his bed, and when she wasn't there, it was Brandon.

When he finally roused without the crushing pain, to his surprise Ruby sat by his bed.

"Hi," he moaned. "Thought you weren't allowed in the hospital because of infection risk at your age."

She snorted. "I needed to check up on you. And Brandon pulled strings to ensure that I was safe. I have to wear a really fancy biosuit to come in and out of the hospital. Your room is biosecure but getting here isn't."

"How—long?"

"You've been out on sedatives and painkillers for a week."

"It's bad, isn't it?"

That's why you're here, right?

Ruby was the best at breaking medical news. He was afraid to say that, afraid to confirm his suspicions, though. Just in case it was true.

Ruby nodded. "Dr. Pramula wanted to get control over your pain before she started the cyborging process." Her voice caught. "And give you time to recover from what was done to you."

"No chance of healing on its own?"

"I'm sorry, Mikey. Your braces were hacked. Both thighbones just— shattered. Dr. Pramula tried the bone regrowth shots. Had to stop them because things weren't coming together properly. Erratic. Weird. We've had to keep you unconscious because she needed to reverse the process."

Mike winced. "How soon for the cyborging?"

"Give you some time to talk to JoAnn and see Smudgie. Then back under you go and the process starts. The sooner Dr. Pramula can get to it, the more likely she can save your actual legs and the less artificial they'll be beyond the bone structure. The shattered bones have caused problems with blood vessels, nerves, and muscles, leading to potential gangrene, in spite of everything she's tried."

"How—high? Are my hips involved? What about my spine?"

Will I be able to ride horses again? was his real question.

Ruby placed a gentle hand on his arm. "Your spine is still good. Dr. Pramula thinks she can salvage your ability to ride. But that's why we need to start the cyborging as soon as possible. You almost let it go too long before—this happened."

God, as always, Ruby seems to know what I'm thinking.

"Did Dr. Pramula say what process she was going to use?"

Limb cyborging had improved over the past few years, from metallic implants that required amputation and plaskin coverings to nanometallic plastic extrusions that incorporated salvageable tissue and bone. But there were different processes that created the same results. And the fact that bone growth shots had resulted in flawed reconstruction meant the most advanced processes might be—problematic. That there were potential systemic issues in the recipient. He'd read enough of the studies to know what his situation could be. But maybe not. He hoped not.

"Liquid nanobuild," Ruby said slowly, her face going blank. "Otherwise it's amputation and full mechanical replacement. It's just that bad, Mikey. No other options are open."

Liquid nanobuild.

Infusions into each leg that would try to rebuild bone based on existing structures while augmenting nerve and tissue connections. It could work spectacularly well, and he would be stronger than before.

But.

It was one of the riskier methods with his—unique situation.

"It's that bad?" His voice quavered.

He didn't want to face this. No. Maybe Ruby was exaggerating—oh, who was he kidding? Ruby didn't do that. It *was* that bad. But he didn't want to admit it to himself. Not yet.

"Yes." Face still blank. "Mike, you were poisoned using a combination of a topical neurotoxin, the nanobots that hacked your braces, and a psychotropic. It's created complications which rule out the easier protocols. And Lily has escaped." Ruby scowled.

"I thought that facility was secure. That we were supposed to be warned if Lily escaped."

Ruby grimaced. "We weren't informed as quickly as we were supposed to be. Not until after she was able to spread her brew all through your apartment."

"Fuck. Is she involved for certain?"

"Yes. The mix was something she was experimenting with before her confinement. I'd sure like to know how she got her hands on all that."

"Especially since she was locked up.

"Exactly. Fortunately, the neurotoxin failed. DNA traces in your apartment were positive for her, and she tried to hack the security cams. She's not very good at it. Her nano programming was better. Now if it had been one of her minions, things might have been different and you might not have made it." Ruby sighed. "Lily has *definitely* inherited the Barkley tendency to do things the stupid way." She shook her head.

Mike exhaled, not wanting to press further at this point, now knowing what he faced. And Lily's involvement. God, he wasn't going to think about that just yet. His thoughts skittered to Jo.

Jo. Oh Jo.

"How is Jo taking it? I didn't mean to call her for first response. She was just the first number on my comm. It—" His voice trailed off.

He was being unfair to Jo. She wasn't like Gina, or Janet, or Karen. She knew about his problems. But God, he just hated for her to see him like this.

"Michael. She loves you. Bran's had to chase her out so she'd keep up with her coursework. She's worried about you."

He closed his eyes for a moment. "It was just—embarrassing, you know? If I remember correctly, my dinner went all over the floor when I fell. And God knows what else my body did under pain."

"Gabe and I dragged each other to the toilet to puke after we'd had too much to drink when we were younger," Ruby countered. "And going through the G9 and then the anti-aging serum was no picnic. If the love is there, this stuff doesn't matter." A chime sounded and she got up. "And there's JoAnn with Smudgie. We're only allowed in here one at a time, have to go through decontam. Lucky me, I get it both ways because of my issues."

"I'm glad you came. But Bran's not dropping in?"

Ruby shook her head, frowning. "Bran can't be here right now. They're following a lead to run Lily down—close enough that he wants to be there."

"Oh."

Ruby sighed and bent to kiss his forehead and he caught a quick scent of disinfectant from her. "Mike. Just focus on getting through this and getting well. It's not your fault."

"I know. But still...." He didn't know what else to say as Ruby walked over to a biosuit hanging from a hook next to the bathroom.

Ruby stepped into the suit with the ease earned from her long experience of suiting up for the clean rooms at the Double R labs. "Just focus on getting well, please?"

He heard the worry in her voice. "I promise," he said.

"Thank you." She blew him a kiss, then left.

He had a few moments to contemplate what liquid nanobuild was going to be like. Then the door opened, and Mike almost burst out laughing at the sight of his dog in a biosuit. JoAnn freed Smudgie first and hung his suit from an auxiliary hook before attaching hers to the one Ruby had used. Smudgie trotted over to the bed and sat, looking anxiously up at Mike and whimpering.

"Just wait, buddy," he said softly. "Jo will help you up. Don't try it yourself." He tried to roll to his side but the slightest shift of his legs sent pain shooting through him. He bit his lip to keep from groaning too loudly, for both Smudgie and Jo's sakes.

"Mike, don't push yourself," Jo scolded as she finished securing her suit. "I heard that moan."

"I didn't mean—"

"I *know* that you didn't mean for me to hear it. I've learned that you hide your pain when you can. But *don't push yourself.*" She came to the bed. "Just a minute, Smudgie. I get to kiss him first." Jo lowered the bedrail and bent to kiss him, the faint whiff of a decontamination spray briefly wafting around them.

It was a relief to feel something other than pain. Mike tentatively raised his arm and eased it around her back when it didn't hurt, prolonging their embrace as he lost himself in the sensation of her lips against his. Even though her normal spicy scent was subdued under the odor of disinfectant, it was still Jo.

Jo raised her brows and smiled wickedly. "I wouldn't think you'd be able to think about *that.*"

"Kissing you makes me forget the pain," he said. "Seriously. I can't think about anything else when you kiss me."

"Then I guess I'll have to do more of it, hmm?" She kissed him again, then eased back carefully as Smudgie whined. "But there's someone else who wants to see you."

Jo gently helped Smudgie get on the bed next to Mike, another brief whiff of decontamination spray stirring. The heeler squirmed a little but was careful not to jostle Mike, licking his face while Mike laughed.

"Smudgie! Smudgie! Settle down. That's a good boy."

Smudgie lay on his belly between Mike's torso and arm, resting his head on Mike's shoulder as he gazed at Mike. He carefully placed his hand on Smudgie's back. Jo smiled down at them.

"A man and his dog," she said. "He's been fretting a lot."

"Where's Smudgie been staying?"

"Pretty much at your place. Brandon, Ruby, and I have been taking turns being with him." She paused. "He tolerates us, but he clearly doesn't like being alone in your apartment. He's been looking for you even when we're there."

"Maybe he should go to the Double R with Ruby," Mike said reluctantly. "For now. Then he won't be constantly watching for me to come back to the apartment." And that apartment wasn't safe anymore. "Are you safe? From what Ruby said…."

"Brandon had the entire place decontaminated before we started staying in it. I have two of the brothers guarding me instead of one." She sighed. "It's probably a good idea that Smudgie goes to the Double R with Ruby. We tried my apartment, but he hasn't been happy there without you." She rested her hand on top of his. "Neither of us have been."

"Jo, I'm sorry."

"Eh, don't be. We knew that your legs were going to fail at some point." She swallowed hard. "The worst part has been seeing you in such agony. I just—I just wish there was more I could do to help."

"Taking care of Smudgie has been fantastic. And kissing me. More kissing, please."

She grinned. "Now *that* I can do." She bent over to kiss him again. This time Smudgie nuzzled in, slurping across their faces.

"Smudgie!" Mike couldn't help but laugh. Then he exhaled. "More seriously. Ruby told me they were giving me just enough time to talk to you two, and then it's off to cyborging step one." He winced.

"Liquid nanobuild. Long. Slow. Painful. All depends on how good the nanos are. And I know too damn much about the process. It could fail. Spectacularly. Might still have to go the route of amputation and full artificial legs."

"Yeah." Jo straightened back up, resting her hand on his again. "Ruby told me about liquid nanobuild. It sounds—complicated."

"It is." He took a deep breath. "Will you still come see me?" His voice quavered when he didn't intend it to, but damn. *Liquid nanobuild.* Worse prospect than chemo.

"Of course!"

"Even if I'm cranky because of the pain?"

"Mike. I knew what I was in for when I started up a relationship with you, even before we talked about this at the New Year." She tightened her hand on his. "I'm in it for the long haul. We just have to get some stuff—like school—finished first. Plus family and business obligations."

"Thank you," he whispered. "Thank you, my love."

Another chime sounded. Jo frowned. "I guess they're ready."

"Kiss me once more for luck. Please."

"Yes."

He didn't want to stop kissing her, but eventually she straightened up as the chime sounded, several times.

"I think they're getting impatient," she said.

"You'll be back soon?" he asked, hating how weak he sounded.

She ran her hand across his forehead, delicately stroking his face and his eyes. "I'll be here when they let you wake up. I promise."

"Okay." He patted Smudgie gently. "And you. Take care of Ruby for me, okay? I'll see you when—I can." His voice wavered. Smudgie licked Mike's face, then whined softly as Jo lifted him off the bed. She didn't suit back up but gathered Smudgie's biosuit.

"It'll be all right, Mike," she said, hesitating at the door.

He smiled weakly at her.

Liquid nanobuild.

He didn't want to think what the next steps would be like if it failed.

<hr>

THE PAINKILLERS WEREN'T STRONG ENOUGH. MIKE SCREAMED HIMSELF hoarse as the nanobuild infusions flowed into place in his feet and ankles, triggering fiery waves of agony combined with spasming muscles that crescendoed until he passed out, only for him to revive and go through the cycle again.

"Smudgie. Jo. Smudgie. *Jo,*" he sobbed when he wasn't shrieking wordlessly and gasping for breath between pain pulses.

And worst of all, he was on his back, his legs strapped down hard so he couldn't move them while the nanobuild worked, no matter how hard his muscles twitched in resistance. He *hated* being on his back. It brought back shadowy memories of those blood draws for Philip.

At least his upper body was elevated so he could breathe more easily, but oh God. This was worse than lungs and heart. Worse than arms. Worse even than chemo. It was every bit the hell the literature described liquid nanobuild as being. Did this degree of agony mean it wasn't working?

Last resort before amputation and complete mechanical replacement.

Sometimes that was the only thought that kept him from screaming for it to stop.

Last resort. Last resort. Last resort.

"*Jo.*" All he could do was moan her name now, gasp for breath. "*Jo.*"

"Shh. Shh." Was he imagining her contralto voice, her body easing on the bed with him? Murmurs as she talked to someone else, her hands steady on his shoulder, then one arm sliding under his back, her body pressing against his as she stroked his forehead. Was this his imagination? Sound. Touch.

"Mikey. I'm here." And now her spicy scent. Gentle pressure of her lips on his forehead. Either real, or his best damn hallucination yet, to include scent and touch as well as sound.

"Jo. Oh God, Jo." He burst into tears, unable to say anything more.

"They brought me in to see if I could help," she murmured. "Can't do anything else for painkillers and you're fighting it so hard...oh

Mikey. Please. Just lean on me. Lean on me. Please don't scream. Please. Don't scream."

Mike nodded, clutching to the reality of the contact of his head with her chest. He couldn't stop sobbing from the pain, but having Jo holding onto him helped Mike separate from the agony. He focused on her soft words, not caring if they made sense. Pain ripped through him but Jo was there.

It was an eternity but Jo was there.

AT SOME POINT PAIN EBBED, AND MIKE FELL INTO SLEEP. EVEN WHILE asleep he was half-aware of Jo coming and going, sometimes in bed with him, sometimes in the chair by the bed, and other times not there at all. But he was so utterly drained and weary that he couldn't open his eyes or move, just half-surface, be aware whether she or someone else was there or not, then fall back into a deep slumber.

He blinked. Fuzzy brain. Warmth flooded through his system, leaving him feeling floaty.

Painkillers finally working.

He swallowed and winced at how raw and scratchy his throat felt. But at least he sensed Jo's presence nearby.

"Jo?" he croaked.

"Right here." She reached for a cup with a straw in it and held the straw to his lips. "Drink."

He sipped tentatively at first, the ache in his throat easing with each swallow. Jo's free hand stroked his forehead rhythmically. He drank until he couldn't extract any more fluid. Jo shook the cup to settle the ice, then went over to the mini fridge set under a counter at the foot of his bed. She refilled the cup from a pitcher of ice water and placed it on the table next to his bed.

"We'll let that melt a little more." She eased onto the bed with him and gently took him into her arms. He sighed and settled into her caress. Part of him wanted to know if the liquid nanobuild had worked.

Part of him didn't, because the next step was amputation if it hadn't. And as fucking painful as the infusions of liquid nanobuild had been, plus the fact that he couldn't feel his legs right now—he dreaded what Jo's answer would be.

And yet the question kept nagging at him.

"My—legs," he said finally. He could shift his arms so the spine hadn't gone to hell. But the rest of him? "Can't feel anything."

"Initial phase worked," she said. "The nanobuild is still forming, according to the latest scan. Well within parameters. Dr. Pramula finally found a nerve blocker that worked and stopped your muscle spasms. But it's a heavy hard-core one that just about paralyzes you."

He heaved a huge sigh of relief. "Pain worth it if works."

"It almost didn't," she said softly. "You kept screaming and passing out, screaming and passing out, and they couldn't give you any more pain meds. Your muscles were spasming pretty bad, and the whole cycle was starting to interfere with the nanobuild."

"That why you told me to stop screaming?"

"Yeah. You settled down enough that they could try different blockers."

He shivered and nestled in closer to her. "Thank you. Thank you for being here." It felt so good to bury his head in her chest, feel her arms around him.

Maybe the worst of it was over.

Realistically he knew it wasn't. This was just the bone formation. Next came retraining his connective tissue and nervous system to work with the new bone.

And there might even be more infusions necessary.

God. What would this mean for Jo's studies spring term, if she had to be here for his sake and not researching? Not going to class? Graduating on time was a lost cause for him right now, but it didn't have to be that way for Jo. Mike noted to himself to bring it up to Brandon for help if necessary, and wearily lifted his head.

And Wes? What about Wes?

"Everything all right with Wes?" he asked.

"He's actually doing better," Jo said. "Eating more. Rae says he's putting on weight. He looks better when I call."

"You're not missing classes and labs?"

"No, hon. I'm not. Brandon comes in when I'm not able to be here. I've been working while you sleep. I got a short leave for remote study."

He swallowed hard. "Did they recapture Lily?"

"No. We're both under heavy guard. Another reason why I was able to get some leave—that and we've found me a project in the hospital tied to my research."

"How on earth does that work?"

She kissed his forehead. "I'm researching nanoized cyborging processes. Translating agricultural nanobot programming to medical usages. Ruby granted me access to the RubyBot base algorithm that she and Gabe created all those years ago. There are some interesting processes which you might want to take a look at when you feel better. Ways to improve both the RubyBot and the Swaitbot."

"Sounds good." He let his head drop on her chest. "Tired." There were more questions lurking but he couldn't summon them.

"Go ahead and sleep some more, Mike. Rest." Her voice quavered slightly.

"How bad was it, Jo? Especially since it nearly stopped the nanobuild?"

She shivered and gulped. "We almost lost you because of a sneaky effect of the neurotoxin, Mikey, which also delayed the effectiveness of the nerve block." Her arms tightened around him. "You were overclocking your heart and lungs. Side effect of what that bitch Lily did to you. Please. Rest."

THINGS GOT BETTER.

The next nanobuild infusion three days later was painful but shorter and not as horrific as the first—this one was to reestablish his nervous system links as well as tendons, ligaments, and muscles. Mike clung shamelessly to Jo while it happened. Any reserves he might have to tough it out were fried by now.

At least this time the painkillers functioned like they should

"The nanobuild is working," Dr. Pramula finally said.

Now it was simply a matter of waiting for the build to finish connections. He was still under painkillers because now it was nerves and connectors rebuilding themselves.

Brandon dropped in at least once a week, usually when Jo was off at school or in the labs.

"You look like hell," Mike said to Brandon on his third visit. By now the fuzz was clearing from his brain and he could think about what was happening beyond his legs.

"Lily's just—disappeared," Brandon said, shaking his head. "Seth has increased security for all family leaders, because there have been attacks. Mike, I think we should close up your apartment and send what you don't need back to the Double R. Have you move into Justine's compound."

"I'm good with that. But what about Jo? Her family?" He had been afraid to ask where she was staying now, and, frankly, until this morning hadn't had the brain power to remember.

"She's already closed her apartment and moved into Justine's place. Not that she spends much time there. Al and Carl are protecting her. And as for the Swaits—it didn't take much for Jeff to ramp up their protections. We're consulting with him and Deontae, but they've always been running under a lot of security due to their work in the indentured uprisings."

"That's good." Mike exhaled. "How's Smudgie? And Ruby?"

"Mom is spoiling Smudgie rotten. But he still wants to sleep on your bed at night, and Mom says he's looking for you. Mom is—Mom. Having Smudgie around is a good distraction and keeps her from marching down here to take over watching you. Not that I think JoAnn would yield her place easily—which is another thing that keeps Mom at the Double R and not here."

"I'm glad to hear that." Ruby didn't need to be in the middle of this. She wilted a little bit when she was away from the ranch.

They talked for a little bit longer, then Brandon left.

For once he was alone. Mike exhaled, thinking hard about the future. The thread of despair that had plagued him during his last cyborging stirred, and he pushed it back ruthlessly.

He wasn't a teenager any more. He was an adult. He had things to do. A degree to finish. A woman who loved him—and, damn it, if Jo had stuck around during this, then she wasn't going to be scared off very easily.

Would she want him to join her at Justine's, once he could leave the hospital? Despite everything, he was afraid to ask.

Before he could think about it further, Jo came into the room. He grinned at her as she slipped out of her lab jacket and hung it up.

"Good research day?"

She startled. "Mike! You're awake."

"Yeah, Brandon was just here. I didn't realize you'd moved out of your place."

"I have told you, but you haven't been retaining what anyone's said to you."

"God. I'm sorry."

Jo sat in the recliner by the bed and took his hand. "Hey. Dr. Pramula warned me you were going to be a little fuzzy for a while. Sounds like you've moved past it."

"Thank you for everything." He kissed the back of her hand. "I couldn't have gone through this as easily without your help. I'm sorry to have been such a pain."

"Mike." Her voice was firm. *"Stop apologizing.* Every damn time you've been awake for the past two weeks, you've been telling me you're sorry. I want you to stop doing that. This wasn't your fault."

"Sorry."

She growled.

He sighed. "All right. I get it. But I am so damn grateful, darling. This can't have been easy for you."

"It wasn't, but nothing near like what you have been going through." She squeezed his hand. "I'm good with it. It's part and parcel of being with you."

He exhaled. "No one's talked to me about when I'm getting kicked out of here."

"It's gonna be a while yet. Mid-May is what the doctor is saying." Before he could ask, she added, "And today is April twenty-fifth."

April twenty-fifth. He'd nearly lost the entire month. But still. A few more weeks and he'd be *done.*

"So not that much longer." He grinned, almost giddy at the prospect. "But what about physical therapy?"

"Justine's building a facility. She and Brandon want to get you out of here."

He shook his head ruefully. "Damn."

"It's an extension of what she already has on site for her and Ruby. She thinks that it may be useful in the future. To quote her: *'Serg, Ruby and I aren't getting any younger. I want to make sure there are safe facilities on site.'* In other words, she sees future uses for it." JoAnn paused. "She's been hardening the compound. It's looking like Lily and her pals are shaping up to be a long-term threat."

"Brandon told me they've not been able to track them down yet."

Jo nodded. "Justine is making provisions for all family members to stay there when they're in the area." She took a deep breath. "My apartment in the compound is set up for handicapped access and it's big enough for both of us. And I've already got a queen-sized hospital bed." She fixed him with a glare. "And before you start making noises about *I don't want to impose*, you're not an imposition. All right?"

"All right," he conceded. She bent over the rail and kissed Mike. When he would have reached up to hug her, Jo shook her head and tapped his nose with a finger. "Don't move around too much yet. It's not the time. I'm going to shower and change. Then we can *safely* cuddle." She grinned wickedly. "You're at my mercy, Michael Martiniere."

"And it's a pleasure," he responded. "Do with me as you will."

Jo grinned big. "Now *that's* the Mike I know." She kissed him again. "Damn, but it's good to see you smiling and remembering things again. I'll be right back."

<hr>

NOW THAT HIS BRAIN HAD CLEARED, MIKE CONTACTED DR. OLMOS AND they laid out a plan for Mike to do research and remote coursework while he was still confined to a hospital bed. Luckily he was just down to one class and his thesis project, thanks to the hours he had already spent. But the final work needed to be deferred until Mike could get into a lab—most likely at the Double R. Security was going to be too difficult to continue that part of his work here.

At least Mike had years of experience studying while under medication. He had his corrections, his checks, the memory coping strategies to fall back on.

And as he worked and went through physical therapy, he clung to the knowledge that soon enough, he'd be in Justine's compound. Sharing an apartment with Jo.

He hoped she could handle having him underfoot.

That will be the real relationship test.

MAY-JUNE 2080

Age: 26

MIKE PUSHED HIMSELF IN PHYSICAL THERAPY, AND WAS DISCHARGED ONCE scans showed that the cyborg bone and nerve replacements were fully integrated. He thought about bringing Smudgie back, but there were only a few weeks before he'd be returning to the Double R.

And Jo was on track to graduate this spring. Mike's goal was to be able to attend her hooding, even if was only in a wheelchair. At this point, it was a matter of physical endurance.

But he had another agenda. The night before her family and Ruby descended upon them for her graduation preliminaries, he fixed them dinner. Romantic, with faux roses and electric candles. He could have afforded the real thing, but at this point he wasn't very thrilled about displaying Martiniere privilege—there'd be plenty of that in evidence over the next few days. Soon enough he'd be back on the Double R to finish his recovery and live the quieter life he preferred.

Jo startled as she entered their apartment. "Wow. Mike."

"Last night before everyone shows up," he said. "A thank you."

"You didn't have to," she said.

"I wanted to. You're graduating on time, in spite of having to take care of me."

"You would have, too, if this hadn't happened." She gestured at his legs.

He now mostly used a cane around the apartment and compound, unless it was a bad physical therapy day and fatigue drove him to using the walker. Outside of the compound, he still used a wheelchair for safety's sake. Except for mandated therapy times, he no longer needed braces.

"Yeah." He kissed her. "Go get comfortable."

She grinned and headed for their bedroom.

Nerves kept him from eating too much. Jo eyed Mike, a speculative expression on her face, but didn't say anything as they cleared dishes, then settled on the couch together.

He took Jo's hand. "I—um—kinda wanted to talk about what's next." It was still awkward for him to shift sideways—he had to stop and think about moving his legs instead of it coming naturally. That was supposed to improve. But he managed to turn so that he could face her.

"Yeah?"

He couldn't read her expression. "Yeah." His rehearsed speech went completely out of his brain—blame meds for that, he guessed. "I —well, we've both got paths outlined ahead of us. You for Swait and me for Barkley-Martiniere, once I graduate this summer." He fumbled for words. "But I've loved this. You. Us. Especially the last few weeks."

"Me too," she said softly.

That gave him hope. "Knowing the commitments we both have— it's not gonna be traditional at all. We'll have to spend time apart for the next three years because of our loan obligations—but—" he gulped. "Jo. Can you stand to marry me? Once I've graduated? I don't want to wait longer than that. Not with—me. What could happen."

"Oh Mikey." She choked, half-laughing, and leaned forward to kiss him. "Can I stand to marry you? What kind of proposal is that? *Of course* I can stand to marry you."

"So—yes?" He wasn't certain he'd heard her right.

She rested a hand on his cheek. "Ask me properly. None of this "can you stand" bullshit."

He swallowed hard. "JoAnn Breonna Swait, will you marry me?"

She laughed again and took his head in both her hands before she leaned forward to kiss him. "Michael Marcus Martiniere, not just yes, but *hell yes*, I can stand to marry you. Now don't you start backpedaling and equivocating about your health and the Martinieres and all that baloney. We stayed together during liquid nanobuild. Can there be anything worse than that?"

He leaned his forehead against hers. "I owe you so damn much, Jo. I don't know if I'll ever be able to thank you to the degree that you deserve. Oh God, I love you. And I'm in your debt forever. Thank you. Thank you." He fumbled in his pocket. "I hope I'm not presuming by picking this out for you. But I saw that you liked this one at Cartier over New Year's, and thought…." He pulled out the box holding the gold ring with a center ruby and sapphire surrounded by small pearls. *One* part of being a Martiniere that gave him joy was the ability to give this ring to Jo without financial worry. He extracted it and held it up. "May I?"

She nodded, dampness forming in the corners of her eyes, and held out her left hand. He slid it onto her ring finger.

"It's beautiful," she whispered, gazing at the red, blue and gold against her dark skin.

"I loved it when you tried it on," he said. "It looks great on your hand."

"Did you buy this when we were in Paris?"

He shook his head. "I—kinda asked Justine to make the arrangements. I hope you don't mind."

"Mind? Not at all." Jo threw her arms around Mike and kissed him. "But I think we need to find a more comfortable space to talk further."

A happy smirk was on Jo's face as she helped Mike walk to the bedroom. He was pretty damn sure he wore a matching one.

I am the luckiest man in the world, he thought, before settling down to make love to his fiancée.

19 / DREAMS REALIZED

JUNE, 2080

Age: 26

Mike was *really* glad that they were living in Justine's compound as the extended Swait family plus assorted Martinieres descended upon them for Jo's hooding and graduation. If they were still in one or both of their apartments there wouldn't have been any room for guests and lots of worry about hotels and security.

But there were places for everyone in the compound. Ruby and Jeff stayed with Justine, giving the elders space away from the others. Wes, Deontae, and Rae had private apartments for their families. And he and Jo had their own apartment where they could retreat when things became a bit much.

Martiniere communal living.

And the Swaits were much the same. The Martinieres lived with family in big houses or compounds. The Swait family members owned property around a central farm. Perhaps that was one reason he and Jo worked so well together—both knew the swirl and swarm of life in big families, and didn't mind it.

Mike drowsed off in the courtyard the morning before Jo's graduation.

"Mike. Go inside and do your therapy rest," Ruby's call from across the courtyard startled him awake. She followed up with a sharp glare. "Don't make me get up and bully you into it. Or tell Jo."

"All right, all right," Mike grumbled. He went inside. Jo was wrapping things up on campus, and she'd apparently told Ruby about Mike's need to take a twice-daily therapeutic rest. He was going to get to it, but just wanted to have some time outside. He'd spent too damn much time in a hospital room this year.

He turned down the lights and settled in on the couch, propping his legs into the required braces, then sighed and placed the thick blindfold over his eyes, arms at his sides, finally setting the timer.

It wasn't that he actually had to *sleep*. The directions were for him to *rest* in a darkened room with his legs in elevated braces, arms down, and no visual stimulation, for forty-five minutes twice a day. He could talk all he wanted but no movement, no reading, and no videos. Apparently audio stimulation was not considered to be as detrimental to the development of nervous system connections as visual.

It didn't make sense to Mike, but he wasn't going to argue with Dr. Pramula about those details—he certainly didn't know the process as well as she did.

Mike had tried listening to books or lectures. The books put him to sleep and he needed to take notes to retain lecture details. Sometimes he could sleep. Other times, he and Jo would talk. He wished Ruby would come over and tell him a story. Something to break the monotony of lying still in darkness.

Now he was wide awake, brain churning enough that he didn't think he could go back to sleep, bad memories from childhood surfacing as he lay there. It was stupid, but it was times like this when the little clone boy at risk resurfaced in his thoughts.

"Deontae Swait," his comm chimed.

Finally. Someone to talk to.

"Open. Hey D. What's happening?"

"Ruby said you could stand to have some company. Mind if I come over?"

"Oh, thank God. Yes. Please."

Deontae laughed. "Be right there."

Mike exhaled. This was probably going to be D's version of The Talk. But hey, it would keep him distracted and besides, he *liked* D.

The slider rasped open. "It's me," Deontae said.

"I'd offer you something, but as you see, I'm kinda indisposed at the moment," Mike said.

"Nah," D scoffed, his tone joking. "And here I thought you'd been sneaking in dance lessons."

"I wish," Mike sighed. "I asked the doc if I'd be able to dance once this was over. She said sure, as well as I did before. Which is disappointing since I couldn't dance worth a hoot *before* liquid nanobuild."

Deontae chuckled. A soft scrape sounded against the floor as he slid a chair over to sit—apparently by Mike's waist. "Then I guess it's a good thing that my little sis has never been into dancing."

"Yeah," Mike said. "Gabe was a good dancer, but I have no idea about my progenitor. For all I know, Gabe got it from his mother. Oh well."

"Eh, doesn't matter."

Silence fell between them.

Deontae coughed. "So. You and Jo. I kinda wondered how things were heading when she went to spend New Year's with you in Paris. She talked about meeting up with you every Sunday and sounded pretty happy about it. Was missing you over Christmas. Then you two came back from New Year's, and bam. Jo gets set up with Martiniere security. That was a fast move."

"The situation with Lily sped things up a bit, D," Mike said. "I didn't want to take a risk with Jo, and even if we hadn't worked out as a couple—she would still have been a target for Lily. And given what happened to me, even with good security—it was a damned good thing I did it."

D snorted. "No shit. This is a damn shame, Mike."

"The cyborging? It was due to happen anyway. I just got forced into a more aggressive version than I wanted. Slows me down, but once it's done, with any luck and hard work, my physical condition will be closer to my chronological age than my progenitor's age." Mike paused. "I don't intend to be a burden on Jo, if that's what you're concerned about."

"I'll leave that talk to Wes," D said. "If he's so inclined. Sounds like you and Dad already went there. But I'm getting the impression that once you've got your degree, you're taking over the management of Barkley-Martiniere Associates. Is that gonna involve Ruby and Brandon's share of Barkley-Martiniere-Swait?"

"That part depends on Brandon and Ruby," Mike said. "However, things are headed in that direction, especially with me and Jo getting married."

"Which means the three of us working together."

"Yeah. I'm not sure how involved Bran is going to be with BMS in the future, to be honest. He's already pulling out of BMA. And Ruby's getting up there in years. That's one reason for me to be taking over BMA, to ease the load on her. Bran has his hands full with the Group and—" Mike sighed. "With Lily. And raising Ron."

"Man looks like he's aged ten years in the last six months."

"That's from Lily." Mike paused. "Her followers are fucking ugly news, D. They're taking my progenitor's delusions even further. One of the things I've had time to do while being laid up has been diving into his old records." He shivered. "Mind control. Eugenics under the guise of medical remediation, reinforced by body modifications and other things. Shades of our fucking slaver ancestors."

"Fuck. I knew the situation was bad."

"Uh-huh. And I need to take some of the load off of Bran. Plus gently urging Ruby toward retirement."

D chuckled. "Boy do I ever know that one, with Dad. Good luck. So. In all of this, with you and Jo getting married." D paused. "Since Wes is in bad shape, and Dad's slowly declining, I'm next in line to take charge of Swait Farms. Rae has already said she's wanting to back off of it. What's your vision is for Jo's role in all this? Is she eventually going to be Martiniere or Swait?"

"You need to talk to her first," Mike said. "That's her decision."

"I have. Now I want your thoughts."

"We've talked about what role she's going to play in both operations," Mike said cautiously. "In the short-term, Jo will be splitting her time between the Double R and Swait Farms as she works off her loan. Long term—things can change damn fast, and we need to keep our options open. We've all been brought into the mix as we've grown up. *I* want to see BMS continue because your dad, Ruby, and Gabe created some damn fine bots. I see me and Jo getting married as forging a closer alliance between Swait and Martiniere, with the three of us working together to continue that tradition."

"Okay," D said slowly. "Jo's hinted about you wanting to go in a new direction in addition to regular BMS. But she said that's for you and me to talk about."

"Yeah. I'm considering a greater expansion into the security market because there's some openings there. Justine's making noises about wanting to hand off the businesses that she and her ex-husband Donald created. Serg has already talked to me about transferring Vygotsky Security."

"You're thinking BMS for that?" Deontae's voice sharpened.

"Not really. BMS for the ag-related stuff, definitely. Not sure what we would do about absorbing the private security groups into it."

"Mmm, Swait already has a security-related division, Swait Secure, that's covered our indentured rescue programs," D said. "Dad and Wes handed it off to me and Rae. But Rae's burned out on it, and Jo's focus is more on ag. I—kinda want to spin it off to be its own thing."

Mike resisted the temptation to tap his fingers and forced himself to relax. "I'm not willing to see Justine and Serg's operations get absorbed into the general Martiniere Group conglomerate. Independence saved our butts before. It'll do so now. And from what I've seen of your security programs, D, I think they'll make a nice combination. Complementary. Maybe the two of us should combine everything into Swait Secure."

"I think it's something we should definitely look into," D said. "I'll work up a preliminary proposal."

"And I'll talk further with Justine and Serg." Mike sighed. "This isn't going to be a quick thing, D. Not from my end, I'm afraid, especially since I'm not in line to become the Martiniere. But it is something I want to do with you. Because even after we deal with Lily and her crew, there are going to be threats. Things we need to consider. And it's only going to get worse as time goes by."

"You think so?"

"I'm pretty damn sure of it," Mike said. "As long as genomic research keeps poking at means of so-called improvements in the human genome—there's going to be groups out there like the Reals who promote eugenics. And from the standards I see them putting out —I don't think I trust a single one of them to be any better than my progenitor. And then there's the Martiniere mind control stuff. When I look at Gabe's old notes, there's some scary damn things there. And that's an aspect of Philip's work that I don't completely understand. Gabe kept a lot under wraps."

"It's going to take all of us working together."

"Yes," Mike said. He gestured at his legs. "But once these are back on line, I'm more than ready to kick butt alongside you."

"Looking forward to it, future bro-in-law."

Bro-in-law. He sure liked the sound of that.

MIKE INHALED DEEPLY AS THEY STEPPED OFF OF THE PLANE AND ONTO THE stairway down to the tarmac. Clear, clean mountain air.

Home.

Part of it was the scent. Early summer with the distant sweet smell of fresh-cut grass hay curing in the fields. Dry but a faint whisper of damp from the thunderheads forming over the Thunder Mountains.

And the light. Delicate ripple of gold across distant green fields edged with brown, as the grasses dried. It hadn't been hot here yet, not like Southern California.

Mike halted at the bottom of the stairs, holding on tight to the railing, waiting for Brandon to bring his walker. It didn't stop him from *looking* and savoring the familiar wide open blue sky, the mountains outlined against the scudding gray and white clouds to the south, the rolling plains of the end of the plateau country to the north and the Thunder Valley tucked between the two.

Home. Finally.

He couldn't help the big grin spreading across his face.

Home.

And soon enough he'd see Smudgie again. Damn, he'd missed that dog. The only thing that would make it more perfect would be if Jo was here with him. But she needed to work.

Working for our future together, he reminded himself. And she'd be here in two weeks, to report on research progress to Ruby as well as spend time with him.

He sighed again, grinning.

Home.

Brandon chuckled as he offered an arm for Mike to lean on as they walked to the crawlers, instead of unfolding his walker. "That blissful expression on your face is just like Mom's when she comes back to the ranch. If I didn't know better, I'd say you're my mother's son instead of me. I think you love the Double R and Thunder County more than I ever could."

"How could you not love this place?" He clutched Brandon's arm. His new legs were still challenging as the neural connections grew, and for some reason walking across gravel could be the hardest thing to do.

Brandon snorted. "Mom and Dad had money when you grew up and no one was going to screw around with the Martiniere's adopted son." He sighed. "Pretty different when it was just Ma, fighting to keep the ranch alive any way she could. Having to cope with bullies at school. I lived a pretty hardscrabble life and couldn't wait to get away. Moondance is rural enough for me."

"Different circumstances for sure," Mike agreed. "But after what I'd been through...." His voice trailed off.

"Yeah," Brandon said. "For you, the Double R probably looked like heaven."

"Pretty damn close."

Charlie sat at the crawler controls. "Ruby sends her apologies, but she got caught up in a last-minute call with Jeff. Smudgie is with her."

"That's fine." Mike paused. Would his legs obey enough to let him get into the crawler without help? The interface was still learning his neural system. He looked down at his left leg, thinking *lift*.

It worked with both legs. Slow, but he managed to climb into the crawler and slide over to let Brandon join them in the front seat.

"Hey, Mike," Charlie said roughly, giving him a hug. "You doing all right with these?" He gestured to Mike's cyborged legs.

"Recovery takes a while."

"That sucks." Charlie paused. "But hey. Congratulations to you and JoAnn."

Mike grinned, knowing that he looked like a blissed-out fool at the mention of Jo. "I am the luckiest damn man in the world. We're gonna have to travel back and forth for a while because of our obligations—but still—she decided to accept me."

"Smart woman. When's the wedding?" Charlie started up the crawler and they headed for the house.

"December. At Swait Farms. And I am going to do my damnedest to be able to walk without a walker or cane by then."

"That long?"

"Yeah, it's going to take that long."

"If anyone can do it, you can, kid." They pulled up in front of the house.

Ruby waited in the front yard, Smudgie sitting docilely next to her on a leash, until he saw Mike. Then he wriggled, barking loudly, escalating to jumping up and down next to Ruby.

It took longer than he wanted to get out of the crawler, unfold his walker, and hobble over to Smudgie. Mike dropped to his knees just out of the reach of the leash.

"It's okay now. C'mon, Smudgie."

Ruby let go of the leash and Smudgie charged into Mike's arms.

"Oh Smudgie, Smudgie," Mike said, as the dog licked his face, whining and wiggling as close to Mike as he could get. Mike closed his eyes and inhaled the essence of *dog*, of *Smudgie*.

Home.

As Smudgie settled, Mike patted him, then straightened up. "I'm gonna need help getting up," he said. "Some things are harder than others."

"I put up the hammock," Ruby said as she and Brandon took Mike's arms and he levered himself to his feet. "It worked for Gabe those last years—do you think you'll be able to use it?"

Mike glanced over to where the hammock swung between two Jeffreys pine trees. Angled just right with a view of the mountains. The memory of Gabe lying in it during his last summer, multiple comp screens around him as he worked was bittersweet.

Wish he'd lived to see what I've been able to do.

"One way or another I'll make it work," he said. "Make Dr. Olmos jealous because my workspace is cooler than his."

"Is everything all right?"

"Martin's an approved proctor and supervisor. That spendy Caltech master's degree is assured, Ruby," Mike said. "Dr. Olmos is thrilled that I'm working in the Double R labs. He would like approval to visit."

"Not a problem at all," Ruby said.

"I'll let him know," he said.

"Your heart and lungs functioning all right?" Instead of taking the ramp ahead of them she walked up the steps, waiting as Brandon helped Mike up the ramp.

"As well as can be expected," Mike said. "Still under the strain of adapting to more cyborging. Dr. Pramula did some different integration processes." He heaved a sigh as he reached the top step. "But this should be the end of it."

Brandon shook his head. "You'd think by now we'd have figured it out."

Mike snorted. "I was my progenitor's last surviving clone. I reflect his deteriorating physical condition."

"Well, you're here," Ruby said. "Home. And maybe we can get you back into something close to good health."

"I already feel tons better," Mike said—and meant it.

* * *

OCTOBER, 2080

Age: 27

• • •

THE SUMMER FLEW BY. BEFORE MIKE KNEW IT, HE WAS GOING THROUGH HIS hooding and graduation, Jo beaming at him. As he got better and could navigate more efficiently with his walker, he and Jo started alternating visits between the Double R and Swait Farms.

And then his Gotcha Day arrived. Mike was now using canes or walking poles to get around instead of his walker.

"Feel like coming out to the barn?" Ruby asked.

Mike glanced over at Jo. "What do you think?"

She gave him an enigmatic smile. "I think you need to see yourself some horses. Put you in the right mood for the day."

He chuckled. "What's up, Ruby?" Whatever it was, he thought it was likely that Jo was privy to whatever Ruby had up her sleeve.

"Mmm, got a new horse shipped in last night. Now that it looks like your legs are gonna let you be a horseman again, I thought you might be interested. Addition to the broodmare band."

He shrugged. "Might as well check her out."

"All right." He reached for his canes and wrestled himself to his feet. Ruby headed out first while Jo got him situated and helped him down the steps.

"I *will* get past this stage," he told Jo. "I plan to walk unassisted at our wedding."

She smiled faintly, and he knew she was worried about Wes living long enough to see them married. He was worried about that himself —he'd grown fond of Wes during their visits. "I look forward to that, love."

"But we can move it up if you're worried about Wes," he added.

She shook her head. "I think it'll be all right. Just as long as he doesn't get sick."

He nodded.

At last they arrived at the barn. Mike half-figured this would be a special horse—god only knew, he'd gotten enough equine Gotcha Day presents in the past. But he wondered what this one would be. Another gaited horse that would be easier on him during recovery? Ruby had already found a lovely silver dapple Rocky Mountain gelding whose coloring reminded Mike of his first pony, Rose, and he'd started riding Rocky under careful supervision. Rocky was nice and docile—but damn, he was boring.

"Where's this mare?" Mike called to Ruby as he and Jo entered the barn.

A familiar nicker answered before she could speak, and Mike caught his breath.

No. No. It couldn't be.

He didn't let himself hope as he hurried to the stall.

A red dun mare with a buttermilk dun colt at her side gazed back at him, her ears pricked toward Mike. She whickered at him again and moved forward. Mike leaned against the wall, clutching at the bars as he dropped his walking poles, stunned, taking her in. Familiar white star, matched by the one on her son's face. *Spree.* And she clearly remembered him.

He'd followed her show career, her championships. Everything he'd dreamed of for her, she'd accomplished. Only she hadn't done it with him.

"Spree?" he finally choked out, gulping.

"And her colt," Ruby said softly. "I wrote first option to repurchase in the sales contract when you sold her, Mike."

He closed his eyes for a moment. "That must have cost a fortune, given her show record."

"Not as bad as you think," Ruby said. She drew a deep breath. "The Smiths were reluctant to get into a breeding program and didn't have a place for her when she got hurt. I traded them a promising three-year-old ready to start training last year plus cash, in exchange for Spree. Then I sent her to the best damn reined cowhorse stud I could find, Speckles."

"That colt's a Speckles?"

"Uh-huh. And she's bred back to him."

Mike drew a ragged breath and fumbled for the door, using the bars to keep himself on his feet. Jo handed him his poles, then helped open the stall door and was at his side as Spree met them.

Spree pressed her head against Mike, her colt hanging back a little at the unfamiliar people in his stall before joining his dam.

"I just—I can't—" he shook his head, overwhelmed, moving to hug Spree's neck. She delicately wrapped her head and neck around him.

Jo grinned at him when he raised his head from inhaling deeply of Spree. "Happy Gotcha Day, Mike. From Ruby and me."

In that moment he *knew* he was the luckiest damn man in the world. And now there was only one more thing left to fulfill his dreams.

DECEMBER, 2080

Age: 27

THEIR WEDDING WAS INTIMATE, WITH CLOSE FAMILY ONLY. LILY AND HER followers made security challenging. All the same, as Mike stood next to Brandon and Seth, watching as Jeff slowly escorted Jo down the aisle, he had to mark this as the best day of his life so far—with the exception of when Ruby and Gabe had rescued him from Philip.

Mike's hands shook as he lifted Jo's veil to kiss her. She smiled at him, quivering as much as he was.

Best friends. Lovers. Business and research partners.

And now, husband and wife.

"I love you," he whispered as they leaned toward each other.

"Damn right. I love you too," she answered, just before their lips touched and her hands slipped to his waist.

They held the Martiniere Ritual in Jeff's office immediately afterward. Even though Martiniere Family power no longer passed through Mike to Jo in the form of mind control words and phrases—an archaic institution he was happy to see die—all the same he wanted her to be able to speak with the same degree of political influence as he would have within the Family. Tears streaked down Ruby's cheeks while Justine as the Matriarch prompted Mike and Jo through the oaths.

"I know you don't want to be the Martiniere," Ruby said softly to

Mike afterward. "But all the same...I dearly want JoAnn to be the Matriarch after Justine."

"Unlikely to happen that I'll ever be the Martiniere," Mike whispered back. "Very unlikely to happen."

It was a damn good thing he never held himself up to be a prophet, because he sucked at it.

JANUARY 2081

Age: 27

WINTERTIME AT THE DOUBLE R. RUBY SURRENDERED HER BIG UPSTAIRS bedroom to Mike and Jo when they returned from their honeymoon, settling into the first-floor bedroom next to the offices. Mike heaved a relieved sigh at that choice. Reaching that third floor was a challenge for her, and Ruby wouldn't use Gabe's old floater, insisting that she could still climb the stairs. He worried that she was going to fall one of those days, and while her bone mass was still good, Ruby *was* on the brink of osteopenia.

Of course, broken bones from falling *would* be something Mike worried about, based on past experience.

The three of them fell into winter routines. Jo wasn't due to return to Swait Farms until springtime. She and Mike spent most of their time working on refinements of a project for their new Swait Secure collaboration with Deontae. The Guardian prototype was based on an agricultural security bot. One of their discoveries was that cyborging using liquid nanobuild managed to evade most detection protocols.

Mike wasn't a perfect test for the Guardian's abilities because his arms, heart, and lungs had been cyborged by other processes. But they created liquid nanobuild-based mouse-brained cyborgs—Mborgs—to challenge the Guardian. And thinking about what to do with the Mborgs besides test the Guardian kept Jo and Mike brainstorming.

Mike was reprogramming Mborg Number Two for potential repair functions when his comm chimed.

"Brandon Martiniere."

He clicked it open, not shielding so that Jo could listen in, intending to joke about working with mouse brains, but Brandon's expression cut him off.

"Seth's dead," Brandon said grimly, without preliminaries. "And his wife Clarissa is in bad shape."

Mike gaped, momentarily unable to react.

Shit!

Suddenly, the possibility of his becoming the Martiniere-in-waiting was much more likely. Ron was too young to step up yet, and the other prospects…had health issues.

"What the hell, Brandon? How did it happen?" Jo slipped her hands from the gloved vacuum box where she was working and joined Mike.

Brandon shook his head. "Neurotoxin and psychotropics applied to a surface. The same combination that almost killed Mike."

"Lily, then," Mike said flatly, dreading Brandon's reaction.

Brandon rubbed his face. "Yeah." His voice cracked. "Damn it. Lily."

"Do you have any leads?" Mike asked. "Obviously the authorities can't or won't do shit about catching her. It's up to us."

Jo scowled. "Mike…you're not going to chase after Lily!"

"We've got to stop her, Jo. We're targets ourselves. Bran. What do we need to do?"

Brandon sighed. "Donna-gran and Serg taught Mom about administering psychotropics. Why don't you start by talking to her? Get the details and figure out the way neurotoxins differ." He rubbed his face again. "Knowing how they're administered in settings besides surfaces may help with defenses. We'll start there. Then we'll see if our people can succeed where the authorities have failed."

Mike and JoAnn exchanged glances. "Get us the specific neurotoxin and psychotropic mix," Jo said. "It's possible that we can run the

Guardians to identify it and rig them up to run family security scans. It's a defensive start."

Brandon nodded. "I will get that information to you quickly."

Mike tapped his fingers on the lab table. Jo's mention of the Guardians triggered something—aha.

"Jo. The Mborgs. Bran, if we can get some leads on a location, we've got bots that can not only feed us information, but aren't detectable by the usual means. At least the Guardian can't find them. I don't think Lily's allies have access to anything more sophisticated than we have."

"The Mborgs? To do *what*, Michael?" Jo frowned at him.

"They're supposed to be able to evade the Guardian bots as part of our test protocols," Mike said. "They can carry a payload and they have the RubyBot's reporting abilities. They move like mice. Get a location. Release Guardians to search until we find Lily and her crew. Then use the Mborgs. Have them release an airborne sedative like Deontae's been talking about creating. Boom. We've got Lily. And we can do this with our own security, take custody of her ourselves. Not worry about others being compromised or bribed to let her go."

Brandon raised his brows. "How soon could you set something like this up?"

Jo pursed her lips thoughtfully. "We have twenty Mborgs on hand right now. And—we have more Guardians available. Program the Guardians to pinpoint Lily's location once we have some idea of where she is, then send in the Mborgs for a more specific location and disabling. Yes. Doable."

"That's a relief." Brandon exhaled. "Make it happen."

"We will," Mike said. "Just get us a location. We'll take it from there."

WITH BECK'S HELP MIKE AND JO SPED UP PRODUCTION OF THE MBORGS and the Guardians. Normally January was down time at the Double R labs, when they ran checks on the facilities, preparing for spring bot production, getting in supplies, fixing freezer chambers, and performing other necessary repairs.

But this changed their agenda entirely. Beck cooked up stem seeds to produce the Guardians while Julie cloned mouse brains. Mike and Jo created a production line for the mechanical portion of the Mborgs and worked on programming both the Guardians and the Mborgs, in consultation with Deontae. Ruby and Beck focused on testing the Guardians using assorted psychotropic/neurotoxin combinations.

Meanwhile Swait and Martiniere security hustled to find any trace of Lily and her followers.

"The challenge is that there's still a network attracted to that whole sexual body mod stuff," Brandon sighed when they joined him and Deontae for a conference call.

"Something's covering for them electronically," D said flatly. "It's a worm akin to the old Stuxnet, but updated so that previous countermeasures don't work. It wipes files. But that's not all. It's damn insidious because it has a mind influencing element."

"I haven't seen that," Brandon said.

"You wouldn't," D said grimly. "If I run a check using Martiniere security elements, it doesn't show up. Run Swait Secure programs and it does. It's targeted to the Martiniere family. I tried networking with Serg about it. Every damn time I send him a file, he forgets about it and poof! It's gone. Hell, I've sent you files, Brandon."

Brandon frowned. "I—I've not seen them."

"There you have it," D said. "The files are either erased or else you forget that you've erased them. It's the same thing I'm seeing with Serg. The files don't just delete. Any tracking record tied to them disappears if they go to a Martiniere-connected address. Complete erasure. I've seen it happen with my Barkley-Martiniere-Swait address. No matter what I do, I can't catch it in time to stop the deletion."

"Same thing for me," Jo said. "I can see it—and then it fades. However, seeing it really jerks my thought processes around and it doesn't matter which address I use." She scowled. "I can remember its existence. But talking about it makes my head hurt."

"Probably an artifact of the Martiniere Ritual," Brandon said.

"You're part of the family, so you're included in the blockages." He chewed on his lip. "How do we get around it to find Lily?"

"I'll take lead," D said.

Brandon nodded. "That makes sense. You can see the worm where we can't."

"Does Lily have control of the worm or is it an independent agent?" Mike asked. "If we can't grab the worm, maybe its presence can tell us where she is."

D raised his brows thoughtfully. "It's a possibility. While I can't see what it erases, I can see where it goes." He leaned back in his chair. "All right. I'll message when I get some notion of Lily's location. Let's hope to hell that this damn worm doesn't wipe out *those* messages."

Two weeks later, a short message popped up from Deontae while Mike and Jo were testing a run of Guardians.

—*Southeast PDX.*

Mike stared at it, repeating the words to himself silently. *Southeast PDX. Southeast PDX. Southeast PDX.*

"You saw it?" Jo asked tensely.

"Yeah," Mike said.

"I'm answering."

"Good. Beck! It's showtime."

"Where?"

"Southeast PDX."

A rare grin appeared on Beck's face. "Got the payloads ready to roll."

"Good." He messaged the house, where Ruby and Justine were working.

—*Showtime.*

A prearranged code. Then he and Jo helped Beck with the final packaging and transport to the hangar.

They converged at the airstrip, where the flight crew was already unplugging the fully-charged jet and checking systems under Justine's watchful eye.

"I've contacted Serg," Justine said to Mike as Beck and Jo secured the drones carrying the Guardians and Mborgs against the outside of the jet. "He found an address where psychotropic and neurotoxin precursors have been shipped. A warehouse."

"In Southeast Portland, right?"

Justine nodded. "Central Industrial district. In huge quantities." She handed Mike a slip of paper. "I wrote this down immediately— good thing because the message disappeared. This time I *saw* it go away. This is your copy."

"I'll let you, Brandon, and Ruby handle dealing with the authorities," Mike said. "Meanwhile, we're on the move."

"Good hunting," Ruby said.

As the plane took off, he handed the paper to Jo.

Together, they entered the address into the programming matrix for the Guardians, Mike reading it to Jo, then him checking it while she read it aloud.

"You need to be primary control," he told her, swallowing hard. "I don't trust that damn worm."

"Got it," Jo said as she pulled on her hazard suit.

BEFORE THEY LANDED AT THE PORTLAND AIRPORT, THEY MADE A PASS OVER Central Eastside to release the drones. No airspace warning alert popped up, so Mike hoped that meant that someone had spoken to Portland air traffic control and the city authorities. Either that or the place was scarily vulnerable—and either possibility was likely in this era.

Brandon met them at the private hangar, wearing everything but the helmet of his hazard suit.

"All clear," he said. "I didn't share details about Lily with the locals. Simply issued a warning that we'd discovered the likelihood of a major toxin release using Martiniere Group materials, and that Swait Secure and the Martiniere Group were mobilizing to handle it. I told the authorities enough to scare the shit out of them. Hopefully that keeps them from tipping off Lily and her buds. They're not happy about us leading the charge. But they're waiting in reserve should we need them. Anything from the Guardians yet?"

"Should be active like right about—*now*." Jo clenched her fist and a map projected in front of them. "Guardians released."

"Let's go," Brandon said, gesturing to four trucks. The map followed Jo as they headed for the lead truck. The three remaining cyborged brothers waited in the back, in full hazard gear. Al, Frederick, and Carl helped them secure their helmets, then handed them the new SPA-12 rifles.

"Guardians still looking," Jo muttered as they left the airport. Mike watched along with her as the faint lines of Guardian movement scanned the grids around the address.

And then one spot flared red.

"Camera zoom," Jo ordered.

Mike frowned as the image of an empty lot shimmered into solidity. It didn't match what he *knew* should be at that address, since it was under an old freeway overpass.

"That doesn't make sense..." and then his voice trailed off as he spotted the shimmer of a shield generator.

"*There,*" Jo said grimly. "Mborg release."

They watched as the lot remained empty, remained empty, remained empty.

"Deshield," Jo ordered.

Light flashed. The old overpass reappeared, and underneath it, a decrepit warehouse. With people frantically running away from it.

"Aw, *shit,*" Al muttered. "Just showed up on my screens. That's supposed to be a pop-up food distribution site. Appeared this morning. No wonder the locals were concerned. We've got civilians at risk."

"Sedative shouldn't hurt them," Jo said. "Not unless Lily's pals have found the means to aerosolize the neurotoxin."

Mike bit his lip.

Philip would do that, and take hostages, his deepest instincts suddenly said.

"Get them out of there," he said. "Something's making those people run, but we've gotta get them further away."

"What?" Brandon snapped.

"Get them out of there," Mike repeated. "That's Lily's play. They're going to use the folks there for food distribution as hostages."

"Mike—"

"It's what fucking Philip would do, all right?" Mike snarled. "I *know*. Assume that the neurotoxin is aerosolized. Get those people the hell out of there."

Brandon stared at him for a moment, then nodded. He and Al huddled together.

Jo rested one hand on his as they both stared at the projection. Biosuited and armed forces suddenly descended on the people racing away from the warehouse. As the authorities started to escort the people further out of the area, Mike spotted movement in an upper window.

"There!" He pointed to it. "Damn it, I *know* that's Lily!"

"Zooming in now," Jo muttered. Lily's features came clear.

The window shattered. Lily raised her hand. Something round was in it.

"*STOP HER!*" Mike bellowed, a sudden sinking sensation in his gut.

Jo nodded sharply. She thrust her hands into the projection and began inputting commands to the Guardians and Mborgs.

Lily swayed as the unmasked people below her began to fall down. For a moment Mike thought she was going to collapse inside the warehouse.

The sedative must be working.

Then light blossomed as the ball in Lily's hand exploded. The people closest to her started to jerk and twitch. A couple of moments later, the people in biosuits started to do the same.

"No," Mike groaned. "*No.* Jo, we've got to do something."

"Working as fast as I can, Mike." Jo's voice was even and level but he could still hear that edge of anger. "Bitch isn't going to get away with killing all those folks. Got a backup payload that was Ruby and Beck's idea. Possible antidote."

Lily kept swaying. She turned back inside. A pause. Then she faced back out. She peered into the crowd, then screamed, her face twisted in rage as she pointed at *someone*. Flames exploded around her body. The flames enveloped her and she stood illuminated as Brandon groaned next to Mike, futilely reaching toward her.

Then Lily leaned forward and deliberately fell out of the window, fire streaming behind her.

———

Brandon was first out of the rig when they reached the warehouse, Mike and Jo right behind with Al, Carl, and Frederick. The locals had already set up barricades.

"Brandon Martiniere," Brandon growled at the uniformed woman who would have blocked him from passing through the barricades. "I have reason to believe that my daughter Lily is involved with this incident. We saw it on our comms. She's wanted on French and US warrants."

"One moment, Mr. Martiniere." The woman spoke into a comm. "All right. Incident commander will escort you."

The commander was right there. "Only you," he said to Brandon.

"No. Michael Martiniere and JoAnn Swait plus my guards," Brandon snapped. "Michael and JoAnn commanded the devices that kept this situation from being worse than it already is. They need to collect data and see the results. And we're not going in without our own protection. Or would you prefer to discuss this with the Martiniere Group legal team?"

More consultations happened. Then the commander nodded curtly. "Come on."

"How many casualties?" Jo asked.

"Five," the commander said. He nodded to Brandon. "Tentative identification on one is Liliana Angelica Martiniere. The other four— two food distribution staff, two clients."

"Neurotoxin?" Mike asked.

"No. They were shot. Just inside the warehouse."

"Lily wasn't alone," Mike said. "I'm pretty damn sure of it."

"No signatures to indicate that anyone else was in the warehouse with her when she started shooting and threatening people," the commander said. "Haven't done the DNA traces yet."

"They had blockers," Jo said, one hand inside the projection that she was towing along, fingers still dancing inside of it. "Unless you picked up Lily on your scans before I stripped her blockers, you wouldn't see them."

She halted just before they reached the black tarp covering Lily's body.

"And. My data doesn't pick up anyone besides Lily tied to that crap she released," she continued. "What the hell?"

"That can't be right," Mike said, stopping and staring at Jo. "Unless it was a suicide op. She wouldn't be that deluded. Would she?"

"We'll probably never know."

They joined Brandon. He pulled back the tarp and knelt next to Lily's scorched and broken body, shaking his head slowly as he stroked her forehead, pushing aside the strands of straightened dark hair that hid her paler-than-usual face as it stared straight up at the sky.

At last Brandon sighed. He cupped Lily's cheek in his still-gloved hand for a moment.

"My little dancer," he choked. "To come to this end. Oh God, my little dancer." He gulped. Then he rose, facing the commander.

"I confirm the identification," he said slowly, voice quavering as if he were twice his forty-eight years. "This is my daughter, Liliana Angelica Martiniere." He shook his head again. His voice caught as he continued. "And may God have mercy on her soul."

He turned away from the commander, staggering slightly, and reached for Mike's shoulder. Mike steadied him with his other arm, holding firm for both Brandon and Jo.

THE THREE OF THEM SPENT THE NIGHT IN A PENTHOUSE SUITE THAT JUSTINE had hastily reserved somewhere on Portland's West Side, near the Pearl District. After dinner, Brandon took a sedative and retreated to his bedroom, refusing any condolences.

Mike and Jo sat in front of the artificial fireplace, a bottle of local whisky in front of them, not looking out the wall of reinforced windows that provided a cityscape. For once Mike was drinking hard. He wanted to be numb. Especially after the preliminary reports started flooding in. The Mborg antidote payload had been effective against the aerosolized neurotoxin, fortunately. But quick ballistics matched the bullets that killed the four to a weapon in the facility. DNA traces within the warehouse were inconclusive.

"There's no fucking way she did that alone," Mike snarled after finishing his second drink. "Just no fucking way. She couldn't set up all those sensors to hide that building from us on her own. Not targeted to our devices like they were. So where are her allies?"

"Mikey—"

His comm dinged, followed by a soft chuckle that sent chills up his spine.

"Hi, Mikey." Lily's shape took form in front of them as she cooed seductively. "So did ya like the way I eliminated those dregs of society?"

Mike sat straight up as Lily laughed. She was wearing the Black Swan crown and tutu from *Swan Lake*—a facsimile of the one that Angelica had worn in her last performance. And her skin was a pale brown, her features modified to resemble Angelica's. Jo muttered something and pulled up a screen.

"I told you that you were gonna miss out on some fun over a year ago," Lily continued. "But I guess you wanted to go screw your Black slut instead." She laughed again. "Well, you didn't get to have fun with me. Then again, Philip always said that you were a chickenshit. And now I'm going to join him. I'm gonna be purified from my mud heritage. After that, I'm gonna take away everything you've ever loved. And when you become the Martiniere, I'm gonna break you. From the grave. *And you can't do anything to stop it!* Right, darling?" She turned as a shadowy shape coalesced next to her. Mike's skin crawled as Philip's visage scowled at him, even as he embraced Lily.

Rage flowed through Mike and he hurled his glass at the projection. Lily and Philip disappeared.

"Damnit!" Jo snapped. "That was the fucking worm! I had the damn thing and it *slipped away!*"

Mike only half-heard her as he shot up off the couch, growling incoherently, shaking with fury as he stomped around the living room, knocking over furniture, battering his hands against the marble kitchen counters. He banged his head against cupboards and reeled away from them. He wanted to hurt. To bleed.

He came up short as Jo stopped him, hands on his shoulders, fixing him with a hard stare.

"Mikey. *Stop it.*"

He bellowed and tried to slip free. But her hands tightened and she shook him.

"Mike. *That's fucking enough.*"

"I—she—-" he spluttered.

"That's enough, Michael," she repeated. Something in her voice stopped him. As he heaved, half-panting, half sobbing, she continued. "No more bullshit from you. That was a prerecorded, timed message carried by the worm. I almost had it, and then the damned thing twisted free, just before you threw the glass at the projection. There was definitely mind control shit in that message, designed to set you off. And she did it, just about damned perfectly, that little bitch."

Mike stared at Jo, chest rising and falling hard, blinking, suddenly confused. Why was he standing up? Why did Jo hold his shoulders so firmly? Why were his hands bloody and his head hurting? He didn't remember anything beyond finishing that second drink.

"What just happened?" *Something* had set off his rage. But what?

A bemused expression flitted across her face. "Something—I don't know, Mike."

She turned to her open screen as Mike looked around the room, bewildered by the broken glass and the disorder. He rinsed the blood off of his hands—fortunately superficial. The cyborg elements in his hands and arms had stopped the bleeding. He started to set things back in place. His hands felt sore and bruised and his head pounded. But what had set him off? Nothing he saw here could explain why his hands suddenly hurt so much, more than the scratches could explain.

"Mikey." Jo's voice quavered as he was picking up shards of glass.

"What?"

"We just got visited by the worm." She pointed to the data she'd brought up on her screen.

Words in bright red letters.

I MAY BE DEAD BUT THIS ISN'T OVER, MICHAEL. YOU WILL BE MINE. PJM.

The words disappeared.

MIKE'S HEAD ACHED THE NEXT MORNING AS HE STIRRED NEXT TO JO.

"Oh," he groaned.

Her moan matched his.

"How much did we drink?" she asked finally.

"More than we probably should," Mike scowled at the ceiling. "I don't remember anything beyond sitting down on the couch and drinking because I just wanted to be numb, damn it. God. Brandon. Poor fucking Brandon. For Lily to go like this."

He flexed his hands. Something didn't feel right. Why were his hands so sore?

He studied his hands, opening and closing them, opening and closing them. Whatever this was had its roots in his cyborging.

"What's the matter, Mikey?"

"Something's not right with my hands," he said slowly. "Something to do with the cyborging. I've been hacked." He sighed. "I'll send a message to Ruby and Dr. Pramula. I want my hands checked before we go back to the Double R or do anything further of any significance. *Today.*"

"Mike—"

"This doesn't just happen, Jo," he said, even slower than before. "And if we can't remember what happened—do you hurt anywhere?"

"Only my head."

Mike carefully sat up. "I'll check on Brandon."

"You're scaring me, Mike."

"You're scared? I am too, Jo." His head throbbed as he wrestled on a pair of sweats. "It takes a lot for my hands to hurt like this, and I can't remember doing anything to make it happen. Which means—"

Her lips tightened. "The worm."

"I want to ensure that my programming isn't fucked up." He could finally put what he feared into words. "And I can't do that at the Double R or any place that's controlled by the Martinieres. Nor do I think it's safe for D to scan me."

Jo nodded and climbed out of the bed.

A message popped up from Ruby before he went to Brandon.

—*How bad is it? Bran won't answer my calls.*

Mike hurried to the door of Brandon's room, dread tightening his gut. The sounds of retching came from the bathroom. Mike slumped against the wall, relieved, the sudden fear that they had two people to mourn dissipating. Then he returned to their room to call Ruby.

"Bran's throwing up," Mike said before she could respond. "I went to his door but didn't go in. We all—drank pretty heavily last night."

"That bad," Ruby said.

"Lily set herself on fire before she jumped," Mike said. He rubbed his face. "Haven't talked to the authorities yet to find out when they're releasing the body. But I've got to go to LA. See Dr. Pramula. Something's wrong with my hands and I haven't the faintest idea what."

Ruby blanched. "That fucking bad."

Mike nodded. "Jo and I have memory blanks that can't be explained entirely by drinking. We think that's connected to my hands. I've been hacked."

"The worm," Ruby said.

Mike nodded and choked. "Bran—oh God, Ruby. It hit him pretty damn hard. He called her *my little dancer* before identifying her body. I've never, ever seen him in so dark a mood. Not even when Kris died. I did my best to keep him from drinking too much over dinner but it wasn't enough." He gulped and rubbed his face again. "I don't want to leave Bran alone right now."

"Oh fuck," Ruby groaned. "All right. Justine and I are on our way. We'll spell you and JoAnn with Bran so you can get to Dr. Pramula as soon as possible."

"Thank you," Mike said.

"IT'S A GOOD THING YOU CAME IN SO QUICKLY," DR. PRAMULA SAID AFTER running the scan that afternoon in her Los Angeles clinic. "It's a sneaky little bugger. It circumvented your normal programming defenses, and was working on disabling your hand controls. If you let it go, we would have needed to redo all your programming."

Mike scowled. "I knew something didn't feel right in my hands this morning."

"It's a good thing you pay attention to changes in your mechanical state," the doctor said. "Keep it up."

"Can we patch the pathway the attacking entity used?" Jo asked.

"Better than that. I fixed that doorway, and I used what data I could get off that program to write a better protective algorithm."

Mike nodded tensely as she attached the leads to upload the updates directly. "Were you able to isolate the program?"

Dr. Pramula shook her head. "It slipped away. Not before I captured enough to reprogram your defensive protocols." She paused. "Michael. It's some sort of worm that adapts easily. I recommend monthly visits to monitor your programming."

"Don't worry," Jo said. "We'll schedule the next appointment on our way out."

"Good," Dr. Pramula said. "We can do this at the Portland Center, if you'd like."

"I don't think so," Jo said before Mike could answer. "LA is better for this purpose."

After they had finished the final bits and left the office, Jo tucked her hand in Mike's arm.

"It was the worm, Mike. It had to be the worm. But why your hands?"

"I don't know," Mike said. He sighed. "And now we have to deal with the fallout from Lily."

He couldn't explain the foreboding that clutched at him.

LILY'S FUNERAL WAS EXCLUSIVELY FOR CLOSE FAMILY. MIKE TOOK OVER THE responsibility for digging the grave next to Kris's in the family cemetery on the Double R and supervising the vault placement. The pounding rain and snow mix that clattered hard on the cab of the backhoe reflected his grim mood. At least the ground wasn't frozen hard, and for once the equipment cooperated with no breakdowns. It allowed him time to mourn alone so he could be strong for Brandon and Ronnie, without encumbering Jo, who was doing her best to help Ruby and Justine deal with everything.

Jo met him with a steaming mug on the back porch as he came in. Mike took one long swig before handing it back to her.

"Whoo," he said. "Lovely hot toddy and heavy on the whiskey. Thanks, Jo." He kissed her, then unzipped his insulated coveralls and took them off. "Things that bad?"

"Saw the weather and thought you could use some internal heat," she said.

"Absolutely." He hung up the coveralls and took the cup in both hands for another sip. Even with cyborged hands the heat felt good. "But. How are things going?"

"Better. Brandon's still detached but he's dealing now. He's finalizing arrangements with Justine. Ronnie is with Ruby. They're doing all right."

Mike followed Jo into the kitchen. He drained the cup and set it on the counter before reaching for her. They stood together quietly for a few moments.

"It's arranged," Justine said as she came into the kitchen. "I managed to persuade a local priest that Lily was not in her right mind when she committed suicide. Still not going to be a Mass but...." Her voice trailed off.

"When?" Mike asked.

"Tomorrow morning. Graveside only."

Mike nodded.

It was only them plus Lily's aunt Pat at the short service the next morning, in much better weather. To Mike's relief, Brandon and Ronnie stayed over at the Double R for another night, along with Pat.

But filling in the grave was his job and no one else's. His atonement for not doing something—anything—to help Lily. Niece. Great-grand-daughter. He tackled the job shortly after the service. Mike let himself sob now that it was over, thinking of bright little Lily dancing in her studio, trying to copy her great-grandmother, and not about what Lily had become at the end. Killer. Exploiter.

Could I have prevented this somehow?

No logical reason for him to feel this way. And yet—

Jo met him on the porch again when he was done, with another hot toddy, stronger than the one from the day before.

"I could get used to this," he said, trying and failing to sustain a joking tone before burying his head in her chest.

She patted him on the shoulder. "Brandon wants to talk to you. I figured you needed a little fortification."

"Thanks. Where is he?"

"Your office."

Mike hugged Jo, drained his drink, then headed to the office.

Brandon sat in front of Mike's desk, staring down at his hands. Mike paused to rest a hand on Brandon's shoulder.

"Hey, brother," he said softly.

Brandon clasped Mike's hand. "Thank you for everything, Mike."

"As you told me years ago when I was sick, we're brothers. Helping each other is what brothers do."

"I just—" Brandon shook his head. "Oh God, Mike. Where did I go wrong with Lily?"

"I don't think it was you or Kris," Mike said slowly. "Jo and I have memory holes for the night after Lily died."

Brandon tightened under Mike's hand. "That fucking worm?"

"Yes. And something tampered with my hand programming for the same time period. Confirmed by Dr. Pramula."

"How are we ever going to beat this damn thing?"

"We'll beat it," Mike said. "Together. One way or another."

Brandon shook his head again, wearily. "I hope so. Oh God," he gulped. "My little girl, gone along with Kris. My little girl who was supposed to be a dancer, damn it. Not this—mess. If it was the fucking worm that twisted her—Ronnie's all I've got left—oh God!"

Mike reached out to Brandon. He held Brandon tight as he sobbed, staring straight ahead.

If this was your doing somehow, Progenitor, I'll make you pay. I'll make you fucking pay, he vowed.

Not that he had many doubts about the cause. It was just —remembering.

And then the doing.

RUBY INTERCEPTED MIKE ONCE BRANDON HAD GONE TO BED.

"He's still not talking to me," she said softly. "Does Bran blame me and Gabe for what happened?"

"I don't think so," Mike said. "Why would he blame you?"

Ruby bit her lip and looked away, then back.

"There were—problems with Kris when she was carrying Lily. Artifacts from the days when she was still indentured. Hormonal implants that weren't removed until after Kris became pregnant." She swallowed hard. "It wasn't unknown. But those who knew about it and what to do about it were primarily in the indentured ranks, and their way of dealing with it was to let—whatever would—happen in the first trimester. If the fetus survived the first trimester, then it was considered viable and treatments started."

"But Lily survived—"

"Because Gabe, Justine, and I insisted on first trimester treatment." Ruby's eyes glimmered with tears. "Maybe if we hadn't—"

"I don't think that's the case," Mike said. "I really don't. I think Bran's just—devastated by what happened."

Ruby leaned her head against him. "I hope you're right, Mike. Because I've been questioning myself ever since she started having problems. What if we created this situation? What if we just didn't do enough?"

"You're not the only one with these questions," Mike said. "I keep wondering if I could have done something—said something—that made a difference. Changed things somehow. But she was just so focused and so obsessed about Philip and me being Philip's clone—" he shuddered.

"You had to protect yourself. I just wish I knew why she suddenly became so self-hating," Ruby said. "She was so beautiful." She sniffled. "She sure didn't hear anything about—that bigotry she spouted against herself—from any of us."

Mike sighed and put an arm around Ruby's shoulders. "Why was my progenitor so twisted when his siblings weren't? Ruby, the Martinieres have a strong streak of depression and bipolar in their genetics. You've seen it in me."

Ruby gulped. "And it's in my family as well—my father's people— was she doomed to become like this?"

"I don't know," Mike said, and meant it.

MIKE FAITHFULLY FLEXED HIS HANDS EVERY MORNING TO CHECK THEIR operation. He couldn't explain why, but it was tied somehow to the worm and that new monthly regime where Dr. Pramula checked his cyborg programming to ensure that it had not been compromised.

It was only in nightmares that Mike remembered Lily and Philip in an embrace, and the threat that had briefly appeared on Jo's screen. Those memories fled when he wakened, leaving him with a sense of ill-defined impending doom, and a further drive to check the functioning of his hands.

21 / RUBY AND JEFF

OCTOBER, 2083

Age: 28

"I'M GOING FOR A RIDE," RUBY SAID, STICKING HER HEAD INTO MIKE'S office. Smudgie raised his head and padded over to her. "Want to join me?" She absently patted Smudgie's head.

"I'd love to, but—" Mike sighed at the multiple screens clustered around his desk. He *should* go with Ruby for safety's sake. But he was wrestling with a bit of coding. He had promised Cousin Beth in Britain that he'd have the fix to her this afternoon. Plus…he was trying to clear his desk so he could leave.

Jo was in Arkansas because Jeff had suddenly developed an aggressive cancer, would die any time now, and he *should* be with her but… family and business stuff kept him here. Including recent concerns about Ruby's health. Brandon had promised he would come to the ranch and stay with Ruby as Jeff declined, so that Mike could be with Jo. But that was going to be another couple of days yet.

Furthermore, despite her age, Ruby was safe enough—on the right horse, as long as she was careful where she rode. "Where are you going?"

The thought of riding *was* tempting, above and beyond the need to keep an eye on Ruby. They'd been working with Spree's son Starlight and if it was going to be a short ride—going out with Ruby would be good for him. Mike planned to campaign Starlight in reined cowhorse competition next year—his first foal crop had been born in June and they looked promising.

"Homestead field," she said. Well within the restrictions they'd placed on her for riding out alone—something Ruby insisted on being able to do even into her seventies, and arguing with her didn't change her mind one bit. It was further than he wanted to ride Starlight, though. "I can do it by myself, Mike. Just thought I'd see if you wanted to go. But if you're in the weeds with Beth's project and trying to get out the door to be with JoAnn...."

"I'm sorry, Ruby. I really am." He glanced out the window. Another gorgeous September day in the Thunder Mountains. Mild, with just a hint of chill in the air. They were coming up on the twenty-third anniversary of his Gotcha Day, and had safely passed the tenth anniversary of Gabe's death. It should be all right. "Who are you going to ride?"

"Old Legacy is still full of beans." A half-smile played on Ruby's lips at the thought of the old palomino mare. "Might be her last outing, though. Twenty-seven years old. Too bad she's never liked doing dressage patterns. We could have done a Century Ride."

For a moment he considered trying to persuade Ruby to take a shorter ride, so he could join her on Starlight. "That would have been something to see." Mike blinked up his clock. He had a spare moment. "I'll help you saddle up. How's that?"

"You sure?"

"I can always manage that much time for you, Ruby," Mike said. To his surprise, she blushed.

He tossed Legacy's saddle on her back for Ruby, and as she rode off, set an alarm. At most, even if she poked around the field and dawdled there and back, she would be back in two hours.

And if she hadn't returned by then, he'd be justified in looking for Ruby without incurring her wrath at being overprotected.

Stubborn old woman.

But that stubbornness was how Ruby had successfully managed years of the Martinieres.

The timer chimed at Mike just as he hit send on the programming fix.

Ruby's not in the house yet.

Which didn't mean much. She could be in the labs, or communing with the horse herd. But usually, she'd message him on her return from a ride.

Worry tightened his gut. He commed Beck in the lab. "Any chance Ruby's there?"

"Haven't seen her since this morning, Mike. What's up?"

"She went for a ride two hours ago. On Legacy."

"Want me to fire up a crawler?" Beck asked.

"Might not be too bad an idea. I'll check at the barn."

He stopped to pull on hiking boots before striding toward the horse barn. Terri, the ranch manager, met him there, as Smudgie followed along beside him.

"No sign of Legacy or Ruby," she said grimly. "I'm coming with you and Beck. Should we call Brandon?"

"Not until we know what's going on," Mike said as he scrambled into the crawler, Beck at the controls. Smudgie jumped into his lap.

After all, there could be a legitimate reason for Ruby's being late. A sudden lameness. Something that caught her attention on the way. Any number of little ranch projects that she might decide was up to her to do.

But he didn't think this was the case. Ruby had been complaining of feeling tired lately. Had looked stretched and strained. Was nibbling at food instead of diving in with her usual hearty appetite. That was why he and Brandon had huddled together last week, when Jeff Swait had taken a turn for the worse and Jo had needed to go back to Swait Farms to be with her dad.

It's nothing, Ruby had said to him. And Brandon had reported the same response to him.

One of us needs to be on the ranch at all times, had been Mike and Brandon's conclusion. *Something's going on with Ruby. One of us needs to be here—just in case.*

And while Brandon could juggle his duties as the Martiniere, there were still some things that required his attention and personal presence. Mike had to be the primary guardian.

"We need to put a locator on her," Beck muttered as they roared up the hill to the Homestead field at the crawler's highest speed. "But damn it, she won't cooperate."

And then she throttled back. Legacy stood at the edge of the field, head down, unmoving. The golden mare raised her head slightly at their approach, then dropped it again.

Mike rolled out of the crawler before it skidded to a stop. He ordered Smudgie to stay before he approached Legacy. The golden mare's coat was sweat-darkened—*had they been running for a while before it happened?* Ruby wouldn't run a horse like that, unless there was a problem. Or had Legacy been spooked and Ruby fell?

"Steady, Legacy, whoa, old girl," he said softly, heart in his throat as he spotted the still figure that Legacy guarded, as if she had a young foal lying down.

Ruby lay curled on her left side, hands clutched to her chest, one of Legacy's reins wrapped around her left hand. Her eyes stared at nothing, her face twisted in pain—*just like Gabe.* Mike pressed trembling fingers first to her neck, then her wrist. Nothing. Legacy pinned her ears and tossed her head, unwilling to move away, as Terri and Beck joined him, Smudgie at their heels.

"I can't feel a pulse," he said to them.

Beck slid in as he stepped back. Legacy's right rein was wrapped around the horn, while Ruby held the left rein. He carefully gathered both reins and scratched the old mare's white forehead, then checked her over. Sweaty.

No sign of a stumble, so she hadn't fallen with Ruby. Could she have bucked? Not likely, with the right rein wrapped loosely around the horn so Legacy couldn't step on it, and the left rein in Ruby's hand. But the sweat—that wasn't right.

He flipped up Legacy's upper lip. Her gums were pale, and when he pressed on them, they stayed pale.

Colic. She's colicking.

Ruby must have dismounted to check Legacy, and then....

Fast, just like Gabe.

"She's gone," Beck said. "You hear me Mike? She's gone."

He nodded numbly and commed Brandon.

"Hey, Mike, I should be at the ranch tonight—" Brandon's smile faded as he took in Mike's expression. "Is it Mom?"

Mike nodded, numbness spreading throughout him. "Happened at the Homestead field, Bran. She was riding Legacy. Looks like Ruby got off to check Legacy because she's colicking, then—" He swallowed hard. "Right rein wrapped around the horn, left rein around her hand. Legacy was standing over her when we found them."

Brandon closed his eyes tightly and tightened his lips, shaking his head. "Like Dad?"

"Yeah. I *should* have ridden out with her, but I was trying to clear my schedule…." Mike shook his head in unconscious mimicry of Brandon. "She was having a good day today, Bran. Like her old self. I thought it was safe!"

"If it was like Dad, you probably couldn't have done a damn thing even if you were right there, Mike. Especially out riding. Wouldn't have made a difference if she'd been in the house when it happened."

Mike exhaled. "I know. Still doesn't make me feel any better about it."

"Don't beat yourself up. I'll be there as quickly as I can." Brandon signed off.

His next call was to Jo.

"What's happening, Mike?" She looked past him, concerned. "You're out in Homestead?"

"Yeah." He exhaled hard. "Ruby's gone, Jo. We just found her. Looks like a heart attack."

"Aw shit. Mike, I'm sorry." Jo looked away and said something that he couldn't hear. "Look. I'll be there shortly."

"You sure? What about your dad?"

Jo swallowed hard. "I've said goodbye. He's—could be in the next few minutes, could be next week. He's in a coma. I need to see you, Mikey. As much as you need to see me."

"I'm sorry," he said back to her. But, selfishly, he was glad she was coming home. Even if it meant she'd have to go back quickly.

No, damn it. *They* would go back quickly. Because he suspected that when Jo had to go back to Arkansas, it would be to bury Jeff.

And he was not going to let her do that by herself. Just like she wasn't going to let him face this alone.

MIKE LED LEGACY BACK TO THE BARN AFTER HELPING TERRI AND BECK load Ruby's body into the crawler. He called Justine, then the Thunder County Sheriff to report Ruby's death, and finally the vet, as he led the golden mare down the track back to the home place. Legacy moved slowly, her head low. She stopped several times, legs wobbling, and Mike waited for the golden mare to start moving again.

Smudgie whined, seeming to know something was wrong.

"C'mon, old lady," he encouraged Legacy. "Not much farther. Just hold on, girl."

Terri hadn't known how quickly someone could get back out here with a trailer to haul Legacy back—might not even be until the vet got there—and the vet was out on another emergency call. If he could just keep Legacy going, slow and steady, the golden mare *might* get better. Sometimes movement helped with colic.

But the heavy sweat and pale gums suggested otherwise.

They were within sight of the barn when Legacy began to stagger.

"Don't do this, old gal," Mike pleaded, even as the golden mare's eyes went dull. "Legacy! Come on!"

She threw her head up, body angling sideways as Mike desperately tried to keep her on her feet, pulling Legacy around him in a circle. Smudgie barked, chasing Legacy's heels as if he could herd her upright.

Legacy crashed to the ground. Her legs jerked and spasmed, as if she were carrying Ruby on a final gallop. Then they stilled.

It was too much. Mike collapsed next to Legacy, burying his head in her neck.

Not her too, not both of them at the same time.

Smudgie's barks alerted him to the arrival of Brandon and the vet, pulling the trailer behind the vet's truck.

READING THE WILL WAS ANTICLIMACTIC, TO SAY THE LEAST. CHRISTOPHER Trask, a nephew of Ruby's long-time friend and lawyer Remy Trask, went through the few legacies that weren't already covered by Martiniere arrangements.

The one surprise was that she had left the Double R to Mike alone. He had thought that she would split it between him and Ron.

But no. The Double R was all his. Along with the Martiniere emeralds.

"I'm—going out," he said to Jo when they got back to the house.

"You gonna be okay?" She frowned at him.

"I just need a moment. It's all—overwhelming."

She didn't say anything more, but kissed him before he walked out to the family graveyard, now expanded to include Martinieres like the cyborged brothers Daniel and George. Smudgie shadowed him, aware of Mike's distress. He stood by the double marker with the freshly dug grave.

Ruby and Gabe, together again.

He blew hard, looking around.

Mine. All mine.

Unexpected. But who would the Double R go to after him? God only knew when everything would catch up to him, between cyborging and the health problems of his younger years. Another Martiniere? One of Jo's nieces or nephews? Ron? He'd better figure that one out soon. Sale was not in the cards. Not with everyone buried here.

Mike fell to his knees next to Smudgie. "I'll do my best to keep it safe, Ruby, but God—"

"She knew you love this place," Brandon said from behind him. "That's why she left it to you. Of all of us, it matters most to you. You'll do the right thing in the long run."

Mike rose to his feet. "I'm sorry. Ron—"

Brandon shook his head. "With Lily gone, Ron has Moondance."

"I'm sorry," Mike repeated.

"There's another matter. Ron is way too young to be the Martiniere-in-waiting, and I've held off nominating someone to replace Seth for too long."

"Then who will be? Karina? Joshua?" The British Martinieres had some up-and-coming young leadership, most promising of all the cousins around his age—if Ben's health wasn't so sketchy, Mike thought he would be a certain candidate for Martiniere-in-waiting. "Or Juliette or Francis?" The French Martinieres also had prospects.

Brandon shook his head again. "Ruby left the Martiniere emeralds to you. And you have JoAnn to wear them."

Mike stared at him, suddenly knowing. "No. No. Bran, you can't do this. I'm Philip's clone." His voice rose. "Do you know the risks? What if this is enough to turn me into *him?* God, don't tempt me. Especially with that damn worm popping up now and then."

"You are not your progenitor," Brandon said slowly. "And I've had long talks with Alice. Juliette. Francis. David. Justine. We all agree. I discussed it with Mom before she died. She agreed—that's why you inherited the emeralds. You are our best option. The Martiniere Group needs you to become the Martiniere-in-waiting. The Family *wants* it to be you." He sighed. "If Ben's health were better it might be different."

"Fuck. Is this really a good idea, Bran?"

"You're our best option," Brandon said.

"That's not saying one hell of a lot." Mike looked at Ruby and Gabe's shared grave.

What would Gabe say?

He pretty much knew what Gabe's answer would be.

Gabe gave up what he really wanted—a quiet life married to Ruby—to wrench the Group and the Martiniere family away from indenture. Because the Family needed him and would sink into a worse position if he didn't do it.

Gabe would expect no less of a sacrifice from the clone he had raised as his own son. Mike turned back to Brandon. "All right. Do me a damn favor. Stay alive until Ron grows up or another, better, candidate appears."

"I'll try," Brandon said. "But no promises."

THE MINUTE MIKE WALKED INTO THE KITCHEN AND SAW JO AT THE TABLE, head buried in her hands, he *knew*. Smudgie whimpered and went to her, Mike a step behind. Without words he took her into his arms. She buried her head in his belly, shaking.

"Mike?" Brandon said softly. He looked up. "Later. Moondance at seven?"

Mike nodded. He waited until he was certain that they were alone.

Then he slid into a neighboring chair and took Jo's head in his hands. Tears ran down her cheeks as she stared at him, still restraining her sobs.

"Daddy—" she choked. "Just now."

"I am so sorry, honey," he said. "Oh God. I am so fucking sorry. We're alone now. We've got a couple of hours to ourselves to mourn without obligations." He inhaled, then exhaled slowly.

"What did Brandon mean about Moondance?" Jo swallowed hard, sniffling.

"I—I'm the fucking Martiniere-in-waiting." He took another deep breath. "No choice. Family will. Brandon wants me to swear to it as soon as possible. And we'll leave directly for Swait Farms from Moondance. Oh God, honey. I am so fucking sorry. This timing is horrible. But we will honor your daddy. Ruby's buried and I just have to do this one last thing. And then I don't give a shit about anything other than what you need me to do to help you through burying your daddy. And whatever else goes along with it. You okay with that?"

She nodded. "What's happening at Moondance? The swearing?"

"Yes." Mike paused. "Then I put the Martiniere emeralds on you."

"Ruby's emeralds?" she whispered.

"They're your emeralds now."

Jo gulped. Her face crumpled and she began to wail. Mike gathered Jo up and eased her into his lap. Jo buried her head in his chest, keening.

"Oh, honey. Oh, honey," he murmured as she sobbed, doing his best to project a reassuring tone.

Ruby and Legacy gone.

And now Jeff. Mike blinked back tears of his own as he remembered his father-in-law.

Gabe gone. Ruby gone. Jeff gone.

It was the end of an era.

Now it's our turn.

The prospect felt—daunting.

THAT NIGHT, WITH REPRESENTATIVES OF THE OTHER FAMILY MEMBERS watching, Mike swore the oath to become the Martiniere-in-waiting. After that, he put the Martiniere emeralds on Jo for the first time, as tears ran down her cheeks.

It's real now.

They were the Martiniere-in-waiting and his wife.

I hope Brandon lives a good long life.

Then they flew to Arkansas to bury Jeff, and discuss the future of Barkley-Martiniere-Swait Associates with Deontae and Rae.

MARTINIERE

2086

Age: 31

22 / BRANDON

MARCH, 2086

Age: 31

"Are you certain this meeting is safe?" Mike asked Brandon. He didn't like what Bran was doing and still hoped he could talk him out of it. Even if this was the last call before the meeting.

Damn it, at the very least Bran should have me monitoring him, despite Jeremy's objections. I do not like this. I do not like this at all. Why doesn't Jeremy want me to listen in to this inspection? And why insist on Justine being there too?

"Frederick and Carl are with me. Al's at Moondance with Ron." Brandon paused, running his left hand through his hair before pulling on a hat and heavy coat to leave the business jet. "Justine is coming in later. She's delayed, and it can't be helped. Besides, this is Montreal, not LA."

"Maybe you should wait until she's there. Have the power of the Matriarch supporting you." Mike tapped his fingers on the big desk that had once been Ruby's.

Brandon rolled his eyes. "Mike, I'll be *fine*." The exasperated tone reminded Mike of Ruby. "Look. I don't think that Jeremy's people are actually doing interdicted work and cloning full humans instead of regenerative parts. It's just research to improve parts cloning. Jeremy's been open about full disclosure."

"All right, if you say so," Mike conceded.

He still felt uneasy, like he'd missed something in his file reviews. Was it something from that worm Deontae was trying to chase down? Dr. Pramula had been enlisted in the worm's pursuit, but so far, no traces had shown up in Mike's monthly check-ins with her.

"I'll buzz you when we're done."

After Brandon disconnected, Mike pulled up the records from Jeremy's division. He had already reviewed them several times, but there was a pattern that kept evading him. He could see that it led to something important, but what? Sometimes he almost felt like he understood what was happening—but then it flitted away. This sense of *almost seeing it* had been occurring more and more since Lily's death.

And it was tied to whatever Jeremy was doing. The worm? Or something else?

You don't just engage in this sort of research without attempting to implement it.

He knew that *deep* in his cyborged bones. Even though he had been very young, he heard enough about cloning processes while under Philip's control to be aware of that reality.

He was missing something. Had to be missing something. But what was it?

Mike leaned back in his chair, taking a deep breath. Smudgie nuzzled at the hand he dangled over the chair arm and Mike absently patted his head. There were specific steps that separated cloning for regenerative parts from cloning a full human. They had been spelled out years ago, when he was a child. Jeremy's Canadian labs appeared to be following the appropriate regenerative protocols, but something still wasn't right. Certain supplies were skewed. They shouldn't need that size of incubators.

There's really only one other route to go for data if you want to find out how to create clones secretly without flagging monitors. One lab that bypassed the regs.

Supposedly all that data had been mined from those particular records years ago, with the dangerous pieces destroyed. Gabe had made it happen.

But what if someone had accessed the one secure archive documenting the successful *covert* creation of clones? Mike had allowed Bran to talk him out of complete destruction of those records documenting Philip's cloning processes, against all of his instincts.

Mike closed his eyes and shuddered, then brought up the old files that only he could access because they were triply-secured with Philip's hard-locked biometric links—not a problem for Philip's clone.

Subject PJM-A-1-Alan. Mike inputted the *compare* command between this file and Jeremy's records. He kept pulling up the files and issuing the *compare* order for them, all the way through to *Subject PJM-M-13-Michael.*

Then he sat back to wait for the results, and worry. He wished he could have found something more tangible before Brandon went into that damn meeting. He wished Brandon would have let him listen in. Something wasn't right about this situation.

His comm chimed. *"JoAnn."*

He snapped it open, his mood lifting already as her projection took shape. "Hey darling, how are you?"

Smudgie barked his own welcome.

"Hey Mike, Smudgie." Jo smiled at him from one of the Swaitrice fields. A blue bandanna hid her frizzy black hair. Mike recognized it as the one he'd gotten her from the marketplace at last year's Reined Cowhorse finals, when Starlight had won his second World Champion title. "Thinking of you, especially since we've just had a good run on the updated Guardian bot. Need you to come here and help me test."

"Be still my beating heart. An excuse to take a plane to see you."

"Not that you need any excuse," she countered. "But it *is* your turn to come see me, darling. I'm looking forward to this fall, when we can be together again for good. I'm not real fond of long-distance marriage."

"Neither am I." He called up his calendar. "Day after tomorrow?"

"Sounds good—" Her words were cut off by the blare of an alert.

"Just a second, Jo. I've got a scan that's found something." He called up the details. Mike's blood ran cold as he saw the sentence. *Congruence between source file and file PJM-M-13-Michael.* "Fuck," he whispered as he skimmed through the details.

His cloning had been sufficiently different from the others—and damn it, Jeremy's labs were going through the same steps that had led to his creation!

Of course it would be *his* file that they'd cracked and used. The file that only he could open because it was keyed to the biometrics he shared with…*Philip, damn it.* And the profile of the cracker fit what little he could retain about that damn worm.

"Oh crap. Jo, hon, I've got to go. Bran's walking into a trap. *Someone connected with Jeremy is trying to copy me.* And the crack has trace elements of that goddamned mind control worm! Tell D."

"Shit! Good luck, Mike. Call me when it gets straightened out!"

He tried comming Brandon, with no answer. Dread tightened his gut. Was it too late? Best to try another route.

He commed Al. "Get Bran out of that meeting *now*. It's a trap and he's not answering my pings. Jeremy's replicating my creation. His labs cracked the raw data records *that are biometrically linked to me alone.* That fucking worm we've been chasing is involved."

"But—all right!"

He commed Justine next. "Bran's in trouble," he said without preamble once her projection solidified. "I just found it. Jeremy's people accessed my damn file. The raw file, including the genetic sequencing. They're lying to us about regenerative cloning and the worm's connected to it. *Don't go to that fucking meeting.*"

"*Alexander Martiniere,*" his comm chimed.

"Let me switch but stay on the line. That's Al. He was going to contact Carl and Frederick since I couldn't raise Bran. He may have news."

Justine's projection swirled on hold as Al's went live next to hers.

"I'm going to be driving to the Double R with Ron for his safety," Al said without preamble. "Trying to divert Justine before we leave Moondance. Things went bad." He gulped, then knelt. Chills ran through Mike as he toggled the *share* switch so Justine could join the conversation, dread at what he suspected was going to happen next making his heart pound harder. "I, Alexander Martiniere, swear my loyalty to Michael Marcus Martiniere as the Martiniere."

"I—I—" Mike's voice quavered.

No. Fuck no.

"What the *fuck*?" Justine bellowed. Mike heard a matching tremor in her voice.

Al looked up, a tear trickling down his cheek. "Martiniere. Matriarch. Brandon is dead. Jeremy and his staff weren't there. Assassins were. They turned Carl and Frederick on Brandon as part of their attack on him." His voice quavered. "The killers used an old back door mind control program to control them. It—almost got me when I tried to warn them."

"Are you safe? What about Ron?" Mike asked. God. Brandon dead.

I'm the Martiniere. I'm the goddamned fucking Martiniere. Are you happy now, Progenitor? You couldn't destroy Gabe, but your legacy killed his granddaughter and now his son. And your clone is now in your place. God damn you to hell. I hope you're burning to a crisp.

A faint memory of red letters that disappeared popped into Mike's thoughts.

I MIGHT BE DEAD BUT THIS ISN'T OVER, MICHAEL. YOU WILL BE MINE. PJM.

Then it faded away.

Al wiped away tears, neither he nor Justine catching Mike's momentary distraction. "Ron caught the damn thing before it implemented. Stopped the worm in the programming. Bran had me swear loyalty to Ron over him a couple of years ago…if I hadn't…."

Mike blinked, swallowing hard. "What happened to Carl and Frederick?"

"Frederick tried to turn me. I—triggered a termination switch," Al choked. "Before he could do it to me. And I triggered Carl. Just in case."

"Diverting to the Double R," Justine said, her face gone hard and hawk-like Martiniere-predatory. "Mike, I'll see you in an hour, and swear to you in person."

"We'll be there about the same time," Al said.

They clicked off, leaving Mike alone. Smudgie nuzzled at him in concern. Mike absently rubbed the heeler's head with both hands. Then he got up and went into the kitchen, staring at the drizzle outside, clutching at the sink as his lungs tightened and Smudgie pressed against him in an attempt at reassurance.

No. God damn it, no.

He was the fucking Martiniere. He had to stay calm. No luxury for panic attacks anymore.

What role did that damn worm play in all this?

He went through the mental checklist. Justine knew. Ron knew. Who else did he need to tell himself?

David. Juliette. Francis. Alice. Ben. Beth. They were the appropriate Family heads. They could spread the word to the rest of the family and the Group.

Separately or all at once?

All of them together. We need to talk.

And then he needed to tell Beck, Terri, and Julie here at the ranch.

But first…he called Jo. He wanted to see her, hear her. God, he wished she was back home.

"You look like hell," she said. "What happened?"

"Brandon's dead," he said. "Murdered by—oh hell, I don't know all the details yet. But somehow Carl and Frederick got turned on him, and *something* tried to twist Al to kill Ron." He gulped. "I can't talk for long, Jo. Things to do, but oh God. Oh God. I'm now the Martiniere."

"Oh, honey." Her face softened. "Do you want me there?"

"Yes," he whispered. "Please."

"I need to take care of some things, but I'll come to the Double R later tonight. Love you. Stay strong," she said.

"I love you," he said, before switching off.

Fuck you, Progenitor. I will not become you. Even now, as the Martiniere.

MIKE KEPT STUDYING THE EARLY REPORTS FROM SERG'S TEAM AND THE police as darkness fell and the rain intensified to windswept pounding against the walls of the house. Smudgie curled up in his lap and he kept rubbing the old heeler's head. Could Jo make it to the ranch tonight, with conditions like this? God, he hoped so.

But until he knew one way or another whether the plane could land, he was staying in his office because he could not stop the racing of his thoughts. Justine was settled in her usual room, after swearing her loyalty to him as the Martiniere, and Ron with Al on guard in another—not his usual room, not the same one that Brandon would use, either. No need to trigger memories.

He reran the video of Brandon's horrific, brutal assassination. His attackers had recorded it and sent Mike and other family members direct links. Mike thought he'd been able to block the link to Ron, as well as the social media replays. How long that would hold once Ron decided to try to break it, he didn't know. But if he could spare Brandon's kid the damn thing, at least for an hour or two, it was worth it.

Brandon hadn't even made it past the lobby before the assassins struck. They stabbed him until Brandon fell, then cut his throat. Mike reran the video segment by segment, doing his best to focus on the attackers and not Brandon, trying to lock onto *something* that would give him an identity, a tie to Jeremy. Trying to discern if that damn mind control worm had influenced them. Zooming in on the attackers didn't mask the brutality of their actions. And even with the sound off after the first replay, Mike couldn't help hearing Brandon's final gasps anyway.

Dad. Mom. Mike. Kris. Oh God. Ronnie. Ronnie. Ronnie.

Mike shook his head to try to clear it.

The attackers were augmented. Not cyborged, at least. But augmented pointed toward an origin in one of the Martiniere labs, and a higher probability of being affected by the worm. If not Jeremy's lab, then whose?

The Family has been corrupted worse than I thought.

"Mikey?" Jo stood in the doorway, still wearing her long heavy coat slick with rain.

He switched off the feed as Smudgie bounced out of his lap to greet Jo. Mike strode over to slide his hands under Jo's coat and pull her close to kiss her. It wasn't until her body pressed against his that he realized he was trembling.

She reached up and took his head in her hands when they were done kissing. "Are you all right?"

He shook his head. "Fuck no. I want to kill those fucking assassins." He gulped. "I want to see them die very slowly and painfully. I —I don't dare let that loose, Jo. Though it would be so damned easy. So damned fucking easy. I feel Philip raging in me, wanting to tear every-thing down around me. Is that weird?"

"No," she said softly. "But it isn't who you are, Mike. It's not the man I love. Not the man I married."

He focused on her dark brown eyes, the tightly curled black hair, the elegant high cheekbones and the dark skin. JoAnn. Jo. He shuddered as she kept her gaze on him, steady, measuring. He knew that *no bullshit from you now* look. The look that kept throttled those increasing moments of partially-remembered rage that they thought might be assaults on him by the worm.

If my people can cope with generations of oppression, then you can handle whatever the fuck this is with grace, Mikey. It's how we'll end this once and for all. The two of us together.

Words she had said to him many times since Lily's suicide, when rage flooded through him for no obvious cause. Words he took to heart.

He let his breath out slowly, releasing that fury. "It's awful, Jo. Bran fought back. They made sure it was a painful death. Long. Drawn out. Stabbing. Then they cut his throat. I—" he swallowed hard. "He called my name as best he could at the end. Along with Kris, Ruby, Gabe, and Ron." He shuddered.

Ronnie. Ronnie. Ronnie.

He'd do his damned best to keep Ron safe. He owed that to his brother. Grandson. Whatever.

Jo tugged at him. "Come on. You need to be someplace other than the office. Have you eaten?"

"Yes." Dinner had been stunned and silent, with Justine, Ron, and Al. Serg had been calling in reports, but God, he didn't look that good himself. The man was almost as old as Justine.

"Good. How's Ron taking it?" Jo steered him toward the stairs.

"In shock. I'm—his guardian now. He's agreed that he'll be the Martiniere-in-waiting. I need to talk to him tomorrow."

Brandon's dead.

After Mike and Jo had made love, and she had fallen asleep, he lay awake, staring at the ceiling.

I am the Martiniere now. Me. Philip's clone.

If anyone can tear down the structures he created, it will be me.

He would finish the job that Gabe and Bran had started.

He had to do it.

And there was really only one way that he could confront that damn worm himself. He had to take the cyborging all the way.

But how could he tell Jo?

That kept Mike awake for quite a while. Including the wrangling with himself about taking that final step.

I don't want to do this. I really don't want to do this.

But a few months ago, he had quietly asked Dr. Pramula what would be required should it become necessary. She had sent him a report about the work needed and the potential long-term impact on him.

At last Mike got up and reviewed that file, over and over again, until he had it just about memorized. He particularly focused on what the probable outcomes would be—and the eventual price he would pay for maxing out his cyborg implants.

MIKE WOKE WITH HIS HEAD BURROWED INTO JO'S CHEST, HER FREE HAND gently fingering through his hair. For a moment he was disoriented, wondering why she was here instead of working on spring planting and the last year of her loan contract with Deontae at Swait Farms— and then he remembered.

Brandon's dead. And I'm now the Martiniere.

He shuddered, then exhaled. The fate he hadn't wanted. The fate that his progenitor had tried—and succeeded, finally, to force on him.

Seth. Lily. And now Brandon. All direct victims of my fucking progenitor's schemes.

He'd count Lily as a victim, now that he knew more about that damned worm.

Jo slid free and took his face in her hands. She kissed his eyelids, his nose, and then his mouth as he shivered.

"You've been yelling," she said softly. "Something about red letters and Philip."

"Is it bad for me to say that this is one of my worst nightmares come true?" he whispered to her. "That I keep thinking that Philip is dancing with glee in some sort of afterlife?"

"Think of who'd be pulling for you instead," she said. "Gabe. Ruby. Brandon. Dad. And those of us who are still alive and support you completely."

He gulped. "It's still—oh God, Jo. This has to stop. Completely. And I dread what I'll have to become to make it happen."

"Which is?"

Mike inhaled. Exhaled. Remembered his review of the file from last night, and the agonizing over this decision. Closed his eyes, then opened them again.

"Take the cyborging all the way—which hasn't been done due to long-term impact. My arm implants aren't fully activated. And... another dose of liquid nanobuild would do the same thing—full activation—for my legs. My heart and lungs would have to be reprogrammed to support everything."

"*Michael.*" The pain in Jo's voice cut hard into him. "You'd put yourself through that hell again? Why do you have to do this? What does it achieve?"

"I don't want to do it," he whispered. "But that damn fucking worm. If I do this I can integrate with the networks. Work at electronic speed instead of human speed in virtual. It goes beyond virtual, Jo. Taking my cyborging to full activation gives me more physical strength. I don't trust the authorities." He shook his head. "They didn't do a damned thing about Lily. I'm not going to let that happen with Brandon. I have the ability to do it as the Martiniere. I can avenge Brandon myself. *And I will.*"

"Going vigilante, both cyber and physical." Approval in her voice, not condemnation.

He nodded slowly. "And it makes me into one of *them* by making this choice."

"You're not doing it to seize power for yourself. You're doing it to stop them from becoming tyrants."

"But what happens afterward?" he whispered. "If I succeed? What if I become what *he* was?"

"When we succeed," she said. "Mike." She gently shook his shoulders. "You can do it. You can outmaneuver Philip's schemes. And you've got me. Al. Justine. Deontae. Ron. Alice. Beth. Lots of us to support you."

Ron. He needed to talk to Ron right away. Then Al.

"All right." He sighed. "I just—there's doubt, and always will be."

"Mikey." She kissed him. "You've got something more powerful in you than Philip ever had. You have a conscience. Sometimes it gets in your way, but you've got that."

He leaned his forehead against hers, savoring the contact.

"Thank you for trusting me," he said finally. "And kicking my ass when I go wrong." He paused. "But there are other issues, Jo. I haven't fully activated the implants because they *will* drain me. They will eventually kill me—shorten my life—unless I go full cyborg. I won't go that far. I don't want to live forever. I want to live right."

Jo groaned. "Mike. God. Is there another option?"

"Not really. Which is why—the hesitation. The second-guessing." He met her eyes. "God, Jo. I am so fucking sorry. *I didn't want this.*"

She blinked hard. "Is full activation reversible?"

"To a certain degree. I can go five years or so, and then the damage starts to become irreversible. After ten years—nothing can be changed. If what's left of my body can last that long with full activation." He exhaled. "Ron's sixteen. He'll be twenty-six in ten years. Maybe that's enough time to give him the experience he'll need to be the Martiniere. I won't have to be at full activation the whole time. After we beat the worm and avenge Brandon, we have to put things back together, and I won't need the extra cyborg boost to do that."

If I survive getting to afterwards.

But he wasn't going to say that piece out loud.

"Gabe walked away from being the Martiniere."

"And Brandon became the Martiniere when he was older than Ron will be."

Jo didn't say anything further but took Mike in her arms again. They lay together quietly.

But deep inside he was raging.

The red letters appeared again. This time he remembered them for a little bit longer.

AFTER A WHILE THEY GOT UP. WHEN MIKE WENT DOWNSTAIRS, RON WAS in the kitchen, staring morosely into a cup of fake coffee. Mike patted him on the shoulder, poured himself a cup, then sat across the table from Ron. Ron's eyes were puffy and bloodshot. He'd clearly been crying. The do-rag that confined his short dreadlocks was black, not the Martiniere greens and blues that Ron usually favored.

Mike reached across the table and rested his hand on Ron's. "Hey."

Ron looked up, blinking. "Now what happens?" He gulped.

"First, we honor and bury your father, Carl, and Frederick," Mike said.

"And then?"

"We make the motherfuckers pay." Mike's lips tightened. "That means programming to stop that worm. Counters to the mind control. We finish the job that your grandfather started. We purge Philip's influence from the Martiniere Group. Completely."

Ron shook his head. "You make it sound so simple, but—" His voice choked.

Mike clenched Ron's hand. "No. Do not give in to despair. Do *not*. That's the worm's influence."

And our family's goddamn biology.

"And do I have a role in all this?"

"You are the Martiniere-in-waiting. Even at sixteen, hell yes, you have a role." Mike stood up, looking outside. Last night's storm had faded, and it was one of those bright blue spring days in the Thunder Valley, the mountains dusted lightly with fresh snow. "Come on. Let's grab a quick breakfast. Then go for a ride and talk."

Ron gulped. "You sound like Grandma Ruby when you say that."

"Who do you think taught *me* that a good horse can help you work through a lot of problems?" Mike said.

A couple of hours later, Mike and Ron jogged their horses up the narrow road to the Homestead field. Smudgie was just old and arthritic enough for long rides to be a struggle these days, so he stayed behind with JoAnn. Mike rode Starlight, while Ron was mounted on one of Starlight's first sons, Cody, still green to under-saddle work but well within Ron's riding ability. They paused for a moment by the white cross that stood where Mike had found Ruby's body. Then Mike and Starlight turned, heading up the ridge to the Lone Pine field at the edge of the Double R's boundary. The track widened, and Mike looked over at Ron with a grin.

"Wanna race to the gate?"

Ron yelped in response and urged Cody into a gallop. Starlight bolted after Cody and easily caught up with his son. Dun and palomino ran head-to-head, neither horse giving ground or drawing ahead. The lead switched back and forth between the two with one nose in front first, then the other.

They reined both horses in as they approached the wire gate. Ron dismounted to open it wide, leading Cody and waiting for Mike and Starlight to pass through before closing it behind them and remounting.

Mike exhaled. A cool, crisp spring day, air freshly cleaned after last night's downpour. And the final climb up the ridge to the top of Lone Pine, near the old Ponderosa pine, gave them a vista of Thunder Valley at the foot of the snow-dusted Thunder Mountains to the south. He halted Starlight. Ron pulled Cody up next to them.

"Okay," Mike said finally, the momentary exhilaration from the impromptu race fading. "How hard do you want to work to do something about your father's killers, Ron?"

Ron glanced at him, then looked away. "You make it sound like I have options."

"Well, you do." Mike swung off of Starlight and hobbled the stud, loosened the cinch, then slipped his bridle off and hung it on the saddle horn. Ron mirrored Mike's actions with Cody. Palomino gelding and dun stallion grazed next to each other companionably—Starlight's young sons as well as the ranch geldings often spent time in the field with Starlight to keep him company, when it wasn't breeding season.

"Like what?"

Mike wandered over to a rock pile and found a good spot to sit. Ron perched on a nearby rock.

"You're the Martiniere-in-waiting. There's a number of roles I could have you fill. Anything from just showing up to be seen, to active participation in Martiniere and Swait only, to full involvement with MS *and* the Martiniere Group. It's your choice, Ron, and really, any of it helps."

Ron looked down at his hands, then back up at Mike.

"I broke through the block you put on the video of Dad's death. This morning." His voice quavered and he blinked hard, shaking his head. "*I want to make those motherfuckers pay!*" he screamed, dropping his head in his hands, quivering as he tried to hold back tears. "Oh God. Dad. What they did to him. Oh Dad."

Mike knelt by Ron, resting a hand on his neck. Ron gulped and leaned against Mike, sobbing.

"I know," Mike whispered. "Oh God. I know." He rubbed Ron's back, waiting for him to calm.

"And he called for me and Mom at the end. *He called for us. And I wasn't there.*" Deep, body-wracking wails tore at Ron. "Oh God, I wasn't there."

"I was trying to spare you." Mike swallowed hard. "It was damned fucking ugly."

He blinked back his own tears and held Ron as the boy cried. No, not a boy any more. A young man, facing a hard reality.

At last Ron straightened up. He wiped his eyes and fixed Mike with a hard glare. "I want to do whatever it takes to make those fuckers pay for what they did to Dad. I'm in, Mike. I'm in all the way." He choked. "I'm in. Just tell me what I have to do."

Mike got up and returned to his rock. "I'm planning to fully activate my cyborg implants to start with. Upgrade Al's implants. I need you to work with Jo and Justine, plus help me do what I can while that process is happening, because I'm going to be laid up for several weeks during the activation. But that's fine. I want to make all but a select group of people think we're ignoring what happened to your dad because I have health problems."

Ron nodded. "Okay."

"It means you learn Martiniere-Swait, Swait Secure, and the Martiniere Group. But once we announce that you're the Martiniere-in-waiting, no one's gonna think anything is going on other than the kid is being set up to take over at way too young an age, because my health crashed after your dad's death." Mike picked up a pebble, rolling it in his palms. "The only people who will know what is going on are Justine. Jo. Deontae. Serg. Al. Those five besides ourselves are the ones I trust. Everyone else has to earn it."

"You think there's a Family connection?"

"Jeremy to start with. And that fucking mind control worm may have corrupted others." Mike drew a deep breath. "Once I'm activated and ready, then I can get to work. Not sure yet if my first step will be to go after Brandon's killers or the worm. If one or the other of us is attacked—that will determine my priorities."

"I want to go after the killers with you."

"No," Mike snapped. "Al and I are cyborged. You're not. Even though you're younger, our reflexes will be faster."

"But—"

"You're gonna have the harder job, Ron." Mike drew a deep breath. He *hadn't* talked with Jo about this piece and he knew she would yell once she learned what he was planning. "Because when that part of the plan gets implemented, you may end up having to perform the duties of the Martiniere. I don't know what's going to happen. We have to be ready for all possibilities."

He bared his teeth in a feral grin, meeting Ron's gaze. "But. One thing can start now. Too many people think that I'm sick and soft, including Family. They don't realize how much I hide inside of me. As much as I publicly deny it, I am telling you as the Martiniere-in-waiting that there is a very small, very vicious part of Philip Martiniere within Michael Martiniere that gets deflected and contained ninety-nine percent of the time. And when the moment is right, I fully intend to set that part of me loose."

Ron tightened his lips in a matching grin. "I can hardly wait to see it."

Oh kid. If you only knew what that will cost.

"It will take time," he said. "This isn't gonna happen overnight. It is going to be slow, cold, premeditated, calculated vengeance."

Brandon. Lily. Seth.

And those were just the most recent victims.

"I am completely down with that," Ron said. "Those fuckers took my father. *They will pay.*"

Mike shivered at the overtones of Philip in Ron's voice. And yet—Gabe and Brandon both had had those moments.

Maybe this wasn't just Philip's legacy but the entire dark whole of the Martiniere heritage. Gabe had faced it. Brandon had faced it.

Now it was his and Ron's turn.

23 / VENGEANCE

MARCH 2086

Age: 31

IT WAS ONE THING TO PROMISE VENGEANCE. IT WAS ANOTHER THING TO plan it in the midst of preparing for the formal Martiniere leadership transition ceremonies, plus put together a small, very private, funeral for Brandon.

As few people as possible and we're having it here at the Double R, Mike told Justine and Jo after he and Ron got back from their ride. *Not compromising on this.*

Then he shut himself into his office with a pad of legal paper and a pen, making notes, playing one of Gabe's old Willie Nelson music mixes crossed with his own Mongolian heavy metal preferences to help him think.

The red letters flashed through his thoughts yet again.

This time he got them written down.

And when Mike wrote the words on paper, he stared at them for ten minutes. It confirmed the wisdom of the rough plan he and Ron had sketched out during the rest of their ride.

Then he began to devise strategies to implement it.

Time passed. Mike was starting to run out of pages on this half-used pad. Ruby had left a stash of them in the attic. He supposed he'd better go dig them out if his growing suspicions proved to be correct.

They were going to be burning through them. He needed to consult with Deontae about devising protections so that they could create isolated comm networks. If possible. Swait Secure's tools might not be enough.

Someone knocked on the door. Jo opened it before he could answer.

"Mikey. What's going on? You've been in here for four hours. It's time for dinner."

He stared at his pad, not wanting to look up at her. He wasn't ready to talk to Jo.

No. Be honest. He was *afraid* to talk to Jo right now.

She shut the door behind her and came to the desk, her arms crossed.

"Michael."

She wasn't going to let him dodge it. Mike sighed and flipped the pages of the pad to the one where *those words* were written, then handed her the pad. He slumped back in his chair with his arm over his eyes, turning the chair sideways.

"Don't say it out loud. Any of it. I haven't figured out safe parameters yet."

Now that he'd written those words down, he could visualize them constantly. They burned deep inside of him, stirring a fear he'd thought was long-gone.

Fuck you, Progenitor. I am going to defeat you. For good. You do not have power over me.

"*Shit.* Oh Mikey."

Mike dropped his arm and spun back to face her.

She pointed to the transcribed words. "Is this…?" Her voice trailed off.

He nodded grimly.

Jo scowled. She flipped the pad to a blank page and reached for the pen. Then she wrote something, handing the pad back to him, pen on top.

Now I remember it, too.

He looked up. Their eyes met. He picked up the pen and refocused on the pad.

I'm sorry, Jo. So sorry, but—I have to do everything I've written here. I'm trying to script it out. I don't know who I can trust except for you, D, Justine, Serg, Ron, and Al. Please look it over closely, because you have a role to play in all this.

He slid pen and pad back across the desk. She raised her brows at him. He nodded. She sighed, and flipped back to the beginning. This time he didn't cover his eyes while she read, but watched her reaction.

She gasped. Covered her mouth. Looked up at him. He nodded again. Her jaw tightened and she shook her head, but went back to reading. Turned pages back and forth, her frown intensifying.

Then she dropped pen and pad into her lap and buried her face in her hands. She sat like that for a moment. Then she lowered her hands, a determined expression on her face. She picked up the pen and wrote, pausing for a few moments before continuing to write, several times. Then she sighed yet again and shoved pen and pad back at him, crossing her arms once more.

He dreaded to pick it up, to read her reaction—and yet he had to.

Michael. Part of me wants to call this pure, unadulterated bullshit. You should not need to be playing these fucking games as the Martiniere.

But then there's what we both now remember from the aftermath of Lily's death. That damn worm.

Still. You playing dead, all by yourself? No. No. NO. We need to talk to D. We need more strategies than this. I'm not sending you off with just Al for support while I pretend the widow's walk.

I DON'T AGREE TO THAT.

Those five words were underlined, several times.

He looked up at her. She shook her head, lips pressed so firmly together that they almost disappeared. She gestured for him to keep reading.

I get your reasons for leaving me behind. I'm not cyborged, and there's no time for me to go through the process. Or a logical reason for me to do it. I can't contribute that way. But damn it, I'm not going to let you face Philip alone. If what we saw was correct, he has Lily. It's only fair that you have me. I love you and I am going to fight for you. I am not going to play the grieving widow unless you are dead for real. I won't do it. More than that, I know how to do the underground shit. I grew up Swait. I grew up hiding indentured workers fleeing their contracts and at times running with them to provide cover.

I will play dead along with you.

<u>I KNOW HOW TO DO THAT.</u>

Find another solution that includes me at your side. That's non-negotiable. Period. You shut me out when you got sick during our teenage years. You are <u>not</u> doing this to me again. I do not want to constantly worry who's won, you or Philip. This is the final battle.

<u>FIND. ANOTHER. SOLUTION.</u>

He exhaled and placed first the pad, then the pen, on the desk.

"I mean it, Mikey. Every single word," she said softly.

He slowly walked around to the front of the desk, leaning against it. She stood, facing him, tense. He sighed and opened his arms.

"Okay. I yield. You're right."

Jo flung herself against him, wrapping her arms tightly around Mike while he clung to her.

"That was Ruby and Gabe's mistake early on," she said softly. "Gabe didn't share with her. She didn't push to find out more about his past, and it allowed Philip to break them apart. I won't do that. I won't let go of you. I am going to push you when you get into that damn Martiniere secrecy fetish."

"God damn it, I love you," he whispered into her ear. "Even when you're bound and determined to do things the hard way."

She pulled back slightly and tapped his nose with her index finger. "Swait women don't sit on the sidelines, Mikey." And then she leaned in close and whispered in his ear. "And my gut tells me that you will need my help by the time we're finished."

He sighed and kissed her.

To be honest, he was relieved.

He didn't want to be separated from her, either. And he had honestly forgotten about the underground aspect of her Swait heritage.

"And before we implement that final piece?" she murmured into his ear again. "We have the tools to do it. Swait Secure, baby. Swait Secure. Philip won't know how to deal with that."

MIKE CHECKED THE SECURITY SCREENS AND ELEVATED THEM TO FULL POWER before he called Al into his office. He leaned against the front of his desk, crossing his arms as he waited. He was pretty certain that Al was clean—he and Ron had run through the checks and the records from Brandon's death just half an hour ago.

But it was best to make sure. And Jo was on alert just in case.

Al flinched a little as he came through the screen. But no alarms flared. No warning codes.

"I'm planning to fully activate my cyborg implants and start training practice," Mike said flatly. "I want you to upgrade so we can practice together."

As he expected, Al recoiled. "Mike. Why? It could destroy you."

"That's not what Dr. Pramula says."

"Mike. Do you realize what you're asking?"

The red letters flashed through his thoughts again.

"Fuck, *yes!*" Mike slammed his hands against the desk's edge, suddenly irritated for no good reason—

Stop. Get control, Mike, get control. This is clearly a trigger straight from Philip. Assume your reaction is being monitored by the worm or forces aligned with it when you react like this. Make them think you're irrational. You've got to run with it just enough to be convincing.

"God *damn* it, Al." He drew a long, heavy breath, pacing across the room before whirling to face Al again. "I can't—I won't—fuck. *No.* This cannot go without a response, and it has to come from me. *I will be the tool of their destruction.*"

He slapped his hands against his sides. Smudgie paced beside him, whining softly at Mike's agitation.

If I can fool Smudgie….

Though he didn't feel good about that. And he had to leave Smudgie behind. Much as that thought hurt, Smudgie was too old and too well-known as *Mike's therapy dog.*

"What does JoAnn think about this?"

Mike exhaled, hissing through his teeth. "She understands. She supports me."

"Does she understand what it does to you?" Al raised his left arm and snapped his fingers. The plaskin covering his cyborged arm faded away to reveal the metal underneath. Green and blue lights flashed up and down it. "Does she understand what this means?"

Smudgie growled.

"Easy, boy," Mike said.

"She understands and she approves." Jo straightened up from the doorway where she had been standing, unnoticed by Mike, Smudgie, and Al. *One of us must have triggered her alerts.* "We've already talked about it. My father spent too damn much of his life fighting these assholes along with Gabe, Ruby, and Brandon. It's past time to do something about them." She crossed the room to stand by Mike. Smudgie pressed against their legs, taking up a defensive position between them and Al.

Al turned to face Jo. "There are problems."

Jo stared at him. "I know, Al."

"But do you really understand? *Do you really understand?*" Al gulped, almost sobbing.

Mike and Jo's eyes met. Jo frowned, worry furrowing her brows.

How affected by the worm is Al?

Keep pushing, Mike decided. *I need to know what's driving this reaction.*

"Al. Stand down. I'm an adult now. I don't need you protecting me."

Al spun back to face Mike. "You and Ron are the only family that I have left now that Brandon and my brothers are dead." Al's voice broke and he shook his head, closing his eyes and grimacing before opening them again. "God. Mikey. I can't lose you too."

Mike met his eyes. "Not doing anything will bring about just that, Al."

"Not if I protect you."

"They got Carl and Frederick. Who's to say what's going to happen with that damned worm the next time? Upgrading my cyborging will protect you."

"But why do you need to do it?" Al's anguished voice rose to a higher pitch.

The threat of loss. Loyalty. That's the key to Al.

It's time, Jo mouthed to Mike.

He nodded and picked up the pad where he and Jo had written out what they wanted Al to know. Mike handed it to him.

Al raised his brows as he saw what Mike had printed in big red letters.

DO NOT SAY ANYTHING. WRITE EVERY RESPONSE TO THIS AFTER YOU HAVE READ THE WHOLE THING.

Jo crossed to stand beside Mike as Al stood there, reading the notes. At last Al looked up, raising his brows in question.

They both nodded.

He put the pad on the desk, picking up the pen, bending over to write. Then he handed them the pad. Al had listed several statements, leaving blank space underneath each statement for a response.

Let me get this straight.

1.) You have reason to believe that the entire Martiniere Group has been compromised by that mind control worm.

Mike and Jo exchanged glances. He picked up the pen and wrote *Yes.*

2.) As a result, you only trust certain people with this information.

Mike wrote *yes* again.

3.) You want to appear less able than you are right now as a cover for upgrading your cyborging and not immediately reacting to Brandon's death. And once that's done, you and JoAnn are going to go underground to fight not just the worm but take care of Brandon's killers.

Another *yes.*

4.) That portion of the plan still needs to be developed in accord with Deontae, and will depend heavily on Swait resources for implementation.

Yes once again—and that was the last of Al's statements. Mike handed the pad back to Al.

He wrote a few words and handed the pad back to Mike and Jo.

All right. I'm in. When do we start?

Mike grinned.

Now, he wrote. *Don't be surprised by anything I do or say from this moment on. It's all part of the game.*

Only it wasn't a game. Not really.

Unless one viewed a fight to the death as being a game—and that might be the key to understanding Philip and his motives.

THAT LEFT JUSTINE, SERG, AND D TO BRIEF. JUSTINE COULD STILL WALK out of range of any monitors on the crawlers using her walker, if the conditions were right. More than that, Mike thought that suggesting a trip to the Double R's informal shooting range to blow off steam not only would fit the pattern of *Mike emotionally affected by Brandon's death,* but that Justine might also want the same sort of relief.

He just had to get her out there without too many trigger words, or having to prematurely disclose his plans.

"Justine. I really need to blow off some steam," he said the next morning after breakfast. "Want to show me the newest SPA rifle variant?"

"I don't know, Mike, we're still organizing Brandon's funeral and the transition," Justine said, studying her screens.

"God damn it, I need to get out!" Mike snapped.

Justine raised her brows, followed by a worried furrow of her brows as she looked at Jo.

"I've got it under control," Jo said. "Mike needs to get out and I can't go with him. I have Swait stuff to work on. Justine. Please. I don't want him doing this alone in this state of mind." *Not what it looks like,* she mouthed to Justine. *Play along. Please.*

"If you're sure," Justine said, eying Mike cautiously, then looking back at Jo.

"I'm sure," Jo said. "Just get Mike out of here for a while. Please. He's going to blow if you don't."

Justine sighed. "All right." She glanced outside. "At least it looks like a semi-decent day."

"I'll drive the crawler up," Mike said. "Meet you around front."

"Thank you," Justine said.

He made sure to swear about the sticky crawler charger plug as he wrestled it loose, then spun out a little on the gravel while driving to the front of the house, screeching to a halt next to Justine.

"Are you sure you should be driving when you're in this mood?" she asked.

"I don't give a shit," he growled.

That earned him a speculative look and a frown.

He raced the crawler out of the barnyard and up to the gates.

"God damn it, Mike, would you stop driving so crazy?" she snapped. "It *hurts* when you jerk me around like this!"

He leaned over. "It's a fucking front, Justine. Play along. Explain later," he whispered into her ear. Then he flung himself out of the crawler and opened the gates. But he was careful not to lurch the crawler quite so much, even though he still drove erratically.

Justine kept watching him with a measuring expression he did not see on her very often. When they arrived at the parking space for the crawler, Mike remained silent, unfolding her walker and handing it to her before carrying the weapons far enough out of range from the crawler that they wouldn't be overheard, then going back and lending her his arm to help her walk faster.

She stopped hard once they were out of line of sight from the crawler, jerking him to face her, stronger than he expected.

"All right, Michael. Why the *hell* are you acting like Daddy-fucking-dearest? This is not you, and I know better. You may be his clone, but *you are not my fucking father*. You weren't raised like this."

Mike drew a deep breath. "Security. The Martiniere Group is compromised by that mind control worm. I don't know who I can and can't trust because of who it's affected. It has affected me. And Jo. It played a major role in Brandon's death. I'm going to fucking end it, but in order to do it, we have to go completely stealth. We can't trust anyone else in the Group."

Her eyes widened. "Shit."

He nodded. "The day Lily died? I received a video supposedly from her. Jo saw it with me. Lily threatened to take away everything I ever loved. That when I became the Martiniere, she would break me from the grave, and that I couldn't do anything to stop it. The video ended with her embracing Philip."

"*No*," Justine whispered, blanching. "Oh God."

"It gets worse," Mike said grimly. "I went on a rampage after that. The video carried emotional triggers designed to set me off. I tried to hurt myself. Jo stopped me. She tried to trap it, had identi-fied the video as being carried by that damn worm. She almost caught it." He drew a deep breath. "The last thing we saw was a statement. 'I may be dead but this isn't over, Michael. You will be mine. PJM.'"

"Why didn't you tell anyone?"

"Because we both forgot about it. I've been dreaming about it, and the memory returns in bits and pieces." He shuddered. "I didn't get those words down until yesterday—and then I remembered everything. When I showed the words to Jo, she remembered them too."

Justine twitched. "Fuck. Fuck." She exhaled, leaning hard on her walker. Then she straightened back up, fixing Mike with a sharp-eyed gaze that provided a surprising amount of relief in its familiarity. *Justine's ready to roll. Good.* "All right. What's the plan?"

"I'm going to be acting like an idiot for a while. Irrational. It's also going to look like I'm having health problems. We're going to make it appear that I'm not responding to Brandon's death because I'm incapacitated, both physically and mentally. But that's a cover for me maxing out my cyborg elements and doing what I can to track that damn worm down online while I'm in recovery from cyborg enhancements."

Justine nodded. "Got it."

He bared his teeth in a grin. "At that point, I will *personally* ensure that Brandon's killers die. We had to take care of Lily ourselves. I am assuming the same holds true for those fucking assassins. *I will not let this slide.*"

Justine shivered, not looking away from Mike. "When you say that, you sound like Philip. You *look* like him."

"There has always been a small piece of me that is completely Philip," Mike said softly. "I've just kept it under hard-core lock and key. Once this begins—the wraps come off." He laughed bitterly. "Who better to eradicate Philip's legacy than his clone?" He sighed and released the bitterness. "Justine, if there's anything—*anything*—in records or accesses that you have as the Matriarch that could help me with this—I need it."

Justine reached up and rested her hand on his cheek. "Mikey. I am horribly afraid for you. Do you understand how pervasive my father's influence can be? If you walk down this road, will you be able to return?" She swallowed hard. "I've watched you fight against him ever since you were five. I don't want to see you lose yourself in him."

"Jo will keep me straight-minded." Mike shook his head as Justine dropped her hand. "Seeing that video of Lily triggered me hard. And the fact that both Jo and I forgot about it until I managed to write those words down scares me. What's to keep it from driving me to doing something stupid so that I get killed like Brandon? He should never have gone to that damn meeting. I tried to talk him out of it."

"So did I."

He swallowed hard. "What if there's just enough of Philip in that worm that I lose myself? That he really does manage to take me over if I do nothing about it? I'll kill myself before I let that happen."

"I hope it doesn't come to that." She sighed. "All right, Mike. What do you need from me, beyond the Matriarch's records?"

"Get this damn funeral and swearing done quickly with the minimal number of attendees and as little family drama as possible," Mike said. "Except for the pieces I provide. Help Jo while I'm going through cyborg upgrades. Work with Deontae to set up our security. Protect Ron. What about Serg? He's one of the others I trust."

Justine shook her head. "Serg needs to be on the outside, Mike. His health isn't going to support what you need. I'll tell him what he needs to know, but other than that...."

"I didn't realize he was in such poor shape."

"He spent too many years ignoring the demands on his body," she said. "He didn't take care of himself. And—if this worm is that nasty, I have to wonder to what degree it's affecting him? Affecting me?"

"I don't know."

"What about Ron?"

"If he ends up having to act as the Martiniere, he's going to need every bit of support you can give him."

"I promise to do that, Mike." She sighed. "Though I hope it doesn't come to that." She paused. "Well. We came out here to shoot. After this discussion, I really, really need to shoot something. Let's do it."

"Your wish is my command, Madame Matriarch," Mike said in French, bowing low, then sweeping one arm toward the gun cases.

It was refreshing to hear one of Justine's rare, real laughs.

DEONTAE WASN'T ABLE TO GET TO THE DOUBLE R UNTIL BRANDON'S funeral and the swearings. Mike was too laden down to try to figure out secure comms before then.

And then there was the challenge of the role he was now playing. Illness wasn't so hard. He'd been sick enough of his life to know how to behave as if his health had taken a sudden turn for the worse. Not feeling well was enough of an excuse to hide out in his office while JoAnn and Justine got the rest of the family off of the Double R after the ceremonies.

He struggled with the heightened emotional piece. It made him want to hide out, to minimize those occasions where he had to role-play a reactiveness that, to be honest, scared the crap out of him because it was so easy to get sucked into it.

As a result, the time post-swearings and funeral was another situation where he wanted to drink himself numb, because he'd spent too damn much time *feeling*. Mike idly wondered if that might cause another manifestation of the worm as it had after Lily's death. He studied the bottle on his desk, one of the last from the first lab manager Martin's distilling, and glanced out the window. He and D would have time to go for a ride if Jo was able to get the message to him discreetly. Either horseback or crawler—*crawler*, he decided. Not quite enough light for horseback to a good place to talk. Unfortunately.

He ignored the bottle and leaned back in his big chair, practicing controlled breathing. Smudgie whimpered at his feet and Mike helped him into his lap. Then he closed his eyes, hands on Smudgie, focusing on his dog, savoring these moments because soon enough he wouldn't have Smudgie at his side.

Smudgie was getting old. He needed to think about bringing up his replacement. Sadie was due to whelp one of Smudgie's litters soon. Maybe there'd be a pup in that batch that he could start training. Mike opened his eyes and scratched Smudgie's neck, feeling guilty as he studied how the black had become grayer in his coat. Once he left without Smudgie....

"Mike?" D entered the office. "Jo said you wanted to talk."

"I did." Mike urged Smudgie down. "Let's go for a crawler drive."

This time he let D take the controls. He was already getting tired of this damned role play. Maybe it was time to start acting sick. Mike leaned back in the seat as D drove, not talking except to give directions to the Ladyslipper spring.

"Park up top," he said to D. They carefully descended into the draw and headed toward the spring. Mike spotted a likely-looking downed Ponderosa and headed for it. He straddled it like he would a horse. D did the same.

"What's—" D began, but Mike held up a hand. He carefully checked for the possibility of any monitoring from the crawler, then, to be safe, cast a shield around them.

D raised his brows.

Mike exhaled. "How much has Jo been able to tell you?"

"She showed me an outline that the two of you had written down," D said. "The mind control worm is targeting you for certain and possibly others in the Martiniere family. That it played a role in Brandon's death. And that you are maxing your cyborging out with plans to chase down Brandon's killers and eliminate that worm once and for all—along with renegades within the Martiniere Group. Pretty much correct?"

"That's the gist of it," Mike said. "Did Jo tell you that she and I may have to go underground?"

D nodded. "How bad do you think this infestation is, Mike?"

"Jeremy's division in Canada has been problematic for quite some time," Mike said. "Started in France in 2077, moved to Canada in January of 2081 for reasons that didn't make sense to me, but..." he sighed. "That was before Seth's death. He and Brandon signed off on it. I couldn't convince Bran that it was a bad idea."

D side-eyed Mike. "You think Brandon was under influence at the time?"

"Yes," Mike said. "In retrospect. But I think it goes beyond Jeremy. Family heads in both Britain and France have been attacked. I need to get some idea of how severe this is before we take off."

D tapped his chin thoughtfully. "So at least nine years that this thing has been running around in the Martiniere databases."

"If not longer. I think we need to be looking at what's been going on since Philip's death." Mike shuddered. "That video of him and Lily. Some sort of algorithm created that. Had to. Could it have been all Lily?"

"You're not gonna know until you get your hands on that algorithm," D said.

"Am I being crazy?" Mike asked. "And can we pull this off?"

D pursed his lips. "No, I don't think you're being crazy. Something's been trying to probe our Swait Secure databases as well as the Guardian algorithms for the last three months. The Martiniere pieces are vulnerable."

"That confirms what I've feared."

"Yeah." A thoughtful expression akin to one Mike recognized in Jo crossed D's face. He tapped rhythmically on the dead Ponderosa's bark. Then he stopped.

"All right, Mike. First thing, I need to scan your entire network here. I've the tools to do it—been working under triple screens to improve security protocols to Martiniere links because of those probes. That worried me. I should be able to upgrade your shielding at the Double R so that we don't have to keep running out of the house to talk without being monitored. Or writing everything down. The writing is a vulnerability in itself. Physical storage available to anyone who gets their hands on it. Yeah, the Double R has controlled access but that may not be good enough."

"Thanks," Mike said.

D waved it off. "You're my brother-in-law. Which made Brandon my brother-in-law too." He grimaced. "I want to see those motherfuckers pay for what they did to him. Brandon was a good man. He didn't deserve to die like that. And I want to see my sister stay safe. So. I'm part of this fight as well. Whatever it takes, man." He sighed. "I'll get Rae to talk Aunt Carrie back into managing the Swait side of Martiniere-Swait. Then I can focus on Swait Secure and this situation."

"You sure?"

"Bro, it's a business threat as well as personal. We've got to do something about it."

Mike held out his hand. "Agreed."

They clasped hands.

Mike glanced at the light. "We'd better be heading back." He sighed. "And back to the role play for me. Damn, I'm tired of acting like a crazy man. Maybe it's time for me to start looking sick." He slipped off the log.

D clapped him on the shoulder as they walked back up to the crawler. "I'll get you enough screening so you don't have to keep up the act. Jo's worried about the effect that hiding everything and playing emotional imbalance is having on you."

"Thanks, man. She's right."

Mike sprawled back in the passenger seat as D drove back. The sunset was one of those spectacular Thunder County ones, with bright reds and oranges as the sun sank behind the mountains.

Mike drank it in, storing the memory. Who knew how soon he'd have to leave his beloved home?

24 / VISITATION

APRIL, 2086

Age: 31

"God damn it!" Mike snarled as the mind control worm's data disappeared from the screen and a shock stung his cyborged fingertips. His screen went solid black. He slumped back in his chair, growling wordlessly as he shook his hands to banish that tingle. Damn upgraded metallic cyborg fingers didn't feel everything, but they sure felt *that*.

Fucking black shield again.

The upgrades in his arms had finally completed—easiest of all of them—and he had *thought* that maybe it would be enough to trace the damn worm. It was like it dropped into some sort of shielded black hole, always disappearing after leading him on a merry chase through just about every damn Martiniere network in the world before disappearing behind that shield.

Three attempts and there's still no different result.

This time he had almost caught the damn thing, come so close— and then it just twisted away. How the *hell* did his progenitor manage this sort of programming? Was this a facet of the mind control algorithms?

They were running out of options. Jo had already tried to break through that shielding with no results. Serg had collapsed—connected to the worm or finally brought down by age, Mike wasn't certain which it was. He wasn't about to enlist Ron's hacking skills because Brandon's death was too new, too raw and Mike didn't want to risk the kid just yet. If the Martinieres were to have a future, then Ron would be key to rebuilding the Group in a new and better mold. He needed to be kept safe.

Mike continued to fret as he spun away from the screen projected over his desk to stare out the window at the snow-dusted Thunder Mountains. Two weeks. Two damned weeks since Brandon's murder, and ten of those fourteen days had been dedicated to the easier upgrades to the cyborging in his heart, lungs, and arms.

Meanwhile, Justine and Jo did their best to track down the source of that mind control worm so that he could use his new abilities to isolate and kill it. All that pain—and the next set of agony he'd have to endure to upgrade his legs—should have been worth *something*. Even though he was now able to navigate data flow at electronic instead of human speed, *it still wasn't fucking enough*. Why?

He reviewed his options. Al had the speed but not the ability to work live in digital networks to trace actual routing instead of diversion routing. Jo and the others needed digigloves to do it and they were just too damn slow. What Jo *was* able to do, since Mike now had the ability to illuminate the routes the worm took, was trace possible copy hideouts.

But each damn pursuit took different paths. The Martiniere databases were so fucking huge that scanning them to find the worm's hideaway would take forever—and it was time they might not have.

The leader of the French Martinieres, Juliette, attacked again yesterday. The family of the British Family head, Ben, attacked the day before. Juliette's attack cyber-based, Ben's a straightforward assassination attempt. The description from Ben fit Brandon's attackers, equipped with refined versions of the body mods that Gabe had banned from Martiniere production lines years ago and that Patricia Markey had gotten interdicted worldwide during her time as the President of the United States.

This is someone or something within the family who's been able to hide dissent for damned near twenty-seven years. Since Gabe became the Martiniere.

And Jeremy had finally, *finally* been arrested by the Canadians for his role in Brandon's death. But Jeremy denied any connections, including involvement in hacking the old files that held the raw data behind Mike's creation. The only reason Mike wasn't doing more as the Martiniere to encourage legal enforcement was to lull his opponents into thinking he was weak.

But his opponents also had official support. Hell, taking things into their own hands was the only way that Gabe and Ruby had triumphed over his progenitor.

It was up to him. Him, Ron, Jo, D, and Justine.

And once the new liquid nanobuild started tomorrow, he'd be out of commission for at least a week.

"There has to be a way for me to do this," he grumbled, staring at his metal fingertips. Plaskin was growing from the wrists down but he still needed to pull on protective gloves when he wasn't working in digital networks. He already missed the tactile sensations from his *real* hands, when they were his own flesh and nerves over the metal cyborg bone replacements. Plaskin was supposed to replicate that.

He sure as hell hoped it did. He yearned to feel Jo's skin against his fingers again.

But that was gone forever. Unless plaskin could replicate the sensation. It was supposed to be able to do that. God, he sure hoped it did.

A flicker from his screen caught his attention and Mike looked up. A bright red filename flashed at him from the middle of the blackness.

MMM-Martiniere activation.

What the hell?

Mike scanned the file. Nothing untoward appeared—it seemed to be a video. But the size was awfully damn big for it to be just that. And yet—the creation date and time weren't recent. The last time anyone had worked with this file was—the day Gabe died. And Gabe was marked as the creator.

Another fucking file that just popped up out of nowhere.

God, he was sick of this.

He should call on Jo for backup. Just in case this was another manifestation of the worm. But she was buried in Martiniere-Swait business today while he chased the worm. At least she had D here to help her.

Besides, he should be able to handle something simple like another bombshell file. Shunt it into a mirror that isolated the payload—if any—from his systems. Mike activated the mirror, then sent a command to sort the file into it, maintaining quarantine against expected covert viruses.

He took a deep breath. "Open MMM-Martiniere activation," he said.

To his surprise, Gabe's image appeared. Sallow. Brown skin yellowish. Like he'd been at lunch that last day of his life, though color had returned as he ate, while Ruby teased him about it being the thirteenth anniversary of their remarriage. And then he'd been dead two hours later.

Gabe rubbed his face, and sighed. *"Michael. I am so sorry. Since you are watching this right now, then the worst-case scenario has happened and you have become the Martiniere. I fucked up. I fucked up bad. And it's going to kill me."* He shook his head. *"You watching this means that Seth, Brandon, and Ruby are dead. And me as well."* He leaned forward and rested his arms on the desk. *"By now you know that Philip—my father, your progenitor—managed to activate a mind control worm in the Martiniere databases before he died, with hidden payloads to exploit the remnants of family mind control programming structures."*

Gabe turned, tapping on an icon. *"The fact that you're the one seeing this video means that no one else has gotten this far in tracking down the worm's hiding place."*

Mike paused the video to pace around the room, frustration welling up inside of him.

What the—why? Why didn't Ruby or Brandon know about this? Or Justine?

Why had Gabe been so fucking paranoid about *this*, of all things?

He shook his head and started it up again.

A rueful smile touched Gabe's lips. *"I have a pretty damned good idea of what you're thinking. Why didn't I say anything before now to Brandon or Ruby?"* He leaned back in his chair. *"In a nutshell—the damn thing has been working on all of us. Including me. Every time I wanted to say something to them, I kept forgetting about it. Except when I'm videoing. And even now, there's a piece missing."*

He grimaced. *"Some of the Martinieres are more vulnerable than others. It hasn't been until the past few days that I figured out how to get around that. And when I started..."* he shook his head again, looking down. Then he looked back up. *"Today's a special day. I just can't start something new today. Tomorrow is when I talk to Brandon and Ruby. Obviously, since you're watching this, we failed."*

A pause. *"It's worse than a simple worm. Philip wrote an algorithm that replicates him as a digital clone. I don't know how effective it is, but I have my suspicions. That digital clone may have had an impact on Lily. On you."*

The hair on the back of Mike's neck prickled.

I'm not imagining it, then.

What could a digital clone do? Did it have more power than that mind control worm? He shivered.

Could a digital clone possess my body?

Was that the explanation for what happened the night of Lily's death—an attempt to possess him by Philip's digital clone? For those unexplained rages and that sense of Philip deep inside him?

Gabe sighed again. *"I'm forgetting something. Or someone. That forgetting is important and I wish I knew why. And I am so sorry to dump this crap in your lap. But if you're seeing this video, it's already been piled on you. Good luck, Mikey."*

The video winked out, its icon popping up next to that of the file. Mike mechanically saved both within the mirror—safest location for now. He locked it down hard.

He'd think about the implications of that algorithm later, because there was a bigger problem that Gabe *didn't* mention.

Justine. Gabe didn't say one word about Justine. Was she the one that Gabe kept forgetting? Or did he not mention her because Justine's also implicated in all this shit?

He needed to talk to Jo. If Justine was dirty, then they had problems. Huge problems. They needed Justine to serve as Ron's guardian, sign off on his decisions as the Martiniere if they went underground.

Deontae needs to know too.

Non-Martinieres close to the family had to know about this. Just in case.

Gabe had died before he could talk to Ruby about this discovery.

That mistake couldn't be repeated. If the worm—or the digital clone—could kill, then *this had to be shared.* He needed to consult with Jo and D—*now.*

Mike went to Jo's office. She and D pored over separate screens, flicking files and comments back and forth. He paused in the doorway, waiting for an opening in their workflow. Even with the urgency tightening Mike's gut, the way brother and sister worked together was a treat to watch. He and Jo often did the same thing, but even after six years of marriage, seven years as a couple, he didn't think their workflow match was as smooth as when she did it with D. The siblings had grown up designing and managing systems together.

Soon enough Jo looked up. "Mike?" Her eyes widened. "What's wrong?"

"I want you and D to see something in my office, as soon as you've got an opening. I—I need feedback and I don't want to influence your reactions."

Deontae and Jo glanced at each other. JoAnn arched a brow at her brother. Deontae froze his screen.

"I think we're at a good place now," he said, as Jo closed hers.

"Don't freeze it, D," she said. "Close it. This is bad, isn't it?"

"I—don't want to influence you in either direction," he said.

She came up to him and took Mike's hand, not flinching away from the metal. Damn it, he'd forgotten to pull on his gloves. Not that it mattered, except that he wished she could have at least the semblance of touching flesh instead of the metal.

"I forgot my gloves. I'm sorry."

"It doesn't matter. But it does tell me how worried you are. Let's go see this."

The three of them silently walked down the hallway to his office.

"D. Please raise Swait Secure," he said when they were inside. "Highest possible level inside of my shields."

D raised his brows. "Bro, really?"

Mike nodded. "I—you'll see why."

"Damn." A quick flick of screens, and the shields raised.

Mike exhaled with relief. If Justine *was* dirty, it would still take her some time to break through both sets of shields, should there be some sort of alert to catch her attention.

"This popped up when I hit the worm's shield wall this time," he said, before opening the video.

It wasn't any easier to watch it again. This time Mike observed Gabe's body language, not listening to his words. Gabe was clearly agitated, his upset showing in the way he moved his hands, more expressive than he usually had been. But was he frightened or angry? The way his right brow twitched when he mentioned forgetting something or someone—no. Gabe wasn't afraid. Wouldn't he be fearful if Justine were dirty, given the degree to which she dominated the Martiniere security protocols?

Gabe was pissed about not remembering, he decided. *And frustrated.*

"Fuuck," D said slowly when the clip ended. "Mike, when was this made?"

"The morning of the day that Gabe died."

"So he never got to talk to Ruby and Brandon about it."

"No."

"I'm concerned about that algorithm piece, but there's a bigger issue. Why doesn't Gabe mention Justine?" Jo said, twining her fingers together thoughtfully.

"That's my concern right there," Mike said. "I'm worried about that algorithm. But that's nothing. Justine."

"You think she's dirty?" D asked.

"I hope to hell she's not. And that the worm's influence on Gabe made him forget about her for a reason."

"What would Philip be thinking about Justine before he died?" Jo asked.

Mike exhaled and leaned back in his chair, studying the ceiling. "I know that both she and Ruby talked about his dismissive attitude toward women. That's one factor. My progenitor *knew* that Justine was working against him, that she supported Gabe to be the Martiniere. Hell, she led the arguments to depose my progenitor as the Martiniere in that Family meeting. I was there. I saw it. Wouldn't that make her a major target for the worm?"

"I've heard both Justine and Ruby talk about Philip," Jo said. "My inclination is that he would underestimate Justine until the very end. Would he have had time to subvert her somehow during that meeting?"

Mike chewed his lip thoughtfully.

"I don't know for certain," he said finally. "Remember, I was only five and very isolated, without normal socialization at the time. I remember Donna-gran—his mother, no, *our* mother—leading me into the meeting. Him screaming at me. I yelled back that I would bite him if he tried to touch me. I'd gotten pretty good at biting as resistance when his doctors tried to force me into doing something." He paused. "There was a lot of arguing. The vote. And then Philip ripped open his shirt to show the suicide vest he was wearing. That got disarmed, and he took poison."

"Hmm." D tapped his fingertips together. "Have you had any questions about Justine's actions until now?"

"No," Mike said firmly. "But if she's a deep sleeper agent, it wouldn't show up."

"If she's a deep one then we're all fucked anyway, given the degree to which she's integrated into our security systems, including Swait Secure," D said. "More likely the worm would have the same influence on her that it had on Gabe, causing her to forget important information. Justine has done too damn much good to support Philip's opposition for her to willingly be one of his agents. And if she's being subconsciously influenced—she has the right to know about it."

Mike exhaled. "All right. Let's call Justine in and show her the clip." He got up. "I'll fetch her."

Justine was working in the kitchen, at the old green Formica and chrome table that was her first choice for a workspace whenever she stayed at the Double R.

"What's going on, Mike?" she asked.

"Something to show you in my office."

She frowned at his expression as she reached for her walker. "Something bad."

"Possibly," he said.

"All right." She shut down her screens and followed Mike. He tapped the programming open to let her in. She raised a brow at that. "Martiniere *and* Swait screens?" And then she spotted the video with Gabe's frozen image, and inhaled sharply. "Gabie? What the hell?"

"This was recorded the day he died," Mike said.

Justine blinked hard and took a deep breath before taking a seat between JoAnn and D. "All right. Run it."

When the clip was finished, she leaned forward, scowling. "So why the fuck didn't he mention me? That's a huge omission. Serg I can understand—Serg has never been in line to inherit. And Gabie was not the sort of sexist who would discount me. No. It's something else. Mike. Run the clip again, but please focus on his hands. I don't need to hear the words—no, I'd better, to coordinate with the timing. But zoom in his hands."

Justine leaned closer as the video ran again, lips tight. "All right," she said as it finished. "Rerun to the first mention of Brandon and Ruby. Still zoom on his hands. Slow-mo it."

Mike obeyed. Justine chewed on her lip, then raised her hand. "Again. Even slower."

Mike did it.

"All right. Next mention. That slowest speed."

This time she nodded to herself.

"Final mention."

When it was done, she slumped back. "All right. Let's go back to that final mention." She got up and stood next to the video. "I think it's subconscious that he doesn't *say* my name. But Gabie is throwing old Martiniere hand security codes when he mentions Brandon and Ruby." She held her hands up, copying Gabe's hand motions. "This means *protect*."

D moved forward. "Yes. I see it." He looked at Justine. "But is there more?"

She nodded. "My name." She signed it, and they all saw the movement replicated by Gabe's hands.

"*Protect Justine?*" Jo frowned.

"What the *hell* is that supposed to mean?" Justine stared at the screen as she tapped her chin with her index fingers. "What *were* you thinking, Gabie? Why didn't you mention me except for handsign? Damn you for being so fucking obscure sometimes. Why didn't you find a way to talk to Ruby at noon? Give her some sort of fucking clue? *Why?*" Her voice cracked and she buried her head in her hands.

"Protect Justine," D said, tapping his fingers on a chair arm. "But he couldn't say it. And then there's the algorithm. How the *hell* do we deal with *that?*"

Justine raised her head. "And why protect me?"

"You still know where a lot of the family bodies are buried," Mike said. "Maybe that's a clue about the algorithm."

"Or it's Gabie's last flourish at being my protective big brother." Justine chewed her lower lip. "Let me poke at that link, Mike."

"I'll set you up," Mike said.

"It'll take time," Justine said. "But maybe I can figure it out. This digital clone thing scares me."

"Me too," Mike said.

LIQUID NANOBUILD WAS HELL. NO TWO WAYS ABOUT IT. EVEN THOUGH this was an upgrade and not the full experience, it still hurt. And he was too chicken to go through it without Jo by his side.

Luckily, this one was a day surgery in Portland, just like his other upgrades had been. And it helped promote the line that something major had happened to his health. Justine had already told the Family that there were many decisions that would come through Ron with her approval, because Mike was having a major health relapse in the wake of Brandon's death. Mike had signed the order that gave her the authority to serve as Ron's guardian in his absence or severe illness, including approving Ron's decisions as the Martiniere.

"Aha!" Jo said in one of his moments of clarity. "Mike. You able to understand?"

He nodded, gritting his teeth against the pain. There'd be another swell of agony soon—it came in waves.

"Got—a few—minutes."

"Brandon's killers are based in Las Vegas."

That sharpened his awareness. "Can—you—keep track?"

The sharp, feral grin she gave him just before another wave of pain blacked him out was his answer.

25 / A TOSS OF THE DIE

MAY, 2086

Age: 31

"You're sure Brandon's killers are still in Vegas?" Mike asked. Jo, D, Justine, Al, and Ron had gathered in his office after his return from Portland for Dr. Pramula's final checks on his cyborg upgrades, including reprogramming accesses should they be compromised.

D nodded. "Been monitoring their activity since Jo tracked them down. They spend a lot of time in Vegas and LA. They occasionally disappear. Fit the profile of professional assassins, but nailing something on them is tough. They have body doubles that have gone through Martiniere body mods, to the degree that it takes a full body scan and very detailed DNA probes to tell them apart. You rarely see all of them together. At least one man and one woman are visible in Vegas at all times. To provide alibis, I suspect."

LA and Vegas.

Not Jeremy's turf. Not like Montreal had been. Mike chewed on his lower lip for a moment. Several of the cousins had taken over Philip's labs in Los Angeles. Were they all compromised?

It is where Philip's strongest supporters were based.

And Lily had escaped from the hospital there.

But Dr. Pramula was also located in LA. She'd passed every damn clearance possible, and proven herself trustworthy.

All the same, Pramula was an independent agent. Not a Martiniere affiliate—her retainer was directly from him now, had previously been from Gabe and Ruby until Mike became a legal adult and had direct access to his Martiniere funds. Was that a factor?

"Are they clones?" Mike asked tensely. "Wouldn't a DNA match identify who's an original and who's a double?"

"Pretty sophisticated body mods," D said. "Not clones. But it takes a deep DNA scan to discern the differences. Law enforcement doesn't have those resources because it's usually not necessary." He frowned. "They also use DNA distorters so it's hard to get a full DNA reading on any traces they leave at any scene. That enhances the doubling effect."

"I've been working on quick ways to sort the doubles from the originals," Justine said. "As of yet I've not been able to tie specific ones to Brandon's murder." She grimaced. "It's going to take at least another month to trace down and bypass those distortions."

Mike nodded curtly. "And meanwhile, they stroll around Vegas—or are they pretty low key?"

"Oh hell no," Jo said. She snapped up a screen. "They're big, flashy players. Not at the big venues but they do stand out where they're regulars—and fortunately their favorite places contract with Swait Secure. Here they are right now."

Mike watched, fingers tightening on the arms of his chair as Jo highlighted Brandon's killers from the Secure cam feeds, throwing dice at one of the smaller casinos. Always a man and a woman together. Rarely more than four of them at once. He could have sworn he saw at least six in that damned video. So where were the others?

"You're sure of the ID?" he asked finally. Not that he doubted.

But there was more than that.

Mike would be willing to bet that if he went back and looked at the videos from Lily's death, he would see those killers in the crowd that watched her leap. She had pointed to someone before jumping. Absently, he wondered if a review of other videos of Lily after her escape would show them in some combination.

Jo bared her teeth at him in a feral grin. "As far as I'm concerned, our big problem is going to be making sure we get the ones responsible for Brandon's death."

"Doubles are just as complicit as the originals, as far as I'm concerned," Justine said. "There were more than just those two originals present at Brandon's death. Six of them. Yeah, we've only seen four. I'm concerned about where the other two—and any more out there—are hiding."

Mike exhaled.

It begins.

"Jo. My health requires that we take a trip to Vegas."

She raised her brows. "As ourselves?"

"To begin with." He glanced at Al. "You've got the skin-darkening option figured out?"

Al nodded. "Still need to print plaskin face masks and I'll need covers for my real hand. You will need the face masks as well."

Jo made a face. "I hate those nose covers."

"At least you can make do with partials," Mike said.

He hated the plaskin, but they had already decided that any underground work meant that Mike and Al passed as either Black or Hispanic to keep Jo from standing out. It was easier for them as cyborgs to modify their appearance. Mike's cyborg structures allowed him to change skin shades on his arms and legs. Al's were limited to his cyborged arm and leg. But both of them had to wear full face masks to change their skin shade and features. Jo just needed to change facial shapes.

"All right, then," Mike said. "Let's lay the groundwork, make the face covers, and then off we go to Vegas."

Justine rolled her eyes. "Just don't emulate Gabe and Brandon by developing a taste for gambling, all right?"

"I don't think that's going to be a problem," Mike said. "I absolutely hate the idea of taking this much of a chance on things. At least until I need to do it."

MIKE TOOK AN OVERSIZED NUMBER OF REGULAR MARTINIERE SECURITY with them as they traveled to Vegas. He held Jo's hand the entire flight down, not wanting to talk.

This was it.

Not his first time in Vegas, mind you. He and Starlight had performed at the great Dreams Come True casino arena for the Reined Cowhorse World competitions. But Mike had not set foot in the town other than for competition. He wasn't very interested in casino gambling.

He followed his usual pattern and reserved the penthouse in Dreams.

"Mr. Martiniere! What a pleasure to see you here—but I'm surprised you haven't come to show your horses," James, the night manager, said as they checked in.

"Unfortunately, I'm here to get a break for my health," Mike said hoarsely. "Need sun and heat."

James laughed. "Well, we have a lot of that here."

"That's what I'm counting on," Mike said. He leaned on his cane and held Jo's arm. Al and Martiniere security escorted their luggage to the elevator. Jo guided Mike to the main casino.

"Cards, dice, roulette?" she asked.

God. He hated this. He sucked at cards, always had despite Justine, Gabe, and Ruby's best efforts to teach him. And roulette was too random for his purposes.

"Dice," Mike said firmly. With cyborged fingers, it was pretty easy to manage the throw. He could control dice. He'd practiced enough with them since his cyborg upgrades.

Just in case.

AFTER TWO HOURS OF PLAYACTING BEING SICK, QUERULOUS, AND PRONE TO losing at dice, Mike was more than ready to retreat to their suite. He'd lost enough money at the tables to attract the assassins' attention—or so he hoped.

Al met them at the suite's door. "Shields and mirroring established," he said after closing the door, checking them for bugs, and raising the shields. "Swait Secure confirmed."

Mike sighed and straightened up. He leaned his cane against the wall, glad to be free of it. "Any sign of our *friends* showing interest?"

"You had two of them trailing you," Al said. He snapped his fingers to bring up the link to the Swait Secure cams. Mike flinched as he saw himself, apparently drunk, yelling at Jo and pitching a fit, waving his cane angrily.

"Hon. I am so sorry," he said to her. "I was an absolute ass out there."

Scary because I got too deep into it.

"You were supposed to be one," she said, her focus on the cams. "No offense."

"But I still feel like a shit for treating you like that." He put his arm around Jo as they watched. Al didn't need to point out the two assassins lurking on the edge of the crowd around the table watching Mike Martiniere make a fool of himself. Mike recognized them from the video of Brandon's death. "Jo, Al, can we tell if those two are the originals or the doubles?"

Jo slipped away from Mike and tapped the images of the two—one man, one woman. A yellow line outlined the man while a green did the same for the woman.

"The man's a double. Woman's the original," she said. "Notice how she hangs back, and how he looks to her before doing anything? She's the controller. They're mixing up their team, looks like. I wonder if that's a standard operating process?"

"I wish we could tap into their conversations," Mike muttered. "It would be nice to know what to expect."

Jo shrugged. "We know they intend to attack you. They'll want to lure you somewhere like they did Brandon. If they do it on the casino floor—especially *this* casino, where you're known and have relationships—then they run a high risk of interference and failure."

"We need to move our action to a different casino tomorrow," Mike said. "Tonight—well, all right. But I don't want to poison the waters too badly, just in case I come back as a competitor. I *will* make things tough if I keep up that sort of performance."

"Easy enough to deal with," Jo said. "Tomorrow morning, you go down alone and tip everyone in sight while having breakfast and a drink. Apologize profusely to everyone, stop by the front desk and talk to the manager. Blame your health and overdoing. Then I'll go down afterward and do the same thing, drop a few cues that you've been having health issues and the prognosis is pretty gloomy. We're booked into a last-chancer's quack cancer treatment clinic tomorrow afternoon. D's discreetly leaked that your cancer has returned. We can stop at one of the assassins' favorite smaller casinos on our way back from the clinic to pull the same show, until I drag you out with much fanfare and drama."

Mike gave her a startled look. *That* had not been in any plans he had known about.

Jo smirked. "Mike, D and I have run this type of operation in Vegas when managing the indentured underground. Why do you think Swait Secure is so popular here?"

Mike kissed her. "Damn, Jo, just when I think I know everything about you, another facet emerges. What else are you going to surprise me with?"

"Now that's a secret," she said, her smirk spreading to a bigger smile. "You'll just have to wait and see."

He grinned back at her. "Al, how likely is it that we'll have to deal with an attack of some sort tonight?"

"Mmm, about 40% probability for a physical attack. We've already had some probes that I've deflected to the mirror sims. Right now the sim shows you and JoAnn in a nasty argument."

Mike shuddered. They had recorded different versions of arguments while still at the Double R, under D's supervision, to have available for the mirrors. Bad enough to have to fake that kind of thing.

His now-restored memories of the meltdown triggered by the video the night after Lily's death were worse.

And I almost lost myself doing the fakes.

That was even more frightening.

"At least those are sims," he said softly to Jo. "And I hated doing them."

"Me too," she agreed.

STARTING THE MORNING WITH ALCOHOL WASN'T HIS USUAL THING. BUT Mike managed to choke down his whisky, thankful that the latest cyborg upgrades seemed to have adjusted his metabolism so that he didn't feel the alcohol. The apologies were easier—he just remembered the times that Gabe had to apologize to Ruby and channeled that.

All the same he was in a hurry to shower again once he went back to their suite, putting off both Al and Jo until he had cleaned up, changed, and run another check on his systems. He had to debug two snoopers.

"You had followers," Al told Mike when he was done and had come back into the living room. "The two women this time."

Mike took a moment to kiss Jo before she went downstairs on her rounds. "Just a sec, Al." He leaned his forehead against Jo's. "I really, really need to make this up to you when we're all done," he said quietly. "I feel like shit. All of this makes me feel crappy. I feel like I'm becoming what I'm pretending to be."

"It's just role play," she said softly, resting her hand on his cheek. "And that's why I wanted to be here with you. To keep you from being twisted. Especially since that damn algorithm is floating around."

After Jo left, Mike turned to Al. "So. Same thing as last night, only two women?"

Al nodded, once again focused on the cams. "The men are now on the scene. Following JoAnn." He glanced at Mike.

Mike shivered. "I sure as hell hope they stay clear of Jo."

But they didn't.

Mike clenched his hands as the men approached Jo. One came close and talked to her while the second stayed apart.

I don't care. If they touch Jo, I'm out of here to protect her.

The discussion grew heated. Jo flashed a hand signal and Martiniere security moved in, followed by casino security. Mike relaxed as the two men were escorted out.

On the other hand, that's gonna make it difficult to run any ops out of Dreams, he cautioned himself. But—Jo's safety was paramount.

The in-house com rang. Mike got it, audio only.

"Hey Mike. There was a spot of trouble with someone harassing your wife," Sally, the day manager, said. "The offenders have been banned from the casino."

"I appreciate it," he said. "Thanks so much, Sally."

"Not at all." She hesitated. "Are you two having problems? There were some issues last night. Not your usual behavior."

"Um—just my health. I'm not feeling well and we've got an appointment with Dr. Fuhran's clinic this afternoon," Mike said.

A sharp intake of breath from Sally. Fuhran's clinic was well-known for catering last resort health options, especially among the wealthy like Mike who could afford his mostly quackish remedies.

"I am so sorry," Sally said.

"It's to be expected, considering who and what I am," Mike said.

"If we can do anything—"

"I'll keep that in mind. Thanks for watching out for JoAnn. I appreciate it."

"We appreciate your business, Mike." Sally disconnected. Mike exhaled and sent her a big tip.

He paced the floor until Jo was safely back in the suite, had debugged herself and showered.

"Are you all right?" he demanded as she came out of the bathroom.

She shivered and he took her into his arms. "They knew who I was. But the man—Gene, he called himself—propositioned me. Offered me a lot of money to go to bed with him."

"Oh, honey."

"The sims worked. Gene referred to our fighting last night. But the motherfucker was crude as hell. He called me a Black slut for hire to the highest bidder, and hinted that if I betrayed you, I'd get an even higher payout."

"That's pure Philip," Mike said grimly.

"Did he give any hint about a plan?" Al asked.

"Nothing. I suspect they're going to try to separate us," Jo said.

"Well, we'll see what happens after we go to Fuhran's," Mike said. "Damn it, in a way I wish we'd exploited that body mod tech ourselves. I know, I know—" he raised a hand as Jo started to protest. "But it would be convenient for us if we could run doubles."

"That's how the slippery slope starts," Jo said, a sharp note in her voice. "Convenience. I am *not* going to let you make that mistake."

It almost sounded like something Ruby would say.

Oddly enough, that made him feel better.

THE VISIT TO DR. FUHRAN MADE MIKE GRATEFUL THAT HE HAD NEVER been this fucking desperate for real.

All the same, he felt as cruddy as he should have if the falsified diagnosis of cancer returning was real, combined with a creepy-crawlie sensation of being watched. Fuhran prescribed several supplements that Mike recognized as prime quackery, and said so. They ended up yelling at each other, and Mike stormed out of the doctor's offices. As planned, but it still made him feel lower than a snake's belly. He didn't like making scenes like this.

Jo caught up to him on the street. "Come on," she said, a false note of cheer in her voice as she slid her arm in his. "Let's do a late lunch at the Starshine. It's on our way. Maybe you can catch up with your losses there."

"Whatever," he grumbled.

"Being followed," Al said into the ear com that Mike was wearing. *"Man and woman. Primaries, not the duplicates."*

Mike clucked back once, their prearranged signal. Jo tensed her arm slightly. He wanted to pat it but no, not a good idea. Didn't fit the image they were trying to portray.

Their tension made a good cover for them to act appropriately, though.

As they walked into the Starshine, one of the female duplicates intercepted them—and her appearance differed from the original. Her short, white-blond hair with bangs reminded Mike of Al's mother Mariah—at least what little he remembered of Mariah before her death. She wore a shimmery sleeveless silver sequined dress slit up the sides, and the low-cut neckline front and back left little to the imagination.

"My God, she's practically a copy of my mother," Al said grimly, confirming Mike's impression. *"Did the motherfucker clone her too?"*

Mike wanted to answer Al but no—not now.

"Mr. and Mrs. Martiniere," the woman gushed.

Jo flinched. "I'm Ms. *Swait*, not Mrs. Martiniere."

"Oh. I'm sorry, Ms. Swait." But the apology sounded false to Mike's ears.

"Maybe we should just leave, Jo," he said sharply. "If they won't respect who you are…."

"Oh no, no, no, that's my mistake," the duplicate continued. "Can we offer you lunch to make up for the insult? Free."

Mike and Jo exchanged glances. "Free *is* a good price," Jo said.

"If you're all right with it, then I am," Mike said.

"Good. I'm so pleased that you chose to patronize our establishment," the duplicate said. "My name is Martina and I'd be happy to help you have the best experience possible at the Starshine. Would you prefer our exclusive dining room or one of our private dining areas?"

"Martina. Fuck. She is *a copy of my mother. Same mannerisms. Maybe not a clone but damn it,"* Al growled. *"You be careful!"*

"Private," Mike said sharply. He wasn't sure how well he could hold it together in public right now. Even in an exclusive room.

"We have just the thing for you." Martina guided them past the big dining areas and into a gaudy, golden room that reminded Mike of an old French chateau. But it was a tawdry imitation of the gilt and glamor of the old Martiniere family holdings—and a closer examination revealed that it *was* just that, an imitation of the dining room in the main Martiniere chateau near Versailles.

Interesting.

He wondered how long this decor had been in existence, and just who within the Family had licensed its use—it wasn't supposed to be duplicated. Mike exchanged a glance with Jo as they sat. He jerked his head toward the walls and she nodded.

Good. It wasn't just him who noticed it.

Cheap copies. Decorating and—Martina?

He ordered a light salad for lunch, sounding cranky the whole time, and a drink.

"Mike." Jo frowned at him. "You need to slow down your drinking."

"What? After that encounter with that quack Fuhran, I want to drink *something*," he snapped back.

"Mike," Jo sighed. "You can't just blow up like that."

"If you say so," he grumbled, noting how Martina watched them carefully.

Neither of them spoke after she left. Mike kept glancing around the room.

Danger. Danger.

He couldn't explain what it was that set him off. The decor? Martina? Something else?

Martina acted as their server. Mike clucked his cyborging into scan mode and checked his salad surreptitiously for drugs or toxins with a brush of his index finger, grateful that he now had the ability with his cyborging upgrades.

—*Soporific in the dressing,* the alert whispered into his ear. It identified the specific drug but Mike clucked it to *save.* Specifics weren't necessary at this point.

They're not fucking around. That worried him. Accelerating the time-line? *Shit.*

Nothing in the drink. He needed to check Jo's food, *now.* And he had to make a scene to cover for it.

"I don't want this crap salad." He shoved the plate across the table, knocking over both his and JoAnn's drinks, and did the same test for her salad, running his finger through her dressing.

A red light only he could see flashed.

—*Neurotoxin,* his cyborging whispered as he wiped it off on the tablecloth. His gut tightened as Jo dipped her fork into her salad.

No!

Mike smacked the fork out of her hand before she could take a bite.

"Mike, *stop.*" Jo's voice was shaky. Real or feigned?

Mike grabbed her and stood up. They had to get out of here, *now.* This situation was a game changer. They needed to be in public, *fast.* Never should have gone private, but then again, would the exclusive dining area have been any safer? They should have just stuck to gambling—but would it have then been something on the dice? Cards?

"I've changed my mind. Let's gamble."

"*Mike,*" Jo protested as he dragged her away from the table.

He leaned in close. "Your salad was poisoned. Dressing. Mine had a soporific. Don't fucking react wrong because we're in trouble!" he whispered into her ear.

"I wanted to eat that salad!" she protested loudly, but gave him a quick nod, her lips tightening.

"Don't want that crap food anyway," he grumbled.

Martina hurried after them.

Before they could reach the main floor Gene and the other two blocked their way.

"If you're not going to do it the easy way—" Gene began.

Mike swung at him before he finished speaking.

Be careful of knives.

This was a mistake. God damn it, they'd set themselves up. He had thought the assassins would take longer to get around to—whatever they had planned for him. And the neurotoxin in Jo's salad just plain pissed Mike off as well as frightened him.

They will pay for trying to kill her. They will pay.

"*On my way!*" Al yelled over the com.

Four against two. And they were in exactly the situation he hadn't wanted. They didn't dare stay engaged with these four, not here, not like this....

—*Max levels,* he clucked to his cyborging, scared to death for Jo as the two women ganged up on her.

"Jo, *run!*" he bellowed.

"Like hell!" she shouted back. She tore her necklace free, twisted, and wrapped it around Martina's neck.

The rest of the fight was a blur.

Another flashing red light.

—*Silent Swait Secure alert,* his cyborging whispered.

Mike grabbed Jo's upper arm and ran, noting that at least one of their attackers were down.

"Mike! Mike! *Mike!*"

He dragged her along, not wanting to stop despite her protests.

This was a fucking God damned trap. They knew we had identified Bran's killers.

When Jo slowed him too much, he swept her up in his arms and ran as hard as he could, even once they were safely outside the casino. But he could feel the draw on his energy. He couldn't keep this up much longer.

Honking distracted him and Mike slowed. Al pulled the rig up in front of them. Mike shoved Jo inside and collapsed on the floor. The last thing he remembered before passing out was Jo and Al dragging him the rest of the way inside the vehicle. He went limp, unable to help them at all, his head pounding.

He must not have been out for long because he could hear sirens as Al drove like a madman, swerving fast and alternately accelerating and braking. Mike lay on his back, still on the floor of the big SUV, gasping.

"Jo?" he croaked, fear grabbing at him. Had she consumed any of that neurotoxin?

"Mikey," her voice quavered.

"You're—all right? You didn't get any of that neurotoxin in you?" He glanced around, trying to see her better from his angle on the floor. Was she all right?

"*That* was what set you off?" She bent over and he saw the scratches and blood on her face.

"Oh God. Jo. Are you all right?" He tried to sit up but Al cornered hard and rolled Mike into the back of the front seats.

"Don't move, Mikey. Not at this speed. Not safe." She rested her hand on his cheek. "We are well and truly fucked right now. D's doing his best to clear us but we are on the run. As you can hear."

"God." He closed his eyes. Worst case scenario and beyond. He'd never thought that they'd have to take off like this. "But you're all right? You didn't get any of that neurotoxin in your salad dressing?"

"No, you knocked the fork out of my hand before I could take a bite." Her voice shook more than ever. "I didn't think they'd dare try anything that blatant, even in a private dining room. Fuck."

"What's our situation?" Now that he knew Jo was all right, he could focus on other things. "I assume that's the police I'm hearing—but both Justine and D should have kept them from coming after us. So somehow that arrangement got fucked."

"We left at least two people down. I'm pretty sure I killed Martina, and if you didn't kill Gene, you left him in damn poor shape. The other two are pretty beat up...Mikey, what the hell did you do?"

"Full activation of my cyborging," he said, staring up at her.

"It's fucking impressive. You were moving so fast that you were just a blur."

"The problem is that you burn out pretty damn fast with full as opposed to half or three-quarter," Al said from the front seat. "As you just discovered. We've gotta get some food in you right away."

Mike drew a deep breath. "At least it worked."

Sirens coming from the other direction. How screwed were they now? He blinked. Things were blurring out around him again. His arms and legs hurt as full-body shakes tightened his muscles.

"Thank God," Al said as the sirens passed them. "At least *that* jurisdiction stayed in our camp." He paused as the sound of sirens faded. "Getting directions from Justine now. Heading north. There's a safe house in a small town called Caliente. Only one night and we'll have to move on. Gonna need to drive for a while as it's a hundred-eighty miles from here by the most discreet route. JoAnn, there's a cooler in the cargo compartment behind your seat. Grab it."

Jo turned, fumbling in the back before she pulled the cooler over the seat. "Got it."

"There's a tube of Liquid Protein in there. Mike needs the whole damn thing. Get it into him fast."

Jo uncapped the tube and stuck it into Mike's mouth, squeezing gently. After the first few swallows he took it from her, rationing the flow. The gray blur sharpened into clarity and the shakes eased—though *damn*, he still hurt all over, as if he'd been beaten hard. He heard further rustling as Jo replaced the cooler in the back.

"I think I can get up now," he said.

"Don't," Al said. "Slight change of plans. We'll be swapping vehicles. D has someone meeting us in an hour. Hold on, Mike. You're gonna be tired even with the Liquid Protein, but at least you won't have the shakes. Turn on your side and take a nap. You'll feel better for it. Trust me. I've been there."

He didn't want to sleep on the floor. He really wanted to crawl up on the seat and lean on Jo. But if it was necessary, it was necessary.

Mike sighed and maneuvered himself through what it took to turn on his side in the cramped space. *Ow.* Something hurt on his left side, not as bad as a rib but he bet it was bruised. And now he was cold.

That didn't matter. They had made it out alive. But still. Was Jo all right or had she been hurt? He wasn't satisfied with what he'd heard so far.

"You're all right, Jo?"

"Nothing that can't wait."

He heard rustling. Then she bent over again. "Raise your head, Mike."

He obeyed and she slipped a folded jacket under his head. He took her hand. "You're all right?" he repeated.

Now he could see how she favored one hand, and her beautiful nose had a slight crook in it that hadn't been there before, dried blood under her nostrils.

Jo got hurt.

That sent tendrils of fear through him. And what if she had been compromised? Gabe's old *WTH* file had noted that Gabe had been infected with nanos that facilitated mind control through sex *and* physical contact—and that Ruby had possibly been infected through contact with. him. Was Jo clear? Gabe *had* developed protections against that years ago. He'd been taking his doses. Had Jo?

"Hush." She spread an old woolen blanket over him.

"Jo. Please. Are you all right? I'm worried about you being infected by nanos. You've been taking your NanoProtect doses, right?"

"Yes, Mike." She swung her legs up on the bench seat. "Here." She reached down to move the coat. "Go ahead and stretch out a little bit. I need to rest, too. Let's get situated and then we can talk."

With Jo's help, he moved so that he wasn't so cramped. She pulled at the blanket so that he was better covered by it, then adjusted another one over her and lay down, resting her hand on his torso.

"It's nothing that I haven't had to deal with before, Mikey," she said finally. "I hurt. But nothing's broken besides my nose. And yes, I've been taking my NanoProtect so you don't have to worry about compromise from that direction." A sharp, rueful chuckle. "At least I won't need to use nose covers as often now."

He took her hand. "I'm sorry, Jo."

"Eh, it can be fixed once this is done." Her hand tightened on his as she moved slightly so that he could see her better. "This is a fine mess, isn't it?"

"No kidding."

"But at least two of them are down. Maybe more. Maybe we won't have to do anything other than hide out for a night, and then it will all be straightened out."

"Maybe," he said.

But his instincts suggested otherwise.

He didn't want to close his eyes and sleep.

However, there wasn't anything else that he could do right now.

26 / ON THE RUN

MAY, 2086

Age: 31

THEY SWITCHED VEHICLES TWICE ON THE WAY TO CALIENTE. THE SAFE house was a tiny cabin on the edge of town, a small single space with two beds that obviously once had been part of an ancient roadside motel—several other cabins survived next to it. At least they didn't have to check in—the second vehicle swap was remote, with all the required information provided along with an analog room key instead of the usual digital code.

Mike still felt shaky and tired as he helped Jo and Al lug suitcases and coolers into the cabin. Al had packed up their suite at Dreams—how he had managed to do it so quickly Mike didn't have the faintest clue, or enough energy to inquire further.

"We need to take care of your face," he said to Jo. "And I want to confirm that you didn't pick up anything from that attack, even with the NanoProtect."

"I can do it," Al said firmly. "Mike, you need to rest. Running on full activation sucks you down. You look like hell. And you need to be checked too. JoAnn, sit down."

"We did clear any prospective trackers or bugs, right?" Mike asked as Jo sat at the small, ancient table that looked almost as old as the kitchen table at the Double R. Just not as well-preserved. He dropped into the other chair.

"Before the first switch," Al said absently as he sponged away the blood on JoAnn's face, then checked the scratches on her cheek.

"Ow!" Jo said as Al poked at her nose.

"Sorry." Al delicately felt her wrist and hand. "Needs a brace." He dove into a backpack and retrieved a brace.

"Don't put it on yet," Jo said. "I want a shower."

"Hurt anywhere else?"

"Yes. I'll have Mike take a look in the bathroom," Jo said. "Doesn't feel like anything worse than bruises."

Al nodded and turned to Mike, examining his hands and face.

"What's our status?" Mike asked.

"Either D or Justine will contact us in an hour," Al said. "Right now, we're gonna lay low." He scowled. "I thought something didn't feel right, so I got everything packed and ready to go after I dropped you off at the clinic, had our security load the rig. Good thing I did."

Mike pushed himself up. "Jo, let's do that full-body check in the bathroom, and then have Al screen us for nanos. Once I eat something I'm down for the count. And I'd like to get showered before I do anything else."

"Me too," she said quickly.

They gathered up personal items and a change into nightclothes before they went into the small bathroom. Mike winced as he unbuttoned his shirt. Not just his side hurt but also his shoulders where the cyborging tied into the flesh.

"Let me help you with that," Jo said. She helped Mike slide off his t-shirt—only then did he notice the blood on both his shirt and tee. "Holy cow, is that ever a big bruise."

He flinched just looking at it in the mirror. It covered most of the ribs on his left side. Jo poked at it but at least the ribs weren't broken. And the blood—definitely someone else's, not his.

The shower was barely big enough for two, but without saying anything they both crowded into it. Jo leaned against Mike as sobs shook her body. He held her close, savoring the warm water, shivering a little in reaction as well.

"Oh God, Mikey," she finally murmured. "They meant to kill me. If I hadn't been wearing that garrote necklace…and what the hell did they plan to do with you?"

"Apparently they wanted me alive." His shudder was stronger than it had been, because he could well imagine what they wanted to do to him. He stroked her cheek. "You gonna be all right?"

She nodded. "Not my first time."

"I hope you managed to keep that necklace. We may need it again."

"I grabbed it before you yanked me out of there." She rubbed her shoulder.

"Did I sore you up? I'm sorry."

"I'm surprised you didn't dislocate it." She gulped. "But better that than dead."

"Fuck yes." He kissed her.

She leaned against him again. "I don't think this is gonna be over any time soon, Mike. Not with the second car switch. I've been in these situations before. Something's happened that we don't know about yet. Something bad."

"We'll see what we learn when we check in, okay?"

She nodded, but he knew she was right.

Well, you thought going underground would be necessary. At least you're prepared for it.

It was Justine who called. Mike knew it was bad news just from her expression.

"You're gonna have to move on tomorrow under new identities," she said. "Deontae and I are working the courts, but right now there's warrants out for your arrests. All three of you. God, I miss Remy Trask. She could work the system so slick, but her nephew Chris just doesn't have her prosecutorial experience…." Justine shook her head. "Two dead. Other two in bad shape. But those aren't the only ones out there, Mike. We've found more."

Two down for Brandon at least, Mike thought grimly. "We got ambushed, Justine. They tried to kill Jo. Neurotoxin. Same one that killed Seth."

"Fuck." Justine rubbed her face. "All right. Forward the data. I'll see if that helps anything. But. We've uncovered some of the Family linkages. It's definitely Jeremy's operation. Jeremy and—" she paused, sighing. "Juliette's granddaughters Marie and Monique. There's a big batch of hidden, modified Loyal Indentureds sworn to the Family—a whole cluster of them in the LA and Vegas area. I had no damned idea. Juliette is *pissed* about what her granddaughters have done, and is running her own checks."

"That fucking worm has contaminated a lot of our structures," Mike said grimly.

"Mike?" Ron moved into the cam's range.

"Hey, Ron." Mike sighed. "Justine. I think we're going to need to implement that contingency plan."

Ron's jaw tightened. "Me as the temporary Martiniere?"

"Yes," Mike said. "Ready to record, Justine?"

"Yes."

He took a deep breath. "Implementing transfer of authority now. I, Michael Marcus Martiniere, due to circumstances, temporarily transfer my authority as the Martiniere to Ronald Marcus Martiniere, the Martiniere-in-waiting. Because Ronald is underage, the Matriarch, Justine Solange Martiniere, is hereby appointed as Ronald's guardian and given the authority to approve decisions Ronald makes as the Martiniere. This transfer of authority is only temporary, and lasts either until I rescind it or my death or incapacity makes it permanent."

Ron straightened up, pulling his shoulders back. "I accept this temporary transfer of authority, with the understanding that it lasts either until Michael Martiniere rescinds it or becomes permanent upon his death or incapacity."

Justine rose and put her hand on Ron's shoulder. "I accept my role as Ronald's temporary guardian and agent. I understand that my role lasts only until Michael rescinds it, or is permanently incapacitated by death or other means, or Ronald reaches the age of eighteen." She paused. "Recording confirmed and switched off. Now sending it to all Martiniere links with my authority as the Matriarch."

Mike heaved a sigh. "Ron, I hope to keep your tenure short. Justine. Where do we stand? Do we need to execute a death fake?"

Justine shook her head. "Deontae and I have already taken care of that situation. That's why you went through the second car switch. It will go off of a cliff sometime in the morning, before sunrise. You went ballistic and suicidal after handing authority over to Ron, and took Jo and Al with you. And I fudged your swearing location, so no one knows where you are now."

Jo's hand fumbled for Mike's and held it tight. He clenched it, remembering when they'd recorded *that* video.

"Leave tomorrow morning, early, under new identities," she said.

"Yes," Justine said. "And keep moving for a few days." She sighed. "We'll see if our opponents accept Mike's apparent death, without a body."

"Next check in is in forty-eight hours," Al said. "We'd better sign off. Have to keep it shorter after this."

"Good luck," Justine said.

"Stay safe," Ron added.

Their images faded.

———

IN SPITE OF EVERYTHING, MIKE FELL ASLEEP FAST, WITH JO IN HIS ARMS. HE still felt dazed and groggy upon awakening. A quick breakfast and coffee didn't help, either.

Jo helped Al apply the plaskin for their first disguise while Mike went into the bathroom to use the depilatory before it was his turn. He stared at his features, suddenly aware that this might be the last time he would see his own face in the mirror for a while.

And then it distorted. An older version of his face leered out of the mirror.

"*You will be mine,*" Philip snarled. "*Just wait. You will be mine.*"

"No!" Mike yelled, grabbing hard at the sink's edge to steady himself.

"Mike? You all right?" Jo called.

Mike took several deep breaths before answering as the image settled into his own reflection.

"Nothing, Jo," he responded. "Just dropped the depilatory."

He looked down and shook his head. Was he truly going over the edge? Or was this the worm? The digital clone?

When he looked back up, Philip's image had returned.

Mike flipped him off with both middle fingers.

"You're not gonna win, motherfucker," he growled. He didn't look in the mirror again as he applied the depilatory with shaking hands.

After he was done, Mike went into the main room so that Jo and Al could put the plaskin on his face. It felt weird and stiff at first, but gradually warmed and melded with his regular skin. When Mike went back into the bathroom to look in the mirror, the unfamiliar face of Jose Olmos stared back at him.

Not Philip.

He was grateful for that small grace, and hoped it would continue as long as he wore Jose's face—and any other he might have to assume.

THEY TRAVELED AS JOSE AND ERICA OLMOS, WITH JOSE'S BROTHER TOMAS. The last vehicle they'd switched to was an ancient crew cab truck that fit their identities' profile of traveling former indentured workers for hire outside of the usual labor pools. While climate change and heat had wiped out a lot of the former ranch hand jobs in some areas, in others the ranchers had adapted and learned to cope with the heat.

Not that they were looking for work very seriously—all three of them carried a significant amount of cash and had access to burner debit accounts tied to their pseudonyms.

They needed to figure out what was happening in that outside world. But they also had to stay hidden until their next check. They drifted toward the Dineh Free State, the old Navajo and Hopi reservations, where the Swait underground linkages were strongest. Jo knew of several places along the route where they could camp out for free in the backcountry and have water access.

The land was redder in hue than the Double R. Mike noticed that as they set up camp next to a narrow gorge that cut through the rugged country. Cliffs rose high above them. He was used to desert country—the southeastern part of the Thunder Mountains was a high sagebrush and forest complex. This country made the arid Thunders look like the moist Oregon Coast Range in comparison. Red dirt everywhere he looked. Very little cover except tucked in the deep ravines that held water and shelter from the sun.

The truck came with bedrolls and a wall tent of the sort he knew from camping in the Thunders—a big tent with an internal frame and a fireproof hole for the small cookstove's vent pipe. Several tattered rugs covered the ground to keep the dust down. The tent was older than the one he used when camping with Al and the brothers as a teen, the white canvas stained in places, faintly stinking of mildew.

Mike surveyed the tent once the beds were unrolled and the tent secured.

"You sure this isn't too fancy?" he asked.

Jo laughed. "Just wait and see. We're appropriately shabby. Come on. Let's get water."

They had filled up their jugs before leaving the little cabin that morning, but needed to refill what they used during the day. Mike followed Jo along a well-trodden narrow path that wound its way down the gorge wall to the bottom, carrying battered plastic water jugs. A couple of times they paused when rattlesnakes buzzed at them, waiting to let the snake relax and retreat. That at least was familiar. He knew rattlers.

The bottom of the narrow gorge was cooler than he expected, given the heat above. But he saw why as they climbed up the bottom to where a small spring trickled into a tiny pool.

"Not drinkable without treatment, for safety's sake," Jo said. "But it's a reliable source with good water, except for any bacteria seeping into it, and that's a rare thing in this country."

Jo filled one jug and handed it to him. Then she filled the other. He took it before she could lift it.

"M—Jose," she said, continuing in Spanish as voices echoed down the draw. "I can carry it."

"Let me do it, Erica," he said back to her in Spanish, counting his lucky stars that he spoke Spanish as well as he did French. Now if it had been Russian....

They encountered another couple with empty jugs about as beat up as theirs on the way back up.

"Gracias," Mike said to the couple as they stepped aside to let him carry his load past them.

When they reached the top, he saw the second camp set up several hundred yards from theirs, made up of two tents with young children milling about as several women and men unloaded two trucks about the same vintage as theirs, only their tents looked newer.

Al looked up from cooking as they returned to camp. Mike retrieved the treatment tablets and dropped them into the jugs before putting them in the truck cab. That would be tomorrow's water.

"Connectivity sucks here," Al said as Mike returned. His Spanish was not quite as good as Mike and Jo's.

"We need to disappear, anyway," Jo said as she rummaged in a box for utensils. "Sit down and relax, Jose."

"Makes me nervous," Al said. "Sleep with weapons at hand tonight."

"That's a good idea anyway," Mike said. "There's snakes around, Tomas."

"And some are two-legged," Jo added. "Still. Poor connectivity means that anyone trying to ping us won't connect—and that's what needs to happen right now. We need some down time." She eyed Mike, mouth tightening. "You saw Philip this morning, didn't you?"

Mike sighed. He'd hoped she hadn't figured that out. "Yes," he admitted. "In the mirror. The usual *you will be mine* thing. I thought I'd been quiet."

"Your yell got my attention, and then I saw you flipping him off," Jo said. She paused by Mike and patted his shoulder. "You need a good night's sleep without ghosts. Digital or otherwise."

He couldn't argue with that.

As dusk fell, two men from the other camp cautiously approached them. The older identified himself as Manny and the younger as Jorge. Mike talked to them while Jo washed dishes and straightened things up in the tent. Al sat silently and repaired a frayed rope. Mike shared a six pack of beer with Manny and Jorge. Al turned down Mike's offer of a beer.

"Are you looking for work?" Manny finally asked after a long, circular discussion in Spanish about traveling, camping, the weather, the water, and some other things.

Mike was grateful that Gabe had insisted that he practice everyday American Spanish over the years, even if the European relatives looked down on his lack of a pure Castilian accent—Gabe could do both, but Mike had never gotten Castilian down. Near as Mike could tell, he didn't sound any different from Manny and Jorge.

"Depends on what it might be."

"Ranch work," Manny said. "Not a long job, but needs someone who knows how to work with bots."

Mike hesitated, tension tightening his muscles. Had they been betrayed? Had their foes managed to track them down? Could this be a trap? He had to think about what to say next.

"Not my strength," he said. "I am better with animals."

Manny laughed. "Alas, my friend, I am in the same position, though Jorge here is better at bots than I am. The same employer needs a few stock hands. And that is most of us looking for work right now, so there is much competition." He shrugged. "You bear the mark of the modified. Many who do have bot skills."

Mike glanced at the simulated tattoo on his hand. "I'm one of the exceptions," he said.

"Maybe one of your—companions?"

"Not my wife or my brother, alas," Mike said. "We managed to escape before much was done to us. That included learning about bots."

"How about sheep and goats?"

"More of a hand with cattle. I've used horses and dogs in herding."

Manny nodded. "You'll need to keep going to the Dineh Free State."

"That's what I had thought."

"When you get there, look up these people." Manny reeled off several names.

Jo tensed as she mended a hole in a pair of jeans.

"I thank you," Mike said.

Manny nodded, tapping the brim of his hat. "You are welcome." He and Jorge rose and returned to their camp.

Jo got up and watched them, the tension in her body warning Mike. Then she switched on the bright solar lamp hanging from the ridgepole, closed the tent flap, and activated a bug scan, her lips rolled tight with worry.

Neither Mike nor Al spoke as Jo deactivated several listening devices where Manny and Jorge had sat.

At last she switched on a low-level shield.

"Are we betrayed?" Mike asked.

Jo shook her head. "Not yet. But those names Manny gave you— bounty hunters. We've been tagged."

"ID switch?" Al asked. "Gonna be a pain without running water."

"Not yet," Jo said. "I'll work up a sim of Manny's tags. I didn't expect this to happen so quickly. It's normal enough. We hadn't been marked, so Manny did it." She grimaced. "My fault. I've lost the discipline. Too many years away from the underground. We should have been tagged before we left the cabin this morning. Then Manny wouldn't have done it, and we wouldn't have attracted his attention as unlabeled migrant travelers."

"Hey, that goes along with my miscalculation at Starshine," Mike sighed, reaching out to hug her. "You aren't the only one."

She leaned against him. "Let's hope we're done with those. We've been lucky so far."

Mike frowned. Luck only went so far, and they'd made two stupid mistakes already. Sooner or later the missteps would catch up to them.

MIKE WOKE WITH A START FROM A NIGHTMARE MIXING THE STARSHINE fight with Philip's appearances, sitting up with his heart pounding hard. A bright light outside illuminated the walls of the tent. For a moment he tensed for a fight, then relaxed as it remained steady and he recognized it.

Moonlight, not headlights or someone with a bright flashlight too close to the tent. He slumped back in the bedroll. JoAnn murmured and turned over.

He lay still, breathing deep and slow to calm himself. Finally, he gave up trying to go back to sleep anytime soon. Might as well get up.

Mike slid out of the bedroll, careful not to disturb Jo, eased past Al, pulled on his pants, and shook out his boots before putting them on. Then he untied the door and went outside.

The full moon rode high in the sky. A familiar sight from sleepless nights at the Double R—but the alien landscape it illuminated made Mike edgy rather than soothing him. It brought back memories of the first time Gabe had rocked him to sleep, curtains eased open just enough to watch the moon and stars. He'd woken from a nightmare— actually one a lot like the one that roused him tonight, with Philip rising from the dead to leer at him—*I may be dead but this isn't over, Michael. You will be mine.*

Mike shuddered. He'd forgotten until now that he'd dreamed those words *that* night. How long had that damn digital clone been active? Since Philip's death? And what had it buried in him?

He stepped several paces away from the tent and exhaled. He was already homesick for the familiar Thunder Mountains, the canyon country he knew like the back of his hand, the prairies...*Smudgie, Starlight, Spree.* The longing for *home* stuck in his throat, making him swallow hard.

God damn it, you're a grown man not a kid. You're a fucking Martiniere, not a baby. You're the *Martiniere. Act like it.*

He knelt and picked up a handful of dust to connect with the earth, a centering technique that usually worked to calm him.

Not this time. It even *felt* different from the Double R's soil. Ruby had taught him to keep in touch with the land, to do more than look at it and the stats from the RubyBot. Measure it in his hand. Get the land's *feel.*

Mike stirred it with a forefinger, idly activating his cyborging scanners to measure the dirt's composition.

So different from home.

Everything felt wrong. Sure, two of Brandon's killers were down. But there was so much more ahead for him to do. So many things to fix.

And then there was that rage deep inside of him. How much of it was Philip? Or was the family craziness finally stirring within him?

You are not Philip.

That had been everyone's mantra ever since Ruby and Gabe had rescued and adopted him.

You are Michael.

But there had been that tiny little core deep within Mike that was so different from the rest of him. That part of him capable of exploding into a destructive, killing fury.

Mike clenched his hand into a fist, then opened to slowly let the dust spill out.

We've already made too many mistakes. We can't afford many more.

Had this been one great grandiose mistake caused by his arrogant assumption that he could avenge Brandon on his own and purge the Martiniere Group? That it was up to him instead of the authorities that seemed to ignore *everything* they had been told? Doubt pulsed through him.

What was worse was that the *different* small spot deep inside him was growing, had been expanding since Brandon's death. Since he had become aware of Philip's threat.

What happens when I lose control of it?

It was definitely a case of *when*, not *if*, it broke free.

It had already broken loose once before, that night of Lily's death. What was he going to do when it took him over?

That's what it wants. Me.

Mike shuddered again. He had to stop that growth, and there was only one way he knew of to make that damned shadow shrink, at least temporarily. He didn't want to walk too much further in the direction of the other camp, and he couldn't go too far behind the tent without stumbling into the gorge. But he had to get further away.

He carefully made his way around the tent. Even with the full moon, he didn't trust himself to go too far. Too many possibilities of falling into a drop-off he didn't know about. He just had to get the right distance from the tent, so that no one would hear him.

At last, he was far enough away. Carefully, precisely, he raised his left hand to his mouth and fit his teeth on the fleshy part below the base of his thumb. A familiar action, though it had been ages since he had felt the need to do this.

Need to make sure that you don't break your teeth on your cyborging, a distant part of him cautioned. That would cause problems difficult to deal with while on the run.

He bit down carefully, until he was certain that it would block sound.

Then he screamed, biting down as hard as he dared to muffle his shrieks.

Screaming felt good. He shuddered as he kept screaming into his hand, the shakes growing in intensity. Mike dropped to his knees and doubled over, shrieking. Screech to banish his fears about something happening to Jo—*if he had been too late to keep her from taking a bite of that salad!* Shriek his rage at Brandon's senseless death. Scream his growing helplessness in the face of this damned worm, this fucking worm that wanted to strip him of his sense of self. Bellow his frustration at the digital clone that wanted to make him nothing more than the reincarnation of *Philip fucking Martiniere.*

I'll kill myself before I let him have me.

That prospect seemed all too damned real in the alien moonlight. Had he fought to stay alive in defiance of Philip all these years just for nothing? Should he have given up and died in order to thwart that fucking digital clone? Had Ruby and Gabe's efforts been in vain?

His teeth broke skin and the sour taste of blood trickled into Mike's mouth, along with the bitter tang of shredded plaskin.

He kept screaming as he fell sideways on the ground, the unfamiliar soil grinding into his cheek as he twitched. At least he wasn't inflicting this on Smudgie.

He couldn't stop, even as his mouth tightened even more on his hand. He was locked in that spiral as childhood memories crashed over him. Sobs mixed with the screams now, his whole body wracked with tremors.

Soft footfalls. Two sets of them. He'd screwed up and made too much noise. Now he was discovered.

Another damned fuckup.

"Oh Mikey," Jo whispered as she knelt next to him. She and Al raised Mike to his knees.

"Oh God," Al groaned.

His fingers were familiar, firm, as he pressed on Mike's jawbone joints, enough to make him release the grip on his hand. Mike whimpered, gasping for breath as he sagged against Jo, still shaking even as she gathered him into her arms.

"Sorry," he gulped. "Sorry I'm so fucking weak."

Al took his hand, shaking his head. "I'll get the first aid kit. You really did a number on yourself. Gonna have to keep it wrapped until the plaskin regenerates."

"Sorry," Mike repeated. "I'm so damned weak."

Jo stroked his forehead. "Mike. Like hell."

"If you'd eaten that salad…."

"But I didn't, thanks to you. I'm here, Mikey. God damn it, don't do this to yourself," Jo whispered. "Don't fucking shut me out! Especially when it gets to be too much for you! We're in this together and that means you *fucking talk to me!*"

Now he could move his arms. His hand hurt like hell, but he could still slide his uninjured arm around Jo and bury his head deep in her chest as he gasped for breath, shuddering as the black fit passed, flowing back into that tight little core inside of himself. At least it was smaller now.

Al returned with the first-aid kit and busied himself treating Mike's hand. "You didn't chew it up this time. Just a scratch, thanks to the plaskin. You'll need to run a scan later to make sure you didn't screw up any nerves. I'm going to wrap it."

"Thanks," Mike mumbled.

"Mike. What the fuck is going on?" Jo asked as Al wrapped Mike's hand.

"Did we make a mistake doing this?" he asked. "Is this one of those dumbshit grand gestures when I should have stayed locked up at home and sent out proxies? Like any sane rich guy would have done? Not played at being an Eastern Oregon cowboy?"

Al grunted. "Stop second-guessing yourself, Mike. That's not who you are."

Jo took his head in her hands. "If that had been the case, we would have stopped you before this went too damned far. You should know that. Mike. Come on. This is more than self-doubt. What the hell is going on?"

He swallowed hard, staring into those familiar, loving eyes. It was time to come clean. To both of them.

"He's in me, Jo," he said finally. "An opening for that fucking digital clone to possess me. And I—I'm just. So. Fucking. Afraid. Terrified that I'm going to go down Lily's path. That I'll lose myself to him. That's what he wants." He gulped, shuddering. "I'm trying to fight it. I really am. This is the only way I know of to make it shrink —temporarily."

"Fucking hell," Al growled. "Mike, you can do it. You've got both of us. I'm taking the kit back to the tent." He left.

"Oh, Mike." She pulled him to her again once Al was gone. "I won't let that happen. I won't. He won't take you over. I promise."

"You may have to kill me if it does happen," he whispered. "If I can't do it for myself."

"*No.* Oh God, *no*, Mikey," Jo groaned.

"It may be the only way to stop him," Mike said.

"I won't let that happen. *I won't.*" Her voice remained soft but grew more intense. "That's why I'm here, Mike. I refuse to let this happen to the man I love. I will fight him for you."

He shuddered. "You may not be able to do that, Jo. I'm serious."

"No matter what, *I will find a way*, Mikey. No matter what."

"I hope you can."

"I will if it's the last damned thing I do." Her arms tightened around him. "Now. Let's get back to the tent. Gonna be daylight soon enough. Let's eat, pack up, and get to our next site."

It took her help to get him back to his feet. But once Mike was standing, he was able to walk back to the tent, leaning on Jo.

"Whatever did I do to make you love me like this?" he whispered. "I swear, I'm the luckiest man in the world."

Jo choked. "By being who you are, Mike. By just being—Mike."

"I hope I can live up to what you see in me."

She reached up and cupped his cheek in her hand. "You already have, Michael."

He leaned into her hand and drew a ragged breath. "Oh, Jo. You are a queen among women. I love you so much. So damn fucking much."

MIKE STRETCHED OUT ON THE BACK SEAT OF THE CREW CAB, LOOSELY belted while he concentrated on first the scan and then triggering the nerve regeneration in his hand. He really had done a number on it. At least Dr. Pramula had installed self-repair nanos and left him with extras that he could inject himself at some point.

But regeneration required rest. Mike couldn't sleep very well because of the roughness of the unpaved backroads they were traveling—and even when he did sleep, Philip haunted his dreams. He woke up yelling several times.

Their contact with D was quick and hurried because there were others coming into the campsite as they spoke. So far, the authorities were distracted by the possibility of their deaths.

"That won't last long," D said. "You need to switch IDs, and soon. Sending next rendezvous for vehicle change to you, Al."

"Got it," Al said.

"Keep to the forty-eight hour check ins," D continued. "Things are moving fast. Signing off now. Stay safe."

Mike mechanically went about his share of the camp chores. When bedtime came, Jo handed him a sleeping pill.

He shook his head, but she scowled at him. "You need sleep without dreams," she insisted.

"It doesn't always work," he objected.

"Even one night will make a difference." Her face was set into stern lines.

Mike yielded.

That night his mind was fogged over and dull, and it continued into the next day. He felt like he was sleepwalking through the world. Jo insisted he take another pill the next night, and the night after. Soon Mike felt detached from everything.

The worst part was that the pills stopped blocking Philip.

Sometimes he even appeared to Mike during the day.

Mike stopped taking the pills after the first daytime appearance.

It didn't make any difference.

27 / INTERLUDE: JUSTINE AND GABE EX MACHINA

JUNE, 2086

THIS ISN'T WORKING.

Justine bit her lip as she studied her screens in the Double R's kitchen, windows wide open to let in the cool evening breeze after the day's heat.

The nice neat plan was falling apart. And she was stuck at the Double R supervising Ron and being the adult in charge of the under-aged Martiniere instead of actually doing more than chasing that damn worm through the databases. Didn't matter that she now had the power of the Martiniere, something she had quietly yearned after for years.

She hadn't wanted it like this.

—*I'm at an impasse,* Deontae had messaged her last night. —*I can't go any further in fighting that damn worm, and I've lost track of Jo and Mike. I'm worried that Ron may end up becoming the Martiniere for real.*

But that wasn't the only thing. More than ever, she kept feeling like Gabie was nearby. Her brother's shadow haunted her, resonances of his presence all around her to the degree that she almost expected to have him glide into the kitchen and startle her. Like he used to enjoy doing.

"God damn you, Gabie," Justine muttered out loud as once again she followed the electronic traces that Deontae had managed to uncover so far. "Why the hell didn't you *talk* to someone before you died? Given us some sort of warning about that damned worm?"

Oh, she knew the possible reasons for Gabe's choice to keep silent until he achieved—whatever it was he had planned to have happen. Ruby had been juggling her roles as grandmother, mother, and wife as well as ranch and corporate responsibilities. Gabe would have seen an early disclosure about the worm without offering solutions as one more burden on Ruby.

But it still would have been helpful if you'd said something about that damn fucking worm and the digital clone possibility then, Gabie. Especially since you knew it was possibly killing you. And it would have been nice to have Ruby's programming eye on this crap that our fucking father created before she died.

She sighed and pushed her chair back from the table. Gabriel. At first a cousin, then discovered to be her actual brother. And the motherfucker was just as evasive as their father at times. Frustrating as hell.

Had been, not was, she corrected herself. The sense of Gabie's presence was stronger than ever. She didn't believe in ghosts, but Ruby had reported the same sensation after his death—days when he seemed to be just out of sight.

Justine eyed her walker. By doctor's orders, she *should* be getting up and walking around. That should banish any of the *Gabie* feelings. She sighed and got up, preparing to make her circuit. Pausing at Ruby's old office, now Mike's, where Ron was doing classwork and monitoring his responsibilities as the temporary Martiniere.

"Any news?" he asked, his brows raising hopefully.

She shook her head. "Just moving like I'm supposed to do. How about you?"

"Nothing other than schoolwork and the operations decisions that I forwarded to you for approval. I'm worried."

"So am I, Ron, so am I." Justine sighed. "When I hear something, you'll be the first to know."

His lips tightened and he turned back to his screens. Justine hesitated. Like Brandon, Ron bore a close resemblance to Gabie. Oh, Ron was slightly darker-skinned than Brandon and Gabie had been, with fuller lips and short dreadlocks, but otherwise…it was like looking at a younger version of her brother.

She moved on. Living room, where she had spent so many delightful evenings with Gabe and Ruby, Mike and JoAnn over so many years. It seemed unnaturally quiet now. Neither she nor Ron had wanted to spend time there since Mike and Jo had left for Vegas—was it only six weeks now?

No. Four weeks.

It seemed like much longer.

Justine turned back, rolling her walker to the kitchen.

More resonances here, beyond Gabie startling her. Gabie cooking to relax. Him and Ruby laughing as they shared their pleasure in preparing food.

God. I miss them. They died too soon.

She collapsed back in her chair, frowning at her screens, the frustration that the walk had briefly deferred returning.

Damn it, Gabie. Why didn't you tell anyone what the hell was going on with that worm? Why did Deontae have to discover it?

Perhaps she was being far too harsh on her brother. After all, he had only figured out what was happening with the worm on the last day of his life. Had written the algorithms and programming just before stopping to spend time with Ruby on their thirteenth wedding anniversary.

Ruby and Mike were right there, at lunch. Why didn't you tell them when you had the opportunity?

Justine wearily shook her head, and scooted up to the table. She knew why. Because Gabie thought he had enough time to indulge in savoring that wedding anniversary before breaking the news. Because that damned worm had blanked it out of his thoughts. But still, damn it….

She studied the links she had been able to track. Then she bit her lip as a thought occurred to her.

Query that last link Deontae discovered.

It might be worth a try. Some of the links they'd encountered had been bare-bones interactive like that one apparently was, with a space to type questions. She hadn't tried it with this one. Yet.

—Gabie, why didn't you tell anyone? she typed into the link. Then waited.

Nothing.

Justine was about ready to give up when another link in red popped up. *Tine-GMR.*

Gabe's occasional nickname for her and the initials he used for his most private communications, reflecting his mother's Hispanic heritage. All the same, Justine scanned it to ensure safety, annoyed that she was quivering slightly with anticipation.

Clear.

She tapped the link.

Gabe appeared.

"Tine." He sighed. *"I suppose that it's you and not Mike at this point means that things are well and truly fucked. Your question has triggered an interactive algorithm. It's not completely me, it's based on an algorithm intended to create a simulacrum, and it's part of the digital clone creation process. Not a full digital clone—yet. We're at the point where drastic measures are required."* Another sigh. *"The simulacrum will ask questions. You can elaborate a little bit but not a lot. Just remember. This is a simulacrum, as life-like as it may seem. Not me. I'm definitely dead. First. Fingerprint and retina scan ID."*

What the fuck, Gabie?

How had he managed to create a sufficiently complex algorithm to do this? Was it real? It *sounded* so damned much like her brother.

An identification scanner appeared in front of her. Justine didn't think a fake would ask for an identity check, and Gabie *had* possessed the programming chops to create a digital ID scanner. She reacted like she would to the usual Martiniere request for a scan and leaned forward, eyes wide open, forcing herself not to blink at the bright light, then extending her fingertips for a full scan.

Besides, now she was curious. How the hell had Gabie managed to do all this? If this was really him.

"Identity confirmed. First question. Is Mike alive? I can't track him anymore."

"To the best of my knowledge, yes," she said.

"Sounds like you have some doubt. Elaborate." Gabe's image frowned at her.

"He has gone underground to track down the worm and Brandon's killers. He's missed several prearranged contacts."

Deeper scowl. *"Does he have support, particularly from the Swaits? Again, things are obscured and we lack sufficient data."*

We? Justine wondered, even as she answered. "Yes. JoAnn married Mike a few years ago. She is with him and Deontae has been providing coverage for them after they went underground."

A faint smile that wasn't entirely programmed. She could almost think that Gabie was truly talking to her, not a simulacrum. Wait. He said—was this part of the digital clone creation process? Her pulse quickened. She needed to remember to ask him that.

"Who is the current Martiniere-in-waiting?"

"Ron. He's acting as Martiniere since Mike disappeared."

"How old is Ron now?"

"Sixteen. As the Matriarch, I am required to approve his actions."

Gabie scowled. *"Him being underaged creates a problem. Has Deontae Swait lost track of Mike?"*

"Yes."

Another scowl. *"Not good at all, especially since it's Deontae with all of his skills. Elaborate. Number of missed check ins and everything else you know including last known location and identities."*

She drew a deep breath. "Three check ins missed during the past week. Mike, JoAnn, and Al were last in Arizona, in the Dineh Free State. I don't know what identities they are using. Lack of check in may be an issue of connectivity."

A pause. Gabie's image froze.

Finally it moved. *"Enough detail for us to find."*

Us? What does Gabie mean by "us"? He never was this casually careless when speaking in life. A problem with the algorithm?

Gabie continued. *"Thanks, Tine. I'm able to figure out what's going on with them now. They were using the identities of Nat Cruz, wife Maria, brother Chris."*

The image froze again.

"They are safe. Identity gone to ground. Chris Cruz apparently killed in

truck accident. Nat and Maria discharged after hospital treatment for superfi-
cial wounds. No further records. No record of them in custody, either visual or
coded. No further appearances of the Cruz identities. No further appearances
by anyone matching their biometrics."

"Has Chris Cruz been identified as Alexander Martiniere?" she asked, a chill sweeping through her.

Al dead. Last of the cyborged brothers that had been created to protect her father and his clones. She was not, not, not going to think about the possibility that Mike had identified himself as Chris instead of Al.

"Death is assumed. No body found in the vehicle wreckage."

A link popped up and she skimmed it. The vehicle—an old gas-fueled internal combustion truck—had gone over a cliff off of a steep canyon backroad in what had been the old Navajo reservation and was now the Dineh Free State. It had caught fire. Nat and Maria Cruz had been picked up hobbling away from it.

That's not right. Both Mike and Al spent too damn much time cruising *around Hells Canyon. They know how to drive those kinds of roads.*

A deliberate attempt in order to change identities, or the result of an attack? Clearly not what it seemed.

"Al may still be alive," she mused.

Surely some part of Al's cyborging would have survived even a fire. Or Mike's. Either one. Whichever, this meant JoAnn was still alive. A minor consolation. With any luck, both Mike and Al had gotten free.

"Probability of 83%." Gabie rubbed his face—another mannerism so much like the live Gabriel that it hurt.

"What the hell do I do next, Gabie? I don't know how far Mike's gotten with avenging Brandon's death. He and Jo took out two of the assassins. Maybe more. None of us can get a handle on the worm. I'm weeding it out of the Martiniere databases and locking the back doors but the process is as slow as fuck even with Ron and Deontae's help. And then there's that fucking digital clone. It's been three fucking months since Brandon died. How much longer is this going to take? I'm getting old and I'd like to see Daddy-fucking-dearest's influence gone before I die. And then there's that fucking digital clone."

The image froze again. This time the freezing lasted long enough that she thought she'd lost the connection.

At least I have some idea about why they might not have checked in. I'll have to pass that information on to Deontae.

Just as she reached into her screen to disconnect and call Deontae, the image moved again. A second image joined Gabie and Justine gasped in shock, covering her mouth with both hands.

Ruby. Oh my God. Ruby.

Only a younger Ruby, the age Ruby had been when Justine first met her through Ruby's work at horse trainer Lora Smith's barn, without either of them knowing the significance until years later. How had Ruby managed to create an algorithm like Gabie's without Justine knowing? God, if she'd known she could access Ruby she would have done so ages ago.

"Does Mike own Spree again?" Ruby asked.

Justine frowned at that question. "Yes. Ruby, you know that! You bought her back and gave her to Mike."

The Ruby simulacrum shook her head. *"I'm missing a lot of information. The worm destroyed many of my records, and I can't access data originating after Gabe's death with any dependable accuracy. Did Spree have any foals that Mike has been riding?"*

"Yes. Her son, Starlight. Mike's shown him. They've won several reined cowhorse championships. Starlight is here on the ranch, standing at stud."

That earned a faint smile from Ruby.

At least that much remains of her. The living Ruby would have been much more excited about Mike and Starlight!

"Does Mike still have heelers that are descendants of Smudge?" the Gabie simulacrum asked.

"Yes. A Smudge grandson who is elderly. Here on the ranch, not with Mike. Pups that Mike hasn't seen yet."

Another moment where Gabie's image rubbed his face. Then the two images exchanged knowing glances. Gabie raised his brows. Ruby nodded. Gabie smiled and she grinned back.

That made her ache. She missed Gabie and Ruby, and seeing this interaction so much like when they were alive brought back fond but painful memories.

"*That's a piece of good news,*" Ruby said.

"Why?"

"*Sleeper genetic modification in Spree that Gabe and I created which would pass on to her foals,*" Ruby said. "*Same for Smudge and his descendants. Targeted specifically to Mike, useless for anyone else.*"

"What the hell are you talking about?"

"*Support mechanisms for Mike using Spree and Smudge descendants,*" Ruby said. "*For just this sort of potential situation.*"

"*My data says that Mike fully activated his cyborg units—arms, legs, heart, lungs. Correct?*" Gabie asked.

"Yes."

"*Good.*" Another long, frozen pause before Gabie spoke again. "*All right, Tine. Information processed, all of it. I need you to type down what I say, read it back to me, then print it out so you have hard copies that won't disappear. I will speak of the algorithm. That's me and Ruby combined and not the simulacrums you are seeing now. Not digital clones yet, just the potential for digital clones.*"

"Okay," she said. She set herself up. "Ready."

"*First. Mike needs to come back to the Double R. The showdown with the digital clone should be there. He needs the support of his horses and dogs. They will keep him centered.*" Gabie's image paused again, shorter this time. "*Ah. Trace worked and their current identities recovered. Now traveling as Steven Rodriguez, father, with son Carlos and daughter Alicia. Very brief flash.*"

Hope surged. "All three of them?"

"*Yes. Now in southern Utah, traveling north. Second. Our combined algorithm will contact Mike. Third. Our algorithm is sending a message to you and Deontae Swait. There will be a link. Type in the word fulfillment. Both of you simultaneously. You need to follow those instructions exactly.*"

"What purpose does that serve?"

"*It will temporarily freeze the worm and let Mike get to the ranch safely without further interference. Unfortunately, we have not found a means to permanently eliminate it. That will be the job of the Martiniere, whether it's Mike or Ron.*"

The voice no longer sounded like an exact copy of Gabie. "Excuse me. You are not sounding right. Run self-check."

"Advice accepted. At this point you are speaking directly to our combined algorithm and not material that Gabriel Marcus Martiniere has previously recorded. Continue with self-check?"

"Yes."

A long pause.

"Self-check complete for both of us. Match for algorithm-generated information and not prerecorded material from Gabriel Marcus Martiniere and Ruby Marie Barkley. Continue?"

What the hell. She might as well find out what the rest of these instructions were. "Yes."

"Fourth." The projection halted as Ron entered the kitchen.

"What on earth?" He reached out, almost touching the two images, then pulled back. "Grandma? Grandpa? What is this?" His voice quavered.

"Identify new person."

"It's two interactive simulacrums that your grandfather created before his death," she said to Ron. "They are giving me instructions about what to do next."

"Like Grandpa's earlier video?"

"Similar. You need to identify yourself for it to continue. Security protocols."

"All right." Ron swallowed hard and straightened himself slightly, projecting that sense of *presence* that Justine had seen Gabe, Brandon, and Mike do when acting officially as the Martiniere. "I am Ronald Marcus Martiniere, Martiniere-in-waiting, currently serving as Martiniere in the absence of Michael Marcus Martiniere."

"Retina scan and fingerprint, please."

Ron stepped forward and inclined his head for the ID check, then extended his hands for the fingertip scan.

"Identity confirmed. Do not speak further until instructions have been concluded. Fourth. When our algorithm contacts you, Justine, and you, Ron, you must go to the place indicated. Bring the horses Starlight and Spree, and the dog Smudgie and his pups. Repeat these instructions."

Justine obeyed.

"Very well." The tone of the voice changed to sound more like Gabie. *"Justine. Print those instructions out promptly."*

"Doing it now, Gabie."

"Grandpa. Grandma. My dad—is he with you?"

"No, Ron. He—" Gabie's voice trailed off, sorrow dominating his expression.

"We can't build a core algorithm. Too much is missing," Ruby said.

"Brandon's files are even more corrupted with trigger viruses than Ruby's were," the Gabie simulacrum said, the anguish in his voice again sounding so much like the real, long-gone Gabriel, that Justine gulped, surprised by the wetness forming in her eyes. *"It was sheer luck that I could recreate Ruby. The worm didn't damage her files as much as it did Brandon's."*

"Oh, those bastards," Justine growled as Ron suddenly sniffled. "Those fucking bastards."

"We'll make them pay," Ruby's simulacrum said grimly.

Gabie smirked at her. *"Yes. We will."*

Tears ran down Ron's cheeks. "Can't you even *try*? I'd be willing to work with your algorithm to fix it if that means we can get Dad back—even in this form."

Ruby sighed. *"What's left would create something even worse than Philip and Lily's simulacrums if we try to revive it. We don't have enough for a core digital persona. I wish—I wish I were more substantial so that I could do a better job of comforting you."*

"What was done to us was bad enough, Ron," Gabie said. *"Your father—the worm's goal was the utter destruction of him both physically and electronically. To my dismay, it succeeded. Philip tried to do it to me, too. He failed. Mike is his target now. Philip wants to download as a digital clone into Mike's body—that's been his goal for a physical clone. He and Lily are laying siege to Mike in order to break him down. Mike's fighting, but even with JoAnn's help—Philip enlisted the help of those supporters that Mike and JoAnn managed to kill. They're using that extra strength to overwhelm him."*

"No," Ron groaned. "Not Mike too!"

"We won't let that happen," Justine said firmly.

Her comm chimed. *"Deontae Swait."*

"Open," Justine said.

Deontae scowled as the link opened. "Justine. I just got a message from that friendly algorithm to call you, with a link."

"I'm talking to it—*them*—right now."

"Them?"

"Gabriel *and* Ruby. Simulations created by that algorithm."

"Does that mean that Bran too—?" Deontae's voice trailed off hopefully.

"He's gone, Deontae," Justine said. "They can't restore him."

Deontae closed his eyes for a moment and shook his head, grimacing.

"The good news is that Mike and Jo are alive. In southern Utah. They have to come here. We have to enter the code word into the link at the same time to temporarily freeze the worm. Mike has to finish the job, but we can pause that damned thing."

"Well, that's a bit of good news," Deontae said. "How soon? I'm ready to do it now."

"All right," Justine said. She opened her matching message. "My link is open."

"Mine is too," Deontae said.

"All right. Entering it." She typed the word *fulfillment* into the link. "Done."

"Done," Deontae echoed.

"Pressing enter—now!"

For a moment she wondered if they'd see any results. Then Ruby and Gabie's forms shimmered, fading slightly. Her screen quivered.

Then everything returned to full brightness. Ruby and Gabie smirked, smacking their palms together in a silent high-five as they became more solid than before. Gabie's form scooped up Ruby's and swung her around him.

"We did it, Ruby-girl, we did it, we did it, we did it! We're now full digital clones!" he exulted as he released her. *"I am so damn glad I could reconstruct you. I couldn't have done those last steps alone!"*

"Could you ever have?" She grinned at Gabie. Then she shook her finger at him. *"But Justine is right. You should have fucking told me and Mike about this before you died! Damn it!"*

"I know. I screwed up again. I miscalculated how long I had and didn't

calculate that the worm would kill me that quickly. But I'm a lot better gambler with your support. And we did it. We have a fighting chance now."

"Fighting chance?" Ron said slowly.

"Yes." Gabie turned to face them, expression turning solemn. *"It was a gamble. That worm is really difficult to defeat, and I underestimated the power of digital clones, especially over their physical counterparts."*

"Can downloading digital clones into existing bodies really be done?" Deontae asked. "Or are we just talking hypotheticals?" He grimaced. "Mike's my brother-in-law and Jo's running underground with him. I need to know if my sister is safe."

"Mike's upgrades of his cyborg parts kept Philip from killing him outright, and provided the ability to resist. But that is breaking down. Mike needs his horses and his dogs to make it stronger. He has to return to the ranch. JoAnn is still safe."

"Gabe, I don't like the *still* in that comment." Deontae scowled.

"Deontae, that's why they need to get back to the ranch. As soon as possible."

"So it is possible. Can you two—?" Justine asked.

"No, we won't download into living bodies," Ruby cut Justine off before she could finish talking.

"Absolutely not," Gabie added. *"Not going to establish precedent. The morality of downloading into a living body and displacing the person in it sucks. I won't do it. Not even to stop Philip."*

"Neither will I," Ruby said. Her form shivered. *"We ran simulations, Justine. The results are hideous because the mind twists. A constant battle between the existing mind and the possessing mind which drives both entities insane. There can't be multiple digital clones of a single personality. We're working on means to stop anyone from ever being able to create the possibility of downloading into a live body again—that's what happened to Lily. Philip possessed her."*

Justine shuddered. "God. Ruby. I wish we'd known."

"Another way that I was a dumbass," Gabie growled. *"I should have been following what was happening with Lily more closely. But I just didn't want to think about it."*

"You were sick," Ruby said firmly. "And the worm kept us from concen-

trating on Lily. We can talk about that aspect later. Right now we need to focus on killing the worm—plus Philip's algorithm."

"Tine. Philip has attempted multiple downloads into Mike that have failed," Gabie said. "Combining with Lily gave Philip more strength. JoAnn and Mike together have been able to stop them, but that ability is fading under continued assault. Talk about perfect timing for querying me, Tine."*

"So why didn't you give me any clues sooner?"

"Tine, I tried. That's why I wanted you protected. I fiddled with my video to send the message to protect you. With Ruby dead, you were the only one I could reach reliably, and even then, it took me until now to get through to you."

"Not Mike?"

"Not even Brandon. We still have a problem. Ruby and I can't initiate contact after we shut down to recharge, and it takes us a while to restructure when we do get activated. That's not the case with Philip and Lily. They're running continuously. We aren't. We've been trying to work around that."

"How can we change that situation?" Ron dropped into a chair across the table from Justine and brought up one of his screens. "Is it a matter of keeping a link open at all times? Or can we modify your programming to override that element?"

"Can't do that from our side," Gabie said. *"And long-term links degrade. It's a question of how I did the programming to differentiate it from that damned worm."*

"Okay," Ron said, frowning. "So why don't we just send a plane for Mike and JoAnn, get them here sooner?"

Good boy, Justine thought. He'd make an excellent Martiniere once he was older.

"Too much hackable programming," Gabie said grimly. *"Can you help us match Philip and Lily's programming stability?"*

""We need to create a non-degradable, stable portal for you from this side of the link. Right?"

"Right."

Ron bit his lip, frowning into his screen. "Is it something that I can do as the Martiniere? After all, that damned worm seems to be able to generate its own portals."

"The methodology that worm uses is unstable," Gabie said.

Ruby frowned at him. *"It's more than unstable. It's chaotic."*

"D, what do you think?" Ron asked.

"What do you mean by 'the methodology is unstable/chaotic?" Deontae frowned at Gabie and Ruby. "The portal, the links, or the worm's processes?"

Justine drew a ragged breath as she watched the four—two living, two digital reconstructions—brainstorm further. It wasn't her area of strength.

Maybe everything would turn out all right after all.

Maybe.

She'd believe it when Mike and Jo were safely back at the Double R and that damned digital clone of her father was destroyed.

28 / STRIKING BACK

Age: 31

THIS ISN'T WORKING.

Mike could barely think for the racket in his head. He bit down hard on the towel to muffle his screams, rocking back and forth in the bed despite Jo's arms around him. Philip and Lily screeched in his mind, blocking out Jo and Al. And it was almost too damned late. He couldn't hold out much longer against Philip's *presence* pushing on him.

God. Now he had complete and utter sympathy for Lily and her voices. Her self-destructiveness. A part of him could observe from on high but it couldn't touch the man having a meltdown in the motel bed. How had Lily managed to hold out against Philip for so long? Why couldn't he be that strong?

At least Jo had substituted a towel for his hand to bite down on. That distant, rational part of Mike was not only grateful for that, but cringed at what he was putting her through. Occasionally that piece of himself could emerge and take control before things got too bad. Not now.

He wasn't fighting it anymore. He had been able to hold this meltdown off until they had gotten into the room, for Al and Jo's sakes. However, he could sense it coming, had warned them about it in one of his coherent moments that afternoon. They had decided then and there to find a motel room, damn it all, because all three of them were drained. They needed showers. Real beds. Bathroom. No energy for getting water, setting up camp, and digging latrines. Not all that and somehow endure this meltdown.

That stupid truck wreck hadn't helped, either. Al had managed to salvage some of their things before burning the truck. Not enough, though. And it was his damned fault for freaking out at absolutely the worst damn time to cause that damned wreck. Had almost hurt Jo *bad*, and it was his fault. The resulting panic had been enough for Mike to resist the siege from the voices for two days, but now they were back, worse than ever.

There had to be a means to break through all this. There *had* to be. But Mike was so exhausted when the clamor ceased that he could do little more than sleep.

It wasn't how they had planned it. It wasn't what he had planned at all. Something had gone seriously wrong.

Sometimes he thought he sensed Ruby trying to break through the clatter. That had to be yet another hallucination. And yet that sense of Ruby's presence was a welcome precursor to the moments when the din eased just enough for him to be rational again.

But it wasn't enough. The silence never lasted for more than a few hours. And then the cacophony raged stronger after that brief reprieve.

"Mike." Ruby's voice. Stronger than it had been until now.

He groaned as Lily and Philip shrilled louder.

"Michael." Ruby's stern tone.

The next step would be his full name and he'd get his butt kicked but good. Oh God. If only this were real and Ruby was there. Mike would take any degree of scolding if he could hear Ruby's voice again. Something sane. Something different.

He'd tried to kill himself this afternoon in a clear moment, because the voices were just too overwhelming. Philip was so damned close to winning control. Sooner or later he would force Mike to turn on Jo. Hurting Jo as a means of finally breaking Mike to his will.

That was Philip's plan. He taunted Mike with it.

Mike had warned Jo and Al about that scenario when Al had

wrenched the gun away from him, as a justification for the attempt. Begged Al to kill him and get Jo to a safe place. Broke down crying when Al refused.

He had to push the meltdown. Maybe he could overclock the cyborging safety mechanisms and kill his heart. If he couldn't kill himself one way, then there had to be another. For Jo's sake.

In spite of it all, Jo still held him, curled around Mike's back and rocking with him, crooning in a half-broken voice that wrenched his heart when he could pay attention to it. That physical contact was the only thing that provided him with the barest link to reality.

"Michael Marcus Martiniere, knock it off!" Ruby's full bellow. The *I'm-fed-up-and-you-need-to-listen-now* tone.

It stopped his screaming. But he still shook. Still rocked. Still bit down on the towel.

The babble in his head ceased abruptly, followed by a sensation that almost felt like Ruby's hand stroking his brow. Whatever it was, it brought a peace he hadn't experienced for some time.

Mike stopped rocking and sagged into the bed, grabbing the towel out of his mouth and hurling it across the room because he couldn't stand its rough texture against his lips and tongue for another moment.

If only this were real. But at least maybe he could catch his breath for a moment, gain some strength against a continued assault. Peace. Calm.

Jo's gasp snapped his eyes open. Mike stared at Ruby's kneeling form in front of him, her pixelated hand brushing his face, *and he could feel it.* Not the old woman she had been when she died, but Ruby when he'd first seen her. And it was a *solid* touch.

"This can't be real," he mumbled, barely able to move his aching jaw.

"I see her too, Mikey," Jo's voice quavered. "Al?"

"If this is an illusion, all three of us are seeing it," Al said.

"About fucking time," the Ruby image said. She straightened up and stood, arms crossed. Gabe joined her—a younger version of him.

"What the hell?" Mike asked wearily. Had his craziness infected all three of them?

"You're fighting competing algorithms helping Philip's digital clone," the Gabe form said. *"They've upped their strength by consuming others in order to attack you and hold us off. We finally got through to Justine, and now we're full digital clones. We're digital simulations of what we were when we were alive, and we can do limited physical manifestations. Have some effect on physical bodies, not much. We're still dead, though."*

"Wait, what?" Jo sat up, resting her hands on Mike's side. He was too tired to do anything more than lie there and stare at Ruby and Gabe.

"I wrote an interactive algorithm based on what analysis I could make of Philip's worm on the day I died," Gabe said. *"You saw the video. That was the first part. But in order to keep it safe, I had to disable certain aspects of Philip's worm in my duplicate programming."* He winced. *"Unfortunately, that's the part that has kept his worm active and allowed him to accumulate allies. He possessed Lily and borrowed from her. It wasn't until Justine finally fucking listened to my hints and activated me that we've been able to create a workaround resulting in complete digital clonehood for Ruby and me. Still working on it."*

That was enough to energize Mike to sit up. "Lily was possessed?" It confirmed his suspicions.

Both Gabe and Ruby's images nodded.

"Fuck." Mike exhaled. "That explains a lot." Then hope grabbed at him. "Were you able to retrieve Bran?"

"No." Sorrow tinged Ruby's voice. That was enough to send Mike crashing back onto the bed in despair.

"Philip targeted Brandon like he is doing to you, Mike," Gabe said. His expression went flat. *"Philip's been able to recruit more strength from the assassins you killed. Bran—Philip would do the same thing to him. Make Bran his. We don't dare reconstruct him as a result. Meanwhile, Philip's followers are sacrificing themselves to give him more strength."*

"So it's not just Philip and Lily coming after Mike," Jo said, rubbing Mike's back.

"No. It's not. We were able to freeze the worm temporarily, which locks up Philip's digital clone. Deontae and Ron are working to give us equal ability to Philip in physical form, without sucking energy from living people or killing them. Meanwhile, you need to get back to the ranch, Mike. You need the

support of your horses and dogs as well as JoAnn. We've programmed that capacity into their genetics. Spree and her descendants, Smudge and his."

"Best case scenario is that the freeze gives you four days to get there," Ruby added. *"Worst case—I don't think Philip can crack what we did in less than forty-eight hours."*

Mike heaved a heavy sigh and pushed himself up. "Then we'd better get going. The way everything's been going wrong—"

"Mikey, you can't. Gabe, Ruby, we can't just pick up and leave right now," Jo said. "Mike's been fighting this for days, and he's wiped out. We're exhausted from helping him. We need to rest. Why can't Justine send a plane to get us back to the Double R?"

"The problem is that there aren't any planes that aren't hackable by Philip's damned digital clone," Gabe said. *"Even with him frozen. Latent links. Too big a risk."*

"Oh. Shit." Jo frowned.

"We'll do what we can to fortify you from our side, and keep the freeze going if it takes you longer to get back," Ruby said. *"You'll need to go in through the back door because the main routes are watched by Philip's people. You will have to deal with lack of connectivity so you can't draw on our resources consistently—but that will affect Philip's manifestations as well. Just get yourself to Thunder County, Mike. The mountains. The land. Take the time to rest tonight. Then go like hell."*

"We'll be watching over you," Gabe added. *"As best as we can."*

"Good luck," Ruby said.

The images winked out. Mike tensed against another possible onslaught of the voices.

Nothing. And he didn't even have that lingering sense of that dark side of himself. It wasn't there.

He exhaled. "It's gone, Jo. The voices are gone." He gulped, suddenly overwhelmed. "Oh God. If this is true—"

"It *has* to be true," Jo said grimly. "I won't accept anything less." She bent over and kissed his temple. "Meanwhile, Mikey. Rest. We'd all better do our best to get a good night's sleep."

Mike pushed himself up, suddenly aware of how gritty and sticky he felt.

"I want to eat and shower first." He inhaled. Exhaled. "And I'm taking off my face. We all are. If this is it—if this is the final showdown —then I'm going as myself. All three of us are supposed to be dead, so we won't be dealing with authorities looking for us. Running a disguise takes more energy than I'm willing to give right now. My focus has to be on getting the hell to the Double R and preparing for that fight."

It was telling that neither Jo nor Al offered an argument as he hobbled over to his suitcase to pull out underwear and a t-shirt to change into.

"You gonna be okay showering by yourself?" Jo asked. "Because I'm gonna plot our trip home. If we can query Ruby and Gabe, and D's hooking into them, then I can as well."

"I should be fine," Mike said.

He hurt all over from the meltdown spasms, but it was a hell of a lot better than going through liquid nanobuild.

Al got up. "I'm checking the rig. Tires, fluids, charge. Make sure we have enough supplies for a long haul. Last thing we need is a breakdown."

"Think we might be able to get something in better shape to replace that junker?" Mike asked.

"In this town? Gonna take luck and cash," Al said. "Unless you want to pull on the credit. But that'll flag us."

"Take the emergency fund in addition to your debit," Mike said. "I'll transfer the rest of my debit funds to you—Jo, do the same. Get a rig that will hold up to backroads. If we're going in the back way to the Double R—well, you know that country, too, Al." He paused, quickly authorizing the money transfer. "It can be old. Plain vanilla farm truck that isn't beat to shit. You know what we need."

Al nodded curtly. "Got it."

Mike flipped through the remaining wad of cash he kept in his suit-case. He held out just enough for food and fuel—then hesitated. Took more from that pile.

Their last charge or refuel could be credit. By then it wouldn't matter. A better vehicle was more important. He handed the cash to Al.

"Get us the best damn vehicle possible with this."

Al nodded again and left.

THE PLASKIN STUNG AS HE PEELED IT OFF IN THE SHOWER. MIKE RUBBED the pieces of plaskin between his hands until it dissolved and ran down the drain, then lifted his real face gratefully to the lukewarm water trickling out of the shower head. He took deep breaths as he washed. The cleansing felt symbolic. An erasure of the failures. The mistakes.

That damn worm had its hooks in me, too.

Just as it had pushed Brandon to his death, it had been trying to break him as well. Only death hadn't been its goal for him.

Lily was possessed. Philip tried to possess me. And tried to get Jeremy to copy me.

Now the pieces all fell together. He suspected that this had been a long-term plan on Philip's part, a last-chance attempt at longer life. If not immortality. If Gabe hadn't somehow managed to put the pieces together on that last day of his life....

And when did Philip start programming me for this likelihood?

Mike stepped out of the shower and dried off as best as he could with the far-too-small, ragged towel that Jo had stuffed in his mouth. He hung it up and went to the sink, gripping the rim as he looked into the mirror, half-anticipating Philip's sneer.

Nothing. The face staring back at him was gaunt and drawn, almost skeletal, with red patches on his cheekbones where the plaskin had irritated his skin. Thinner than he'd been during cancer. He had lost too damn much weight over the past month, between being on the run and fighting against being possessed.

But it was *his face*, not Philip's. Not Jose, not Nat, not Carlos or the other identities that now blended into one over the past month.

I am Michael Marcus Martiniere. No one else. Michael. Husband to JoAnn. Michael. Brother to Brandon. Michael. Uncle of Ron. Michael. Son of Gabe and Ruby. Michael. And I will prevail.

He pulled on his clothing, then hesitated as an idea came to him.

"Gabe?" he said softly.

Could he be so easily summoned? Gabe might know whether

Philip had been trying to program him for possession from the beginning. One way to find out.

Pixels shimmered in front of him. Then Gabe was there. *"Mike."*

"Are you in an afterlife?" An irrelevant question, but all the same, elation rose in Mike. It worked.

"Not really. It's an assembler algorithm. It becomes more real with more data and contacts. We seem realistic because a lot of recordings exist for our algorithms to draw upon to create a digital clone."

"I think," Mike began slowly, thinking as he spoke. "That a susceptibility to this worm might somehow have been programmed into me from the very beginning. I've always sensed a part of me that was—Philip, for lack of a better description. Now I have to wonder about that. Especially since I don't feel it at all since the worm's been frozen."

"It's entirely possible." The Gabe image rubbed his chin, just like the real Gabe had done. *"It would be in your creation file."*

"Someone hacked that file just before Brandon's death. Could the Philip digital clone do that?"

"Very possible. Those files were locked down solid. None of us could get into them. I've always wondered how your creation file was available for you to find when you were a kid. It wasn't visible in your directory before you first saw it. That would point to the likelihood of the algorithm manipulating that file."

"I think I had some sort of back door built into me," Mike said. "Mind control programmed into a developing clone. Is there any possibility we can do something about it before the showdown?"

"We need time. You'll have to open the file for us while you still have connectivity."

"We're going to be on the road for a while. I'd feel one hell of a lot better if we can do something about closing or at least barricading that hole before I go head-to-head with Philip. It's a vulnerability."

"Worth a try," Gabe said.

"Then we'll do it," Mike said firmly.

"All right." Gabe grinned. *"But you'd better get some food and rest. Especially if you're planning to hack yourself while traveling."*

"Okay. And Gabe—thanks. For everything."

Gabe's lips tightened. *"Just eliminate my fucking father. For what he did to me and Ruby. To Lily. To Bran. To you. Make damn good and sure he's dead. Avenge us."*

"I will," Mike promised, as Gabe's pixels shimmered away.

Jo looked up as Mike entered the main room, her face tight and worried. "I heard you talking."

"To Gabe," he said, noticing how the worry faded from her face and her shoulders relaxed once he said that. "Making plans." He wrapped his arms around her neck and shoulders, resting his head on Jo's.

"I'm glad you're feeling better," she said, leaning into him.

"Yeah. I had a thought while showering, which is why I called him up. That hack into my file just before Brandon's death. There's— always been something of Philip in me. I don't feel it now. Gabe and I talked about the possibility that there might be a mind control back door programmed into me that got hacked. We're—gonna work on it while traveling."

"Hmm. That angry piece you've talked about?"

"Uh-huh."

"I think the back door might be older than that. The night after Lily's suicide."

"I realized I was a clone when I was ten," Mike said. "When that file first surfaced. Now I've gotta wonder, because a couple of years later another nasty file popped up."

"You're going to work on this with them, I hope?"

"I don't think I dare do this without Gabe and Ruby's help," he said.

Her hands slipped up and tightened on his. They stood like that for a few moments. Then Mike sighed, and went to rummage in the cooler for food. He could tell he was not that far away from crashing, and he didn't want to do it on an empty stomach.

FOR THE FIRST TIME IN WEEKS, MIKE SLEPT WITHOUT BEING AWARE OF HIS dreams. It was still dark when he roused, Jo spooned into the fold of his body. She hadn't done that for at least a week, not since the wreck. He wrapped his arms around her, grateful.

She kept faith with him through this nightmare. God, what could he do to pay it back to her?

Fix this situation once and for all. And then you spend the rest of your life doing whatever it is she wants you to do.

Jo stirred and turned to face him. "Mikey," she whispered, reaching out to touch his face. "It's still you. Not—" Her voice broke and she buried her head in his chest, shaking with repressed sobs. Mike held her close, pressing little kisses on her head. At last she shuddered and looked up, her eyes still wet. "This last week. I thought I'd lost you. And yesterday—oh God, I was so fucking scared when you tried to kill yourself. Terrified that I was going to lose you."

"You were," he murmured. "I couldn't see my way out. I—it was worse than when I was at my sickest. When Al took that gun away and I felt the meltdown coming on, I wasn't sure what was going to happen." He swallowed. "I thought—I thought if I pushed it enough, that I'd find a way to overclock my cyborg programming and make my heart stop. I've never been given those codes. But I thought it was possible. I reached my breaking point yesterday afternoon, Jo. I'm afraid that if Gabe and Ruby hadn't intervened—Philip would have taken me, if I hadn't found a way to kill myself instead."

"*Mike.*"

"He was so close, Jo. So damn close. And he would have made me hurt you. Worse than the wreck. I couldn't face that, Jo. I just—couldn't."

Jo gulped. "I am so damn glad that it didn't happen. Everything."

"So am I." He stroked her cheek. "Jo. When this is done. I owe you so much. We'll do whatever it is you want to do. Without reserve. I will do anything you want. Give you anything you want. Blank check. You call the shots."

"A quiet life with you, Mikey," she whispered. "That's what I want. That's all I've ever wanted." She tried and failed to smile. "Maybe a vacation. We've never had more than a week off. And time with the nieces and nephews. Maybe helping other kids too."

"I'd like that," he said. "Wherever. Your choice."

The thought of helping kids sounded really good to him. A means to pay back all those people who had helped him.

"Let's just get through this in one piece first, okay?"

"Okay."

They lay together in silence after that, arms around each other.

MIKE SPENT THE DAY STRETCHED OUT ON THE BACK SEAT OF THE NEW truck, a plain crew cab that had clearly seen better days. Most of its issues were cosmetic, though—the engine purred along and best of all, the systems were simple enough that the three of them could hack quick repairs for it if necessary.

He was half-aware of Al and Jo's occasional conversation in the front, but most of his focus was on the file he had opened as well as the programmable parts of himself. He'd never gone into the details behind his creation before except for quick looks.

"Should have done this when I was still alive," Gabe muttered at one point. *"Would have been easier."* The two of them were deep into a programming sequence that *could* be disabled via algorithm.

"I didn't investigate this file further because every damn time I looked at it when I was younger, I risked a panic attack," Mike said.

"Yeah, and we were busy dealing with your physical legacy. Gotta be delicate with this matrix, Mike. Philip set it up for digital clone involvement, anticipating the possibility of possessing you in ways that he couldn't do with others, even Lily. But he wasn't trying to preserve your personality structures."

Lily. Whenever he thought of how Philip's digital clone had set out to seduce her to his cause, Mike felt sick. He understood the process better by hacking himself, and it turned his stomach.

Hell, the degree to which mind control structures had already been programmed into his biology from earliest development made him ill. How had he managed to resist? Al and the brothers had played a role in his resistance. The further he dug into his files, the clearer it became that they had not followed the script to make little Michael compliant to Philip's demands.

Lucky clone number thirteen.

Lucky because the cyborged brothers were sick of watching Philip exploit and destroy his clones, and had the independence to do something about it.

Lucky that they had deliberately sabotaged Philip's goals, even though they hadn't been fully aware of his plans for *this* clone.

Lucky being raised by the Matriarch and the Martiniere. Lucky with Brandon as his big brother.

By accident, the community that raised him had saved him from this fate.

Lucky thirteen.

BY MIDDAY, MIKE WAS READY TO TAKE A BREAK. HE AND GABE HAD BEEN able to defuse the worst of the programming elements. The back-door access wasn't completely locked off, but it was less vulnerable than it had been. The rest required biologic intervention and would have to wait until he was back at the Double R, with the support of the labs and his companion animals.

That was another protective piece. His animals. The immediate attraction to the horses and then the dogs.

Mike exhaled and sat up, Gabe momentarily silent as his algorithm followed another trace.

Barren basin land still, though there were mountains looming ahead.

"Where are we?" he asked.

"Getting ready to leave Utah," Al said. "We could go faster on the main routes."

"Can't do that. Watchers," Jo said. "Ruby's flagged them. They don't have our current vehicle ID, but it won't take long to track down." She turned in her seat. "How's your work going, Mike?"

He exhaled. "Worst of it is defused. I still need to do more, but that's all biologics." He shivered. "Al. If you and the others hadn't resisted following the programming Philip wanted me to undergo, things would be a lot worse. Thank you for everything you guys did. Until this morning I didn't realize how important that was."

"We were tired of what was happening," Al said, his words short and sharp. "Sick of seeing little kids die. Sick of what Philip put you and your Befores through. It was time for all that to stop. Plus me knowing who my mother was, unlike my brothers, also made a huge difference. I could be independent in a way that my brothers couldn't."

"It was crucial in keeping me myself and not a vessel for Philip," Mike said. He fumbled in the cooler for yet another tube of Liquid Protein. "If I never suck down another tube of this stuff it will be too soon," he muttered.

"What's that?" Al growled as Mike finished the tube. "Cars blocking the road ahead of us. Official?"

Jo faced back forward, her fingers dancing in a projection. "Not from what I see."

"Get in the back seat, JoAnn," Al ordered. "On the floor. Mike. Arm up."

Mike and Jo switched seats. He reached under the glove box for the SPA-29 case magnetically attached there, popping it open and quickly assembling the short-barrel (and highly illegal) automatic rifle, shoving extra ammo clips into his back pockets.

"Ready," he said, eying the blockade. Room to get around off the road if they went into four-wheel mode. "Jo. Still no official IDs?"

"Barely close enough to scan," she said.

Ruby popped up between Mike and Al. *"I've got them. Loyal Indentured IDs. Discontinued. But augmented. Matching those fucking assassins."*

Mike reached through her projection to pop open the sunroof that had a drop-down brace for someone standing up (*and why on earth did anyone want that feature in a work truck? Along with the self-inflating tires. There'd been something screwy about this rig supposedly just for four-wheeling but now he was grateful for these extra features. Even if it meant Al had bought it from a smuggler*).

—*Activate half levels and blur shield,* he clicked to his cyborging. "Going up, Al. Half levels and blur shield."

"Done, for me as well," Al answered.

Mike slid up and locked into the brace. If he'd had any doubts before, the data available to him with partial cyborg activation confirmed the blockaders as Loyal Indentureds. They alerted, starting to raise their weapons as he popped through the sunroof.

He elected for quantity over quality and blasted the blockaders. Didn't get them all—he saw two of them duck into their vehicles.

My cyborging's faster, even at half levels.

Good to know.

The survivors fired at them. Mike shot back as Al veered off of the road. Jolted as Al came to an abrupt halt.

"Run up on a rock—gotta reverse!" Al yelled.

There were more survivors of his first spray of shots than he thought, breaking free from their rigs and running toward them. Mike ejected one clip and jammed in another, firing at the runners as Al backed up, then accelerated through the rough terrain, though not as fast.

One of their shots hit his left shoulder. He slammed against the rim of the sunroof but the cyborging quickly shut off the pain and the brace kept him upright. Mike emptied another magazine, raking not just the runners but their vehicles.

He disengaged the brace and ducked back down as Al ricocheted back on the road, fumbling in the case for grenades. He couldn't throw one far enough—*wait a minute, you're cyborged, and strength is part of it.* He just had to remember to immediately ramp it down for his body's sake.

—*Max levels*, he clucked to his cyborging. Armed the first grenade and threw it.

The cyborg-assisted strength was just enough to land the grenade in the middle of the vehicles.

—*Half levels*, he clucked to his cyborging. The second grenade landed in the middle of the road. Two more, the last one a comm disrupter to give surviving pursuers issues.

—*Normal levels.*

Then he dropped back to his seat, breathing heavily, grateful that he had sucked down that tube of Liquid Protein just before this.

—*Damage alert*, his cyborg com flashed in red letters, accompanied by a projection showing the extent of his injury. Most of it was in cyborging, not flesh.

—*Acknowledged,* he clucked back.

"You okay, Jo?" he asked, twisting around to look at her.

"Yeah," she said shakily, straightening up. "Oh Mike. You've been hit."

"In my cyborging," he said.

"Come back here and let me check it."

"Gotta secure weapon first. Al, you okay?"

"Thanks to you, yes," Al said.

Mike disarmed the weapon, still leaving it assembled. Then he crawled into the back and slumped against the seat while Jo fussed over his shoulder.

"It's right at the interface," she fretted.

"Bandage what you can. I'll take care of the rest of it." He closed his eyes as she worked, fatigue washing over him. Even half-levels sucked energy.

But another thing to be grateful for—all those years of weapons training thanks to Justine and Serg. The Martiniere habit of learning weaponry and packing it. Justine's secretive weapons division. He'd have to thank her once they got to the ranch.

Reaching the ranch seemed much more possible now.

29 / SHOWDOWN

Age: 31

TWO DAYS LATER, THEY WERE FINALLY IN THUNDER COUNTY, AFTER encountering two more barricades and experiencing a breakdown. Mike and Jo managed to repair it but it was definitely a cobbled-up fix. The three of them took turns driving, Mike and Al more than Jo since the rough mountain roads required more experience with this terrain.

Both nights they snatched a quick rest break off the main roads. Connectivity was iffy, so they didn't always have Ruby and Gabe to call upon. But as they got closer to Thunder County, the roads became more familiar and connectivity improved.

Mike took the wheel for the last stretch, slipping into the National Forest from the north instead of the east—too many opposition watchers in that direction.

At some point we've got to run out of watchers.

But at least they were on familiar ground. And Ruby sat on the console between the two front seats, shrunk down to fit, pointing out the old forest roads leading to the Double R.

They *had* picked up armed followers. But these followers had learned caution after a couple of skirmishes, and stayed back just far enough to be out of weapons range.

"Gonna have to cut across the Reed place to get home," Ruby said. *"No way around it. You have the sensor codes?"*

"Unless they've changed," Mike said as they approached that gate from Forest Service land. He rolled to a stop and climbed out. When Jo opened her door, he waved her back. "Gotta input codes, Jo. Better let me do it. Drive the truck through when I get the gate open, then get back into the passenger side."

He tapped the codes into the nearest sensor, relieved when they flashed acceptance. Only then did he unfasten the three-strand wire gate and pull it across the narrow track. After Jo drove it through, he refastened the gate and changed the security to highest levels, sending an authentication message to Corey Reed, adding, *your fences are likely to get blown. Sorry. It's a Martiniere thing. Send me the repair bill. Mike.* As he ran back to the truck, Mike chuckled to himself, imagining Corey's *what the hell, Mike's supposed to be dead!* reaction.

Not that there was any time left to dawdle. Highest level security on that gate meant the followers would have to cope with autoweapons. Another piece of secretive Martiniere security that had been extended to the Double R's neighbors. The followers might get through, but it would cost them.

All the same, Mike drove faster than he would normally across the dirt track, just because it ran across the ridgeline well within the range of a decent shooter on the other side of the Reed fences. Hell, someone had nearly hit Ruby while shooting from that location years ago, during the AgSuperhero competition.

So close to home now. So close. He'd reviewed the activation file Ruby had given him yesterday.

Just then, a shot smacked the truck cab.

"Shit!" Al whirled in the back seat to try to spot the shooter.

"Jo, *get down!*" Mike snapped. Damn it, just as he'd feared. And there was that last gate to get through, still in plain sight. Unless he rammed it.

What the hell, Corey already knows the fences are screwed.

"Going up," Al growled, grabbing the SPA-29 as he popped the sunroof and activated the brace.

"Got it." Mike accelerated, wrestling with the wheel as the truck jounced along the rutted track. Jo slid down and knelt, holding on, head buried in the seat almost like she was praying as Al began to shoot.

Then Al yelled, abruptly cut off. The SPA-29 clattered to the floor as Al collapsed, the brace broken.

"They got Al!" Jo shrieked, startling up.

"*Damn* it!" Mike snarled. How had those damn followers gotten through the Reed defenses so easily?

Al. Damn it, Al.

But he didn't have time to think about that now.

Another round shattered the back window. Heavier round, or else the previous hits had weakened the reinforced window. Jo grabbed the SPA-29 and reared up to shoot through the back window.

"Jo, *don't!*"

"Cyborging doesn't protect against a head shot!" she screamed back. "Al proves that! If I shoot, they're gonna stay back."

"They've got heavier weaponry than before," Mike muttered.

And now there was the gate to the Double R.

"Hold *on*, Jo!" He floorboarded the accelerator.

God, hopefully someone at the ranch was watching the sensors and had turned off the defenses…thank God, *yes!* They weren't getting hit with friendly fire as they crashed through the gate. Now they were in the Lone Pine field and getting the hell *off* this ridgetop soon. *Home*, damn it.

He murmured the activation code for connecting to his animals that he'd gotten from Ruby. Just as suddenly, he was aware of *presences* in his mind, friendly and *not Philip*. Starlight, regal and kingly, straining against Ron's hold on the lead rope, bellowing a stud's welcome as he became aware of Mike. Spree, foal at her side, skittering and dancing as Justine tried to hold her. Smudgie, rising to his feet and growling defiance, along with smaller beings Mike didn't know.

And then the truck stopped just as the road ducked below the ridgeline, the front end raising several feet before crashing down, like the universal joint had broken and jammed itself into the ground. Mike clung to the wheel. Jo yelped as she was flung toward the broken window, then against the seat backs.

Not surprising given the rough treatment they'd given this rig. U-joint, axle, something in the drive train had finally given out.

"Jo! You all right?"

"I'm fine!"

"What about Al?" Mike whirled, seeing Al's prone body in the back, face blown off, his chest a bloody mess. "Oh God."

"He's dead, Mike, we've gotta go!"

Jo turned to him, the SPA-29 in hand. Mike grabbed its counterpart that had been secured between his seat and the door, then grabbed the last three of their grenades. He set them on a thermal/motion sensor.

—*Half levels,* he clicked to his cyborging.

At least they were below the ridgeline now.

He and Jo burst out of the truck, weapons ready. Mike tossed the grenades onto the track behind them, aiming for a spot at the top of the ridge.

That should take care of those motherfuckers if they get through the damned gate.

By now he was certain that Brandon had been well and truly avenged, and this last piece would take care of Al's killers—*damn it, Al, to die this close to safety!*

That just left Philip's digital clone.

They sprinted down the narrow track. He whistled for Starlight as they ran. As they rounded the ridge's end, he spotted Starlight galloping toward them. Spree followed her son, her foal at her side, Cody behind Spree. The adult horses wore saddles and bridles.

Mike slowed his steps as Starlight approached. The dun stallion dropped to a trot, then a walk as he drew close, nickering a deep, throaty welcome. And then Starlight was *there.* Mike wrapped his arms around Starlight's neck as Spree and then Cody joined them, nuzzling Mike's back. Starlight squealed.

"It's okay, it's okay," Mike murmured. "Jo. Get up on Spree. Cody will follow us. Hand me the weapon first."

He held it while Jo mounted, handed both weapons to her, then leapt up on Starlight's back. As he reached for the SPA-29, a loud BOOM sounded. Two more. The horses' heads jerked up, but they didn't startle.

"Well, that should take care of our followers," he said to Jo as he spun Starlight around. They galloped along the track, welcome strength pouring into Mike from both horses, their presences a surprising boost.

Movement on the hillside. Mike glanced up to see Martiniere security in camouflage taking up positions. A longed-for sight.

"Freeze breaking up," Gabe's voice warned. *"Worm active shortly."*

Mike's response was an inarticulate yell. They rounded a corner and, just as he'd hoped, Ron and Justine waited with another group of Martiniere security and a crawler contingent. Smudgie stood next to Justine.

Then Philip appeared. His form solidified as he stood in the track between them and the others, hands on his hips, glowering at Mike, even as that small, angry part of Mike stirred awake.

What the hell?

This was a stronger physical manifestation than Ruby or Gabe could do!

"This isn't over yet," Philip growled. His arm elongated as he reached toward Jo.

Spree blew a long, rolling warning snort, her head raised high as she half-reared to evade Philip, striking at his arm and deflecting it.

"Whoa," Mike ordered Starlight.

—*Max level*, he clucked to his cyborging.

He dropped the SPA-29—useless against Philip. It would take clone strength to defeat his progenitor. Clone digital abilities. He jumped off of Starlight.

"It ends now!" he yelled at Philip, intercepting the extended arm before it could grab at Jo again.

Starlight reared and struck Philip with both forefeet, giving Mike the opportunity to drag his progenitor closer to him. Power pulsed through Mike—not just his cyborged strength which extended into the electronic pathways Philip exploited but Gabe. Ruby. The horses. Smudgie, growling and snarling as he approached Philip from behind.

Starlight grabbed Philip's shoulder with his teeth and wrenched a piece away.

Lily. Her algorithm shattered into pieces.

Philip diminished slightly, but other pieces of him battered at Mike's cyborg protections, seeking the back door. Spree screamed and double-barreled Philip with both hind legs, sending those other parts flying. Mike staggered backward, away from Philip. Before they faded away, Mike recognized Gene. Martina. The other attackers he'd killed.

Ruby guarded Mike's back door. Gabe's hands superimposed over his as Mike reached for Philip, at first thinking to throttle him.

His target changed with Gabe's input. Slipped down to the chest. A faint tendril of doubt crept into Mike's thoughts as Philip swung at him, electric jolts radiating through him as Philip made contact.

Ignore it.

But the shocks were strong enough to slow him.

Then Smudgie grabbed Philip's leg, whining and darting back as it shocked him, too. A tiny blue-gray copy of Smudgie issued mighty growls, snapping at Philip. It yelped as it got shocked, but Smudgie launched himself at Philip again.

The canine harassment was just enough to distract Philip. Mike's hands slid inside Philip's chest. Closed around the heart. Pulled it free.

Poured every bit of energy he had into zapping every single pixel of it out of existence. The Philip form faded slightly, movements slowing. But it didn't go away.

"Brain, damn it! I got it wrong!" Gabe bellowed.

Mike didn't mess around trying to yank the brain out, but put both hands on Philip's head. Philip latched on to Mike's torso, sending searing electric jolts through him. He gasped for breath and then Starlight's nose was on his back, lending Mike just enough strength to incinerate Philip's head.

"You—" But Philip's voice was just a whisper that blew softly away as his form dissipated.

The small alien piece of Mike disappeared again.

Smudgie whined and licked Mike's face as he sagged to his knees, followed by the blue-gray fluff ball that had joined him in attacking Philip. Starlight nudged Mike. And then Jo and Spree were there, Jo running to Mike, Spree nuzzling him just like she would her foal.

Mike leaned against Jo's legs as he hugged Smudgie.

"It's done," he said. "He's gone."

—*Normal levels*, he clucked to his cyborging, just before exhaustion crashed over him.

MIKE KNEW EVEN BEFORE HE OPENED HIS EYES THAT HE WAS BACK *HOME*. The familiar feel of the bed. Jo's hand on his chest as she lay by his right side. The whisper of a summer breeze through the branches of the Jeffreys pines that circled the ranch house—from the angle of the sun, it was late afternoon. The faint scent of dog as Smudgie snuggled tight in the crook of his left arm, with that squirmy smaller fluff ball presence next to him.

Home, without the weight that had pressed on him for so many years. Mike almost felt like a feather floating on the surface of the bed. Was it really over?

He shifted his weight, groaning as multiple all-over-his-body aches made themselves known.

"Hey, Mikey," Jo said. "Welcome back to the land of the living."

That snapped his eyes open, as Smudgie and the pup both whined, squirming against Mike.

"What? Don't tell me I actually overclocked my cyborging after all," he said, barely able to do more than whisper. His throat was surprisingly sore.

"No, you just drained yourself," Jo said. She sat up and held a squeeze bottle to his lips. "You've been out for two days straight."

"Oh," he groaned, after draining the bottle. "Shit. How big a mess is it?"

"Not as bad as you think," she said.

He tried to sit up and found he had to scoot himself up against the headboard to do it. Smudgie and the pup objected.

Mike grinned down at them. "I guess I've got a new little buddy, hmm?"

"Spot wouldn't leave her papa's side," Jo said. "She's been standing vigil over you. Just like Smudgie and me."

Mike rubbed Smudgie's head, then Spot's. He took Jo in his arms.

"It's really over?" he asked.

"Except for winding up the connections," she said. "It'll take a little while to clean up all the linkages in the Martiniere databases, but killing that worm? Exposed a lot. Ron and Justine have been busy, along with Juliette for the French Family and Ben for the British Family. They've been getting guidance from Ruby and Gabe. They'll have things to report to you, including the precautions that Gabe and Ruby have been developing so that this doesn't happen again."

He sighed. "I guess I'd better get to it."

"Not for a day or two you aren't," she said. "It's *done*, Mikey. And now it is time for you to take a break."

"Is that an order?" he asked.

"Damn right it is," she said, tapping his nose with her index finger. "You made me a promise. It's time for me to collect."

"I need to know some details first. Al."

Jo blinked and Mike thought he saw dampness in her eyes. "He was dead when we left him, Mike. Per his will, he's being cremated. Ashes to be scattered on the Double R."

Mike shook his head. "Damn it. He almost made it to safety. Fuck." He exhaled hard. All the brothers gone now. "I owe so damn much to him and the others, and I didn't know just how much until—" he shook his head again. "I wouldn't be here without the brothers."

"I know," she said softly.

"We've got to honor him." Al's mother Mariah was buried in Los Angeles, and she'd been sold to Philip as a teen, so there probably wasn't any other family to track down. Mike and his family had become Al's family.

"Agreed. Just waiting for you to wake up before we plan anything."

"Any survivors from that last group following us?"

"No." She pressed her lips together tightly. "Security checked them out. I didn't ask questions, and Justine hasn't said anything other than they were ex-Loyal Indentured. And dead."

"Current business status?"

"Now you can let *that* go, damn it, Mike. Justine and Ron have it under control." She shook her finger at him. "You don't need to pick up the Martiniere's mantle right this damn minute. They've got it covered. You and I need time to rest and recover."

Mike laughed. "I can hardly wait to start." All the same, he resolved to have a quiet chat with Justine and Ron soon.

At that point he needed to get up. "Gotta use the bathroom." God, his body ached and he was barely able to throw back the covers, much less move his legs. "What the hell did I do? Is this cyborg crash?"

"Philip hit you with some hard electric shocks." That worried note crept back into Jo's voice. "Dr. Pramula says that if you hadn't maxed your cyborging at the end, Philip would have killed you—at the very least crippled you enough to possess you. Even with the protective links, you took a big jolt and your systems—biological and cyborg alike—were impacted. That's another reason why you need to rest. Take it easy for a while. Recover."

"Oh." Mike sat on the edge of the bed, leaning hard on his hands. Smudgie and Spot fussed at his feet. Jo hurried around to help him. "I think I want to take a shower, too. Unless there's some reason not to."

Jo wrinkled her nose. "Sounds like a good idea. You *stink*, Mikey. Got your bloody clothing off but that's it."

"Then I'd better do it."

By the time they made it to the bathroom, supervised by a worried Smudgie and Spot, he could stand without shaking too badly.

Jo helped him out of the pajamas he'd been wearing. Mike gasped as he saw the blackened skin on his chest and ribs.

"God. No wonder I hurt." He gently brushed his hand against it.

Bruising, thank God, not burns. The wound in his shoulder was mostly healed in the cyborg area, and the non-cyborg portion was now neatly stitched.

He took a long, leisurely shower. By the time he came out, Jo had set out sweats for him to wear. Mike managed to wrestle them on by himself. He studied his face in the mirror afterward. The irritation from the plaskin was already starting to fade. But it was still too gaunt, reminiscent of his cancer face.

Already, though, it looked less like Philip than it ever had.

Mike laughed.

Free. Free at last.

He hadn't felt this free since that first time he sat on a horse's back.

With Jo's help, he made his way to the kitchen. Justine was there, as he expected. Ron sprang up to stride across the room and give Mike a big hug.

"He's avenged," Mike said to Ron. "We left a swath of his killers' bodies across the Southwest, but he's avenged."

Ron blinked hard. "I was scared shitless there at the end, Mike. When we lost track of you."

"It was close. But it's done now." Mike exhaled. Hugged Ron again, then stepped away. He walked over to Justine and hugged her carefully, suddenly aware of how frail she was.

"Thank you for everything," he said.

Deontae thundered into the room. "Mike? You're up! Damn, man, it's good to see you again!"

More hugging. At last Mike broke free.

"We couldn't have done it without Gabe—and Ruby."

Justine nodded. "We've done a lot of mapping over the past two days."

Mike blinked. "So that's it, then."

"Oh, there's still things to do," Justine said. "But nothing more that requires your attention for a couple of days, at least."

It felt weird. Mike turned to Jo. "How are Starlight and Spree?"

She chuckled. "Come on, Mikey. Let's see the horses."

He needed to lean on her as they left the house and walked to the stallion field. Starlight was alone for once, allowed to rest and recover with his buddies just over the fence.

Mike crawled through the fence and whistled. The dun stallion raised his head and nickered. And then he galloped across the field to Mike, sliding to a precisely calculated stop just a foot away.

Mike laughed. "Hey, fella," he crooned softly as Starlight lowered his head.

The stud delicately placed his head against Mike's chest as Mike rubbed and scratched around his ears. They stood there for a timeless moment, man and horse communing silently.

Starlight broke the mood by raising his head slightly and nudging

Mike, black-lined ears pricked forward. Mike laughed again and slipped the stallion a treat. Starlight snorted.

Movement caught the stud's attention and he turned away to watch the geldings in the field next to him run along the fence, playing as the day cooled. With a flick of his head, he half-reared, called to them, then took off galloping, tail held high. He bellowed a challenge as he dropped to a high, springy trot, whipping his head around and posturing.

Mike snorted. "I don't think he's getting much rest. Showing off for his buddies."

"Doesn't look like it," Jo agreed.

He crawled back through the fence and they walked arm-in-arm back to the pen where Spree and her filly waited to be turned out with the broodmare band. Mike buried his neck in Spree's neck after feeding her a treat, taking liberties that he wouldn't do with her son because stallions shouldn't be treated that way, savoring the familiar, beloved scent of *horse*. Spree tucked him into her neck and they stood there silently, until the filly poked at him. Mike rubbed the filly's forehead, gave Spree another treat, then finally joined Jo, who had been leaning on the fence watching.

"So, what do you want to do now?" he asked.

She laughed. "We still have details to clean up for a couple of weeks. But after that...I want at least two months with nothing to do. Away from people. Just us."

"Name the place and we'll do it," he said, bending over to kiss her.

"Absolutely, Michael Marcus Martiniere," she said softly. "And then I look forward to being the mistress of the Double R ranch and the wife of the Martiniere."

He sighed and slung an arm around her shoulders as they walked back to the house. "No time in Paris? No exotic tropical islands? No shopping sprees? Just hanging out here at the ranch? Is that gonna be enough for you, Ms. JoAnn Breonna Swait?"

"Oh, I'm sure we'll find something to do," she said. "We still have businesses to run. People to manage. Ron to prepare for leadership. But for now? A nice, quiet, *ordinary* life—or as ordinary as the two of us can manage—is enough for me."

He laughed and snugged her tight. "I can agree with that."

"And one thing I want to do," she said, musing. "Ron and Justine appear to be getting along pretty well. They've been talking about returning to Moondance and Justine living there, especially since he's the Martiniere-in-waiting and you two shouldn't be living together. But—" she hesitated. "Wes's kids. Robyn's working her rear off but as a widow with four kids, that's a lot. I'd like to help her, maybe bring the kids to the ranch. Rae's helped, but she's got her own kiddos to deal with."

"I've got no problem with that," Mike said.

"It's something I'm considering expanding, too. Not here at the Double R. But there are a lot of kids out there in struggling families. Indenture may not be a threat any more, but we haven't abolished poverty. Now that we've gotten past the worst of the Martiniere family drama, we should turn our attention to future generations."

"Especially since we can't have kids of our own."

"Exactly," she said.

"I don't have any problems with setting up programs here. Find tech-oriented kids. Expand Ruby's intern program beyond locals. You know, that might solve one issue."

"What's that?"

He exhaled. "What happens with the Double R after I die. If the Double R transitions to becoming an educational program, benefiting kids in poverty, then that's a fine legacy. At least I think so. Is that something you'd want to do?"

She stopped and turned to face him. "You asked me what I'd want after all this. And yes. This is what I want to do."

Mike leaned forward and kissed her. "Then it's going to happen." He sighed. "Give me a few years to finish prepping Ron before I can fully participate. But there's no reason why you can't get started on building it."

"Oh, Mikey." The glow of her smile was well worth it. "I love you."

"And I think it's a damn fine usage of my heritage," he said softly. "I love you and your vision. I want to build something positive."

And maybe, just maybe, helping kids might counterbalance the shadows of the Martiniere legacy. At least it was worth a try.

He knew without asking that Ruby and Gabe would approve. A worthy outcome for their rescue of the crippled clone boy from the man who had brought them so much misery.

And the ultimate fuck you, Progenitor.

Mike tensed, just in case *something* would stir.

Silence.

Perhaps he was finally free, for real.

THE END

NEWSLETTER SIGNUP

Like what you've read? Want to follow Joyce either through her monthly newsletter ?

Sign up for Joyce's newsletter here:

https://tinyletter.com/JoyceReynolds-Ward

Or follow Joyce's irregular blog posts on her Substack, here:

https://joycereynoldsward.substack.com/

Interested in a different one of Joyce's universes? Check out Martiniere Stories on Substack.

https://joycef1d.substack.com/p/an-introduction-to-martiniere-stories

BOOKS AND PUBLICATIONS

The Martiniere Legacy

First Meetings: A Martiniere Legacy Short Story
Inheritance: The Martiniere Legacy Book One
Ascendant: The Martiniere Legacy Book Two
Realization: The Martiniere Legacy Book Three
A Belated Christmas Honeymoon: A Martiniere Legacy Short Story
The Enduring Legacy: The Martiniere Legacy Book Four

The People of the Martiniere Legacy

The Heritage of Michael Martiniere: An Agripunk Thriller
Broken Angel: The Lost Years of Gabriel Martiniere: An Agripunk Thriller
Justine Fixes Everything: Reflections on Mortality: An Agripunk Thriller

The Martiniere Multiverse Books

A Different Life—What If?
A Different Life—Linda's Story (Release Date—Fall 2022, currently serializing on Vella)
Dreamwalker: Gabriel (to be determined)
The Cost of Power (to be determined)

Goddess's Honor titles currently available (chronological order):

The Goddess's Choice: A Goddess's Honor Short Story
Beyond Honor: A Goddess's Honor Novella
Exile's Honor: A Goddess's Honor Novelette
Birth of Sorrow: A Goddess's Honor Short Story
Pledges of Honor: Goddess's Honor Book One
Return to Wickmasa: A Goddess's Honor Short Story
Crown Anniversary: A Goddess's Honor Short Story
Challenges of Honor: Goddess's Honor Book Two
Cleaning House: A Goddess's Honor Outtake Story
Unexpected Alliances: A Goddess's Honor Rough Draft Outtake Story
Choices of Honor: Goddess's Honor Book Three
Judgment of Honor: Goddess's Honor Book Four

Netwalk Sequence Author Preferred 2022 Editions
Life in the Shadows: Book One
Netwalk: Book Two
Netwalker Uprising: Book Three
Netwalk's Children: Book Four
Learning in Space: Book Five
Netwalking Space: Book Six

Bright Star Fair Witches
Becoming Solo: A Bright Star Fair Witches Novella

Non-Series Titles currently available:
Alien Savvy: A Western SF Novella
Klone's Stronghold
Beating the Apocalypse

Vella Titles:
Falcon of the Martinieres (part of *Justine Fixes Everything*)
Bearing Witness
Beating the Apocalypse
A Different Life—What If? An Alternative Martiniere Legacy Novel
Becoming Solo
A Different Life—Linda's Story: An Alternative Martiniere Legacy Novel

Audiobooks Available:

Alien Savvy: A Western SF Novella

Released from other publishers:

"Queen of the Snows," in *Once Upon A Winter: A Folk and Fairy Tale Anthology*, edited by H. L. Macfarlane

"My Man Left Me, My Dog Hates Me, and There Goes My Truck," in *Black-Eyed Peas on New Year's Day: An Anthology of Hope*, edited by Shannon Page

"Lost Loves," in *All Worlds Wayfarer*

"The Wisdom of Robins," in *Whimsical Beasts: A Campcon Anthology*, edited by Joyce Reynolds-Ward

"The Cow at the End of the World," in *Well...It's Your Cow*, edited by Frog Jones

"To Plant or Pull Up Stakes," in *Pulling Up Stakes: A Campcon Anthology*, edited by Joyce Reynolds-Ward

"The Notice," in *Children of a Different Sky*, edited by Alma Alexander

ABOUT THE AUTHOR

Joyce Reynolds-Ward has been called "the best writer I've never heard of" by one reviewer. Her work includes themes of high-stakes family and political conflict, digital sentience, personal agency and control, realistic strong women, and (whenever possible) horses. She is the author of *The Netwalk Sequence* series, the *Goddess's Honor* series, and the recently released *The Martiniere Legacy* series as well as standalones *Klone's Stronghold, Alien Savvy,* and *Beating the Apocalypse.* Samples of her Martiniere short stories/novel in progress and her nonfiction can be found on Substack at either Speculations from the Wide Open Spaces (general, writing) or Martiniere Stories (fiction). Joyce is a Self-Published Fantasy BlogOff Semifinalist, a Writers of the Future SemiFinalist, and an Anthology Builder Finalist. She is the Secretary of the Northwest Independent Writers Association, a member of the Science Fiction and Fantasy Writers Association, and a member of Soroptimists International.

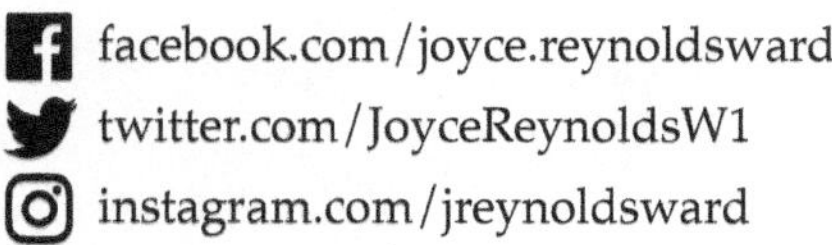

facebook.com/joyce.reynoldsward
twitter.com/JoyceReynoldsW1
instagram.com/jreynoldsward